TED CC C

GW01017690

THE
REUNION

outskirts
press

The Reunion
All Rights Reserved.
Copyright © 2021 Ted CC Odom
v4.0

This is a work of fiction. Names, characters, businesses, places, events, locales, and incidents are either the products of the author's imagination or used in a fictitious manner. Any resemblance to actual persons, living or dead, or actual events is purely coincidental.

The opinions expressed in this manuscript are solely the opinions of the author and do not represent the opinions or thoughts of the publisher. The author has represented and warranted full ownership and/or legal right to publish all the materials in this book.

This book may not be reproduced, transmitted, or stored in whole or in part by any means, including graphic, electronic, or mechanical without the express written consent of the publisher except in the case of brief quotations embodied in critical articles and reviews.

Outskirts Press, Inc.
http://www.outskirtspress.com

Paperback ISBN: 978-1-9772-3671-5

Cover Photo © 2021 www.gettyimages.com. All rights reserved - used with permission.

Outskirts Press and the "OP" logo are trademarks belonging to Outskirts Press, Inc.

PRINTED IN THE UNITED STATES OF AMERICA

"The past isn't dead, it's not even past."
William Faulkner

The Atlantic Ocean, Off the Coast of Key Largo

Friday, April 14, 2016

11:59 pm

"MAYDAY, MAYDAY, MAYDAY!" she screamed into the phone. "This is Leanne Piper, oh God, oh God, please. Mayday, mayday, mayday"

A few seconds passed before a voice responded, "What's your position?"

"I don't know. I don't know. I don't sail, I don't know. Off the coast of Key Largo is all I know," she said, the fear and agitation in her voice increasing as she spoke.

"What's the name of your vessel?"

"The Sweet Revenge."

"What's the nature of your distress," the coast guard officer asked evenly in an effort to calm the caller down. But before she could respond, violent thuds, pounding and shouting could be heard over the radio telephone. Again, the officer asked, this time urgently, "What's happening?"

"My husband, Scotty Piper, he's trying to kill me and now I'm locked in a stateroom and he's trying to break in. He's got a gun and..." Another loud thud, more pounding. "Oh God, he's going to kill me. He's going to kill us all..." Then the sound of more thuds, wood shattering and sickening, horrific screams before the radio telephone went silent.

Bayou Derkin, Louisiana

October 1975

It's hot in southwest Louisiana on autumn afternoons. The bracing morning chill slowly fades into hot, still air by afternoon. Children who made their way to school wearing jackets and sweaters have dropped and dragged them by mid-afternoon as they made their way home on baking concrete sidewalks.

Amelie had had a good day. Jimmy Fisher gave her his old pocketknife and then hung around through most of recess even though she hadn't encouraged him to. She'd had fish sticks for lunch, a favorite, and since it was Friday there was music class with Mr. Allen whom she considered a musical genius. But best of all she'd won the Bayou Derkin Elementary School spelling bee, again, and was awarded *The Bobbsey Twins at Snow Lodge*, the fifth in the series of books she'd been reading. She was pondering the day's success when she heard Annie call out for her to wait up.

Amelie turned to find Annie and Charlotte Claire running breathlessly towards her. "You have to come with us," Annie panted when they'd reached Amelie. "It's Timmy, those bullies beat him up again. I think he ran down by the river. They punched him in the stomach and busted his lip."

"When he fell down they started kicking him," Charlotte Claire added. "We need to find him. He may need to go to the infirmary."

Immediately the three girls ran in the direction of the river that snaked through the woods on the outskirts of Bayou Derkin.

The foursome had been best friends and each other's protectors since first grade. Every afternoon, weekends and all summer they were together; riding bikes, swimming in the river, or just hanging around one or the other's houses.

"You promised you wouldn't tell," Timmy cried when the girls reached him. He was squatting by the river's edge beneath the long, graceful branches of an old willow, splashing the brown river water on his mouth. His lower lip had already begun to swell, and the strap of his denim overalls was torn.

"I didn't tell," Annie replied. "It's just Amelie. Not the same as telling. Anyway, we need Amelie. Her house is closest. We can go there and get you cleaned up before Miss Lou gets home from work." He stopped dabbing at his lip with his sleeve and looked up at his three friends. He pulled the flap of his overalls over his face and began to cry.

"Oh Timmy, it's okay," Amelie said reassuringly. "It was Tom Burnett and Scotty Piper, wasn't it?" Timmy nodded, still hiding his face in his overalls.

"I think we should tell Mr. Fontenot," Charlotte Claire announced, "or your Mama and Daddy or..."

"No!" Timmy shouted abruptly. "I don't want them to know, I don't want anyone to know."

"It's nothing to be ashamed of. *You* didn't do anything wrong," Annie said.

"It's nothing to be ashamed of Timmy," Amelie repeated.

"It is," he said, pulling the overall flap away from his face and looking at his three friends. "I am."

TIMMY

New York, June 2015

HE WAS FEELING pretty good about himself these days. He'd published seven books, become a talk show regular and a minor celebrity. His most recent book was on *The New York Times* best seller list and his agent had just negotiated the biggest book advance of his career. Now he was headed home on a perfect summer day to celebrate his book deal with Joe, aka "the one" with whom he shared a life of domestic bliss that included two step-children, two dogs and a fashionable triplex apartment in Manhattan's Chelsea neighborhood.

His journey to that Manhattan neighborhood had begun as a painful one. His childhood was something he recalled with sadness. Bayou Derkin Louisiana was a hard-up town in the 1970s, and while it wasn't exactly poverty it wasn't prosperity either. His mother was by turns doting and cruel but, as children sometimes believe, he thought all mothers were like that. She was bitter about where life had taken her, was relentlessly critical of her husband and children, and she made sure they knew they were a disappointment to her. She seemed to derive pleasure in setting one member of the family against another and the result was that Timmy and his three older sisters were never close. His father, who was a farmer and an alcoholic, was a kind man, but beaten down by an unhappy wife and a joyless marriage. Rage filled fights between his parents punctuated Timmy's young life. Their home was a place of tension and conflict, accusations and blame, manipulation and guilt.

Timmy's method of coping was eating and by the time he was 12 he was a fat kid. As a boy he didn't know what homosexuality was, but he knew from an early age that he was different from other boys. Being called a "sissy," a "fatty" or, best of all, a "fat sissy" was a regular and humiliating occurrence. By the time he reached his freshman year of high school the occasional taunts had turned uglier and sometimes violent. They called him "faggot" and "queer" whenever they passed him in the hallway at school. Tom Burnett and Scotty Piper hounded him incessantly; they had since third grade. Timmy did his best to avoid them, but they sought him out. He felt stalked, living in fear of his tormentors. He quit the band after they started attacking him on the bus several times after out of town games. Eventually he quit all his other extracurricular activities to avoid them. He even withdrew from Amelie, Annie and Charlotte Claire. The shame he felt would not allow him friends, only isolation.

The spring of his freshman year Timmy got his driver's license and used his savings, $300, to buy a 1976 Plymouth Valiant. The car became the sole source of joy in his life. It meant freedom and the chance to escape the stifling unhappiness of his life at home. Every afternoon after school he drove the back-country roads for hours; windows down, radio cranked and the wind blowing. The sun shimmering on the flooded rice fields and the vibrant, green rice erupting from the water's surface was the only beauty he saw in his life. It was the only time he felt like a kid his age, free of fear, free of sadness and shame.

A week after he got his car he was invited to get together with his old group. It was Annie's birthday and she was having the group over to celebrate. At first Timmy said he couldn't come, making some excuse about a term paper that was due. "It'll be fun," Annie insisted. "Come on. I never get to hang around with you anymore. We all miss you." Sensing the reason for his hesitation she pressed on, "It' just me, Charlotte Claire and Amelie. It'll be just the four of us, promise."

"Okay," he said, with some reservation.

The night of the party Timmy was the last to arrive. He found the girls on the patio behind the neighborhood bar where Annie lived with her two elderly aunts. The three girls shrieked delightedly when they saw him, and he felt instantly at ease. The patio was decorated with colored lights and music drifted in from the open windows of the bar. An old wash tub filled with soft drinks sat on the ground and wire net domes covered the food on the picnic table to keep the flies at bay.

For an hour and a half, they played records, danced and gossiped about their classmates. Timmy couldn't remember the last time he'd laughed so much. By 9:30 the mosquitoes had become intolerable, so Annie decided to move the party inside. Just as they entered the apartment they heard the loud rumble of a car pulling into the driveway. "Who on Earth?" Annie wondered aloud, but Timmy knew right away that it was Tom Burnett and Scotty Piper. He recognized the loud engine of Tom's old Ford pick-up.

"It's Tom and Scotty," he said to Annie. "Did you invite them?"

'No, Timmy, I promise. I would never have done that."

Timmy turned to Amelie and Charlotte Claire. "Who invited them?" he demanded, becoming agitated. "Who invited them? Is that why I'm here? Did they put you up to this?" They both spoke at once assuring Timmy that they hadn't. "They must've seen my car in the driveway. I don't know what to do. Annie, you can't let them in."

"Don't worry, I won't," she assured him. "Y'all just go on with the party. I'll take care of this." Annie stepped outside as the two boys were climbing the old wooden stairs that led to the apartment. "Oh, hey Tom, hey Scotty. What are y'all up to?"

"We heard you were having a party. Thought we'd come check it out," Scotty said, his tone velvety and sexy, the voice he used on girls.

"Oh, who told you that? It's not a party, just a couple of people over for cokes. I'd invite you in but Aunt Idelle said not one more person, you know how she is."

"Who all's in there?" Tom asked suspiciously.

"Charlotte Claire and Amelie."

"Is that faggot there?" Scotty demanded.

"Now you listen to me Scotty Piper," Annie said firmly. "I don't want any trouble from you. You and I have always gotten along, so let's just leave it that way. Or I can go get Aunt Daisy and Aunt Idelle from the bar downstairs and you can deal with them."

"Alright, alright. Don't get your panties in a twist. We're leaving."

"Alright then," she replied in a conciliatory tone. "See y'all at school on Monday. Night."

As soon as Annie opened the door Tom and Scotty started yelling, their voices thick with rage, "We'll get you faggot! Count on it! Queer!" Several tense minutes passed before they heard Tom Burnett's pick-up roaring out of the driveway.

"It's my fault," Charlotte Claire said, fighting back tears. "I told him you'd be here. Not like that, not on purpose. I just said who all was going to be here. But I'm so sorry, Timmy. It was just in conversation. I wasn't thinking. I should have known better. But I didn't invite them, I promise. I would've never said a thing about you being here if I thought they were going to show up."

"Why won't they just leave you alone?" Amelie asked in puzzlement.

"I don't know," he said dejectedly. "I'm going home."

"Don't leave now," Annie implored. But reading the look on his face she could see that he was about to cry and didn't press him further.

Timmy walked slowly to his car, looking around to make sure he wasn't walking into a trap. In the light of the lamp post he could see that something was smeared on the door handles of his car. As he got closer he could see-and worse, smell-that it was feces. That's why it took them so long to leave, he realized. They'd smeared shit on all the door handles. He didn't know if it was animal dung or their own shit, but he was disgusted and horrified. He could no longer hold the tears back. He walked back towards the patio, got the garden hose and hosed down the car, crying as he did so and wishing he were dead.

Timmy pulled out of Annie's driveway and started for home. Good thing I locked the car, he thought, no telling what they might have done to the inside. As he pulled away from a stop sign a car parked on the side of the road turned on its lights and began to follow. The car continued to follow him to the next turn and then the next. Timmy pulled onto the highway and sped towards home but the car behind him sped faster until it was tailgating him. Despite the glare in the rear-view mirror Timmy could see that it was Tom's old Ford and it was getting dangerously close. He was sure that their next move would be to run him off the road. It was a lonely stretch of highway and Timmy knew that if he pulled over, so would they and there'd be no one to help him. As Tom flicked on his high-beams, light flooded Timmy's car, and the glare in the rear-view was blinding. Tom gunned the engine and swerved into the opposite lane. Just as Tom's truck caught up to Timmy's car, Scotty leaned so far out the window, his entire upper body jutting out of the truck. With the wind whipping his hair and shirt, his face animated with hatred and delight, he screamed, "I'm gonna kill you faggot! You hear me? I'm gonna fuck you up, faggot! You can't hide from me, fat queer!"

Tom jerked the steering wheel, veering over into Timmy's lane. Instinctively Timmy jerked his wheel sharply to avoid him, sending him spinning half way around, rubber burning and tires screeching. He jumped the drainage ditch at a powerful speed, landing in a rice field with a monstrous thump. Timmy's head smashed against the windshield as he came to a violent stop. Tom made a quick U-turn and the truck sped away.

The night around Timmy was dark and quiet except for the hissing of the radiator. He reached up and felt the warm blood trickling down his forehead. He tried to start the car, but the engine wouldn't turn over. Resigned, he eased himself out of the car and walked, slowly, toward the highway, keeping close to the drainage ditch in case Tom and Scotty came back for him. He was seven miles from home when he spotted a patrol car coming toward him. The officer slowed down, made a U-turn and pulled up beside him.

"What are you doing out on the highway at this hour, son?"

"I had an accident. I'm walking home."

"Where do you live?"

"74 Little Farm Road."

"Get in. I'll take you home. Shouldn't be out here on the highway this late." Timmy climbed into the back seat of the cruiser and the officer pulled away. "What happened?" the officer asked him.

"I swerved to miss a deer."

"Oh, yeah," the cop said sympathetically, "Got to be careful this time of year."

After the accident Timmy fell into a profound depression. He spent his afternoons in his room or driving the back-country roads until it got dark. He thought a lot about death, and about how joyless his life had become. His three friends reached out to him, but he rebuffed all their attempts.

One steamy spring afternoon, a particularly oppressive feeling of hopelessness overtook him. He went into the kitchen for a snack, and found his mother sitting at the table reading a magazine. She put the magazine down and looked over her reading glasses at Timmy. "Why can't you be like other boys your age? Would it be too much for you to play a sport or something? Call someone! Do something, anything!" she wailed, a look of disgust on her face. "Why can't my children be like other children? No, mine are always the dumb one or the selfish one or the *odd* one!" The way she emphasized "odd," he knew that she meant him. "Go do something," she continued. "Go for a walk, or better yet, a run. You could stand to lose some weight. I'm sick of watching you mope around this house." Timmy stood, tugging his shirt away from his protruding belly and staring at her with a stricken look on his face. "What's wrong with you?" she screamed. Timmy considered his response. He could be honest, or he could say nothing as he always had before. He knew that honesty was a risk.

"I'm not happy," he said at last.

"You're not happy?" she chided. "You're not happy? Well if you're not happy you've no one to blame but yourself." She looked at him scornfully, picked up her magazine, and continued reading.

Timmy was crestfallen. He went to his room, got his car keys and left the house by way of his father's office so he wouldn't have to see his mother again. As he reached his car his middle sister, Aiden, drove up and blocked him in. She sat behind the wheel, laughing at her practical joke.

"Can you move your car?" Timmy asked.

She rolled down the window and said, "What was that? I couldn't hear you."

"I said, can you move your car?"

"Mm, don't think so," she replied, laughing playfully.

"I said move your car!" he shouted. "I have to go!"

"No can do."

"Move your car!" he screamed. "I have to go! I have to get out! I have to go!" He threw his car keys at her car and darted toward her in a fury. She quickly rolled up the window and locked the doors as Timmy pounded on the driver's side window and screaming, "I have to go! I have to get out!" He began to sob, "I have to get out! I have to get out!" His sobs turned into guttural wailing. He felt as if threats were rushing at him from all sides. He turned and ran to the chain link fence that surrounded the house and clung to it, wailing. His sister Bridgett, hearing the racket, stepped out onto the porch. Aiden got out of her car and the two sisters looked on in disbelief.

"Go get Daddy," Aiden told her sister.

His father rushed to where he clung to the fence and placed his hands on Timmy's shoulders. His sobs began to dissipate. "It's okay Buddy. It's okay." His father gently pulled him away from the fence and, with an arm around his shoulders, walked Timmy back into the house. "Here, now, just lay down a while until you feel better," his father said when they'd reached Timmy's room. He sat on the edge of the bed and rubbed Timmy's shoulder comfortingly.

"What's wrong with him?" his mother asked from the doorway.

"We need to get him to a doctor," was all he said.

The psychiatrist told Timmy's parents that he'd suffered a nervous breakdown. Because his mother feared the small-town gossip, he was briefly hospitalized under the guise of appendicitis. His psychiatrist, Dr. Hurd, listened to Timmy's stories of pain and humiliation with a sympathetic ear. After weeks of counseling Timmy finally opened up about all the issues that led to his emotional collapse: his mother's harsh criticism, his not being like other boys, and the bullying. Years later Timmy would guess that the doctor was himself gay and recognized a kindred soul. Dr. Hurd suggested that Timmy begin to document his feelings in a journal and, if that were too painful, to create stories that spoke to his feelings. Timmy took up the task of journaling with seriousness and consistency and soon he began writing poetry, then short stories and essays. He read more, studying the ways of professional writers. Writing became his passion and his savior. He was still isolated, but this new isolation was one of choice and fulfillment.

In their senior year of high school Timmy, Amelie and Annie took college level English classes at night at a nearby community college. He applied to Loyola University in New Orleans and was accepted. Before he even graduated, Timmy was living in New Orleans and preparing for the summer semester. He'd gladly skipped commencement in his eagerness to leave the little town where he'd experienced so much pain. He was walking away without a backward glance, to live in a world that didn't include Scotty Piper and Tom Burnett. There was nothing there that he would miss...except Amelie, Annie and Charlotte Claire.

For Timmy, college was the opposite experience of high school. At Loyola people 'got' him. He was surprised by the ease with which he was making friends. He felt accepted. He had an active social life, met other gay students, even began to date. He wrote constantly, for the school newspaper, literary magazines and journals, and even had articles published in the *Times-Picayune*. By the end of his freshman year he'd lost 80 pounds. He was happy for the first time in his life.

He got his degree from Loyola and entered the Masters program in English at nearby Tulane University. He finished the program in 18 months and headed straight to New York and a job in the mailroom of Alfred A. Knopf. Every moment of his free time was spent writing. He was soon publishing articles and short stories in literary magazines and working on his first novel. It took two years to finish the book which he showed to one of the editors he'd befriended at Knopf. To his surprise, the editor wanted to publish it. After a year of editing and re-writes, it was published, received positive reviews, and was even moderately successful. He quit the mailroom to write full time.

Timmy's literary star continued to rise. Each book did a little better than the last. He was invited on talk shows to promote his books and was becoming a minor celebrity. Everything in his life was going as he hoped except for one thing: He wanted someone to share it with. Growing up, the idea that he could ever marry seemed impossible. But the world had changed, and he knew that now it was within his grasp. He'd had relationships over the years, but nothing long-term seemed to click. He wondered was he too picky, were they too picky? Maybe it just wasn't meant to be.

In 2006, Timmy appeared on *The View* to promote his third book, a collection of short stories based upon his life growing up in Louisiana: *The Autobiography of No One in Particular*. Waiting with him in the green room was a tall, good looking WASP he recognized from MSNBC. His name was Joe Briarcliff, a well-known financial analyst, regular contributor to *The Wall Street Journal,* and prominent member of the Manhattan gay community. Timmy had always thought Briarcliff was attractive, but in person he was even more so. Timmy couldn't help but notice that Joe had picked up his book and was reading it. In an uncharacteristically bold move he asked, "How do you like it?"

"Well I just started reading it. They're giving them away to the audience, so I snagged one. So far, I like it," he said, looking up at Timmy and making direct eye contact with twinkling, hazel eyes.

"What do you like about it?" Timmy asked flirtatiously.

"You're funny."

"Yes, yes, I am," Timmy agreed. There was a palpable chemistry that neither man could deny. Timmy waited in the green room until the show was over and invited Joe to lunch. Conversation flowed easily, and their mutual attraction was electric. After lunch Joe invited Timmy to the Cindy Sherman exhibit at the Museum of Modern Art, and after they continued on to dinner at Timmy's favorite restaurant in Chelsea. After dinnner they walked around for some time until they reached Timmy's apartment. "Would you like me to come up?" Joe asked.

"Yes...but no."

"Too soon?"

"Maybe just a little."

"Too soon to kiss you good night?"

"Probably...but let's anyway." They kissed tenderly, then Joe smiled and walked away. "I'll take a rain check on the coming up part," Timmy called out.

"I'm holding you to that." In all they'd spent twelve hours together that day. What started as a conversation blossomed into a relationship- and ultimately, a life together.

There were moments Timmy couldn't believe the course his life had taken, as if the place he started and the place he ended up had no connecting roads; as if that fearful, introverted kid from Bayou Derkin, Louisiana was someone else altogether. But of course there was a connecting road: His 'girls,' as he liked to think of them. Amelie, Annie and Charlotte Claire had always been there, would always be there. Except for his darkest periods in high school there had never been a time, from first grade to that very day, that they were not a part of his life. Their friendship had been maintained over great distance through letters and phone calls, then emails and text messages, their contact was constant. They'd been there for each other's life events: Marriages, children, deaths, and career highs and lows. And since 1990, they'd taken summer trips together. Every year they met at the beach; be it a condo rental, resort or someone's beach house, the idea of meeting anywhere other than a beach never came up.

Timmy walked into his apartment, threw his keys on the credenza and began shuffling through the mail when Joe walked in behind him.

"There's the face I love," Timmy said.

"And there's the face *I* love," Joe told him. "And congratulations Sweetie, I knew they'd cave."

"What? Oh, the advance. It helps to have a barracuda for an agent. But thanks. I'm just glad the negotiation got wrapped up before the trip. I didn't want to be constantly on the phone while I'm on the Cape."

"Oh, heavens no," Joe said, teasingly. "Can't have anything come between you and your girls. Remind me of the dates."

"Five weeks from today, exactly. Can't think of the actual date though. It's in my travel file."

"What did you plan to do while you're there?"

"You know, same old, same old. Talk all morning over coffee, make sandwiches and a pitcher of Crantimmys for the beach, and laugh all afternoon. Maybe go out to dinner if we're not too drunk. That reminds me, would you excuse me Sweetie, I need to call Perry's and order a case of champagne for the Cape before I forget."

"Sweetie, you know you have five weeks to order champagne."

"If I don't do it while I'm thinking about it...who taught me that? It'll just take a minute."

"Go ahead, I'm going upstairs to shower and then I'm taking you out to celebrate." As he climbed the stairs, Joe said, "Sheesh, a case?"

The Atlantic Ocean, Off the Coast of Key Largo

Friday, April 15th, 2016

Midnight

"Mayday, mayday, mayday, do you read me?"

"Yes, I read you," the Coast Guard office replied. "What is the nature of your emergency?"

"This is Timothy Tyler. I'm on The Sweet Revenge. We are off the coast of Key Largo. A man, Scotty Piper, has a gun and is threatening his wife. He's trying to break down the stateroom door to get to...to hurt his wife. He's..." Pounding could be heard in the background. "He has a gun. I can hear him now, trying to break into the stateroom!" Timmy shouted.

"Where are you?"

"We're locked in another stateroom. There are four of us. There's..." Shots can be heard, and then screaming. "Oh my God, I just heard gun shots. We need help!" Timmy cried.

"What are your coordinates?" the coast guard officer asked.

"I don't know! Annie, what are our coordinates?" The pounding got closer, louder. "He's trying to get to us. He's trying to get into our stateroom. He's..." The coast guard officer heard the thwack of Timmy's cell phone hit the floor of the stateroom and the shouting of the people inside it.

"Are you there?" the coast guard officer asked. But all he could hear was the frantic voices of people in fear.

"Get the mattresses, get the mattresses..."

"Put them against the door...hurry!"

"He's going to kill us..."

"Are you there?" the officer shouted. "Are you there?"

CHARLOTTE CLAIRE

Houston, Texas

June, 2015

CHARLOTTE CLAIRE WAS not in a particularly good mood. The fitting hadn't gone well, and it had made her late. The clerk at Nieman's had given her the wrong shopping bag, and she had to go back to the store and swap out the bags. Her stylist had taken an insufferably long time with her hair, yammering on about God knows what, she couldn't even remember. Whatever, she thought, I don't have time to think about that now. Tonight, she was hosting a five-course dinner for potential investors in Stanley's new company and she needed to get home and check the table settings.

"Alma, I'm back," she sang out, dropping a pile of shopping bags on the center hall table. She paused for a minute to admire it, the Lalique crystal table had been quite a splurge. She turned to the grand, curving staircase and let her gaze drift toward the 20-foot ceilings. "Do you pinch yourself sometimes?" Timmy once asked her. "Yes," she'd admitted, "I do."

"Alma?" she called out, as she strode across the foyer. "Meet me in the dining room." She circled the dining table, noting every detail. The linens were perfect; the flowers were perfect, the crystal, perfect. Then she spotted it.

"Alma, the soup spoon is at the right, followed, working from the outside toward the plate, by the fish knife and fork, the meat knife and fork, and the salad knife and fork. Can you fix that?"

"I'm sorry Miss."

"Spare me the labor pains. Just bring me the baby," she said pleasantly.

Charlotte Claire Parker had grown up in a remote area, miles outside of Bayou Derkin. Though her's was a stable home with loving parents, she'd always felt the sting of being poor. She longed for the advantages she saw her classmates enjoy. From an early age she became an acute observer of the haves and have nots. She was determined to rise above her circumstances.

When she was eight years old she went to play with a classmate, Leanne Reed, whose family had just built a sprawling new home. It was on 6th Street in a nice part of town. All the houses on 6th Street were substantial and sat on perfectly manicured lawns, banked by colorful azalea and hydrangea. As Charlotte Claire walked slowly toward the house she took in its great height, its impressive columns and the deep, wide veranda. She'd never been inside a house as magnificent as this. She rang the doorbell and was delighted by the resonant chimes that signaled her arrival. Leanne opened the door and directed her in with a wave. Charlotte Claire stepped into what she thought was a vacant living room with a wide set of curving stairs. Leanne closed the door with a gentle push and said, "This is the *foyay*."

"What's a...*foyay*?" Charlotte Claire asked.

"It's the room that comes before the other rooms. Follow me and I'll show you around." Leanne led her across the foyer and through a pair of French doors. Charlotte Claire had never seen such an elegant room. The floor to ceiling windows were hung with great lengths of fabric, vivid eruptions of colorful flowers emblazoned upon them. There was a huge marble fireplace and a grandfather clock. The room looked like something she'd only seen on TV or at the movies. "That's the living room," Leanne said after giving her time to take it in. Leanne directed her back through the foyer and through another set of French doors. "And this is the dining room," Leanne told her with great satisfaction. Charlotte Claire found the dining room every bit as impressive as the living room. The gleaming mahogany dining table looked as long as a football field to her and she'd never seen upholstered dining chairs. The large sideboard was laid out with a sparkling sterling silver tea and coffee service.

"Is this where you eat?" Charlotte Claire asked incredulously.

"We only eat in here on holidays or if we have company." She motioned for Charlotte Claire to follow her and they stepped through a hallway with cabinets and counters running the length of the space. "This is the butler's pantry," she said as they passed through.

"You have a butler?"

"Not right now, but we might get one."

"We're not getting a butler, Leanne," her mother called out from another room.

"But we've got a maid," she said defiantly. They stepped into a sun-filled breakfast room. Through the bank of French doors she saw a manicured, flower filled back yard. "And here's the kitchen." The gleaming white kitchen had white marble counter tops and the wall mounted cabinet doors looked like windows through which you could see a plethora of matching china and glassware.

"Look!" Charlotte Claire cried. "You have a stove like the school cafeteria...and an ice box like the school, too."

"Hello Charlotte Claire," Leanne's mother said. "How's your mother?"

"She's fine, Miss Betty. Thank you for asking."

"Oh Charlotte Claire, you have such good manners. Tell her I say hello."

"Yes ma'am. Where'd you get that stove and ice box. I've never seen ones like that outside the school cafeteria."

"We got them from a restaurant supply. They're what's called professional grade for the home. I guess I'll have to do a lot of cooking to justify the purchase."

"You never cook," Leanne said cheekily. "Hazel does."

"Leanne!" her mother cried.

"We're getting all new furniture too. I'm getting a canopy bed. That's because we're rich. Mama says I'm not supposed to say that even though it's true."

"Leanne!" her mother admonished. "I have told you and told you, we don't talk about money and what we have. It's impolite."

"We're rich, too," Charlotte Claire replied defensively.

"No, you're not. You're poor. Your daddy works for my daddy at the gravel pit. Your mama works in the lunch room. My mama doesn't have to work. She's in the Garden Club."

"Leanne, I want to talk to you right now, in the living room!" her mother said through clenched teeth. "I'm sorry Charlotte Claire. Would you excuse us for a moment?"

When she returned home, Charlotte Claire raced to the kitchen where her mother was preparing dinner. Her mother kissed her on top of her head and continued with her work. Charlotte Claire plopped into a chair and sat silently at the kitchen table. Her eyes fell on the unlined, calico curtains that her mother had made, and the old Formica countertops that were cracked and marked. She looked at the old four-burner stove where her mother stood and then the small pine kitchen table where she sat. "Mama, are we rich?" she asked earnestly. Her mother stopped what she was doing and turned to her daughter with a quizzical look.

"Why are you asking, Charlotte Claire?"

"Leanne Reed said we're not rich. Are we rich?"

"Well, there are all sorts of ways to be rich," her mama

explained gently. "We're rich in love. We're rich in family. We're rich in faith."

"But what about money? Are we rich in money?" she persisted, staring at her mother intently.

"It's not polite to talk about money. Now go wash up for supper," her mother told her before returning to her cooking.

"I want to be rich in money, too," Charlotte Claire said as she left the kitchen. In her room she unpacked her book sack, kicked off her shoes and fell on her single bed. Her eyes moved from object to object in the tiny room; the wobbly desk where she did her homework, the painted wood floors, the faded wall paper that was probably there when her parents bought the small house, and more homemade curtains. Looking up at the ceiling she could not help but think of Leanne's canopy bed. "And I will be too," she muttered.

Charlotte Claire grew from a spunky, precocious child into a shy, serious teenager. An idea had taken root that day at Leanne's house and it grew over time; that she was *less than*. She'd walk the halls of Bayou Derkin High with her head down and her school books clutched to her chest. If a classmate said hello as they passed, she'd look up and muster a timid 'Hey' and keep moving. She envied the attention that Annie got from boys and Amelie's easygoing, good natured personality which made her popular among their classmates.

In her sophomore year Charlotte Claire was not allowed to date. The subject had become and ongoing tug of war with her parents. They'd conceded that she would be allowed to begin dating after she entered her junior year, but it was only October which meant eleven more months dateless. Most girls in her class had begun dating in their freshmen year, so to Charlotte Claire this penalization seemed unfair and unnecessary. It prompted the first stirrings of rebelliousness in her.

On an unusually warm fall afternoon after the pep rally, Charlotte Claire was in the gym talking with Amelie and Annie when Scotty Piper walked over to them. She assumed he was coming to flirt with Annie; all the boys flirted with Annie. Scotty was popular with the girls and Charlotte Claire was attracted to him. Though she hated the way he treated Timmy, she found his bad boy swagger appealing. He stood for several seconds looking at the three girls when Annie said, "Well, are you going to just stand there, or do you have something to say?"

"I'm just taking a few seconds to drink in the beauty," he said smoothly.

"Oh, brother!" Amelie groaned. "Where'd you get that line; the second-hand store?"

"You just haven't learned to appreciate my debonair charms, Amelie."

"Well I'll get right on that."

"Hey Annie, Stoner's having a kegger after the game tonight. Want to go with me?"

"Thanks Scotty, I already have a date."

"Your loss," he told her playfully.

"Is that another sample of your debonair charm?" Amelie asked.

"Amelie, I don't think you get me," he replied before turning to Charlotte Claire. "I'd ask you for the pleasure of your company, but I believe Daddy's little girl is still not allowed to date."

"No," she told him. "I'm allowed to date." Annie and Amelie looked at Charlotte Claire in astonishment. "Yes, they changed their minds. I mean they decided it was fine...if I dated."

"Well, that's good news for the boys of Bayou Derkin High. So how about it? Want to come with me to the kegger? It's gonna be fun."

"Sure, it sounds like fun."

"Great, great," he said. "I'll pick you up before the game, say six-thirty?"

"No," she said urgently. "I'll meet you at the stadium just

before the game."

"Great, see you there."

After he'd walked away Annie asked, "Your daddy decided to let you start dating?"

"You didn't tell us that," Amelie added. Charlotte Claire said nothing for several seconds.

"He didn't. I lied."

"Charlotte Claire!" Amelie cried. "Are you crazy? If your daddy and mama find out, you are going to get in so much trouble."

"I don't care," she said petulantly. "I'm one of the only girls, besides the Pentecostals, who don't get to date. I'm taking matters into my own hands."

"She is woman, hear her roar," Amelie said playfully.

"Annie, I need your help."

"Name it."

"Can I come home with you until the game and can I spend the night at your house?"

"Well yeah, but I've only got that little single bed. One of us is going to have to sleep on the floor or the couch in the living room."

"Let's go to my house," Amelie suggested. "We've got plenty of room and I hate missing anything."

"Perfect," Charlotte Claire said. "I'll tell Mama and Daddy we're having a sleepover at Amelie's. I don't think they'll say no since it's not a school night. Annie, you can help me with my makeup."

"What makeup?" Annie asked.

"Exactly," she replied. "So, you can help me with your makeup. And Amelie can I borrow some clothes? Something... sexy."

Charlotte Claire was all nervous excitement when she arrived at the stadium that evening with Amelie and Annie. "Do you see him?" she asked.

"Four o'clock," Amelie said.

"I'm a little nervous," she confided.

"Don't be," Annie told her. "You look great. We need to get our band uniforms on. We're late. Mr. White is going to kill us. See you at the kegger."

Charlotte Claire walked over to where Scotty was talking with Andy Stoner and Tom Burnett. "Hey," she said.

Scotty whistled when he saw her. "Who are you?" he asked flirtatiously. "We'd bettter get out of here before my date shows up."

"Ha ha, very funny," she said.

"You look real good," Tom told her.

"Yeah," Andy agreed. "I've never seen you dressed like that before."

It was true. Her homemade clothes were always loose fitting, what her mother referred to as wholesome; nothing like the blue jean mini skirt and midriff sweater that Amelie and Annie insisted she wear. After she'd dressed and saw herself in the mirror she couldn't believe how she looked. The clothes accentuated her curvy breasts, her small waist and her round bottom. Plus, she thought the makeup brought her face to life.

"Back off, losers," Scotty said proudly. "This one's mine."

As soon as they got to the kegger Scotty excused himself to get their beers. Annie and Amelie made a bee line to Charlotte Claire. "Well?" Annie asked excitedly.

"It was great!" Charlotte Claire told them. "He was so sweet. He held my hand part of the time and put his arm around me too. And he flirted a lot. He kept telling me how sexy I looked. No one's ever told me that before."

"That's because you dress like a nun," Amelie said.

"Shut up, Amelie," Annie told her. "You look great, Charlotte Claire. I'm glad you're having a good time."

"I'm glad you're having a good time, too," Amelie said. "I

just don't like him. I hate him for the way he treats Timmy. I don't think he has a conscience."

"I know," Charlotte Claire said. "I feel kind of bad about Timmy. Don't say anything about this if you talk to him. I think he'd feel betrayed. But Scotty is so cute...and sexy, too."

"Don't think about Timmy tonight," Annie told her. "Just have a good time."

"Here *it* comes now with your beer," Amelie said.

"Hello ladies," Scotty said when he'd reached the girls.

"Hey Scotty," Annie said.

"Hi," Amelie said, grudgingly.

"Hey, let's go hang by the fire pit for a while," he suggested to Charlotte Claire.

"Okay."

"See you girls later," Scotty told Annie and Amelie.

After they'd gone Amelie said, "Not if we see you first."

"Man, you really don't like him."

"No, I don't. I wouldn't trust him as far as I could throw him. I think he's a sociopath. And I think he's cruel."

"You just think that because of the way he treats Timmy. I don't know why boys always feel like they have to pick on someone to make themselves feel...tough."

"All boys don't," Amelie said. "Just assholes."

They'd been at the party for a little over an hour when Scotty suggested they go for a drive. Charlotte Claire knew it was code for "let's go make out." She'd never gone "parking" before but she said yes anyway. She felt adventurous and a little light headed from the beer. Scotty drove towards the river, his arm draped across the top of the plank seat of his father's old Oldsmobile. Charlotte Claire wasn't sure if that was a signal that she should scoot over beside him, so she placed herself midway between Scotty and the passenger's side door. "You can come a little closer," Scotty said amusedly. "I don't bite." She slid over next to him and he put his arm around her shoulder. "Open Arms" by Journey was playing on the radio.

"I love that song," Charlotte Claire said.

"You do?" Scotty replied. "Not me." He turned the radio dial past several stations and stopped when he heard "Hurts So Good" by John Cougar. "Now there's a good song."

"Oh yeah," was all she said but, in truth, Charlotte Claire hated the song.

When they'd reached the river, Scotty turned off the engine and left the radio on. Without saying a word, he pulled Charlotte Claire next to him and began kissing her forcefully. She was startled by the suddenness with which he did so but, having no point of reference, she figured that was the way it was done. After several minutes he stopped and looked at Charlotte Claire with a smile. "Let's sit in the back seat. This steering wheel is kind of uncomfortable." She hesitated at first but didn't want him to be uncomfortable. Now in back, he took her in his arms and they resumed. He was kissing her even more forcefully than before, thrusting his tongue deep into her mouth. She felt his hand on her breast. She pushed his hand away, but he immediately grabbed her again. She pushed his hand away again and this time he put his hand up her skirt. She tried to tell him to stop but each time she pulled her head away to speak he leaned further in until she was on her back.

Finally, she turned her head away from him and said, "Stop, I want to go home."

"Oh, you don't want to go home," he said dismissively. "Just relax. We're going to have a good time." He sat up briefly and in one swift motion swung her legs on to the seat and rolled on top of her. When Charlotte Claire tried to scream Scotty put his forearm across her throat: with his free hand he reached up her skirt and ripped her panties off. He unzipped his pants, pushed them down to his thighs and brutally forced himself inside of her. Pain shot through Charlotte Claire as he continued to violently thrust himself in her, his face wild with, something like anger or rage. Filled with terror and barely able to breathe, Charlotte Claire was sure that he was going to kill her. She closed her eyes and turned away from him, so she wouldn't have to see his face. After a few minutes he groaned loudly and quickly pulled himself out of her. He reached down to pull his pants up and said, "What the fuck?" He sat up suddenly, his penis protruding from his pants and covered in blood. "Shit!" he yelled. "There's blood everywhere. Are you on your period? Why didn't you tell me?"

"I'm not on my period," Charlotte Claire said weakly. She pushed her skirt down and sat up clutching the arm rest with both hands.

"What? You're not a virgin, are you?"

"Yes, I...."

"Fuck, there's blood all over the seat. My Dad is going to kill me. Why didn't you tell me? I'm going to have to go somewhere and clean this up before I go home. Shit! And I guess I'll have to take you home. You can't go back to the kegger like that. Fuck! You'd better stay in the back. I don't need blood in the front seat too."

Charlotte Claire stared out the window and into the darkness through the long, silent drive home. When they'd reached her parent's house Scotty started to say something, but Charlotte Claire was out of the car and up the front walk before she could hear what it was. She opened the front door carefully so as not to make noise, but her mother heard her and called out from the bedroom.

"Charlotte Claire is that you?"

"Yes Mama."

"I thought you were staying over at Amelie's."

"I changed my mind. I don't feel well."

"Let me get the thermometer."

"No, don't get up," she said, realizing she was still in Amelie's clothes. "I'm just going to wash up and go to bed. I'm sure it's nothing. I'll see you in the morning."

"Okay then, night-night."

"Night-night." In the bathroom she took off her clothes and drew a bath. She looked at her reflection in the bathroom mirror. She was different now. She'd never be the same again. I'm not a virgin anymore, she thought to herself. Then she began to cry for the first time that evening.

The next morning, she carried on as usual. She was not going to think about Scotty or that terrible night ever again.

For Charlotte Claire, like so many others, college was an opportunity for reinvention. She colored her hair and got her own make-up. In high school she'd had a good figure but covered it in the baggy clothes her mother made for her. With Annie's help she now chose more colorful and figure flattering outfits. Her confidence soared, and she was no longer the timid girl who felt invisible-she was outgoing, vivacious and fun to be around. She pledged a sorority and her circle of friends increased exponentially. Many of her sorority sisters were from wealthy families and through them Charlotte Claire got a glimpse of what life was like for the other half.

In her sophomore year she began dating Adam Collins, a quiet, studious and handsome boy she met through one of her sorority sisters. Adam was from a prominent local family. His father owned several car dealerships, and his mother was regularly in the social pages. On their first date Adam picked her up in a brand new red Mustang and took her to The Plantation House, an exclusive, members-only restaurant. Up to that time her dates were more likely a burger and a movie. Now she was dining by candlelight in an antebellum mansion with 14-foot ceilings and velvet drapes.

Adam continued to pursue her. She loved the old fashioned, gentlemanly way he courted her. He opened doors for her, both literally and figuratively. He brought her to parties and dinners in some of the town's finest homes, including his own. When he asked her to meet his parents she realized that the relationship had become serious for Adam and though she loved dating him she wasn't sure if she loved *him*. Plus, she wondered how his parents would feel about *her*. They were rich and she was a poor girl from a small town. She borrowed an expensive dress and heels from a sorority sister, determined to make the best possible impression. But when Adam arrived to pick her up he was wearing khaki shorts and a polo shirt. Perhaps she'd miscalculated, she thought, but they were running late and there was no time to change. "You look beautiful," he said amusedly. "Kind of dressy for barbecue."

"You said lunch with my parents...not barbecue with my parents. I wanted to make a good impression," she told him. "Guess I over did it a bit."

"Well, you look amazing. And don't worry, they'll love you."

"From your mouth to God's ears," she said weakly.

They pulled into the circular drive in front of a large, red brick colonial home. They passed through the porticos great white columns and into the formal entry hall where marble floors ran from the front to the back of the house. Adam's mother and father were having cocktails on the large covered patio which faced an Olympic sized swimming pool. His father, who was tall, solidly built and dressed almost exactly like Adam, rose to greet them. His mother, dressed in a flowery, sleeveless shift, (which Charlotte Claire would later learn was a Lilli Pulitzer staple) with sandals and a small strand of pearls remained seated. She was a petite, fine boned woman, her perfect shade of blonde hair pulled back in a neat ponytail.

"There's my boy," his father said to Adam warmly.

"And here's my girl," he replied. "Mom, Dad, this is Charlotte Claire Parker."

At last Adam's mother rose to greet her. Charlotte Claire felt her face flush. "Hello," she said timidly, extending her hand.

"It's great to finally meet you," Adam's father said.

"Yes," his mother offered. "Welcome to our home."

"It's so nice to meet you as well, Mr. and Mrs. Collins."

"Oh, please, call me Bunny."

"And I'm just Mike," his father added.

This made Charlotte Claire uncomfortable. No one from Bayou Derkin would ever dream of calling their friend's parents by their first name.

"Cora!" Bunny called out. "My dear what can we get you to drink?"

"Whatever you're having, Miss Bunny." said Charlotte Claire apprehensively. Bunny glanced at her husband in amusement. A middle-aged black woman in a maid's uniform appeared on the patio with a tray of hors d'oeuvres. "Cora, Charlotte Claire will have a vodka and lemonade. Adam?"

"Same."

Charlotte Claire had never had liquor but was too nervous to say so. "Come," Bunny continued. "Let's sit." Charlotte Claire worried that she should have asked what they were drinking or that Bunny would disapprove of her having alcohol. But no one seemed the least bit fazed, so she supposed it was okay. She tried to relax but could feel Bunny's eyes on her, assessing her, and probably laughing inside that she was overdressed. She hadn't felt this nervous since she left Bayou Derkin; she was 'less than' once again.

"Adam tells us you're a business major," Bunny said.

"Yes ma'am."

"Smart girl," Mike added. "That's a degree that'll gives you lots of options."

"Yes sir."

"You don't need to ma'am and sir us," Mike said warmly. "Mike and Bunny is fine."

"Yes sir," she repeated prompting mild laughter. "I mean, yes Mike."

"You'll get the hang of it," Adam told her.

"Your home is lovely," Charlotte Claire offered. "How long have you lived here?"

"Dad's lived here his entire life," Adam said. "His grandparents built this house and passed it on to his parents and so on."

"One day Adam will live in this house," Bunny said, as if baiting a hook. "And where are you from, dear?"

"Bayou Derkin-well just outside of Bayou Derkin," Charlotte Claire said. "It's about forty miles from here."

"Oh, yes, I know it," Mike said. "Friend of mine, Landon Reed, owns the gravel pit there. There's a lot of money in gravel." Charlotte Claire began to shift in her seat. She touched the back of her neck nervously and took a sip of lemonade.

"Oh really?" she went on. "What a coincidence."

"And what do your parents do?" Bunny asked. This was it, the moment Charlotte Claire had been dreading. But what could she do? She could lie or embellish, but it would only be worse when they found out later—and they would find out later.

"My Daddy works at the gravel pit, the one that your friend owns. His daughter, Leanne, was a classmate. How's that for a small world? And my mother works in the school cafeteria. We live near the gravel pit, so my Daddy can walk to work. Mama has to drive into town, but it's not that far."

Bunny and Mike exchanged a glance in the brief silence that followed before Adam came to her rescue. "Well," he said earnestly. "I can't wait to meet your folks. They have to be pretty great if they're your parents." He took her hand in his and gave it a little kiss.

"I'd better check on Cora in the kitchen and Mike you'd better start the coals," Bunny said. "Will you excuse me, Charlotte Claire?"

"Can I help?" she asked.

"No, dear, I have help."

Charlotte Claire was mortified. She'd rambled on so. Why

hadn't she just answered the question and moved onto some other topic? Was Bunny trying to embarrass her? Did she already know what her parents did? If Adam were to ask her, would Bunny ever approve of her son marrying a poor girl from Bayou Derkin, a girl who would live in this very house and inherit Bunny's life? "Where is the bathroom?" she asked Adam.

"I'll show you," he said, taking her hand and leading her back into the foyer. "She shouldn't have said that. I'll talk to her."

"No, don't," she said, tears welling in her eyes. "It may just make it worse." In the powder room she dabbed at her eyes, touched up her makeup and fussed with her hair. She looked at her reflection in the mirror and sighed. "Back into the lion's den." As she approached the patio she heard Adam speaking angrily.

"She's a great girl and in part because she *didn't* grow up rich like those spoiled brats you want me to go out with."

"I know you are young and this is all very romantic," Bunny said. "But when you get older these differences in your upbringings will be a source of conflict. You are from different worlds. God knows what her family is like. Her father works at a gravel pit."

"That's enough Mother!" Once it was quiet Charlotte Claire returned to the patio, sat down beside Adam and took his hand.

Charlotte Claire's discomfort and nervous rambling only served to further endear her to Adam. And Bunny's objections solidified his resolve. Within months they were engaged.

The wedding was a huge affair. This was Bunny's show and she wanted only the best, so Adam's family paid for everything, including Charlotte Claire's wedding gown-which cost more than her parents' car. Bunny had input on all decisions: Invitations, china patterns, trousseau, venue, menu, orchestra. Ordinarily she'd have resented Bunny's control, but Charlotte Claire knew she was out of her depth. The wedding would be covered extensively in the social pages, so Charlotte Claire, also, wanted everything to be perfect and Bunny could do that. It did pain her, though, to see her own mother so overwhelmed by all the fuss, which came second nature to Bunny.

After their honeymoon Adam and Charlotte Claire moved to Houston. He entered Baylor School of Medicine and she took an administrative assistant's position at HT Technologies, a cutting-edge company. Most of the staff at HT were in their 20's and 30's, and the office culture was a very social one. Charlotte Claire enjoyed the quick banter and good-natured ribbing that peppered her work day. Adam's schedule at the medical school was grueling which left her free to spend many evenings out with her co-workers.

Within months of moving to Houston, Adam's schedule and Charlotte Claire's social life had left a gulf between them. She tried to initiate outings with Adam, but he was usually too tired or needed to study. They rarely fought and still made love, but Charlotte Claire could not help thinking that something was missing; a spark, a connection, chemistry. Adam's courtly pursuit of her before their marriage had all but vanished. It felt as if now that they were married, he didn't need to make an effort. She wondered if Adam was unaware of the change in their relationship, or if, like her, he was going through the motions and saying nothing. Charlotte Claire began to think that she'd jumped into marriage too soon; she hadn't given herself a chance to experience an independent life before settling down. She started to question if she really loved him. She tried to push those thoughts away, but the more time passed the sadder she was and the harder it was to ignore.

Charlotte Claire had been at HT Tech for two years when she met Stanley Latimer, a big, gregarious Midwesterner who transferred from Chicago to manage her division of the company. At first, she maintained a deferential distance from her new boss, but he was quick witted and warm, and soon she found that she liked him. He was an easy boss to work for; professional yet laid back. He treated her as a colleague rather than an employee and he expanded her areas of responsibility.

Being single, Stanley regularly joined the office happy hour crowd and through that he and Charlotte Claire became friends as well as colleagues. Sometimes they'd go to a quiet area of the bar and talk about more serious things; their upbringings, their families, their lives. It was in one of those conversations that Charlotte Claire confided her unhappiness in her marriage.

It was mid-summer when Charlotte Claire realized she was falling in love with Stanley. She'd been batting the thought away like an annoying fly for a month. But one Friday morning when Stanley stuck his head into her office to say good morning it hit her-his smile, his sweet face, his laugh. She was with him every day. How could she not fall in love with him?

The following week the office crowd met for a typical happy hour gathering. Charlotte Claire found herself surreptitiously glancing at the door, hoping Stanley would appear. After an hour he walked briskly into the bar and directly to where she was sitting. His grave expression made Charlotte Claire think something terrible must have happened. "Stanley, what is it?"

"Can I talk to you outside?"

"Of course."

They walked into the humid summer night. Stanley was walking with purpose, two steps ahead of Charlotte Claire. She glanced up to see the night sky filled with stars and a half moon. When they'd reached the parking lot Stanley stopped beside a car. He seemed to be searching for what to say. For a moment Charlotte Claire thought she might be getting fired. She leaned against the car and began to pull a tissue from her purse when Stanley turned suddenly, took her in his arms and kissed her. When they stopped kissing he said, "I'm in love with you."

Having an affair was something Charlotte Claire could have never have imagined herself doing, yet here she was. Being with Stanley had convinced her that she wasn't in love with Adam. But divorce was another thing she couldn't see herself doing. With Stanley she'd discovered the "something missing" in her marriage to Adam. She couldn't wait to get to work each day and hated coming home in the evenings. Their sexual relationship was passionate and intense. Their love for one another deepened. She'd struggled to break away from Stanley, but the pull was too strong.

She lived for months in a state of turmoil and guilt. In her mind there played an endless loop of the same question; What do I do, what do I do? If she left Adam she'd break his heart, if she stayed with him she'd be unhappy for the rest of her life. She knew if she got a divorce her parents would be disappointed in her. They were old fashioned and believed that when you married it was for life. Her emotions veered wildly; joy when she was with Stanley and despair when she considered what to do about Adam and their marriage.

She'd been sleeping with Stanley for six months when everything changed. She'd mentioned to a co-worker that she'd been nauseous for several days, and the friend suggested a home pregnancy test. That afternoon after work Charlotte Claire went to CVS, bought the test and went directly home. She sat on the side of the tub anxiously awaiting the results. She was pregnant. She knew the baby was Stanley's, she hadn't had sex with Adam in months. Now her dilemma took on a greater sense of urgency.

Over the next two weeks the gradual acceptance that she was going to have a child slowly sunk in. Her emotions were so extreme and her thoughts so conflicted that she was having trouble sleeping. Stanley kept asking her what was wrong, but she'd resolved not tell him anything until she came to some decision.

It was a Friday and Stanley was out of town on business. Charlotte Claire and a co-worker were in the ladies' room freshening up when she felt a violent pain in her abdomen. She grabbed her stomach and looked at her friend.

"Are you alright honey?" her friend asked.

"Yeah, I think so. That's so weird. I just all of a sudden..." Another violent pain, and this one was worse. "I'm having a lot of pain," she said weakly.

"Why don't you go sit down and I'll get you some water."

"That's a good idea," Charlotte Claire agreed. But before she could leave the ladies' room another pain struck, so violent she collapsed onto the bathroom floor. "Oh!" she screamed in pain. "Call an ambulance. I need to go to the emergency room."

The doctor who treated her was an older man with a kindly face and a soothing voice. "First, I want you to know that you'll be fine," he told her, holding her hand in his as he did so. "But I'm sorry to tell you've that you lost the baby." Charlotte Claire gazed absently out the window as he spoke. "There's no reason you can't have a completely healthy baby in the future. But we need to get you back in tip top shape, so you'll be our guest here for a few days. Try to get some rest now." The doctor left the room without Charlotte Claire ever having said a word.

The day she was to be released from the hospital she called Timmy. "What should I do?" she asked plaintively, nearly crying. "Mama and Daddy will be so let down, and Adam, what about Adam, he will be..."

"Hurt, he will be hurt Charlotte Claire. It happens to all of us. There's no avoiding it. At some point in all of our lives we will be hurt." After a few moments he asked, "Do you love Adam?"

"No," she said softly. She'd known it for some time but,

had never said it out loud to another person.

"Do you love Stanley?

"Yes, Timmy, I love him."

"Here's the thing Charlotte Claire," he said thoughtfully. "I would rather live the rest of my life with the hope of finding real love than spend the rest of my life settling and knowing I would never have it."

It was the clarity she needed to move forward. She felt the weight of the world had been lifted from her shoulders. When Adam arrived to pick her up she sat him down and told him that she was leaving him, that though she loved him, she was not in love with him and that she would be moving out. It was the hardest thing she'd ever had to do, but of one thing she was now sure-she had to do it.

That night she packed a bag and checked into a hotel. Within a week she'd moved into Stanley's apartment and within a year, they were married. That was twenty-four years ago. During that time Stanley's rise in the tech industry was meteoric. Their early life together was a succession of re-locations. Each new city meant a larger house, nicer cars, fancier country clubs and more and more money. Charlotte Claire quit working when they decided to have a family. They had two children, a boy named Tyler (for Timmy) and a girl, Amelia Anne. As Stanley's profile rose, so did Charlotte Claire's. She was in demand for charities, women's clubs, fundraisers and numerous, sought-after boards. She evolved into a world-class hostess who was equally envied and admired. The little girl who grew up by the gravel pit had made it big time and she was happy.

Yet there was something long buried, and she could feel it, fighting its way to the surface.

The Atlantic Ocean, Off the Coast of Key Largo

Friday, April 15th, 2016

12:05 AM

"Mayday, mayday, mayday," Timmy said. "Do you read me?"

"Yes, I read you," the officer said.

"I called earlier to report an incident with a man named Scotty Piper."

"Yes, we've noted the earlier calls. We need your coordinates."

"We're locked in a stateroom," Timmy said, excitedly. "We can't get to the pilothouse to get the coordinates. There were shots fired but now it's quiet. He's not saying anything but we're afraid to leave of the stateroom. We don't know if he's out there waiting for us. Please!" he cried, "You've got to help us. You have to send someone out here."

"Sir, we can't help you without your coordinates. We won't know how to find you. We have aircraft out looking for you but it's a lot of area to cover. If you think you're in danger, just stay where you are. We'll continue to search. If, at some point you're certain that you're safe, call us with your coordinates"

"I understand. I can't talk right now. We'll give it a little more time and then we'll check. We'll call back."

ANNIE

Los Angeles, July 2015

"CUT!" CALDER CALLED out.

"Oh, thank God, those lights were frying me. I start the scene looking like me and finish it looking like George Hamilton" Annie said, prompting everyone on set to break up. She'd just started filming season three of a highly rated legal drama for a prolific writer and producer who had four other highly rated dramas on the air. She'd hated going to TV after having had a successful film career, but there had been fewer and fewer offers coming in and even those weren't enticing. She had no interest in playing mothers of adult children, spinsters or small supporting roles that would most likely be cut to pieces in the editing room. She was only 45 when the film industry deemed her obsolete. So, when she got the script for *Philadelphia Law* she'd had to reconsider television.

It was a hit from the first episode and revived her career in a way, no movie could have, she thought. As the show became more successful her salary got fatter. There were endorsements-her name and face became associated with hair and make-up products, high-end fragrances and even jewelry. She was financially secure before *Philadelphia Law,* but now she was out-and-out rich. And it turned out that it was a great part. She won a Golden Globe an got an Emmy nomination for season one, and won the Emmy and Globe for season two. The show routinely got great reviews and was deemed a "watercooler" show by the entertainment media. She could see it going for six or seven years; after that she could retire or choose to work when the material was good.

Another perk of the show was its director, Calder West. Though several years older, he was ruggedly handsome and intelligent. Sex between them was explosive and near-constant. They started seeing each other shortly after they began filming season one, and became exclusive within a couple of months. They decided to maintain separate residences, as both wished to maintain their independence, and neither of them were interested in marriage. The arrangement seemed to work.

Calder stepped into Annie's trailer, where she sat at her make-up table. He moved silently behind her, lifted her hair and kissed her on the nape of her neck. Looking at her reflection in the mirror, he said, "Hello beautiful."

"Hello handsome," she replied. She spun her chair around and kissed him softly on the lips.

"I thought the cross-examination scene went well today," he said. "How'd it feel for you?"

"Good, no complaints. Well just one. I wish Lucky would stop improvising and stick to the script. It's all well and good to be creative, but if he gets an idea he should bring it to you or the writers, so we can flesh it out. It throws off the blocking. He keeps missing his marks and then we have to re-shoot the scene. It's a waste of time and money. But other than that, hunky dory."

They both laughed.

"I'm going to miss you when you're off on the Cape with your friends next week."

"I'll miss you too," she told him. "But it's just a week."

"Liar," he chided. "You don't miss anyone when you're off with your gang."

"Well, I'll miss you...a little bit," she teased.

"Come here, you." He pulled her close, took her in his arms

and kissed her.

"Well, I'll definitely miss that."

It was true that she wouldn't miss him. She loved him very much, but when the four friends were together at the beach none of them missed anyone very much. It was as if they existed in a parallel universe for a week each summer. Husbands, children, lovers-all seemed characters from another life. It wasn't that they didn't love the people in their lives, but for that week the four of them were enough.

Annie Squibb's life had been tumultuous from the start. She was born during a devastating hurricane which, in retrospect, seemed to her a dark foreshadowing of her early life. Annie lived with her mother in a tiny frame house that consisted of just three rooms and a bath. The house sat next door to the bar and package liquor store owned by her two spinster aunts, Idelle and Daisy.

Her mother's chronic heart disease had taken a toll on her parent's marriage, and her father walked out on them when Annie was four. He moved to the Northeast and disappeared from her life. Her mother tried to fill the void of her father's absence, but it left a hole in her life that she'd been trying to fill ever since.

By age 10 Annie had already started to develop breasts, and it had become a source of humiliation to her. At school the boys made lewd comments and the girls snickered and openly teased her. After one particularly rough day she walked home in tears. When she got home she picked up a hand-full of rocks, sat on the front porch steps and dejectedly threw them, one by one, at the ground. Seeing this through the kitchen window, her mother came onto the porch and sat beside Annie on the steps. "Some one's having a bad day, I think," she said gently.

"No," Annie said, sullenly.

"Maybe this will help." Her mother slipped a chocolate chip cookie from the pocket of her apron. Annie looked at her mother who smiled down at her. She took the cookie and began to eat it slowly. "Want to tell me what's wrong?" Annie pulled at her bra strap. "Oh, *those* are causing you a bad day," she said amusedly. "You may have to get used to that."

"No, I mean the kids at school are...always picking on me about 'em"

"What are they saying?"

"They're calling me their bosom buddy or asking me if I want a tittie-twister or if I come from BRA-zille," she whined.

Her mother had to stifle the urge to laugh. "Well, kids can be mean sometimes. You just try to ignore them. I promise things will change when you get older. Right now, the girls are just jealous, and the boys are...well... nervous."

"But I'm the only girl in my grade with...these," she complained pointing awkwardly at her breasts. "I hate'em. And nobody's jealous."

"All of the girls are going to go through what you're going through. It's just happened to you sooner. You remind them of that when they say mean things. And you might remind them that they better hope they'll go through that. That ought to shut them up." Annie laughed, and her mother joined in. She scooted in closer to Annie and put an arm around her shoulder. "Oh honey, growing up can be tough sometimes, but the good news is that time moves on and you'll forget all about this. And speaking of time I better go in and get supper started. Do you have homework?"

"Just a little."

"Well then, don't stay...," she said weakly, bracing herself against the porch post.

"Mama, are you alright?"

"Just a little dizzy spell," she said, still holding onto the post. "Here, help Mama inside. I'd better lay down for a few minutes."

After dinner Annie stood at the kitchen sink and dried the dishes as her mother washed. Her mother began to hum and after a while to sing, "You are my sunshine, my only sunshine. You make me happy when skies are gray. You'll never know dear how much I love you. Please don't take my sunshine away." When she was finished she turned to Annie and kissed her on the cheek. Annie thought her mother looked beautiful in the moonlight that drifted through the kitchen window. "Okay, time to get ready for bed."

The house was dark and quiet when Annie tip-toed into her mother's room around midnight. "Mama," she whispered. When her mother didn't answer she said it louder. "Mama?"

"Annie," she said groggily. "What are you doing in here?"

"I can't sleep. Can I sleep with you?"

"I guess so," she said. "Crawl in." Annie crawled in under the covers and snuggled up next to her. Her mother put an arm around her and said, "Now close your eyes and try to think of something wonderful so you can fall asleep."

"Like what?"

"Angels. Think of all the beautiful angels in heaven." In a little while Annie fell asleep and dreamed of angels.

When Annie woke the next morning, she was still in her mother's arms. She glanced at the clock on the nightstand, 7:35. Her mother usually woke her at 7 o'clock to get ready for school. "Mama, we're late. Mama," she repeated. "We over slept." Annie sat up and gently shook her mother's shoulder. "Mama, Mama!" She didn't move. Annie shook her again and again, but her mother was still. Her face was drawn and pale. Annie began to panic. She shook her mother once more and then leapt from the bed and ran out of the house and down the driveway, the gravel hurting her bare feet. She ran into the package liquor and up the stairs to the apartment her two aunts shared. She burst through the door and cried, "There's something wrong with Mama! She won't wake up. She looks funny." The two women put down their coffee cups and rushed out the door behind Annie. When they reached the bedroom both women knew right away that their sister was dead.

"Daisy, take Annie to her room so she can get dressed for school," Idelle told her sister.

"I can dress myself," Annie said. "What's wrong with her? Call the doctor!"

"I will sweetie," she said gently. "Now go get dressed." Annie left the room in a state of anxiety. The two women remained near their sister. Daisy began to weep softly. Idelle sat on the bed and held her sister's lifeless hand. "She'll be dressed soon," Idelle said. "Let's wait for her in the kitchen. We need to tell her."

"Oh, no," Daisy wept.

"There's nothing else to do. After that's done you sit with her and I'll make the arrangements."

At the funeral parlor the following day Annie appeared stoic, but in truth she was in shock. A deer in the headlights, her mother would've said. She hadn't even cried when her aunts told her that her mother was dead, or passed, as they put it. At first, she hadn't known what they meant so they had to elaborate. Now Annie felt like a zombie, drifting from the viewing room to the reception room, sitting motionless as if in a trance. She'd never been in a funeral parlor before and she hated it. It smelled like death and wax. Even the roses smelled like death. It was Friday and she was missing school, which she hated. She wondered when she'd go back. In the afternoon she asked her aunts if she could go outside. She'd been inside the funeral parlor all day and it was starting to get to her. She was sitting on the front porch of the funeral parlor when she saw Timmy, Amelie and Charlotte Claire making their way towards her. She was so happy to see them that she began to cry. The closer they got, the harder she cried. By the time they reached Annie her body shook with sobs. Charlotte Claire sat beside her and held her hand while Timmy sat on the other side with his arm around her shoulders. Amelie knelt before her and, looking intently into her eyes said, "We're here."

Annie moved into the little two-bedroom flat her spinster aunts shared above the bar. A large, windowed pantry off the kitchen was fitted with a single bed and served as Annie's room. The old women were oil and water: Idelle barking out instructions, the loving task master, and Daisy alternately swooning or giggling. But their affection for Annie was palpable and she knew she was safe and loved. Still, when she went to bed each night she prayed for her mother, and that her Daddy would come back and be her Daddy again.

After a week she was happy to return to school but nervous about how her classmates and teachers would treat her. Would she be treated as an object of pity or would everyone act like she'd just come back from a vacation? It was with relief that she spotted Timmy and Charlotte Claire standing near the monkey bars. She crossed directly to them and said, "Hey!"

"Hey!" they responded in unison. After an uncomfortable silence Charlotte Claire asked, "How you doing?"

"Fine. It's weird, but I'm fine."

"Yeah, I guess so," Timmy said. "Hey, guess what, you got to miss campus clean-up. So boring and so hot."

"It lasted like two hours," Charlotte Claire added. "It's child labor! There ought to be a law."

"There is," Timmy said dryly.

"Here comes Amelie," Annie said when she spotted her walking across the school yard. As they waited for her, Leanne Reed approached with a group of her friends.

"Well, looks who's back, girls," Leanne said. "It's Little Orphan Annie." Leanne and her girlfriends burst into shrill laughter. Charlotte Claire and Timmy were stunned by the cruelty of the comment but said nothing. Annie's eyes welled with tears. Timmy walked over to Leanne and pushed her forcefully to the ground. "I'm going to tell," she shrieked, dusting the dirt from her dress.

"No, you're not, you hateful cow, or I'll have to tell the reason I pushed you down." Realizing Timmy was right, she changed her tactic.

"You'd never have done that if I were a boy. Because you're a sissy-baby like everyone says, a big sissy who can only stand up to a girl."

"Yeah, well you're a girl and you can't even stand up," he replied, causing Annie and Charlotte Claire to laugh.

"What are you laughing at, Little Orphan Annie?" she snapped before storming off, her friends following in her wake.

As Annie's routine returned to normal, so did she, mostly. Leanne continued to torment her with the cruel nickname for years. She was self-conscious about not having a mother or father. She felt like an orphan and the repeated reminders from Leanne only made it worse. At friends' houses, she would hang back and observe mothers and fathers together. She liked to see how they interacted, if they were affectionate to each other and their children, if they were romantic. She longed for a nuclear family and studied them with anthropological fervor.

As she grew older she became even more beautiful. She was popular with the boys, but other than Amelie and Charlotte Claire, Annie had few girlfriends. She became grist for the high school gossip mill. They said she was a slut, went all the way, was giving blow jobs in back seats, was pregnant. In truth, while most of the girls who spread the hateful rumors were doing all the things they accused Annie of doing, she remained a virgin until she went to college. The rumors, which always got back to her, were hurtful and demeaning. She couldn't help but feel it had to do with the fact that she had no parents and lived over a bar with two eccentric old women.

Annie graduated with a full scholarship and attended the same small college as Charlotte Claire and Amelie. She majored in Drama and began performing in school and community theater productions. The pursuit came naturally to her and she threw herself into her rehearsals and performances with more commitment and dedication than she ever had before. Her passion for acting and love of the craft became all-consuming.

In her junior year she was cast as Maggie the Cat in *Cat on a Hot Tin Roof*. She'd worked hard on her audition piece and had campaigned enthusiastically for the part. The day of the audition she was nervous, but prepared. The director, Benton Craig, was a new professor and Annie was unsure what kind of Maggie he was looking for. Young and handsome, in a scholarly way, he possessed an authoritative, almost arrogant bearing which unnerved Annie. When she'd finished the audition he simply said, 'thanks,' so she was sure she hadn't gotten the part. But when she went to the green room to check the cast list the next day, Charlotte Claire was already waiting for her. "You got it!" she shrieked. "You got Maggie!"

Throughout the weeks of rehearsal Benton's interactions with Annie became more flirtatious. At first, she demurred. She did find him attractive, but he was older and married. His advances continued, her attraction grew and by the opening night of the play their affair was in full swing.

Since he was married and she lived in the dorm, they had to become creative in their meeting places. They met in rehearsal rooms, friends' apartments, back stage, back seats and cheap hotels. Sex seemed to come as naturally to Annie as acting had. She'd had sex with a college boy she dated in freshman and sophomore year, but she'd found the sex disappointing and the boy awkward and selfish in bed. Benton was an experienced lover, alternately aggressive and gentle. He was tall and leanly muscled with broad shoulders and a sculpted chest. Annie loved his body and loved making love with him. She only occasionally allowed the guilt she felt for sleeping with another woman's husband to simmer to the surface. By the time the run of the play had ended they'd been sleeping together for two months.

At four months into the relationship Annie began to feel off. She had low energy and felt slightly nauseous all the time. She thought she might be getting the flu until the time for her period came and went. She'd always had very regular periods. Worried, she called Charlotte Claire who, within an hour, arrived at Annie's dorm room with an early pregnancy test. They sat on her bed and waited for the result. It was true. She was pregnant. She was pregnant for a married man.

"What am I going to do?" she asked.

"Go to the doctor. These test results could be wrong."

"I don't think they're wrong. I'm late, I've been nauseous, tired..."

"But you still need to see a doctor, especially if you *are* pregnant. Do you want me to go with you?"

"No, I think it's the one thing I'd rather do without an audience." Annie laughed weakly.

"Will you tell Benton?"

"I don't know. I don't know anything. I'll see the doctor, and then decide."

The doctor confirmed Annie's fears. She was pregnant. Sitting on her bed with her head in her hands she wondered how she could have let herself become involved with a married man. What was she going to tell Benton? She cared about him, but she wasn't sure if she loved him. She wanted to finish school and move to New York. She wanted to be an actress, not a mother. She looked at her reflection in the mirror and sighed. Pull yourself together, she thought, put on some lipstick and go to class.

"Annie!" a voice called from the hall. "Phone!" She hurriedly put on her lipstick, grabbed her books and went to the phone.

"Is this Annie Squibb?" an unfamiliar voice asked.

"Yeah,"

"This is Sarah Craig."

Annie froze. Her heart was pounding. "Yes?" She couldn't think of anything else to say.

"I believe you know my husband," the voice said evenly. "I believe you're sleeping with my husband. Well, not sleeping. He sleeps with me. I believe you're fucking my husband."

A hot flush surged through Annie's body.

"You're going to stop seeing my husband. I'm pregnant. Do you understand? It's over." Then there was a click and the sound of a dial tone.

She stood frozen for several seconds before dropping the receiver and rushing back to her room. This is over, she thought; she could never tell Benton about the pregnancy now. No one could know about the pregnancy. How could she have allowed this to happen? The old taunts of her high school classmates came flooding back; tramp, slut. She couldn't have a baby, and no one could know about the affair. She was not going to prove her detractors right.

It took a few days and some surreptitious inquiries to find an abortion clinic and schedule the procedure. Timmy came from New Orleans and accompanied Annie to the clinic while Charlotte Claire waited in a motel room for their return. The four friends chipped in for the room and the procedure. Timmy and Charlotte Claire took turns checking on Annie, who mostly slept. The next morning Timmy left for New Orleans, Annie and Charlotte Claire returned to their dorms, and resumed their regular routines as if nothing had happened.

Annie remained in school through the rest of the semester. She and Benton spoke briefly about his wife's phone call and mutually agreed that the relationship was over. But, Annie was changed. Carrying the secret of her abortion around with her, day in and day out, proved to be a weight too hard to bear. Her enjoyment of school had evaporated, and seeing Benton daily in the drama department was like seeing a ghost. She knew she had to move on, but that seemed impossible at school. She decided it was time for New York.

Annie never finished college. She went to New York and shared an apartment with an upper-classman who'd moved there the year before. She got a job waiting tables, enrolled in acting classes and started auditioning. At first, she found work as a movie extra and got walk-ons or bit parts in off-Broadway plays. It wasn't much, but it got her an agent. At her agent's suggestion, she dropped Squibb from her name and used her middle name as her surname. Now she was Anne Renee. Her agent thought it would highlight her sex appeal, like Ann Margret or Tina Louise. Her agent found her a recurring role on a soap opera. It was good money and good exposure. It also allowed her to quit her job and work on her craft full time. The soap was also a good education, giving her some experience in front of a camera. And the camera loved her. Her features popped on screen. Her large eyes, high cheekbones and supple mouth were made even more beautiful through the lens.

As the months on the soap passed, Annie's profile started to rise. She was getting guest starring roles on prime-time series that were filmed in New York, and her role on the soap had been given more prominence. She had become a successful working actor. But now, she thought, it was time to look ahead. She fired her agent and signed with a powerful talent agency that sent her up for prime-time TV and film roles.

Two years after she began, Annie quit the soap and accepted a supporting role on a prime-time sit-com filmed in

Los Angeles. She played Ursula, a sexy office dimwit who was warm and occasionally wise. The show, which was headlined by a successful stand-up comedian, was a huge success and Annie's role was a fan favorite. As Ursula, she was not merely the butt of the joke; the part was actually funny, and Annie captured her character perfectly. Viewers quoted Ursula's lines and mimicked her sexy walk. Annie stole every scene she was in, and was becoming a part of the cultural landscape. She had become a bona fide TV star. After season one was completed she won the Emmy for best supporting actress in a comedy. The prime-time success opened doors to larger roles in TV and film. She was shrewd in her choice of films, conscientiously constructing a ladder of roles designed to elevate her career: Serious supporting roles in high-profile films, leads in romantic comedies, "the girl" in action films, dramatic leads. She established herself as a talented and versatile actress who could bring in box office. Annie was a success beyond her most indulgent dreams. She had money, fame, a fulfilling career and any man she wanted. But occasionally, in her most private moments-when she let her thoughts drift south to Bayou Derkin-she still felt like a motherless child, like Little Orphan Annie.

The Atlantic Ocean, Off the Coast of Key Largo

Friday, April 15th, 2016

12:15 AM

"Mayday, mayday, mayday," she said into the radio telephone. "Do you read me?"

"Yes, I read you," the Coast Guard officer replied. "What is your status? Are you able now to give me your coordinates?"

"We have two people dead. I'm bringing the vessel in to dock in Key Largo Marina. Please have the Coast Guard and the police meet us at the dock. We are no longer in danger. Please, we need help."

"No!" the officer said emphatically. "I need you to stay where you are. Turn on all the lights on the vessel and give me your coordinates, now!"

"Just a minute, let me see. I'm new at this," she said nervously. "Latitude 25, Longitude 80. Yes, I think that's right."

"Good, you're doing fine," he said encouragingly. "Just sit tight and we'll be there as soon as we can."

"Okay," she said, "Okay."

AMELIE

IT WAS 8PM and Amelie was still in her office rifling through a stack of fabric samples. She was creating a new line of bedding to coordinate with her artisan quilts. At this rate, she thought, she wouldn't get home until 11, again. Her business, Amelie Ardoin Home, was a success, but it didn't leave her much time for a life. At least she was able to work with her husband and daughter, so the long hours weren't as difficult. And she was grateful for her success. Someday, she thought, I'll retire, and it will have been worth it.

"Mom," Deedee said, as she walked into the office with more fabric samples, "Don't forget you have a conference call with your gang at 8:15"

"Oh, that's right. Dammit! I just about forgot. Shit."

"Language Mom, Elizabeth is in my office."

"*Sorry*," Amelie exaggerated. "Thanks for reminding me."

"Just doing my job, Boss. I'll set up the conference in five and then I need to get Elizabeth home. Anything brief you need done before I go?"

"No, I'm good. Just buzz me when the call's ready. Oh, and Deedee, close the door on your way out, please."

Amelie made it through a few more samples when the phone buzzed. She slipped on her headphones and took the call. "Who's ready for the beach?" Annie asked excitedly.

"I am!" All three called out.

"Who arrives first?" Timmy asked.

"I get to Boston at 12:30 on Saturday," Annie said.

"I'm 11:30," Charlotte Claire volunteered.

"I'm noon," Amelie said.

"Great, barring any delays you'll all be there in time to make the fast ferry at two. It takes 90 minutes. You'll get to my place just in time for happy hour. Plus, it's a great way to approach P-Town. The views are spectacular."

"I'm so excited," Amelie trilled. "I need a break in the worst way."

"And that's how you'll get it," Timmy volleyed.

"Gnaw, gnaw, gnaw," Amelie returned, in her best Curley from The Three Stooges.

"Oh, here we go," Annie added.

They all laughed. It always felt as if the trip were beginning on these pre-trip calls, all of them so happy to see one another after a yearlong wait.

"Timmy, I can't wait to see your house," Charlotte Claire chimed. "I bet it's gorgeous."

"Thanks to my impeccable taste and my husband's impeccable bank account, you would be correct. Seriously, it's a super casual house, very nice, but modest...more of a cottage than a house. Actually, it is literally a vine-covered cottage. But it has three beds and three baths. Two of you will have to share the large guest suite."

"I'm not sleeping with Amelie," Charlotte Claire said with mock irritation. "She snores."

"Should we arrange for a car to take us to your place?" Annie asked.

"It's a short walk to the cottage from the..." Timmy paused. "Oh, wait; who am I talking to, the queens of the steamer trunks. I have a car; I'll meet you at the dock. I'm so excited. This is going to be a great week!"

Later that night, as she lay in bed, her husband snoring beside her, Amelie thought how unlikely and wonderful that after all these years the four of them remained so close. It was an observation they all shared. So many others had passed through their lives, but no others had lived it with them. An entire life lived together, she thought, that was something.

Amelie's path to her present life was a twisting, turning one that she traveled without benefit of plan or purpose. It was a series of detours that she took optimistically, if not impetuously.

Her father had been a supervisor at the electric plant, and her mother a nurse at Bayou Derkin Hospital. They raised three daughters, of which Amelie was the oldest, followed by Sara and Elizabeth. Amelie's family was Cajun and they enjoyed singing Cajun music together. Her father, Arnie, played fiddle and her mother, Miss Lou, sang in a beautiful, rich contralto, her Cajun accent clipping the syllables when she sang. The three sisters were kind, companionable and highly intelligent There was a kind of innocence about the family, as if that quality had been shared genetically.

Like most of the kids in Bayou Derkin in 1979, Amelie and her sisters were left to their own devices on summer days while their parents worked. At 12 Amelie was charged with her younger siblings' care. On a searing, hot August afternoon, when she could no longer take the heat, Amelie decided to treat her little sisters to an afternoon dip in the shallow river that snaked its way through the little town. She sent them to put their swimming suits on, then called Annie, Charlotte Claire, and Timmy and invited them to meet at the river. The three sisters set out in the glare of the August sun in flip-flops and swimming suits, Elizabeth wearing a little, pink inflatable float in the shape of a swan around her waist. When she fell several paces behind Amelie walked back and took her by the hand. "Try to keep up Elizabeth." They walked a half-mile to the long, narrow strip of woods that ran between the school yard and bordered the river. When they reached the riverbank, Amelie was surprised to find her three friends already there. "Hey," she called out cheerfully. "You beat us!"

"Hey," Annie said. "What took you so long?"

"Elizabeth," she replied. "First it was getting her suit on, then we had to find her float, then I had to blow it up. Sheesh, I don't think I want to have kids."

"You're the only one of us with little sisters or brothers," Timmy said enviously. "I never thought of that before. I wish I had a little sister or brother."

"No, you don't," Amelie replied. "I have to baby sit all the time."

"I don't think I'd mind that," Charlotte Claire said. "And your little sisters are so sweet."

"That's true," Amelie conceded. The group dropped their various belongings on the bank of the river, kicked off their flip-flops and waded into the tepid water where Sara and Elizabeth were already splashing and giggling gleefully. "It's so hot today," Amelie complained. "It almost makes me wish for October."

"No...," Timmy groaned. "That means we would be in school and I hate school."

"I love school," Charlotte Claire said.

"Me too," Annie agreed.

"You can have it," Timmy said grumpily.

"Sara and Elizabeth!" Amelie shouted. "You're out too far. Come back this way. I like school too," she continued. "Why don't you like school Timmy?"

"I don't know, I just don't." He felt a flush rise in his face. Of course, he knew. Of course, *they* knew. It was the unceasing harassment from Tom Burnett and Scotty Piper that made his stomach hurt every morning when he got ready for school.

"Well, maybe you'll like high school better," Charlotte Claire said reassuringly.

"Doubt it."

"Sara! Elizabeth!" Amelie yelled. "You are out too far, I said come back." As the two little girls pushed their way through the muddy water she said, "Why don't y'all go play on the bank for a while."

"Oh, Amelie," Sara whined.

"I don't want to go to the bank," Elizabeth pouted, twisting her pink swan float from side to side.

"Just for a little while," Amelie said gently. "I promise."

"Can we go in the woods and look for arrowheads?" Sara asked.

"Arrowheads, arrowheads!" Elizabeth chirped.

"Okay," Amelie acquiesced. "But stay on the edge of the woods where I can see you." The two little girls made their way across the river bank, Elizabeth lagging behind, her little pink swan waddling as she walked.

The four friends sat in the shallow water near the river's edge and talked. The dappled sunlight streaming through the trees near the river danced playfully on their faces, arms and legs. "I saw Leanne on my way here," Annie said. "I said hey to her and asked where she was going, and she said, 'To the river, not that it's any of your business, Little Orphan Annie' and then she turned her pointy nose up at me and walked off."

"She's a bitch," Timmy said.

"Timmy!" Charlotte Claire exclaimed.

"I don't care," he continued. "She is."

"I can't believe you said that word."

"She is one," Annie agreed. "But your Mama would have a conniption fit if she heard you cuss."

"Well she'll have one about something or other anyway, so it may as well be that." They all began to laugh. As their laughter trailed off Amelie looked towards the woods where she saw Sara digging at the ground with a stick, but no sign of Elizabeth. "Sara," she called out. "Sara, come here." Sara skipped over to where the group was sitting in the water.

"Where is Elizabeth?"

"In the woods," she replied.

"Where in the woods? I don't see her."

"I dunno. She was there a few minutes ago."

"How many minutes?" Amelie asked urgently. She looked in all directions, but she didn't see Elizabeth anywhere. "How many minutes?" she asked again, angrily.

"I don't know," Sara whimpered. Her lip shook, and she began to cry. "I don't know time."

"I need to go find her," Amelie told the others.

"We'll go with you," Timmy offered.

"We'll split up," Annie said, as the group crossed the bank to the woods edge. "Timmy and Charlotte Claire, you go left. Amelie and I will go right. We'll go, say, fifteen minutes in each direction and then circle back and meet in the school yard."

"We'll find her," Charlotte Claire said, reassuringly.

"I know," Amelie said, warily.

When they reconvened 20 minutes later no one had found Elizabeth. It was decided that Timmy, Charlotte Claire and Annie would stay and continue to search while Amelie took Sara home and called her parents. As they crossed the school yard for home Amelie spotted Leanne Reed walking briskly towards the school building. "Leanne!" she called out, but Leanne kept walking as if she didn't hear her. "Leanne!" Amelie hollered. Leanne stopped and turned to her.

"What?" she said, sharply.

"My little sister is missing. Have you seen her?"

"No."

"Can you help us find her? Annie, Charlotte Claire and Timmy are looking for her in the woods. Could you go help them try to find her?"

"Can't," she said flatly before walking away. "Mama wants me home early for supper."

Within minutes of speaking with Mr. Arnie and Miss Lou

the police and volunteer fire department were on the scene. Mr. Arnie sped into the school parking lot, his tires screeching and gravel flying as he came to an abrupt stop. He leapt from his truck and raced towards Clinton Holloway, a police officer and friend from the VFW. "Have you found her, Clinton?" he asked anxiously.

"Not yet, Arnie," he told him, "But we will."

Arnie ran furiously toward the woods, his heart pounding and his mind racing. "Elizabeth!" he screamed, "Elizabeth!" He ran frantically through the woods, pushing through the brush and dodging the trunks of the tall pines. He cleared the woods and stopped on the river bank, sweaty and panting, he looked up and down the river unsure of which way to go. His sense of urgency so acute, he started running south along the river on impulse. He'd run about 400 feet and was just deciding to turn back when a small patch of pink on the river bank caught his eye. He stopped to try and make out what it was, but he was too far. A horrible dread overtook him and he started running double time towards the patch of pink. As he got closer he hollered, "Elizabeth! Elizabeth, Elizabeth!" Now, he could see that it was her. She was lying on her stomach at the river's edge. Her tiny arms and legs splayed awkwardly on the ground, her face in the water. He rolled her limp body over and found a terrible gash in the side of her head. Her eyes were open. He knew she was dead. "No!" he wailed, a sound so guttural, so terrible it didn't sound human. "No! No! No! No! No!" he screamed as he scooped her little body up in his arms, rocking back and forth. That is the scene Clinton Holloway and two volunteer firemen found when they'd reached him moments later.

"Oh, God dammit, God dammit," Clinton said, running his hands over his head. The three men stood there, devastated, and watched as Mr. Arnie stood up with Elizabeth in his arms and walked back towards the woods.

Miss Lou had just arrived at the schoolyard when Mr.

Arnie, followed by the three men, walked out of the woods and towards the parking lot. "Is she hurt, Arnie? Is she hurt?" she called out, as she ran towards him. Her husband walked silently towards her, carrying their baby in his arms. When she reached him, he was sobbing. His tears falling from his cheek onto Elizabeth's.

"She's gone," was all he could say. She fell to the ground, screaming. He knelt beside her and placed Elizabeth in his wife's arms.

The coroner ruled it an accidental drowning. There was a large contusion on the side of her head and that area of the river bank was rocky. They concluded that she must have been playing on the water's edge, tripped, and struck her head on a rock, leaving her unconscious and face down in the water. Almost every adult in Bayou Derkin attended the funeral. Timmy, Charlotte Claire and Annie were there too. Miss Lou and Mr. Arnie were inconsolable. Sara was confused, and Amelie was numb with pain and guilt. Timmy became over-whelmed at the funeral home, fainted and had to be taken to the family room and revived. He awakened to Dr. Stoner sitting beside him on the sofa. Standing behind the doctor were his father, Annie, Charlotte Claire and Amelie. "How are you feeling, young man?" the doctor asked.

"Fine, I guess," he said woozily.

"Do you feel sick, Buddy?" his father asked.

"No, everything started getting smaller and then I don't know what happened."

"Well, I think you'll be just fine," Dr. Stoner said. "These things can be upsetting...overwhelming, and fainting is your body telling you so. Just lay here for a half hour or so and I'll come back and check on you then."

"Do you want me to stay with you?" his father asked.

"We'll stay with him, Mr. Tyler," Charlotte Claire said.

"No, Daddy," he said weakly. "I'll just sit here and talk to my friends for a while. I'm fine." When the adults left the room he asked, "Did y'all see what happened?"

"Yeah," Charlotte Claire said. "You were lucky your Daddy caught you before you hit the floor. You could have banged your head on a pew or something."

"He just swooped you up like a sack of horse feed and brought you in here," Annie told him.

"That must have been a sight," he said derisively. "Daddy carrying fatso out of the funeral." The girls laughed half-heartedly and then fell silent. Timmy looked at Amelie. "Are you okay?" he asked her.

"I don't know," she said. "I don't feel much of anything."

"That can happen if you have a big, emotional event happen," Annie told her.

"I keep thinking if I had just stayed home that day, or if we'd started looking for her on the river bank instead of the woods..." her voice trailed off. "It's my fault," she said. "I'm always going to know that it was my fault."

"It's not your fault," Annie insisted.

"It could have just as well happened on another day," Charlotte Claire added. "My Mama says it's in the Lord's hands and there's nothing you can do about it. When it's your time, it's your time."

"We were all there, Amelie," Timmy said. "None of us saw her slip away."

"It wasn't your job to notice," Amelie said quietly, "It was mine." She looked at the others fixedly and said, "But I can't figure out what happened to her pink swan float. She had it with her when she slipped away, and no one found it. All those people and the police searching in the woods and no one found it." Annie, Charlotte Claire and Timmy surreptitiously looked from one to the other. "I went back to where it happened yesterday and looked again. I looked all through the woods. I looked for hours. Why wouldn't she have been wearing it? She wore it all the time. She even wore it at home sometimes. Why didn't anyone find it?"

The Ardoin family was never the same after Elizabeth's death. Over time they resumed their normal routines, but the joy and innocence that were the hallmarks of their family was gone. Gradually Amelie learned to block out the guilt she felt for her sister's death, but she never forgave herself. She learned to compartmentalize it.

Amelie glided easily through high school, but the small-town, public school education was neither challenging nor engaging enough for her. She could make straight As without cracking a book, and Bayou Derkin had little else to offer but riding around in cars and drinking with Annie and Charlotte Claire. She began to smoke a little pot and hang out with other kids who were into it. She was restless and felt as though she were coasting through life, just waiting for something to happen.

After graduation she enrolled in the same nearby college as Annie and Charlotte Claire. But rather than wait until the fall semester to start classes, as her two friends had chosen to do, she opted to begin the summer semester, so she could move away from Bayou Derkin as soon as possible. That summer was a dizzying whirlwind of drinking, drugs and sex. By the semester's end Amelie had earned below-average grades for the first time in her life. Her sense of restlessness had never been more acute. What she was looking for exactly she couldn't say, but she came up with a plan to find out.

When she returned home to Bayou Derkin after the summer session, Amelie announced to her bewildered parents that she was not planning to return to school. She would like, she told them, to go exploring.

"Where?" asked her mother.

"Not sure. I think I'll just get in my car, take off and see where I end up."

"For how long?" asked her father.

"Not sure about that either. I just know that I need to find out what I want to do with my life. And I don't think I'm going to find that out here, or in college, at least not right now."

After a few days' consideration Amelie's parents acquiesced. They were worried about her safety and the choices she might make on her own. But they also knew that it was important to her, and hoped that after she got it out of her system, she would come home and return to college. Two weeks later they stood in their driveway and said a tearful goodbye. All, that is, except for Amelie. Now she was free, and the liberation was exhilarating. As she drove away she glanced in the rearview mirror and saw her family standing in the driveway, waving goodbye in front of the house she had lived in all her life.

She drove all day until she reached north Louisiana, where she stopped at her grandmother's for the night. When she pulled into the driveway she found her grandmother standing in the front doorway. "*Mais chere Amelie*, what is this I hear? You're just going to take off with no idea where you're going?"

"Nice to see you too, Grandma," Amelie joked.

"Come give your old MaMa a hug." Amelie put her arms around the old woman's broad back and rested her head on MaMa's large bosom. She always felt like a little girl when she hugged her Grandma. "Now come in," the old woman instructed. "I have supper all ready."

"But Grandma," Amelie laughed. "It's only 5 o'clock."

"Well *chere*, you know I'm old and I can't stay up like I used to. So, we'll just have some supper, have our devotional, and then I'll go to bed. You can stay up and watch the TV if you want."

"Grandma, I don't really do daily devotionals anymore."

Her grandmother looked at Amelie in horror. "Don't tell me that. You must always do your daily devotional. You're about to embark on a rudderless journey. The daily devotionals can show you the way and keep you safe."

"Okay Grandma," Amelie lied. "I'll do my devotionals."

After they'd eaten a dinner of chicken and sausage gumbo and potato salad, Amelie's grandmother took out her book of daily devotionals and her bible, both earmarked with little strips of torn paper. She called Amelie back to the kitchen table. Amelie could think of a million things she'd rather read, but out of respect and affection for the old lady she joined her at the table. "I picked these out especially," she told her. "Let's read together." Amelie pulled her chair closer to her grandmother's and the old lady spread out the two books before them.

"From the bible first, from Proverbs," her grandmother told her. They began to read, "Train up a child in the way he should go and when he is old he will not depart from it."

Amelie looked at her grandmother's kind face and was surprised to find herself deeply touched.

"Now the devotional," her grandmother said as she slid the book between the two of them.

"Let us relish life as we live it, find joy in the journey, and share our love with friends and family. One day each of us will run out of tomorrows. I believe that we can find joy in the journey of life if we keep our heavenly father as our guide."

"And just one more, from Psalms, it's short," the old lady told her as she slid the bible before them.

"Thy word is a lamp unto my feet, and a light unto my path." Her grandmother pushed the books away and leaned back in her chair. She turned to Amelie and smiled sweetly.

"Grandma," Amelie said softly. "Those are lovely. How sweet of you to choose those for me."

"I worry about you being on the road Amelie, but I'm proud of you for striking out on your own. I don't know if I'd have had the courage to do that when I was a girl, but I'd like to think I would." Amelie put her arms around her grandmother and rested her head on her shoulder. The old lady patted Amelie on the back and said, "Now it's off to bed for me. You can stay up as late as you like."

"Good night, Gran."

As her grandmother walked away she said, "There's beer in the ice-box if you like."

"Grandma!" Amelie cried, as her grandmother had never offered her alcohol before.

"I used to be young once too," she replied, disappearing into her bedroom.

The next morning Amelie set out early and drove north-northeast on Route 30 until she reached Hot Springs. Struck by the beauty of the Quachita Mountains, she decided to stay for the night. She checked into a motel and set out on foot to explore downtown. Antique shops, bars and restaurants lined the main street, which was filled mostly with tourists. After an hour she'd seen nothing of interest and decided to get a bite to eat. It had turned into a cool September evening by the time she stopped into a little pub called the Hot Springs Burger and Brew. She got a seat at the bar and ordered the specialty, a burger and beer. She looked around the bar and observed a couple of guys playing pool and two chubby girls giggling at a table. A guy at the opposite end of the bar pushed up his cowboy hat and raised his beer bottle in her direction when she happened to glance his way. She turned back on her stool and caught her reflection in the mirror behind the bar. What *was* she looking for? Was this the place? She didn't think so. And she had only just started her adventure. It was too soon to pick a destination.

In the morning she set out again, this time heading east on Route 40. She found the verdant Tennessee landscape so love-ly that she drove most of the day until she reached Nashville. She drove around the city for a while, stopping occasionally to sight-see and have a bite to eat. She was enjoying herself, but she knew this wasn't the place either. It was too big and crowded. She wouldn't mind a city, but a smaller city would be better. The next morning, she was traveling east again on Route 40 when she noticed signs for Asheville, North Carolina and the Blue Ridge Mountains. The idea of the Blue Ridge Mountains captured her imagination. That's it, she thought, next stop the Blue Ridge Mountains.

Amelie reached Asheville by mid-afternoon. The drive through the mountains had been so breathtaking that she was smitten with Asheville before she'd arrived. Driving through the streets of the city, she happened upon the arts district and the residential neighborhoods that surround it. She spotted an old Victorian house with a sign in front that read: THE BONNIE TEAPOT—BED AND BREAKFAST. She pulled her car over and went inside.

She was greeted in the heavily paneled foyer by a slim woman with wiry, salt-and-pepper hair, wearing loose-fitting jeans and a brightly colored t-shirt. She greeted Amelie with a warm smile and kind eyes. "Welcome," she chirped. "What brings you to the Bonnie Teapot? In search of a room, I hope."

"Well, yes," Amelie replied, returning her smile.

"How long will you be with us-well I say with us, it's just me," she chuckled.

"I'm not sure, definitely a few days...maybe longer."

"Ah, an adventurer," she sang. "I like that. You'll fit in fine here. I'm Delia Kendall. This is my place. Isn't it nice? I'd always wanted a B&B," she said, turning to look around the place before turning a beaming smile back to Amelie. "Let me show you around."

The house's interior was old-fashioned and cheerful with lots of feminine touches. After touring the common rooms Delia showed her each of the vacant bedrooms. Amelie selected the smallest, least expensive room. It had a single bed, covered with an intricate quilt, a nightstand, a small painted chest and a dressing table. The walls were covered with pale green, striped wallpaper. The only window was adorned with white curtains, upon which were tiny pink rosebuds with deep green leaves. Amelie went to the window and pulled back the curtain to find that it overlooked a rose garden. This may be the place, she thought, and looked back at Delia with a smile.

Over the next few days Amelie explored Asheville and its environs, seeing the Biltmore Estate and the Blue Ridge Parkway. Within Asheville itself she toured downtown, the historic district and the River Arts district where, she learned, Delia had a quilt shop called Bits and Pieces. Like the Bonnie Teapot, the quilt shop was cheerful and feminine.

By the end of her first week in Asheville, Amelie had decided that, for now, this was her new home. That evening, over a glass of wine, she told Delia that she would be staying on, and that she probably should look for a studio apartment, as the nightly rate at the Bonnie Teapot would be beyond her budget. Delia put her glass down and looked thoughtfully at Amelie. "I have a proposition for you. How about you stay on here and work for me. You can help out here and at the quilt shop, and no charge for the room." Amelie was silent for a moment when Delia said abruptly, "Oh and I'll pay you of course; just not as much as I would if you weren't using a room. What do you think?"

"I think I'd love that," Amelie said, relieved that she didn't have to ask her about the pay.

"Great, it's settled then. Look, it's already Thursday. Take tomorrow and the weekend to do what you have to do and start on Monday."

"Monday it is," Amelie said thinking how all of this was working out better than she could have imagined.

She quickly settled into a happy routine. Monday through Friday she worked at Bits and Pieces. On weekends she helped Delia with breakfast at The Bonnie Teapot, then had the rest of the day to herself. She thought she'd be bored working in a store full of quilts, but she soon found that it felt cozy and safe-rather the way she imagined it would feel in an antique shop or an old bookstore. The quilts were made by local artists, including Delia herself, and some of them were quite expensive. She started reading the quilting books on the shelves and one evening asked Delia if she could teach her how to quilt. Delia was pleased that she'd asked, and began teaching Amelie at the store and on quiet evenings at The Bonnie Teapot.

As with all things, Amelie was a quick study and she blossomed as a quilter under Delia's guidance. There was an easy rapport between the two women of such different ages and experience. Sitting at Delia's big quilting table with glasses of wine, the two women sewed and talked amiably, about their lives, the shop, or the guests at the Bonnie Teapot. Delia was a great story teller and Amelie an enthusiastic audience.

On the Friday before Columbus Day, Amelie walked through the door of the Bonnie Teapot to find a tall, lanky man with long, thin hair standing alone at the far end of the foyer. Her eyes had not adjusted from the bright sunshine outside, so she could only see him in silhouette. She stood near the door, saying nothing and wondering if she should run when Delia stepped out of the kitchen.

"Oh, you're home," she called out. "Come meet Heath."

"Hello," Amelie said as she approached them.

"Heath is a handyman. Isn't that wonderful?" Delia chirped. "He's going to take care of some of the little projects I've been meaning to get around to."

"Hey," Heath said, his hands shoved in his pockets.

Now Amelie could see him clearly. His face, too, was long and thin but his features fine, almost delicate. She thought he looked the way depictions of Jesus always looked. His voice was low and raspy, and when he spoke she noticed that the bottom row of his teeth were crooked.

"I'd better get going," he said. "I'll be back on Tuesday to get started. It was nice to meet you, Amelie. Never met anyone named Amelie before. That's a nice name. Delia."

"Oh great, see you Tuesday," Delia sang out. "Happy Columbus Day!"

"Happy Columbus Day," he replied. But he wasn't looking at Delia; he was looking directly at Amelie.

Over the next few weeks Heath was around a lot. Whenever he finished one project Delia found another. He began doing projects at the quilt shop, too. At first Amelie and Heath went about their work with little more than a nod or a brief hello, but little by little, they began talking to one another. They talked about rock music, TV shows, and their families. They shared a wanderer's spirit; restless and uninterested in a traditional path. Like Amelie, Heath had taken off on his own—after living with his parents in Hot Springs, where he went to work for his father right out of high school. Unlike Amelie, college for Heath was neither a plan nor a possibility.

December came, and the quilt shopped buzzed with holiday shoppers. One Saturday evening after a long and tiring day, Heath came into the shop with a stack of new quilts that Delia had sent over from the Bonnie Teapot.

"Oh, good," Amelie said as he entered. "We're running low. The store has been so busy today. I'm pooped."

"Nice to see you too," he said, half smiling.

"Sorry, nice to see you. Hey, I'm about to close up. Want to get a drink?"

"Sure. Sounds good. Let's walk over to Candy Bar. I could use a beer."

The bar was quiet as the happy hour crowd hadn't yet started to file in. They settled themselves at the bar and ordered two beers.

"So, are you going back to Louisiana for Christmas?" Heath asked.

"No, it's going to be kind of weird though. It's the first time in my life that I haven't been with my family for Christmas.

My parents were really bummed out; my little sister too."

"Why not?"

"Money; I'm short on funds. Not broke, but there isn't a lot of surplus in the cash department."

"Well, that's too bad," Heath said before draining the rest of his beer. "Want another round?"

"Sure, why not."

"Barkeep!" Health called out. "Two more." They sat in silence as the bartender placed their beers before them.

After he'd stepped away she asked Heath, "What are you going to do for the holidays?"

"My parents in Hot Springs. My mom would bust a gut if I didn't come home for Christmas seeing how Hot Springs ain't so far from Asheville. And to be honest, I really kind of like being with my family at Christmas."

Amelie thought that was sweet and she smiled at Heath. She didn't know if it was the beer, but she found herself attracted to Heath. She liked his long hair, his bohemian style, and the slow, easy way he spoke. And the way he looked at her at the bar that night made her think that the attraction might be mutual.

"I got an idea," he said. He slipped a joint out of his blue jean jacket and held it below the bar so that only Amelie could see it.

"Want to?" he asked.

"Absolutely," she whispered.

They walked out into the chilly December dusk and down the alley beside the bar. They sat together on the back stoop while Heath lit up the joint. They began talking about dreams they'd had and what their meanings might be. As their analyses became more absurd they began to laugh in that hard-to-stop laughter that pot induces. The intimacy of their shared laughter caused them both to grow quiet. Heath leaned in and kissed Amelie softly. When she didn't pull away he took her in his arms and he kissed her again.

Half an hour later they were at Heath's tiny apartment over a garage behind his landlord's house. As soon as they were inside they began pulling each other's clothes off amidst a flurry of kisses and embraces, their hands eagerly discovering each other's bodies. Later Amelie would recall that Heath's lovemaking was rougher than she liked, but that night she chalked it up to the pot, the alcohol...or maybe he just hadn't had sex in a long time. When they were finished she said she needed to go. She hadn't told Delia she'd be out late and thought she might worry. And she had to be up early to help with breakfast at The Bonnie Teacup. But when Heath didn't offer any objection she felt disappointed. She got dressed as Heath watched from his bed where he'd lit a cigarette. After she'd dressed she said, "Well, I'll be going now."

"Okay, then," he said. "This was great. Let's do it again." When he remained in bed Amelie walked over and kissed him briefly and left.

Driving home that night she thought that this would probably turn out to be a one-night stand. Heath had been so cool and laid back after they'd made love, she'd assumed it was just sex to him. "Why the hell did I do that? I have to work with him every day." she wondered aloud. "Annie always says, don't shit where you sleep." But the next time she saw him he seemed happy to see her, and suggested that they get together for pizza and beer. After that they began to see each other regularly. One or the other would suggest seeing a movie or grabbing a burger, though it occurred to Amelie that he never actually asked her out as if they were on a date. It felt as if they were just hanging out, except they ended up in his bed each time they did. She decided that he was just not the romantic type, accepted that that was the way he was, and fell in love with him anyway.

Amelie sat on the toilet and waited for the pregnancy test results. "I'm literally holding my fate in my hands," she said to herself as she waited. It had been six and half months since the first time they'd made love. They were always careful. She was on the pill and he wore a condom most times, but not every time. After a few minutes she worked up the courage to look at the test. Her heart sank. She was pregnant. Her mind began to race. She didn't want a baby, she was just 19. She couldn't imagine that Heath would want a child. He was only 20 and, anyway, she wasn't even sure if he loved her. He'd never said it. Should she even tell him? And what was the alternative, abortion? The thought gave her a sick feeling. She thought about calling her Mother but then thought better of it. She needed time to consider all options, and if she were to decide on an abortion she wouldn't want her parents to know.

That night at The Bonnie Teapot she laid out the details for Delia who listened quietly, a thoughtful expression on her face. When she'd finished they were quiet for several seconds before Delia asked, "So what are you going to do?"

"I don't know," Amelie sighed. "I was hoping you could tell me..."

"Oh sweetie," Delia said, taking Amelie's hand in hers. "You know I can't do that. No one can make that decision for you. You need to take a few days to think this through...and then follow your heart. The one thing I would say is that I think you should tell Heath. It's your decision and your body, but I think Heath's reaction may help you to know what you really want."

Though she'd considered keeping the pregnancy from Heath, Delia's suggestion had given Amelie a degree of comfort. It was a place to start and someone with whom to share the load. And if he wasn't willing to share the load she needed to know it.

Heath had spent the better part of the next afternoon building shelves in the stock room at Bits and Pieces. At 5:30 he came into the shop and sat down across the quilting table from Amelie.

"You're quiet today," he said. "Want to pick up a pizza and some beer and go back to my place?"

"That sounds good."

"I'll walk over to Pizza Mike's and pick one up."

"Before you go I need to tell you something," she said tentatively. "And before I tell you, I need for you to know that whatever reaction you have will be fine. Don't react in a way you think I want you to. Just be honest." She gave him a couple of moments for that to sink in before she said, "I'm pregnant."

"It's mine, right?" he asked casually. Amelie tilted her head to the side and gave him a long, silent look as if to say, really? "Yeah, yeah, of course it is. Sorry," he said, standing up and shoving his hands into his pockets. "What do you want to do?"

"Well," she said nervously. "That's what I thought we should talk about..." Before she could go on Heath cut her off.

"Maybe we should get married."

It was May, again, and the bleak winter chill that had enveloped Hot Springs was replaced by iris, dogwood, and dappled sunlight. It had been a year since Heath's proposal, now she was sitting on an old outdoor swing, rocking her baby and waiting for Heath to come home. Amelie had been so surprised by Heath's reaction to the news of her pregnancy that she'd almost forgot to answer his de facto proposal. In fact, everything that happened over those next couple of months was a surprise; Heath's unruffled acceptance of fatherhood, his determination that they should move to Hot Springs to be near his family, and his willingness to travel to Louisiana to be married near her folks. Annie, Charlotte Claire and Timmy had all returned to Bayou Derkin for the wedding.

After the wedding they'd packed up Amelie's car and drove directly to Hot Springs, where they moved into a trailer on land owned by Heath's family. The trailer was old-but clean and well kept, and Amelie made it cheerful with her quilts and curtains made on the new Singer sewing machine that was Delia's going away gift. How sweet Heath had been in those first months as her belly and the specter of parenthood grew larger. She observed that he seemed neither thrilled nor unhappy at the prospect of being a husband and father, rather pleasantly acquiescent.

After Deedee was born things began to change. Initially Heath had seemed thrilled with his new baby girl, holding her for extended periods of time, talking baby talk and helping with feeding and changing. But after a while it was as if the novelty of having a baby had worn off. He'd return from work at his father's garage, give Amelie and the baby a peck on the forehead, then plop down in front of the TV with the first of the night's beers.

By the time Deedee was six Amelie felt like a single mother. Heath would return from work, stay long enough to eat and take a shower before he was out of the door, beer in hand. When she asked where he was going he would simply say 'out' or 'the pool hall.' If she tried to suggest they go out together he generally made an excuse saying that she would hate the pool hall or that they could never get a sitter on such short notice. Eventually she stopped making the suggestion. She was usually asleep, or pretending to be asleep, when he returned home drunk and wanting sex. A few times he had wakened her and forced himself on her. He had even hit her in a drunken rage once when she refused him. It had reached the point that she was happy to see him go out, and didn't much care if he came back.

She spent her days mostly alone, except for Deedee and an occasional visit from her sister-in-law or Heath's mother. Whenever Deedee napped, or was happily occupied, Amelie sewed. She made curtains and quilts to sell to friends and neighbors. The curtains she made were simple rod-and-pocket curtains in florals, geometrics and stripes. But the quilts were intricate, artistic and visually stunning. After Deedee started

Pre-K she began sewing full time. She sewed all day, Monday thru Friday. Word spread, and demand grew so much she enlisted her sister-in-law to work for her. They rented a booth at a weekend arts fair and began taking orders. She was also getting orders from Delia in Ashville, and demand began to grow there as well. Her quilts were beginning to bring in real money, money she could use to get out of her marriage.

For most of the seven years of her marriage, Amelie felt trapped. She loved Deedee, and, in the beginning, she'd loved Heath, too. Though he was never romantic or intellectually stimulating, he was good company and a good husband and father. But his good nature had receded, and his sullenness, bad temper and drinking had replaced it. She was afraid of him now. When he drank he was quick to throw back his hand, as if to slap her, and on a few occasions when he was very drunk, he had. He'd never been abusive when he was sober, but she was aware that domestic violence escalates, and she needed to get out before that happened. She wished she'd left him years before, but she was in her 20s with a small child, no job, and no college education. And she couldn't bring herself to return to Bayou Derkin, divorced-with a baby, to live with her parents.

But things were different now. She was making real money and had saved a substantial amount for an escape fund. She decided to move back to Asheville. Since she'd developed a following in both Hot Springs and Asheville, switching locations would not materially hurt her business. She'd still be able to ship her quilts to her established vendors and customers, Heath's sister could still run the booth at the art fair, and she could go back to work at Bits and Pieces, a perfect venue for her quilts. In fact, she thought, she could get a booth at the Asheville art fair and increase her business there. She called Delia to discuss her business plan. "I'll have to get an apartment and find a good school district for Deedee."

"Nonsense," she said immediately. "You'll live at the Bonnie Teapot. You can have the big room with the window seat next to your old room, and Deedee can have your old room. The bathroom across the hall will be for you and Deedee exclusively. It'll be cheaper than an entire apartment with upkeep and the like, and I'm in an excellent school district, one of the best in Asheville."

Amelie agreed that Delia's points were valid. It would definitely make sense from a practical point of view. But did she want to raise Deedee in a B&B? And though she loved Delia, did she want to share a home with another woman now that she was in her late 20s and a mother? She fumbled for something to say. "But we couldn't intrude. It's asking too much," she said at last.

"Nonsense, I like you and you like me. I love kids. The B&B is not as busy as it used to be, so having a steady tenant would be beneficial to me. You get your good school district, not to mention a big house with a big yard for Deedee to play in. You'd be good company, and if you play your cards right, I might even babysit sometime." It all made so much sense and, after all, she had liked living with Delia before.

"Okay," she said with a laugh. "We're in. But you can't undercharge me, and I insist on helping with the chores."

"Good."

"And, Delia, thank you."

"Oh shoot," she demurred. "I couldn't be more thrilled."

That June, after the close of Deedee's school year, Amelie packed up her parents' old car with their clothes, quilts, Deedee's books and toys, and her sewing machine. Heath put Deedee in the back seat, buckled her up, and gave her a kiss on the forehead. He walked back towards the trailer and watched as Amelie put the last boxes in the trunk. She slammed the trunk and, before getting behind the wheel, looked across the roof of the car to see Heath leaning against the trailer smoking a cigarette. She couldn't help thinking of that night after the first time they'd slept together; Heath sitting in his bed smoking as she got dressed. He'd never bothered to get up to see her out. And she'd remembered what he said to her that night as she was leaving.

"Okay, then," she called out. "This was great. Let's *not* do it again."

The Atlantic Ocean, Off the Coast of Key Largo

Friday April 15th, 2016

12:45 AM

She could see the lights of the coast guard rescue boat in the distance. "They're coming," Annie said to the others. How would they explain what happened? That it was just a recreational outing gone horribly wrong? Just a group of old friends catching up and then...what? The cool April wind whipped across the ocean, slapping water against the sides of the boat, causing it to rock from side to side. Moonlight illuminated Annie's face as she pulled the blanket tighter around her shoulders to keep warm. Timmy put his arm around her and she rested her head on his shoulder. Charlotte Claire and Amelie shielded their eyes from the glaring lights of the rescue boat and watched silently as it circled The Sweet Revenge. Soon they'd tell their story. And they'd have to take them below and show them where two bodies lay dead.

When Coast Guard Captain Max Price and two subordinates boarded The Sweet Revenge, they found the four remaining passengers huddled together, wrapped in blankets for protection from the chill. The shaken group stood looking at him in silence as if awaiting instructions.

"Do you have any weapons?" he asked.

"No," Timmy said. "There was just the one gun and we left it below. We didn't touch anything."

"I'm going to have to verify that," he said. "Please drop your blankets for a moment. Officers Clayton and Reynolds are going to pat you down. It's just procedure." When Price was satisfied they were unarmed, he instructed Clayton to go below and assess the situation.

"Is anyone down there who may need medical attention?" Price asked.

"No," Timmy said. "It's just the two of them. They're both dead. We checked their pulse, their breathing. We felt for heartbeats. They were obviously dead."

"Who wants to tell me what happened here tonight?"

"I will," Annie said.

"Who are you?"

"Anne Renee', this is my boat," she said weakly.

Price looked up from his pad and asked, "Anne Renee'? The actress?"

"Yes."

"Go on."

"We left Key Largo around six o'clock tonight. We were planning to cruise around a while and then anchor somewhere and have dinner."

"Why don't you start by explaining who was on the boat."

"Myself, Scotty and Leanne Piper. They're the couple below, and Timothy Tyler..."

"Wait, the writer?"

"Yes, that's me," Timmy said.

"Amelie Ardoin and..." Annie continued.

"Ah, come on," Price said. "Is everyone on this boat famous?"

"No," Charlotte Claire said dryly. "I'm Charlotte Claire Latimer and I'm not famous."

"We all grew up together, including the Pipers'," Annie explained. "This was a mini-reunion of sorts. We're all staying in Miami. They just arrived yesterday. Timmy is from New York, Charlotte Claire from Houston, Amelie from Asheville, North Carolina, and the Pipers are from our home-town in Louisiana."

Officer Clayton appeared from below deck. "We have two confirmed dead; one male, one female. The female has a bullet wound to the head, and the male's injury to the head looks self-inflicted, like he swallowed his gun."

"Thanks, Matt, go below and make sure the scene is

secure," Price told him. "Go on, Miss Renee."

"I..." Annie's voice trailed off and she began to cry.

"We left Key Largo around six," Charlotte Claire continued. "We had a late lunch at the Pilot House and afterward we sat at the bar for quite a while. We all had a lot to drink, but Scotty and Leanne were drinking especially heavily. At six we boarded the Sweet Revenge and cruised up and down the coast for a couple of hours. I think it was about eight o'clock when we anchored for dinner. Scotty was drinking heavily the entire time. Well, Leanne was too, for that matter, but Scotty more so. He caused such a scene at the Pilot House that the manager had to come over and ask what the problem was. By 11 o'clock he was just a really messy drunk. And that set Leanne off. Scotty was saying inappropriate things to, well, all of us. He is...was a nasty drunk. He was saying sexually suggestive things to Annie and making homophobic comments to Timmy. When Leanne called him out on it, he exploded."

"I'd never seen anything like it," Annie told him. "It was like Jekyll and Hyde. He was a completely different person. In hindsight I think he was in an alcoholic blackout."

"That's when I suggested that he go lay down below in one of the staterooms," Amelie said. "But he just kept railing."

"Leanne was pretty drunk, too," Annie explained. "She flew into a rage and started screaming at him to shut up and go down stairs and sleep it off."

"And that's when he hit her," Timmy said. "We tried to intervene, but he went insane. Leanne ran below crying. She locked herself in Annie's stateroom."

"Scotty went after her, but we thought they would just stay below and scream it out or pass out," Annie interjected. "But he started yelling at her through the stateroom door. When she wouldn't open the door, he started beating on it, screaming and cursing her the whole time. Timmy went down to try and talk him down..."

"But he just shoved me against the wall and then went

back on deck," Timmy said.

"When he came back he went straight for the gun," Annie explained.

"You had a gun on the vessel?" Price asked.

"Yes, for protection," Annie said. "It's licensed and registered with the state of Florida. I only just bought it when I bought my house in Miami. I'm not one of these crazy stand-your-ground nuts, but I thought I'd feel safer."

"How'd he know you had a gun and where to find it?" Price asked.

"I'd mentioned it earlier in the evening and he asked to see it," she explained. "He wasn't that drunk at the time, so I figured there was no harm in showing it to him. I didn't let him handle the gun. I just showed it to him."

"You showed this man who'd been drinking for hours your gun?" Price asked incredulously.

"Yes, but again, I didn't let him handle the gun. I told him he'd had too much to drink. If I had any idea he was capable of something like this I wouldn't have even mentioned the gun. I feel...responsible for all this."

"No, Annie," Amelie told her.

"The gun, which she normally keeps in her stateroom, was still up top, but she had put it in that cabinet and locked the cabinet." Timmy explained. "He just barreled up here like a wild man. I followed him up, thinking Leanne was safe as long as she stayed locked in the stateroom. But he kicked the cabinet in. We were all here. He turned on his heels and pointed the gun at us. We all scrambled. It was terrifying. It all happened so fast."

"Yes," Amelie said, "He went back down to the stateroom and started beating on the door again and screaming for her to open it. Then we heard the first shots and the sound of bullets hitting something hard...sort of a pinging sound. You could hear him kicking at the door. His adrenaline must have kicked in, because we heard the door slam against the wall when he finally got it open."

"We heard the door crash open," Timmy said nervously. "We heard Leanne scream...and then we heard the shots."

"That's when we ran to the other stateroom and locked ourselves in," Charlotte Claire said. "We'd hoped that he'd just fired the gun to scare her and that maybe the sound of the gun going off would bring him to his senses."

"It got quiet, for, like, a few seconds, and then we heard him walking towards our stateroom," Timmy told him. "He was pounding on the door and kicking at it. We were yelling at him to stop, to come to his senses, but he kept banging-and then he shot at the door, or the lock, I don't know for sure. So, we pulled the mattresses off the bunks and put them up against the door. We were panicked, trying any way we could to protect ourselves. But then the banging stopped, and it got quiet. We just sat there waiting...and then we heard another shot. And then it got quiet again. We waited for...probably half an hour before we opened the door a crack to look out. That's when we saw Scotty on the floor in the hallway. Once we got close we could see that he was dead. The gun was on the floor beside him."

"After that," Charlotte Claire said, "We went to Annie's stateroom to see if Leanne was okay, but of course, she wasn't. There was a gunshot wound in her forehead. Her eyes were open."

"Oh," Amelie cried. "Her poor children...and her mother. This is terrible, it will kill them."

"What happens now?" Timmy asked.

"You'll come back to Key Largo on my vessel. Officer Clayton will take the Sweet Revenge back to the marina. Radio ahead and tell them to have a CSI team waiting," Price told him. "The boat will have to be processed for evidence. You'll all need to give statements. I know it's late, but this can't wait until tomorrow. And you'll need to remain in Key Largo to-night. It's a murder-suicide, seems pretty cut and dry, but we need to process the scene and get your statements."

"Whatever we have to do, Officer," Timmy said. "We're glad to cooperate."

"Yes," Annie agreed.

"May I go below and get my bag?" Charlotte Claire asked.

"All of our bags," Amelie added.

"I'm afraid not," Price said. "The scene has to be processed first."

"But we don't have identification...," Amelie told him.

"Or money for a hotel," Charlotte Claire added.

"It's okay, girls," Timmy said. "I have my wallet on me. I will be able to keep my wallet, won't I, Captain Price?"

"Yes, I just don't want to disturb the scene. You should be able to get your things back tomorrow," Price said. "Now let's get you aboard our vessel. Adam, you want to help the ladies and gentleman aboard."

"Follow me," Office Reynolds instructed. Still clutching their blankets, they followed Officer Reynolds, traversing the space between the two vessels. They huddled together in the cramped pilot house as the officer sped off into the darkness.

"It's over now," Amelie said to them.

"Yes, it's over," Annie echoed softly.

June, 2015

Provincetown, MA

Timmy raced up Commercial Street, arms loaded with groceries. He turned onto Brewster and doubled his pace. The girls were arriving that afternoon and there was still so much he had to do. The champagne needed to be chilled, the flowers arranged and hors d'oeuvres made. When he reached number 18, he paused to take in the view of his house. He and Joe bought the house the second year they were together. At first they thought they'd buy one of Provincetown's charming antique homes, but when they saw the 1950s cottage, they fell in love with it. It was obscured from the street by a 20-foot privet hedge, and once they'd passed through the garden gate it felt as if they'd stepped into another world. The small house was surrounded by a lush garden, and in the rear garden was a large two-tiered deck. They'd expanded and renovated the house, so that unlike the antique homes they'd seen, it had a large kitchen and open floor plan. Timmy had spent weeks shopping for exactly the right fabrics, furnishings and decorative accessories. The result of his efforts was a lovingly decorated home that was stylish, comfortable and perfect for entertaining. The crisp white linen sofas, bleached-wood coffee table, sisal rugs and a profusion of blue and white porcelain accessories gave the house the perfect beach ambiance. This would be his first time to host the girls in Provincetown and he wanted everything to be perfect.

Timmy worked quickly through the morning; flowers for the living room and bedrooms, every room spotlessly clean, champagne chilled, hors d'oeuvres done. After a quick shower he drove to the dock in the center of Provincetown and waited for the fast ferry to arrive with the girls. It was a beautiful, cloudless summer day on the Cape. Sunlight bounced off the water's surface and a warm breeze swept in over the ocean. At 3:30 he saw the ferry approaching in the distance. Timmy walked to the end of the dock to scan the passengers on the ferry's deck. Finally, he spotted Annie, her huge, broad-brimmed hat nearly flying off her head, with Amelie and Charlotte Claire beside her. He waved his arms in the air to get their attention when at last Amelie saw him, and they all waved excitedly as the ferry approached the dock. After they'd disembarked and exchanged greetings Timmy asked them, "How was your trip?"

"I loved the ferry," Amelie replied.

"I loved the bar on the ferry," Charlotte Claire joked.

"The views were spectacular," Amelie went on.

"It was crowded, though," Annie said. "And people kept asking to take selfies with me."

"Selfies with celebrities are the new autographs'," Amelie mused.

"Yeah, must be tough being a TV star. Your disguise didn't throw the fans off?" he asked, gesturing toward her hat.

"You'd think," she laughed. "Next time I'll put a bag over my head."

"Better put a bag over your boobs, too," Charlotte Claire said.

"Hilarious," Annie replied dryly.

"Okay, ladies, back to your corners," Timmy said. "Let's finish this rumble over champagne. The car is this way."

"Seriously, Annie," Charlotte Claire said. "I don't know how you put up with it. It would drive me crazy."

As Timmy opened the champagne in the kitchen he could hear the women's laughter from the living room. He turned and watched his three friends for a moment. It was good to have them there, he thought. Their laughter and chatter were a tonic to him. He looked forward to their beach vacations all year, and now that it was here all he could think of was how fast the week would pass. Don't think about it, he told himself, just have fun. "Let's get this party started," he said as he entered the living room.

"Woohoo!" Amelie sang out.

"Fill'er up," Annie added.

"Girls, I've been looking forward to this all year," Timmy said, filling their glasses. "I'm so glad y'all are here."

"Me too," Charlotte Claire said. "Timmy, your house is beautiful."

"Aw thanks," he said proudly. "I love this place. It really is a dream come true."

"Is it always this perfectly presented?" Amelie asked, thinking of the piles of fabric samples, quilting supplies and paperwork that seemed to be everywhere in her house.

"Pretty much. I'm totally anal when it comes to my homes."

"Me too," Charlotte Claire said. "I can't stand anything out of place in my house. I think Alma, my maid, is dyslexic. She's a good cleaner but I have to go behind her and put everything back in the proper order. You'd think she would get a clue after five years."

"You can keep a maid for five years?" Annie laughed.

"I don't even have a maid," Timmy said.

"You don't have a maid?" Charlotte Claire asked in astonishment.

"Why not?" Amelie asked, incredulous.

"Because I work at home," he said. "I can't stand having them there when I'm writing. It's too distracting. Plus, I feel like I'm invading *their* privacy."

"How's the new book coming?" Annie asked, refilling her champagne glass.

"Just getting started, really."

"What's this one about?" Charlotte Claire asked, holding out her glass for a refill.

"Ooh, tell, tell," Amelie said, excitedly.

"It's about a gay man and the three women he's been friends with since first grade. They go to their 30th high school reunion and kill all the people who treated them like shit in high school." They fell silent for a moment before Timmy started laughing. "God, that would make a terrible book. I don't think I could get an advance for that."

"I don't know," Charlotte Claire said. "I'd read that book."

"Perhaps," Timmy replied. "But I wouldn't write it. I think it's time to open another bottle. What say all of you?"

"We thought you'd never ask," Amelie told him.

He opened the SubZero and paused in amusement. Of the four shelves in the refrigerator, one contained food and the other three were all champagne. He grabbed a bottle and returned to the living room.

"So, what's on the agenda, Captain? Oh, by the way that reminds me-I bought a house in Miami. And a boat!" Annie told them.

"A boat?" Charlotte Claire cried. "What on earth are you going to do with a boat? A motor boat or a sail boat?"

"A yacht, actually."

"Ooh, la la," Amelie trilled.

"And a house in Miami?" Timmy asked.

"I bought a house on Star Island Drive. It's sort of like an island between Miami and Miami Beach; very toney, very beachy. There are a lot of actors there. I think Madonna might own a house there...or used to. Anyway, it comes with a dock, so Calder and I thought it would be fun to have a boat. You know, just to cruise around in the bay or take out on the ocean. We thought it would be fun to take it to the Keys, and a lot faster, too."

"I think it's a great idea," Amelie said. "We should go down there one summer for our beach week."

"Count me in," Timmy said. "I was just surprised, that's all. We'll have to start calling you Tugboat Annie."

"That beats Little Orphan Annie, I guess," Annie said.

"Did you and Calder buy it together?" Charlotte Claire asked.

"No," Annie said firmly. "We agreed we are not mixing money or real estate. We want to keep things simple. He has a boat in Malibu that's his. I needed an investment and we'd been talking about spending time in Miami. I mentioned that to my financial planner and she said real estate would be a good investment. That's why she recommended Star Island Drive. The houses there don't lose their value even when the market's bad. The boat is just a treat to myself...and because the house came with a dock. Anyway," she said giggling. "I interrupted myself. Now what's the plan for tonight, Timmy?"

"Let's see, first we're going to drink a couple more bottles of champagne. Then we'll get ready for dinner. I'm taking y'all to The Mews, one of my favorite restaurants here. Then we'll come back here, have a few drinks and cackle like a bunch of old hens."

"Sounds perfect," Charlotte Claire said.

"And tomorrow I'll make a giant batch of double Crantimmys and it's off for a day at the beach."

"Count me in," Amelie said.

"Me too...uh, three...uh, four!" Annie declared.

In the morning Timmy was up first and padded to the kitchen to put the coffee on. He worked steadily, putting out muffins, yogurt, fruit and berries. He took out blue and white porcelain cups and saucers, put them on a driftwood tray and placed them beside the coffee maker. He opened up the French doors that led to the patio and breathed in the fresh beach air. Why, he wondered, did beach air seem so different from regular air? Maybe it was the smell of the ocean mingled with the sand and sun. Or maybe it was just in his head. Then he noticed the throw pillows on the outdoor furniture in disarray and his contemplation of the sea air came to an abrupt end. He moved around the deck efficiently restoring them to order, then returned to the kitchen to prepare a picnic basket for the beach.

By noon the group was piled into the car and off to the beach. The women chattered and laughed as Timmy fiddled with the radio and navigated the back roads of Provincetown to Herring Cove beach. He found a radio station playing "Build Me Up Buttercup" and everyone sang along. With the windows down, the wind blew pleasantly through the car, and Timmy felt happy and young. It was as if they'd all become teenagers again.

Once they reached the beach they piled out of the car and unloaded the trunk. Burdened with umbrellas, beach chairs, towels, picnic baskets and a cooler, they made their way like pack mules to the beach. After they settled themselves Timmy said, "Okay, first order of business, Crantimmys!"

"Woohoo!" Amelie cheered.

"Double Crantimmys, I hope," Charlotte Claire asked.

"No," he replied.

"What?" Annie asked in mock horror.

"Triples," he replied slyly. "I had a weak moment." He filled their plastic cups and then his own. Then he raised his cup and toasted. "To weak moments!"

"To weak moments!" they echoed.

By 3 o'clock they were sufficiently buzzed. The conversation, as it often did on their beach trips, turned to Bayou Derkin. "Are you going to the 30-year reunion?" Charlotte Claire asked.

"Oh, good Lord, no!" Timmy groaned.

"I want to go," she responded. "Shove it in their faces." She began to giggle. "I want to shove some of my husband's hard-earned millions in their faces, especially Leanne. That bitch. She was always so hateful to me. She was constantly pointing out how poor we were and how rich they were. She made fun of my Mama because she worked in the cafeteria, and my clothes because they were homemade. God, I hated her. I think I'll bring our stock portfolio and shove that in her face." The others began to laugh.

"So, I guess I'll have to shove a book down her throat, and Annie will have to shove an Emmy down her throat," Timmy said.

"I'm not that cruel," Annie told them. "The Golden Globe will go down much easier." Their laughter continued to build.

"Oh, we've got to stop," Amelie said. "My stomach is starting to hurt."

"I'm leaking," Annie giggled.

"Me, too!" Charlotte Claire howled.

"And, we've got a movie star in our posse," Amelie said boastfully.

"We've got a movie star in our pussy?" Charlotte Claire shrieked. Now their laughter was self-perpetuating. After a few minutes the hilarity subsided.

"TV star, I used to be a movie star but now I'm almost middle aged, which means I'm a TV star."

"*Almost*?" Charlotte Claire squealed.

The group erupted in drunken laughter again. Annie was initially stung, but within seconds was laughing at herself. "I'm 47, which is pretty much the definition of middle age."

"If you are lucky enough to live to 94," Amelie blurted through her laughter.

"Oh shit," Annie said. "I'm almost elderly and I didn't even realize I was middle aged yet." Then she let out a loud whoop. They were all drunk, laughing uncontrollably until they were too spent to laugh anymore.

After a moment Timmy said, "No, seriously, why would you want to go back for that? We're not friends with any of those people. We have nothing in common with them anymore. Maybe we never did. And didn't we all suffer enough at the hands of those assholes? I still think about how Scotty and Tom tormented me-no, *stalked* me- and bullied me for most of my life; from third grade until I went to college."

Charlotte Claire looked at Annie, who turned to Amelie. They were all thinking the same thing. Timmy had never recovered from his childhood in Bayou Derkin. In some ways each of the women could say the same. Yet, somehow, they'd managed to let most of it go. The pain that Timmy carried into adulthood seemed deeper, darker. The thought gave Charlotte Claire a new resolve. "Well, I think we should go," she said. "I mean, really. We've all done really well for ourselves. Timmy, you've published how many books? You're famous! You look great. You're in great shape."

"She's right," Annie said. "Timmy, maybe going to the reunion will be a catharsis. Maybe you'd see Scotty and Tom be able to bury the hatchet."

"Yeah, in their backs," Charlotte Claire said, giggling.

"Now that is a bit tempting," Timmy said.

"I'm serious; you ought to think about it. I would go if you went," she continued.

"We'd all go," Amelie offered.

"Excuse me," Annie said. "I have a shooting schedule. I can't just pick up and run off to Bayou Derkin."

"It's on a Saturday night," Charlotte Claire said. "Don't you get weekends off? You're the lead, the star; can't you just tell them you have a commitment? You could fly in on Friday morning and be back on Monday afternoon."

"When is it?" Amelie asked.

"August," Charlotte Claire said.

"I could probably get Calder to juggle the shooting schedule. Well then, if Timmy goes, I'll go." They all turned to Timmy who looked back at them silently for several moments.

"Geez...peer pressure much? I'll think about it. I'm not making any promises...but I'll think about it."

"Now that you mention it, I wouldn't mind flaunting these," Annie said cupping her breasts with her hands. "Not bad for 47, and I heard Leanne got fat. Remember, how after my Mama died Leanne started calling me Little Orphan

Annie?"

"Yes, we remember," Amelie groaned. "I have to admit I didn't like her much, but she never did anything to me."

"That's because you're so nice to everyone, Amelie," Charlotte Claire told her.

"Thanks, Charlotte Claire,"

"It wasn't a compliment."

"Everybody liked you, Amelie. Anyway, she still called me Little Orphan Annie behind my back in high school. I'd be walking down the hall and she'd whisper something to her mean girls and they'd all laugh. It was just so hateful."

"Annie, your body isn't bad for 27," Charlotte Claire said. "And yes, Mama told me she got fat. She sees her in town all the time. Mama said she is so phony and *still* a snob. I still can't believe she married Scotty Piper. And you'll love this, Timmy. Scotty's fat too."

"Good. You *are* making this more and more tempting," he replied. "I'll truly consider it. Anyway, if all of you were there that would be reason enough to go. I could see my sister and my Aunt. I almost never go there since Mama and Daddy died."

"Everyone in Bayou Derkin says Scotty married her for her Daddy's money." Charlotte Claire continued. "How else could she get a husband?"

"Ooh, it's hot," Amelie said. "I'm going in the water to cool off. Anyone want to come?"

"I'll go," Annie replied.

"Me too," Charlotte Claire said. "Coming, Timmy?"

"No. I'll stay here and start packing up. We should get back by 4 so we have time to sleep it off before cocktail hour," he laughed.

"I like the way you think," Annie said with a wink. Timmy watched his three friends cross the beach to the ocean and let his gaze drift to the vast horizon. The blue of the water and sky were so close in color that the horizon was almost indiscernible.

He smiled watching Amelie, Annie, and Charlotte Claire splash in the water like happy children. How they'd all changed. Yet watching them now he was struck by how, in some ways, they were the same children that played together in Bayou Derkin all those years ago. Maybe they're right, he thought. Maybe I need to let this go. I'm so sick of carrying this baggage. Maybe I need to confront these old ghosts. Maybe I need to forgive them.

It was past midnight by the time they returned from dinner, drunk and laughing raucously. While the women piled onto the sofas Timmy went into the kitchen to open a bottle of wine.

"Okay, it's time," Charlotte Claire said mischievously.

"Oh, no," Amelie groaned. "Not again."

"Yes," Annie said. "We've played it on every trip we've ever gone on. There's no reason not to play it this year."

"What did I miss?" Timmy asked, returning with the wine.

"They want to play Truth or Dare," Amelie whined.

"Stop whining and have some wine," Annie giggled.

"Well, of course we have to play Truth or Dare," Timmy said matter-of-factly. "We always do. It's a tradition; mustn't fuck with tradition."

"See," Charlotte Claire said, kicking off her shoes. "Majority rules and Amelie drools." She let out the high-pitched whooping sound that she made when she was tickled.

"Oh, all right," Amelie said, surrendering. "I'll play. But I'm not doing anything naked or illegal."

"Okay, I'll go first," Charlotte Claire said. She put her folded hands to her face and with furrowed brow, contemplated her challenge. "Timmy," she said finally, "Truth or Dare?"

"Do you really need to actually say Truth or Dare every time?" Amelie complained. "We already know that it's tell the truth or take a dare. The person called on can just say if they want to tell the truth or accept the dare."

"Oh Amelie!" the others groaned.

"Only you would think of that," Charlotte Claire said, rolling her eyes and shaking her head.

"I'm just trying to...," Amelie trailed off and burst into laughter. "I forgot what I was trying to do. I think I'm drunk."

"I think we all are. Timmy, I love this wine," Charlotte Claire cooed.

"Oh, me too," he said. "There's nothing like a good rosé in summer. And I like the French rosés so much better than the California ones. I...

"Jesus, Mary and Joseph," Annie cried. "Are we going to play Truth or Dare or are we going to talk about the damn wine?"

"Oh, okay," Charlotte Claire said. "You know how I get side tracked; okay, Timmy-Truth or Dare?"

"Well, let's see," he said contemplatively. "I've had too much to drink to do any kind of daredevil stunts, so let's say truth."

"How many men have you slept with in your entire life?"

"Oh my God," he said. "Who the hell knows? I lived in New Orleans in my 20s so...a lot."

"Like 10 or 20?" she asked.

"I would say more in the range of 200 or 300."

"What!" Charlotte Claire cried.

"I'm a man. We're all sluts. Well, I was a slut when I was single. Now I'm monotonous-I mean, *monogamous*." He giggled drunkenly at his mistake.

"Oh, my lord," Annie said slipping into her pre-acting school southern drawl. She always slipped into her Bayou Derkin voice when she'd had too much to drink. "I'm jealous."

"Okay, Timmy," Charlotte Claire said. "Your turn."

"Annie," he said decisively. "Truth or Dare?"

"Dare," she said, instantly.

"Oh snap!" he said. "I was hoping you'd say truth. Now I have to come up with something. Let's see, let's see..."

"Don't take all night," Amelie scolded.

"Okay, this isn't much of a dare but..." he said. "Show us your boobs."

"Alright," she said as she happily unbuttoned her sheer silk blouse.

"Oh, good lord," Charlotte Claire cried. "Those old things? Nobody wants to see your old boobs. God knows I've seen enough of them." As Annie struggled to get her bra off, the others shrieked with laughter. "Look!" Charlotte Claire cried. "She can't get her bra, her brawl...y'all, she can't get her *brawl* off."

"Oh, hell, Amelie," Annie said in frustration. "Unhook the damn thing for me." Amelie leaned across the sofa and unhooked Annie's bra. She pulled her bra off and then turned to the group and exclaimed, "Ta da!"

After a moment of quiet deference, Timmy said, "They're lovely, Annie."

"Okay," Charlotte Claire said. "Now put your brawl back on."

"Good lord, it was hard enough getting it off once," she said. She dropped her bra on the floor and put her blouse back on. "Now it's my turn. I choose...Amelie. Amelie?"

"What?" Amelie snickered. "I'm waiting for the question."

"Oh, for hell's sake," Annie said in exasperation. "Truth or fucking dare?"

"Well, y'all are the ones who insisted on the question," she said sarcastically. "I'm just playing by the rules."

"Amelie!" they all cried.

"Okay, okay...dare."

"Oh, hell! I can't think of a good dare," Annie said. "I was hoping you would say truth. Give me a minute. I'll come up with something."

"Make her chug a tumbler full of vodka," Charlotte Claire suggested.

"Are you crazy?" Amelie said. "I've already had enough to

drink tonight. I don't want to die from alcohol poisoning."

"She's right," Timmy said. "That sounds dangerous."

"Ooh, I know, I know!" Annie called out excitedly before running into the kitchen.

"What on earth is she up to?" Timmy asked.

"She's going to make her eat something gross," Charlotte Claire surmised.

"Oh, great," Amelie moaned.

"Yep," Timmy said. "She got a bowl from the cabinet and now she's standing in the fridge, but she's behind the fridge door so I can't see what she's taking out of it. I hope she doesn't use any of my breakfast groceries."

"Now I wish I'd said truth," Amelie told them.

"I can't wait to see what she comes up with," Charlotte Claire said.

"Okay," Annie announced triumphantly as she returned from the kitchen and set down a small bowl and spoon in front of Amelie.

"What is this?" Amelie asked. She screwed her face up in disgust when she smelled the contents of the bowl. "It looks like mud."

"Mayonnaise, hot sauce, chocolate syrup, caviar and blue cheese dressing," Annie announced proudly, sending the group into fresh peals of laughter. "Sorry about the caviar, Timmy. I'll replace it tomorrow."

"Eat it! Eat it! Eat it..." they chanted. Amelie put the bowl to her nose and sniffed again. Then she took a spoon full of the concoction and, holding her nose, swallowed it down quickly. "That is disgusting!" she groaned.

"You have to eat the whole thing!" Annie demanded.

"No, don't make her," Timmy said. "It might make her sick. Especially with all the drinking we've been doing. Exactly how old are we, anyway?"

"On beach weeks, we're teenagers," Annie told him.

"She's right," Charlotte Claire agreed.

"Aww, my Timmy to the rescue," Amelie cooed.

"Oh, alright," Annie conceded. "Okay Amelie, now it's your turn."

"Charlotte Claire," she said turning in her direction. "Truth or Dare?"

"Truth!" she replied immediately. "I've no intention of eating something gross."

"I was prepared for this one," Amelie said slyly. "I thought it up before I left Asheville."

"Uh, oh..." Timmy said ominously.

"Hit me," Charlotte Claire said.

"Tell us something you've never told us before. Something you've always kept secret from us."

"Oh, that's a good one," Annie said. Charlotte Claire paused to consider what to say as the other three looked from one to the other in anticipation. Timmy couldn't imagine there was anything they hadn't told each other. But Annie and Amelie were titillated at the prospect of something juicy. Charlotte Claire put her hands to the sides of her neck and turned her gaze towards the floor. She remained that way for nearly a minute. When she lifted her head to speak her expression was sober and thoughtful.

"When we were in tenth grade," she said slowly, "Scotty Piper raped me."

"You can't make stuff up," Amelie scolded good-naturedly.

"Right," Annie concurred, laughing. "Only non-fiction secrets are acceptable."

"Y'all," Timmy said, his tone growing serious. "I don't think she's making this up. Is this really true, Charlotte Claire?"

"Yes," she said. "It's really true. I've never told anyone. I never told my parents or my brothers. I never told Adam and I've never told Stanley."

"Oh, Charlotte Claire," Annie said gently.

"Why didn't you tell someone?" Amelie asked.

"Or go to the police?" Timmy added.

"I was ashamed," she responded unemotionally. "I was humiliated, embarrassed and...ashamed."

"But you didn't do anything wrong," Timmy argued. "You had no reason to be ashamed."

"Well, I know that now, of course," she said. "But I was in the tenth grade and people didn't discuss rape back then, not the way they do now. It was a totally different time, a totally different atmosphere. And it was Bayou Derkin, for heaven's sake, good old, backwards Bayou Derkin. Can you imagine what school would have been like for me if people knew? And he would have denied it and said that it was consensual. They'd have called me a slut and Scotty a stud."

"How'd it happen?" Amelie asked.

"We were on a date," she responded.

"Oh my God; the kegger," Annie said in shock. "Do you remember Amelie? We helped her with her makeup."

"Oh, that's right. And you borrowed some of my clothes," Amelie said. "You were supposed to sleep over and you ended up going back home after the party."

"I never knew you dated Scotty," Timmy said.

"It was only one date," she replied, laughing bitterly. "And what a doozy that turned out to be. I never told you I went out with him, Timmy, because Scotty was so mean to you and I knew how you felt about him. I was afraid you'd get mad at me if you knew. And I really had a crush on him which made me feel kind of guilty, like I was being disloyal to you."

"Was it at the party?" Annie asked.

She took a deep breath and started at the beginning; meeting Scotty at the kegger, the drive, parking at the river. When she got to the part when he suggested they get in the back seat, she raised a hand as if to stop someone from speaking, though none of them had made a sound since she began her story. "Y'all I was young, I was naïve, I had no idea," her voice breaking as she told them. She fell silent for several seconds, wiping away tears before resuming her story; the force with which he pinned her to back seat, the brutality of the rape and the blood. "And I was a virgin," she continued. "I'd never let a boy even put his hand down there. He brought me home, and I had to tell my poor little Mama that I started my period. I'll never forget it y'all. I went into the bathroom and ran a hot bath. I sat in that tub with my arms around my knees and cried and cried. And do you know the main thing I was crying about?"

"What?" Amelie asked.

"I was crying because I felt guilty and ashamed, and because I felt like I let my Mama and Daddy down. They told me I wasn't allowed to date and look what happened when I defied them. That's how I felt. That's why I thought it was my fault."

"How'd that let your Mama and Daddy down?" Timmy asked gently.

"Because I wasn't a virgin anymore," she responded.

"But you didn't give up your virginity," Annie said wiping away tears. "It was taken from you."

"Oh, I know all that now," Charlotte Claire said. "But, again, I was a naïve kid."

"Oh Charlotte Claire," Timmy said. "I wish you could have told us. We've always stuck together. We might have been able to help you see it the way you do now."

"I wish that, too," she said. "I really do. It took me years to understand that I'd been raped and that it wasn't my fault or anything I should be ashamed of. It was in college, when they had those rape prevention presentations, that I finally accepted that I had been victimized, and that it wasn't because I made a bad decision, and that I shouldn't blame myself for it."

"So why would you want to go back for the thirty-year reunion and have to see him there?" Timmy asked.

"Oh, good Lord," she responded. "I had to go back to school that Monday and see him every day for the next two years until we graduated. I just compartmentalized it. After a while I just pretended it never happened. But it's never left me. When I first started having sex with Adam, sometimes, in the middle of it I would just start to feel panicky and have to stop. He never understood, and I just didn't want to tell him. It even happened with Stanley a couple of times. I just tell him that I'm having cramps and have to stop. It makes me so angry that I've had to live with it all these years. It doesn't leave you. And Scotty just goes on with his life like nothing happened. I'll bet he never even thinks about it. And if he does I'm willing to bet he doesn't feel any remorse. I truly hate him for what he did to me. I think he's the only person that I truly hate. And I'll hate him for the rest of my life."

"How does it feel talking about it now?" Annie asked.

"Good, actually," she said resolutely. "It feels good to give up that secret." Timmy crossed to the sofa where Charlotte Claire was sitting, sat beside her and put his arm around her shoulder. Annie moved to the other side of her and Amelie sat on the floor at her feet. They sat quietly that way for several minutes, the faint music from the stereo the only sound. It was James Taylor's "Sweet Baby James". Finally, Charlotte Claire said, "I love you guys."

"We love you too," Timmy said.

"'Y'all are going to have a hard time topping that Truth or Dare," Charlotte Claire said, and they all laughed.

Just as Timmy had expected, the week flew by with blinding speed. What had seemed like an long succession of lazy summer days at the beginning of the week now felt like a blur of memories. On their last day they got up early, and with a bottle of champagne, headed for the beach to watch the sunrise. They sat in a row on the sand facing the ocean like one of those Facebook posts about the beach. Timmy popped the cork and passed the bottle for each to fill their plastic cups. They sat quietly, wrapped in beach towels, and watched the giant orange sun as it rose above the horizon and cast its image on the glassy ocean. Timmy took a sip of champagne and said, "I can't believe the week is over already."

"It flew by like it always does," Amelie said.

"I know," Timmy said. "I hate that. And it always seems like an eternity until our next trip. I spend the whole year looking forward to it."

"Me too," Charlotte Claire said. "But you wouldn't have to, Timmy, if you came to the reunion. That's just two months from now."

"You've had the whole week to think about it, Timmy," Annie said. "What's it going to be? Will you come?"

"Are you really going to go if I go?" he asked.

"Yes," she replied.

"Promise?"

"Promise."

"Charlotte Claire?" he asked.

"Oh, hell yes."

"Amelie?"

"Definitely."

"Oh hell," he said, acquiescing. "Guess I'm going to the damn reunion."

"Woo hoo!" Amelie cheered. "Here's to the class of '85!" They raised their plastic cups and toasted as the brilliant sun rose high above their heads.

Bayou Derkin, Louisiana

August 14th, 2015

It was a complicated stew of emotions that Timmy felt as he crossed the Bayou Derkin town line. 'Bayou Derkin... Crossroads to Everywhere' the welcome sign read. It was the town's same old slogan, but the sign was new. It was evidence of the change in fortunes for the small town of his childhood where he experienced so much pain and humiliation. He'd taken the three-hour flight from New York to New Orleans, picked up a rental car, and drove west for three hours along Interstate 10 and through a network of two-lane farm roads that bordered the rice, soy bean and sugar cane fields that made up southwest Louisiana's agricultural industry. He'd forgotten just how big the sky was here, like a giant blue monolith in every direction. It was, perhaps, the only thing he missed about Bayou Derkin.

He hadn't slept well the night before, thinking about the trip. That morning Joe had tried to ease his anxiety by telling him what a good time he'd have seeing his old classmates. And even if he didn't enjoy the reunion, Joe pointed out, he'd still get to spend time with the girls. He *was* excited to see the girls, but everything else-everyone else-loomed like a haunted house of unpredictable surprises and ghosts from his past.

He decided to drive around before checking into the hotel, to see what had and hadn't changed about Bayou Derkin. A new Native American casino built ten years earlier had brought prosperity to the small town, and the manifestations of the casino's success could be found on every block. The little mid-century town hall of Timmy's childhood was gone, and in its place, stood an immense Southern Colonial building with a portico of great white pillars. The little stucco library, too, was gone, replaced by a new bank, and a big new library stood where Mr. R. G's furniture store had been. There were restaurants, gift shops, jewelry and clothing stores that hadn't been there before. A monument to Vietnam War veterans stood before a gazebo in the perfectly manicured town tri-angle that once was empty, save for dandelion-dotted crab grass. It was heartening to Timmy to see his old hometown re-born. Perhaps, he thought optimistically, it was a foreshadowing of what was to come.

He turned onto the highway and drove toward the out-skirts of town, past the new hotels and housing developments, past the new golf course, and on to the casino hotel where Timmy and the girls had decided to stay. Charlotte Claire still had a parent to stay with, but her mother lived far outside of Bayou Derkin, and she feared driving the dark, country roads at night after drinking. The others' parents had died long ago, their houses gone, or sold and inhabited by strangers. Timmy pulled into the casino's long driveway and parked in front of the hotel. The valet signaled for the bellhop. "No need," Timmy said. "I just have the one bag...and it rolls."

It was an exceptionally bright and sunny day, so it took Timmy a few seconds to adjust to the subdued lighting of the hotel lobby. Once he did he was able to scan the space and make an assessment. I cannot believe this hotel is in Bayou Derkin, he thought. It was luxe, with travertine floors and plush car-pets, and beautifully appointed with modern furnishings and art. While he was being checked in he pulled out his cell and called Charlotte Claire, who was due to arrive first, as she had driven from Houston the night before. She picked up after the first ring. "Where are you?" she asked immediately.

"Wow, that was fast," Timmy said. "Do you keep that thing strapped to your head?"

"I know," she said, laughing. "OCD Charlotte Claire. I just couldn't wait for you to get here."

"I'm in the lobby checking in," he said. "Almost done... wait, strike that, done. Hold on a second." Timmy listened as the desk clerk explained the hotel's amenities, told him his room number and gave him his key card. "Okay, I'm back."

"Let's meet in the bar," she suggested. "I've been with Mama and Aunt Sadie since yesterday afternoon and I need a cocktail."

"I need to unpack," he said. "Tell you what, come to my suite and we'll have something from the mini bar while I unpack. Suite 1015."

"That works. Be there in five."

Timmy had just gotten his suitcase open when the doorbell rang. He opened the door and grabbed Charlotte Claire in a bear hug. "You look amazing, Charlotte Claire!" he said admiringly, noting her chic beige slacks and slightly lighter shade of beige silk blouse, which draped perfectly at the waist. She wore heavy gold chains around her neck and wrist, gold earrings, and the huge diamond engagement sparkler that Stanley gave her to replace the simple one that he'd proposed with. Timmy figured the ring had to be at least five karats. That will drive Leanne up the wall, he thought delightedly. Charlotte Claire embraced her wealth and material possessions, but she did it so openly and joyously that it was impossible for Timmy not to enjoy it too.

"Timmy, you look fantastic," she said. "Always so fit. I wish I had your will power."

"What are you talking about? You look fantastic."

"Thanks, but I have this last five pounds that I need to drop, and it's holding on for dear life."

"Well I think it looks good on you. Hey, mini bar's over there. Improvise a Crantimmy for me and help yourself to whatever you want."

"Remind me, what's in it?"

"Three-parts vodka, one-part cranberry, and lime juice. Have you heard from Amelie or Annie yet?" Timmy unpacked his suitcase while Charlotte Claire mixed the drinks.

"Yeah, Amelie's flight to New Orleans was cancelled, so she

rebooked to Houston and met Annie at the airport. They're driving together. They should be here in about an hour."

"Why did Annie fly into Houston? New Orleans is closer."

"Typical Annie; she waited until the last minute to book and couldn't get a flight."

"Oh, too bad they didn't travel yesterday. You could have all driven together."

"I know," she said. "That would've been fun. I'd have waited a day, but I needed to get here and see Mama."

"How's your Mom?"

"Good, nothing new. She's become so independent since Daddy died. She travels with Aunt Sadie. They went to Las Vegas, just these two old ladies. Can you imagine? Timmy, that jacket is gorgeous. Whose is it?"

"Tom Ford," he said, holding it at arm's length and admiring it. "I love it. I figured I'd do it up right, as long as I came all the way down here."

"You'll probably be the only guy in a jacket...nobody dresses down here. I sent Mama a truck-load of new clothes, so she'd stop wearing her homemade schmattas."

"It's nice of you to be so generous with your Mom. I wish my Mother had lived long enough for me to do that."

"I know," she said sympathetically. "That is too bad. Hey, did you see the itinerary for the weekend? Here's your cocktail."

"Bottom's up!"

"Bottom's up."

"No, I haven't had a chance to look at it yet. I thought it was just the party tomorrow night. I didn't realize it required an *itinerary*," he said, dragging out the word sarcastically.

"Well, then you would be mistaken, my good man," she said, throwing her legs over the arm of the chair and kicking off her heels. "Tomorrow morning there's a breakfast. That starts at nine."

"Nine?" he groaned. "Why so early? Have they never heard

of brunch, for Christ's sake?"

"Some of them want to play golf. You could skip that. I think I'm going to. I never eat breakfast anyway."

"Me either."

"Then there's a luncheon at 1:00. That's in the casino restaurant, which is supposed to be very good. Plus, we can drink as much as we want since we don't have to drive."

"That, I'll do," Timmy said as he put his suitcase away and joined Charlotte Claire in the living room.

"And of course," she continued, "The big deal is tomorrow night, also here in the hotel. So again, we can drink as much as we like."

"I love how you hone in on the really important points."

"Naturally," she said, bowing her head and rolling her hand in a courtly manner. "But wait, I've saved the best for last."

"Do tell."

"The barbecue tonight," she said, pausing for dramatic effect, "Hosted by none other than Scotty and Leanne Piper." Charlotte Claire took a sip of her drink and waited for Timmy's response.

"Oh shit," Timmy said. "I'm not sure I want to go to that."

"You have to go," she said excitedly. "It's outside around their pool! The invitation says bring swim-suits. You have to, have to, have to. Besides, you can show off your buff-ness and make Scotty jealous," she continued. "And, I want to see their house. It's supposed to be hideous, a nouveau riche mini-mansion. Mama said that's what Scotty wanted. It must be killing Leanne. I don't like the bitch, but she had pretty good taste. Well, at least her mother did. She got a decorator from Houston, but that's just lipstick on a pig. So, you have to go. Amelie and Annie are going. Please, please!"

"I don't know, Charlotte Claire."

"Look," she said seriously, "You said you were going to confront old ghosts. So, come to the spook-house with us.

We'll all be there for moral support...which you won't even need. But, we'll be there if you do."

"Well," he considered, "Right into the fire, I guess."

"Oh good," she said jubilantly. "It'll be fun. You'll see. That starts at 7 but we don't need to get there until 8, so you have two hours to get ready and do whatever. On second thought, be ready at 7:00. The four of us can meet in the hotel bar for a drink before we go."

Timmy spotted Amelie and Annie as soon as he walked into the hotel bar. The two women jumped out of their seats and raced across the bar to greet him.

"Hey, Bubs," Annie said happily.

"Hey, Sis!"

"Timmy," Amelie said. "My Timmy!"

"Amawee!" he replied, greetings they'd exchanged since childhood. "How was the drive?"

"Long," Annie replied. "Shitload of traffic."

"At least you didn't have to drive," Amelie complained. "Let's order some drinks. We only have half an hour."

"Order something for Charlotte Claire," Annie said. "She'll be down in a couple of minutes. She's running late...again." Timmy motioned for the waitress and they ordered four Cosmo's.

"Well?" Annie asked, "How does it feel to be back in the big BD?"

"Surreal."

"You just need time to acclimate," Amelie told him. "It'll be fine."

"I hope so," he said.

"Ready for a pool party?" Annie asked.

"I don't think I'm going in the pool," Amelie said.

"I'll bring my suit," Timmy said. "But I'll see how I feel when I get there."

"You *have* to show off that body," Annie said. "That's going to be the talk of the reunion. I'm definitely going in. I haven't had a carb in a month. I dropped five pounds. Oh, look, there's Charlotte Claire." Annie waved her over. The women were exchanging hugs when the waitress returned with their drinks. She gingerly set the glasses down and took a step back from the table. Thinking that she was waiting to collect payment, Timmy pulled out his wallet and handed her his credit card, but she continued to stand there. She nervously ran a hand through her thin blonde hair.

"You're Anne Renee'," she said at last.

"The one and only, honey," Annie said.

"I love *Philadelphia Law*. It's my favorite show. I've seen every episode twice except this season of course because there aren't any reruns yet, but I'll definitely watch those too. My mother thinks you're beautiful and I ..." Annie could feel herself becoming irritated and the others were wishing the young woman would leave so they could continue their conversation.

"Would you like a selfie with me?" Annie interrupted.

"Oh, could I?" she gushed. "That would be great. Mama would never believe me otherwise." Annie stood beside the young woman and smiled broadly as she took the selfie.

"Thanks so much," Annie said, in a tone that made it clear that the conversation was over. The waitress handed Timmy his credit card.

"These are on me," she said sweetly, then walked away staring at her cell phone.

"Well, that worked out," Timmy said. "Free drinks!"

"That wasn't free," Annie said. "I had to pose for a picture. That's work."

"Do people ever recognize you, Timmy?" Amelie asked.

"Once in a while," he replied. "Mostly in airports and stuff. I suspect I get recognized in New York some. There are times I feel like people are taking note of me. But New Yorkers are too cool to approach you. Annie, you should relocate the show to New York."

"And do winter?" she replied dryly. "No, thanks, LA works for me."

"Who's designated driver?" Charlotte Claire asked. "I did it last time."

"No, that was P-Town. I was the DD. But no worries, ladies," Timmy said. "I hired a driver, so drink away."

"Woohoo!" Amelie cheered.

It was already dark when the SUV pulled away from the casino for the drive to the Pipers'. The women chattered happily about who they were most and least eager to see and what they might look like now. Only Charlotte Claire had been to Bayou Derkin over the years, and even then, only to see her mother. Timmy tried to participate in the conversation but was distracted by his growing anxiety. Had he made a mistake coming to the reunion, he wondered? Was he confronting the old ghosts of a painful past or was he really there to say, 'hey look at me, I'm rich, I'm famous, I've got a great body, I'm everything you're not.' And if that really is the reason, he thought, what kind of person does that make me; petty, materialistic, pathetic?

"Timmy?" Charlotte Claire said. "Where are you, man? You seem a million miles away."

"Not quite a million," he said with a chuckle.

"It's going to be fine," Annie said. "Better than fine, even. It's going to be fun."

"Right, Timmy," Amelie added. "What could possibly go wrong?" After a beat they simultaneously burst out laughing.

The SUV turned into a long, tree-lined driveway and traveled slowly towards the Piper residence. It was illuminated in front by powerful flood-lights, giving the house a carnival-like appearance. "Oh my God," Charlotte Claire said. "It's even worse than they said it was." The house was comprised of multiple architectural vernaculars. There were Gothic arched windows, Tudor style brick work, a Greek Revival portico supported by Italianate brick columns, and, worst of all, a Victorian turret.

"What the hell?" Timmy said. "It looks like Disneyland."

"More like a haunted house," Amelie said.

"It's a monstrosity," Annie added.

"Yeah, isn't it great?" Charlotte Claire said, prompting another fit of laughter.

"Ready, Timmy?" Annie asked, as they stood at the front door.

"As I'll ever be," he replied. He pressed the doorbell and electronic door chimes rang out loudly. They snickered but kept their amusement in check. The door swung open, and after a pause Leanne Reed Piper threw her arms open and beamed at the group.

"Oh, my goodness, the out-of-towners have arrived! And fashionably late at that," she said with slight edge in her voice. "I'm so glad y'all could make it. Come in, come in." As she turned to lead them inside, the group exchanged amused looks. Charlotte Claire's intel had been spot on. Leanne had indeed gained a significant amount of weight, which she concealed beneath a long black tunic with a Nehru collar. The pointy nose and chin of her girlhood looked oddly incongruous with her puffy cheeks and jowls. She wore masses of gold chains around her neck and both wrists, and long, dangling gold earrings. Her blonde hair was arranged in a large confection that resembled a Kaiser roll. She looked easily 20 years older than she should.

"Leanne," Timmy said. "It's so good to see you."

"How long has it been?" she asked.

"I haven't seen you since college," Annie replied.

"And Annie, a movie star no less! Well, TV star, now. Or should I call you Anne now that you've changed your name."

"My name *is* Anne. Annie's a nickname."

"Oh. This must be so mundane for you. No red carpets tonight, I'm afraid, Anne," she chortled.

"Well thank goodness for that," Annie said. "And Annie still works. This isn't mundane at all. I've been looking forward to it."

"Well, aren't you sweet to say so. My kids are so excited to meet the star of *Philadelphia Law*. They're going to stop by later with my grandbabies. I hope you don't mind. I think they just want to get a few selfies to show their friends."

Annie surreptitiously glanced at Timmy and rolled her eyes.

"Charlotte Claire," Leanne cooed. "How nice to see you and don't you look *tres' chic*."

"Thank you, Leanne," she sang. "And you, the chains, the tunic, it's just so exotic! Where's Scotty?"

"Out on the patio smoking cigars with a group of men," she replied. "You know how men are. They huddle and talk about sports or hunting and what-not."

"Amelie, welcome," she said, pivoting in her direction. "How sweet of you to come."

"Thank you, Leanne," Amelie said. "And aren't you sweet to host the class of '85."

"Now don't go peeking at my bed linens," she warned. "Sorry to say you won't find Amelie Ardoin sheets. I'm a Frette girl I'm afraid; always have been."

"Well, don't *Frette*, Leanne," Amelie said coyly. "I wouldn't dream of going into your bedroom." Leanne laughed insincerely, then was quiet for a moment, not-so-subtly registering her distaste for the joke.

"But Timmy, I have read one of your books. I can't think which one. Oh, well, it's in the library somewhere. I'll have to see if I can dig it up. Now please make yourselves at home," she told them. "There are hors d'oeuvres in the dining room and the bar's outside by the pool. And do feel free to look around. The house is new, you know. I had a decorator from Houston. Charlotte Claire, I'll have to give you his name. He's a little, well, *you know*," she said with an almost imperceptible glance at Timmy. "But his work is divine. I think you'll agree after you see the rest of the house. Better check on the caterer. See you outside!" She turned with a flourish and strode through the French doors leading to the patio.

"Well, its official," Annie said. "She's still a bitch."

"She looks dreadful," Charlotte Claire trilled. "It was definitely worth the trip."

"And the snarky comments...I've read one of your books. Can't think which one," Timmy said, mimicking her southern drawl. "I was about to thank her when she throws in, 'Can't think which one.' Which is just her way of saying that it was forgettable. Bitch...is right."

"Oh, Annie you're a movie star," Annie mocked. "I mean TV star."

"Don't go looking for Amelie Ardoin sheets," Amelie added. "I'm a Frette girl. She just had to let me know that."

"And did you see all those gold necklaces and bracelets," Charlotte Claire asked. "I wanted to ask her if she'd just escaped from a chain gang."

"Something was needed to break up the giant black monolith that is Leanne," Timmy said. "She looks like an elderly priest."

"A fat, elderly priest," Charlotte Claire snickered.

"Listen to us, we're terrible," Annie laughed. "We sound like those old hens in *The Music Man*." She began to sing, "Pick a little, talk a little. Pick a little, talk a little. Cheap, cheap, cheap! Talk a lot, pick a little more." They laughed guiltily.

"You're right," Timmy said. "We should stop. We're the pot calling the kettle black. We've just taken catty to a new dimension. Let's go get a drink and mingle."

"Good idea," Charlotte Claire said. "I need a drink."

"Sounds good to me," Amelie said.

"Me too," Annie agreed.

"Alright then, ladies," Timmy said. "Into the fray!"

As soon as the group stepped onto the patio they were

besieged by their classmates; particularly Annie and Timmy. For the next hour they fielded questions as if it were a press conference. What's it like living in New York? What's it like being famous? What famous people do you know? Are you going to make any more movies? Are you working on another book? It was all in a day's work to Annie, but their interest and excitement was touching to Timmy. It put him at ease enough to feel glad that he'd come to the reunion. People do change, he thought, look how much he himself had changed. As soon as he could excuse himself, he made for the bar. He ordered a vodka tonic and while he waited for his drink he scanned the patio to see who he recognized. He spotted Scotty Piper on the other side of the pool talking to Andy Stoner and Chaz King, two of Scotty's high school buddies. Avoid that side of the pool, he thought. Deal with those guys one at a time, not en masse. After he got his drink he set out in search of the girls. As he walked past the pergola a man called out to him. Timmy turned to find Tom Burnett leaning against a column smoking a cigarette. Timmy hesitated for a second and then moved towards him. "Hi Tom," he said cordially.

"Timmy, man, it's good to see you."

"And you, Tom, how've you been?"

"Oh, alright I guess. Same old, same old; nothing exciting like what you got going on."

He took a long drag from his cigarette and blew it upward so as not to blow smoke in Timmy's face. Now Timmy could see that Tom was a little drunk. He searched for something to say. Finally, he came up with, "Are you married?"

"Was," Tom said, laughing bitterly. "Divorced three years ago."

"Oh, I'm sorry," Timmy said uncomfortably.

"Don't be. I'm not. What about you? You married?"

Timmy felt himself flushing at the question. It should have been an ordinary question. But standing there with the boy who had made his childhood a living hell, who called him faggot and queer over the course of years, it was enough to make him suddenly nervous. He steeled himself and said, "Yes."

"What's he do?" he asked casually.

"He's a financial analyst," Timmy said, relieved and surprised by Tom's choice of pronouns. "You may have heard of him. They sometime interview him on MSNBC. His name's Joe Briarcliff."

"No, haven't heard of him. But I don't really keep up with financial news. Mechanics don't have much cause to. Well, congratulations on your marriage. I hope you have better luck than I did," he laughed, taking another long drag on his cigarette. After a few moments of silence Timmy thought it was a good time to make his exit.

"Well, it's been great catching up," he said extending his hand. "Hope to..."

"Timmy," he interrupted. "I...I wanted to say I'm sorry. I'm sorry for the way I treated you back then."

"Well, thank you, Tom," Timmy said after a moment. "That means a lot to me."

"I can't tell you how bad I've felt about that. And for a long time too. It was a hateful thing to do. A stupid thing to do and I'm sorrier than I can really tell you."

"You're very kind to do it now. A lot of people would just think of it as in the past and not bother."

"My boy was gay," he said earnestly. "I had to watch him go through the same thing I put you through. He killed himself. He couldn't take it."

"Oh Tom, I'm so, so sorry."

"Karma's a bitch," he laughed, bitterly. "My wife couldn't handle it. It tore our marriage apart. I hadn't been supportive of it, of him, at first. I was embarrassed. You know Bayou Derkin, people talk and it ain't always so nice. But I came around. She still blamed me after it happened. And I guess she was right."

"What was his name?"

"Scotty, can you believe it?"

"Well, sure. You and Scotty have been best friends since we were kids."

"That son of a bitch is no friend of mine."

Timmy was surprised by the harshness of Tom's voice. "What happened?"

"Leanne, that's what happened. Once he married that stuck-up bitch-and believe me, he only married her for the money-but once he married her he was too good to be friends with me. He went to work in her Daddy's company and of course Big Daddy kept the money rolling in. Now that the old man's dead, Leanne owns the company and Scotty runs it. We invited them to the house a few times. Never came. Leanne would see Mary, that's my ex, see her in town and not even say hello. Oh, and the kicker. My Scotty used to hang around with Piper's boy, Matthew. Matthew starts giving Scotty the brush off. After a few days of that, Scotty, my Scotty, asks him why and he says, 'my Dad said he didn't want me hanging around with no damn faggots.' I'd like to have beat the shit out of him, and I would've too if he weren't up the ass of every cop, district attorney and judge in the parish. They'd have locked me up and thrown away the key. No Timmy, he is as big a dick as he ever was. Only now he's a dick with money and he has a cunt for a wife. Huh," he laughed, threw back half a can of beer and wiped his mouth with the back of his hand. "He's a dick and she's a cunt; perfect couple."

"Well...," Timmy said uncomfortably.

"Hell, *she* may be worse than a cunt. *She* may be a murderer."

"What?"

"That's been going around for years; and when she was a kid, too. Amelie's little sister. What was her name?" he said opening another can of beer.

"Elizabeth," Timmy said.

"Yeah, that's right, Elizabeth."

"Gal I'm dating, Carla, is a nurse at Bayou Derkin Hospital. Leanne came in for a hysterectomy a few years back and she got an infection or something, I don't know what, so they had her on IV pain meds. Then she had a bad reaction to the pain meds and was delirious and talking out of her head. Started saying she didn't want to go to hell and she was just a little girl and didn't know what she was doing. She was saying 'She wouldn't shut up and she kept screaming and saying she was going to tell.' And something about hitting her with a rock and I don't know what all. She was saying how she just wanted the float and she wouldn't let her play with it. Carla thought she was hallucinating random shit, but Patty Hammond, you remember Patty Hammond, she's about ten years older than us, she told Carla she thought she was talking about..." Tom paused, searching for the name.

"Elizabeth," Timmy offered.

"Yeah, that she was talking about Elizabeth Ardoin. Carla's not from around here so she didn't have any idea what Patty was talking about, until she told me, and I filled her in. That's about five years ago. Well Carla tells this to someone and someone tells it to someone else and then it sort of got a life of its own, the rumor I mean. I don't know if Leanne or Scotty even know about it. But it's not that hard to believe. Leanne is such a bitch and she was a hateful little snob of a kid. Makes it sort of believable."

"Wow," Timmy said incredulously. "That is quite a rumor. Still, murder is a stretch, especially by a 12-year-old. Like *The Bad Seed*."

"The what?" Tom said slurring.

"*The Bad Seed*, it's an old movie about a kid who's a murderer." Timmy could see that Tom was getting drunker and figured that he had no idea what he was talking about. He'd spent much more time with Tom than he'd wanted, no matter how rewarding the apology. As he searched for an excuse to make a graceful exit Charlotte Claire appeared.

"Hey Tom, how are you?" she asked him.

"Good, good," he slurred. "I was just telling Timmy how good everything is."

"Glad to hear it," Charlotte Claire said. "Can I steal Timmy from you for a moment? There's someone who wants to talk to him."

"Yeah, yeah," Tom said, motioning with his cigarette hand. "I've taken enough of his time."

"It was good talking to you, Tom," Timmy said. "Really good. Thank you."

"You too, man," he said drunkenly. "Stay cool, man."

As they walked away Timmy said quietly, "Thank you. I was just trying to figure out how to get out of there without offending him. We talked for a pretty long time."

"I know," Charlotte Claire said. "I watched y'all for about ten minutes before I decided you needed to be saved. What were y'all talking about for so long?"

"Well, for starters he apologized for the way he treated me when we were kids."

"No! You're kidding. Oh, Timmy that's great. Now see, aren't you glad you came?"

"Yeah, yes I am. Thanks for being so pushy," he said, putting his arm around her shoulder and giving it a little squeeze. "And he told me the wildest rumor that's going around about Leanne."

"Well, now you're in my wheelhouse," she said excitedly. "Tell, tell!"

"Okay, let's go sit at a table. But first I need another drink. By the way, where are Annie and Amelie?"

"They're giving themselves a tour of the house. Meanwhile, Ladonna Frey was getting me caught up on what's going on with everybody. She is a font of information, aka uber-gossip."

Annie sat on the toilet staring at the wallpaper in the

powder room. Black monkeys pulling rickshaws covered the walls. A huge gilt mirror over a marble vanity reflected more of the wallpaper back at her. Good God, she thought, I feel like I'm in a Las Vegas brothel. She flushed the toilet, pulled her pants up and looked at her reflection in the mirror. Makeup's holding up well, she thought, but better touch up the lipstick. When she was satisfied with the result she left the bathroom and walked right into Scotty Piper. "Oh, sorry," she laughed. "I should look where I'm going."

"You can run into me anytime. You sure are looking good, Annie."

"Thanks," she said. "You're looking well Scotty."

"No, I mean you are looking *hot.*"

"Still the sweet talker, Scotty. I guess some things never change."

He moved in closer to her so that her back was almost against the wall. "You know we could duck into that bathroom and see what we missed in high school."

"No thanks," she said dryly.

"Come on," he said, placing his hands on her shoulders and pressing her to the wall. "Leanne doesn't care, so why should we?" When he leaned in to kiss her she could smell the whiskey on his breath. She pushed him back with all the strength she could summon, and his back hit the opposite wall of the small corridor with a thud.

"I said, no thanks," she repeated emphatically.

"Cunt," he hissed. "Everybody knows you're a slut." Then he turned and walked toward the patio. Annie, shaken and angry, rushed out of the little hallway and into the foyer in search of Amelie. When she didn't find her there she went into the library and found her looking over the titles on Leanne and Scotty's bookshelves.

"Oh, there you are," Annie said, her heart pounding in her chest.

"This is so predictable," Amelie said, disdainfully. "They

have all the classics, leather-bound no less, and not a one of them looks like they've ever been opened. Look," she said holding up one of the volumes and bending the cover back so that it made a creaking sound. "Never been opened. They're all like that."

"Amelie," Annie said breathlessly.

"What's wrong?" she asked. "You look like you just saw a ghost."

"Scotty just pinned me to the wall and tried to kiss me. He wanted us to fuck in the powder room."

"Oh my God!" Amelie cried. "What did you do?"

"I pushed him off me so hard that he hit the wall...hard!" When Amelie started to laugh Annie interrupted her. "It's not funny. I was really scared. You know what he did to Charlotte Claire. People like that don't change. He called me a cunt. It was so hateful, so verbally violent. I was really, really scared."

"Oh, honey, I'm sorry. What a prick! I can't believe he would try that with all these people here. What if Leanne had walked by?"

"That's the weird part. He said she wouldn't care."

"Are you alright? Do you want to leave?"

"No, no, I'm fine," she said. "I've handled bigger dicks than that. Wait, that didn't come out right." They walked out of the library laughing.

"The inside is a lot nicer than the outside," Annie was saying as they climbed the stairs to the second floor. "Her decorator does have good taste even though he's *a little too...*"

"Yeah," Amelie said. "I caught that too...so did Timmy. I hate to admit it, but I really did love the kitchen. It's so classic." When they reached the top of the stairs they looked out from the gallery to the foyer below. "That's a little grand for my taste," Amelie said.

"It's all too traditional for me. What's in here?" Annie asked, opening a door off the hall. "Bedroom."

"Too many flowers," Amelie complained. "Flowers on the curtains, flowers on the wallpaper. She should break it up with some geometrics."

They continued down the hallway inspecting three additional bedrooms and four baths. At the end of the hall a pair of double doors beckoned. "Must be the master," Amelie said. "This ought to be good. You think they have mirrors on the ceiling?"

"It would be bad enough to have to have sex with Leanne. But would you want to have to see yourself do it?"

Leanne's bedroom looked like a luxury hotel room. Heavily lined drapes in yellows and greens depicting birds and flowers puddled onto thick carpet, and a king-sized bed ladened with masses of decorative pillows against an upholstered headboard. The case pieces were high-quality, reproduction Louis XVI, and copies of great works of art hung from the pale-yellow walls. A tall gold-leaf mirror hung above a chest-of-drawers, upon which sat Leanne's collection of crystal perfume atomizers and a framed family photo.

"Do people actually use these things?" Amelie asked, picking up an atomizer and spraying a little cloud of perfume into the air.

"I'm sure Leanne does," Annie said. She picked up the framed photo and considered it for a moment. "Luckily her kids got Scotty's looks. One has a kid. Grandma Leanne."

"Hey now, I'm a grandma too."

"Oh look, the master bath." They stepped inside the master bath, which was all marble and glass with a Louis XVI vanity that coordinated with the chest in the bedroom.

"The bath fittings are gold...I hate that," Annie said as she turned to find Amelie opening one of two medicine cabinets. "What are you doing, Amelie?" she cried.

"Exploring, don't you do that when you're in someone's bathroom?" she said matter-of-factly.

"No, I don't," Annie told her.

"You should; you can learn a lot about someone by seeing what they keep in their medicine cabinets."

"Oh, really?" Annie asked skeptically.

"Yeah," Amelie replied. "Like Leanne doesn't have any Midol, so maybe she's gone through menopause or had a hysterectomy. And she has a depilatory...so she has whiskers."

"Oh my God; that's hysterical."

"And she takes Xanax so she's depressed. I bet she's on it right now."

"Is it a recent prescription?" Annie asked.

"Yeah, she just filled it last week. And it's already half empty. See what's in Scotty's."

"No," Annie told her. "Let's get out of here before we get caught."

"Oh, move over, chicken."

Amelie opened the medicine cabinet and looked inside. "Nothing so interesting here; shaving stuff, Old Spice. I didn't think anyone still wore that. Oh, wait. Xanax. They have his and hers Xanax."

"Amelie, let's go!" Annie insisted.

They went back into the bedroom and were on their way out when Amelie noticed a pair of tall doors. "I wonder what's in here?"

"Probably a closet," Annie said.

Amelie opened the doors and the large closet was immediately fully illuminated. She stepped inside.

"This is not just any closet," Amelie said in awe. "Annie, you have to see this." The closet had to be 10 feet by 12 feet. It was outfitted on all sides, from floor to ceiling, with wood paneled doors, so that none of the contents of the closet were visible. In the center of the space was a counter-height storage cabinet of the same paneled wood, surrounded on all sides by drawers and doors. Above it hung an elegant crystal chandelier, the light of which was reflected in the marble countertop below.

"I have to admit it," Annie said after entering the closet. "This is one fucking amazing closet. It doesn't even look like a closet. Where are all the clothes?"

"It looks more like a kitchen without appliances; a very, very beautiful kitchen."

"It seems so much more organized because you don't see all the different colors and sizes and types of clothes, just beautiful wooden cabinets."

"It pains me to say it, but I think I'm jealous," Amelie confided.

"Well, don't tell her, it'll just give her something else to be smug about."

"Can't have that. Do you notice what's missing?" Amelie asked. "Mirrors; where are the mirrors?" They looked at one another conspiratorially. Without speaking each of them opened a cabinet door. "Ah ha, I found the mirror...and the clothes. And her clothes are color coded lightest to darkest. As a quilter I can appreciate that."

"Do you mean, as an anal-retentive neurotic, you can appreciate that?" Annie asked, opening a pair of cabinet doors to reveal rows of shelves above and drawers below. On each shelf were linen-covered containers, stacked two per shelf in neat, vertical rows. "Speaking of anal retentive neurotics. Look at this."

"Okay, jealous for sure now," Amelie said, turning to investigate another closet.

"And she's labeled every container," Annie told her. "I'm sorry, that's just scary. Mother's Day Cards," she said, reading from the labels. "Letters from Mother, Letters from Children, Baby Shoes, Christening Gowns, Pink Swan Float, Kid's Report Cards..."

"Wait," Amelie said as if awaking from a dream. "What did you say?"

"Kids' Report Cards."

"No, before that."

"Pink Swan Float."

"Let me see that," Amelie said crossing the closet and removing the container from the shelf.

"Amelie!" Annie cried. "I don't think you should do that. What if Leanne or Scotty walked in?"

But Amelie ignored her, jerking the lid off the container and removing the neatly folded deflated float. She unfolded it and held it up to examine it. A feeling like a shockwave went through her and she felt suddenly clammy, as if she were going to faint. "Elizabeth," she said softly.

"Amelie, what are you doing? What are you talking about? You're being weird. What's going on?"

"It's Elizabeth's. It's the pink swan float that Elizabeth was playing with the day she died."

"Oh, my God. I'd forgotten about that. I hadn't thought of it in years. Are you sure?"

Amelie held out the underside of the float for Annie to see. There underneath the base of the swan's long neck were two tiny, faded letters: EA.

"But I don't understand," Annie asked incredulously. "Why would she have Elizabeth's float? Where would she have gotten it from?"

"I don't know. Maybe she found it the day Elizabeth died. Remember they never found it. Maybe she came across it first and just kept it. I remember seeing her that day when I was on my way to get Mama and Daddy. She was walking across the schoolyard near the woods, near where they found Elizabeth. I asked her to help us look for Elizabeth, and she said she couldn't because her Mama wanted her home for something or other. I'll never forget it. I was so panicked, and she couldn't have cared less."

"Oh, Amelie," Annie said sympathetically. "What are you going to do? Are you going to take it? Are you going to confront her?"

"I'm not going to confront her. She'd know we'd been

digging around in her closet. And I can't take it. It's too big to fit under my clothes and our tote bags are downstairs. I'd never be able to get it there without someone seeing. I'd try to drop it out the window and then get it outside, but knowing Leanne the house has a security system and we'd risk setting it off. And we don't have a car here, so I'd have to wait until the driver comes to pick us up at the end of the night and everybody will be leaving then. Someone would surely see me coming out from around the side of the house."

"You've certainly thought this through," Annie said.

"No, I'm going to have to put it back."

"Well, hurry then, before someone comes in and catches us."

Amelie held out the float and looked at it one more time. She felt as if she were looking at Elizabeth herself. A feeling of nostalgia and pain overwhelmed her. She hugged the float to her chest before refolding it and returning it to the container. As she slid the box back onto the shelf she couldn't help but think of Elizabeth's burial. It was as if she were burying her all over again.

"Pardon my manners," Scotty said, approaching the table where Timmy and Charlotte Claire were sitting. "I've been meaning to get over here and say hello, but I got caught up in a conversation with Andy Stoner, who by the way is drunk as shit, so I'd steer clear if I were you. Stupid bastard don't know when to shut the hell up. Well, how've y'all been? You still living up there in New York City, Timmy?"

"Yeah, still there," Timmy said cordially.

"Leanne and I been there a couple of times," he said. "Personally, I could do without it; too many people. Buildings are so tall you got no goddamn sky to speak of, and everything cost a fucking fortune. Not that I can't afford it."

"Yeah, I think you love it or you hate it. Obviously, I love it."

"And how are you, Charlotte Claire?" Scotty said, rocking

back on his heels. "You still in Houston?"

"Sure am," she said. "Still loving it."

While he spoke with Charlotte Claire, Timmy took stock of Scotty Piper, the middle-aged man. He was still handsome, though he had a beer belly now. But how incongruous his polo shirt and khakis looked on the poor kid who only wore his brother's hand-me-down clothes, or things his mother found at the thrift shop. Underneath his new, elevated style, Timmy thought he saw the same old Scotty: Arrogant, boastful, mean.

"My husband," Charlotte Claire was saying, "starts tech companies and sells them."

"He must do well at that," Scotty said. "Course, now, cost of living must be a lot higher in Houston. You'd never be able to get a house like this in Houston. It'd cost a mint."

"Oh, I think I could if I wanted to," Charlotte Claire said, whipping out her phone from the pocket of her cover-up. "This is my house." She thrust her phone with an image of her house in Scotty's direction.

"Hot damn," Scotty said admiringly. "You sure married up."

"Likewise, I'm sure," Charlotte Claire said, smiling broadly. "Tell me Scotty, what's the deal with Tom Burnett? He seems so sullen."

"That sorry piece of shit," he said acidly. "He's just a fucking loser; a mechanic. He's divorced now. He's just a goddamned sad sack. It's no wonder she left him."

"He lost his son," Timmy said evenly. "I guess that would be reason enough to be a 'sad sack,' as you put it."

"That was five years ago," Scotty said dismissively. "Life goes on. Get the fuck over it already. By the way, my boy Matthew is playing for LSU. He's got real talent. He's made his old man damn proud. You got kids, Charlotte Claire?"

"Yep," she said proudly, pulling her phone from her pocket once again. "My daughter, Amelia Anne, she's in New York, a struggling actress. And my son, Tyler, is in New York as well. He's a chef. We bought a two-bedroom apartment on the Upper West Side and they share. It's such a comfort to know that Tyler is there to look out for Amelia Anne. In fact, they live a short subway ride from Timmy. He sees them more than I do. Timmy has two kids as well."

"Well, well," Scotty said, looking confused.

"Two step-kids," Timmy clarified. "My husband has two kids. Britt and Leigh, they're still in high school. You may have heard of my husband. His name is Joe Briarcliff. He's a regular consultant on MSNBC."

"Yeah, I know who he is. Well, what do you know?"

"Everybody knows who he is," Charlotte Claire cried. "Everyone knows who y'all are, Timmy. Y'all are famous! Did you know?" she continued, turning to Scotty. "Timmy, or Timothy as he's known professionally, has just published his seventh book and just got a book and movie deal. Can you believe someone from Bayou Derkin doing all that? It's impressive!"

"Well, that's great Timmy," Scotty said dismissively. "You know what? I'd better check on the barbecue. Great talking."

After Scotty was out of earshot Timmy and Charlotte Claire howled with laughter. "I thought that would shut him up," Charlotte Claire said.

"Well, if my success didn't shut him up," Timmy said, "I knew my husband would. Charlotte Claire, you are bad."

"You're welcome. Oh look, there are Amelie and Annie. Yoo-hoo!" she called out.

When they'd reached the table, it was clear to Charlotte Claire and Timmy that something was wrong. "We need to talk," Annie said. "You won't believe what we just found in Leanne's closet."

"What you found in her closet?" Timmy snorted. "What on earth have y'all been up to? Amelie, are you okay? You look as if you've seen a ghost."

"She has," Annie said. "We both have. Do you remember

when Elizabeth died?"

"Of course," Charlotte Claire said.

"No, let me finish, Charlotte Claire," Annie snapped. "Do you remember at the time Amelie kept asking where the pink swan float was?"

"Oh, I had totally forgotten about that," Timmy said.

"How she looked for it and she told the police and they looked for it, but it was never found...well, we found it...in Leanne's closet."

"What?" Timmy exclaimed. "How, wait this just doesn't make any sense. Why on earth, how on earth would Leanne have come to have it?"

"Good question," Annie said.

"Oh, sweet Lord," Charlotte Claire said. "Amelie are you all right?"

"I'm...I don't know what. I'm stunned, confused. I don't know what to make of it."

"How can you be sure it was Elizabeth's?" Timmy asked. "Maybe she had one just like it."

"It had her initials on it," Amelie said. "She'd asked me to put her initials on it. She was afraid she would lose it, or some-one would take it. She loved that stupid float like it was a pet."

"Oh, my God," Timmy said. "Tom Burnett."

"What about Tom Burnett? Timmy, try to stay focused." Annie told him.

"What?" Amelie demanded.

"It's a rumor he heard, but I don't think we should talk about it here," Timmy said.

"Let's go," Amelie said. "I don't feel like being here."

"Understandable," Charlotte Claire said.

"Agreed," Timmy said. "I'll call for the car. It should be here in about 15 minutes. We should all make the rounds and say goodbye to whoever we want to say goodbye to, and thank-argh-Leanne and Scotty. We can talk about this in my suite when we get back to the hotel."

On their way out Amelie stopped short when they'd reached the foyer. The weight of the tote bag on her arm had given her an idea. "Wait," she said. "I've got to try and get that float. I'm going to sneak back into the closet and put it in my tote bag."

"Are you sure you want to try that?" Timmy asked.

"Yes."

"Do you want one of us to come with you?" Charlotte Claire asked her.

"No, better if I go alone. Go on to the car. I'll be quick."

"Are you sure?" Annie asked her.

"Yes! Just go!"

Amelie climbed the circular stair and stepped onto the gallery. She looked down the long hallway that lead to the master bedroom and saw that it was clear. She walked quickly down the hall until she'd reached the double doors. She waited there for a moment to see if she could hear anyone inside the room. When she concluded that the room was empty she opened the doors, glanced over her shoulder to make sure the hallway was still clear, and entered the bedroom. She moved quickly across the room and opened the closet doors.

"Oh, I thought the house tours were over," Leanne said from the bedroom doorway. Amelie froze. "I know, the closet is terribly extravagant, but we all need a little extravagance, don't we?"

"Of course," Amelie said nervously. "In fact, I'm doing some renovating myself and I wanted to get one more look to get some ideas."

"Really?" Leanne said. "How flattering. Well, take a picture."

"What?"

"With your phone; take a picture. Then you won't have to depend on your memory."

"Oh, right," Amelie stumbled. "Great idea; let me see..."

She fumbled through her tote bag, fished out her phone and took a picture of the closet. She looked over at Leanne who remained standing in the doorway. "Well, thanks, Leanne."

"You're most welcome," she said, her eyes fixed on Amelie.

"Well, I guess I'd better be going. The others are waiting for me outside."

"I'm so sorry that you have to go so soon." Leanne stepped aside, indicating that Amelie should exit first.

"Oh," Amelie said in surprise, "Okay then, well, thanks again." Amelie walked past Leanne and out the door.

"It was a pleasure. I'm so glad you could join our little party," she called out to Amelie. When Amelie had reached the stairs, Leanne walked quickly to the closet, opened the closet door and pulled the container from the shelf. She pulled the lid off and saw that the pink swan float was still in its container. She carefully replaced the lid, returned the container to the shelf and closed the closet door. She leaned against the door and let out a long breath.

When they returned to the hotel Timmy opened a bottle of wine and recounted his conversation with Tom Burnett. Amelie sat speechless and overwhelmed. Timmy said, "I don't know what to think."

"Frankly, it sounds kind of far-fetched," Annie said. "I know we all dislike her, but I can't imagine that Leanne, at 12 years old, would kill Elizabeth for her float."

"Little kids have killed for a lot less," Charlotte Claire told them. "Take Mary Bell for example. She killed a little four-year-old so that she could frame him for a break-in she committed. Then she killed a three-year-old and carved the letter "M" into his chest. She was 11. And Jasmine Richardson was 12 when she killed her mother, father and 8-year-old brother after she saw Natural Born Killers. It was a thrill kill. Child murderers are not as rare as you might think. And they tend to kill over petty things...like toys...like pink swan floats. And that's just two of them. I could go on and on."

"Please don't," Annie told her. "How do you know all this stuff?"

"I watch Investigation Discovery."

"Still, it does sound kind of far-fetched," Timmy said. "And Tom was kind of drunk. Though, honestly, he seemed pretty lucid...and emphatic."

"Yeah," Annie said, "And we have no idea what this girl-friend of his is like. She could be a fruitcake."

"Right," Charlotte Claire said, "But Patty Hammond isn't. That's who Tom's girlfriend heard the story from. Amelie, your mom worked with Patty at the hospital. You know her pretty well, right?"

"Well, I used to," she replied. "I haven't talked to her in years."

"Well you're going to talk to her tomorrow. Find out if, in fact, Leanne said those things while she was on pain meds."

"That's a great idea," Annie said. "I'll go with you. Aunt Idelle used to babysit Patty, and Patty used to babysit me. We'll call her and say we're in town and would like to come say hello. We'll bring this rumor up, quote-unquote, coinci-dentally; as if we think the rumor is ridiculous, and gauge her response."

"This is starting to sound a little cloak and dagger," Amelie said doubtfully.

"Maybe," Charlotte Claire said. "But I, for one, would like to hear what she has to say. Y'all call her in the morning and see if she's free for coffee tomorrow afternoon."

"And then what?" Timmy asked. "If you come away from the conversation and think there's some truth to the rumor are you going to the police? Are you going to confront Leanne? I just don't see where you take it from there."

"Frankly, Timmy, I don't know either," Amelie said. "But this is my little sister, my sweet Elizabeth. Losing her was the hardest thing I've ever been through. If her death wasn't an accident I want to know. And if there is some way I can find out, I have to try. Whether or not there's a next step after that, well, I'll figure that out later."

Early the next afternoon Amelie and Annie drove to Patty Hammond's home. It was a modest wood-framed house that sat on the outskirts of Bayou Derkin, on the opposite side of town from the hotel.

"But for the grace of God," Annie said when they pulled up.

"Don't be a snob," Amelie chastised.

"This could have been us."

"It wouldn't be so bad. I bet she's happy. I remember her as being a really nice, good-natured person. She and Mama were really good friends, so I knew her pretty well."

"Everyone in Bayou Derkin knows everyone else in Bayou Derkin pretty well, whether you like it or not. Just another reason that I'm glad I got the hell out of here."

Patty Hammond pushed open the screen door and stepped onto the porch, letting it slam shut behind her. She was wearing a cotton shirt-waist dress and, Annie noticed when she drew closer, make-up. That's for us, Annie thought, I bet she'd normally be in jeans and a t-shirt on a Saturday afternoon. Patty put her hands on her hips and said, "Well, I'll be damned! What a treat! A TV star and the Queen of Sheets! I'll be the envy of the garden club. Come on in girls, come on in. I'm so happy to see y'all." The inside of Patty's house was modest too, but charming and impeccably neat. Patty scurried around busily setting out lemon sponge cake and coffee in the living room. Patty asked Annie the usual barrage of questions about Hollywood, and made a point of telling Amelie that she had splurged on a set of sheets from the Ardoin Home Collection. "Just to think," she was giggling as she joined them in the living room. "Who'd ever guess a Cajun name like Ardoin would become synonymous with fancy sheets!"

The three of them had been talking for several minutes

when Patty put her coffee cup down and leaned forward towards Amelie, a warm smile on her face. "Amelie, you look just like your Mama, as pretty as you can be."

"Thanks, Patty," she said, genuinely touched. "Generally, it's this one who gets the 'pretty' compliments."

"Well, of course she does. Annie, you're a beautiful girl, even as a little girl you were beautiful. I used to love to babysit you. It was like playing with a baby doll. But truly Amelie, the resemblance to Lou is striking. I always thought Lou was pretty, and such a kind, good-natured woman. Everyone at the hospital loved her and loved working with her. It just broke all our hearts when little Elizabeth..." She trailed off and when she leaned down to pick up her coffee cup Amelie and Annie exchanged a conspiratorial glance. "I'm so sorry sweetie. I'm sure that must be hard for you to think about, still."

"Oh, please don't apologize," Amelie said almost too hastily. "I was so young then. I hardly know any of the details of what happened after Elizabeth died. You know, like, if there was a police investigation or any of that. Mama and Daddy were so grief-stricken. They never wanted to talk about it. And they were trying to protect Sara and me from any gossip or rumors that might be going around town. I'd really like to know more."

"Well, there really wasn't much of a police investigation. Everyone at the time just assumed she slipped and hit her head on a rock, and unfortunately, fell into the water face down and drowned. That's what the coroner said, that it was an accidental drowning. They did the autopsy at Bayou Derkin Hospital. I was there when they did it. So was your Mama, she didn't want to leave Elizabeth alone. Your Daddy, well...it was heart breaking."

"No," Amelie said. "He couldn't take it."

Patty fell silent for a few seconds. "He got drunk, very, very drunk. It was the only time I had ever seen Arnie drink, let alone get drunk."

A wave of profound sadness washed over Amelie as she listened to Patty recount the events surrounding Elizabeth's death. But a powerful resolve to find the truth propelled her forward. "Patty, you said that everyone at the time believed Elizabeth fell and hit her head and drowned. When you say, 'at the time'," Amelie said pointedly. "Have there been other theories...or rumors since then?"

Patty set her cup down and looked at Amelie, then Annie, and then back again at Amelie. She let out a breath and paused a few seconds. "Have you heard something?" she asked finally.

Amelie looked at Annie, unsure of what to do. If Patty thought that this was the only reason for their visit, she may be offended and refuse to share what she knew. But before she could formulate a response Annie said, "Yes, Patty. We have heard something, and it involves Leanne Piper."

"Tell me what you've heard," Patty said soberly.

Annie recounted the conversation between Timmy and Tom Burnett in great detail. Amelie jumped in to explain how the pink swan float had gone missing, and that they'd found it in Leanne's closet. Patty listened quietly, then leaned forward in her chair and said, "I never believed Elizabeth's death was an accident. You don't get a wound that extreme from a fall. Remember, I was at the hospital during the autopsy. I saw Elizabeth's body when they brought her in. Elizabeth's wound was blunt force trauma. The coroner had no experience with that kind of autopsy. Hell, I don't even think he was trained as a coroner. He was just a doctor that the parish hired to do autopsies. He had a checkered reputation as a doctor, but I guess the parish thought, hell, at least he can't kill anybody. And I've suspected that Leanne did this, ever since that day in the hospital when she was loopy on the pain meds. The things she said just went through me like a lightning bolt. It all fit. She was a mean child, and terribly, terribly spoiled and selfish in a way most kids aren't. I babysat her a couple of times and I refused to go back. She stuck a fork in the dog. She squeezed her hamster to death. No tears, no remorse. That was the last straw for me."

"She started calling me 'little orphan Annie' after Mama died," Annie said.

"I remember that," Patty said. "I was still babysitting you then. Children can be cruel, but she was crueler than any child I'd ever known."

"Did you suspect her of killing Elizabeth all along?" Amelie asked. "Why didn't you tell anyone?"

"Oh, no, honey, I had no reason to. It never even crossed my mind as a possibility until her rambling in the hospital. And by that time, it had been years and years. But when I heard the things she was saying and remembering what a hateful and selfish child she was, it made sense. Especially because I'd seen Elizabeth's injury and felt strongly that it wasn't caused by a fall. She was a tiny, young girl. She couldn't fall far enough and with enough force to create that kind of injury. No, it was only then that I became suspicious. And if I told that to anybody they would've thought I was crazy. And it was a suspicion I had, but I wasn't convinced until now and the business with this pink swan float. I remember your Mama came back to work telling me how she was worried about you because you kept going back to the river to look for it. She was so worried about you. She was afraid that it was a psychological response, that it was because you couldn't process Elizabeth's death or because you felt guilty because you were with her."

"I did," Amelie said softly. "I still do."

"Oh, no," Patty said. "You can't do that to yourself. You were a child. No, no, please don't do that to yourself. No one else thinks that." The three women fell silent. Then Patty asked, "What are you going to do with this information? I wouldn't confront her. There's no telling what she'd do. And that husband of hers is just as bad, worse. He's not going to let anyone come between him and his meal ticket. He's as hateful as she is. They say Tom Burnett's boy killed himself after he made his boy cut off his friendship with him because Scotty thought he was gay."

"No," Amelie said. "I'm not going to confront her, at least not now. I honestly don't know what I'll do."

"Maybe hire a private investigator," Annie suggested.

"Maybe," Amelie said.

"It's not for me to say," Patty said cautiously. "But honey, I'd leave it alone. If it hadn't been so long ago and if it weren't for the fact that she was just a little girl-which makes this seem so hard to believe-well then, I'd say pursue it. But it's all of those things, and I think you'll put yourself through a whole lot of misery and get nothing for it in the end."

"You're probably right," Amelie agreed.

"You know I've never told another soul about what I believed," Patty said. "I should've known better to say that in the presence of Carla Courville. The town crier, they call her. That girl can't keep her mouth shut. It's probably all over town that *I'm* the one who's been saying it. I guess I'd better watch my back. They'll probably come after me," she said, unable to stifle at laugh at the thought.

"I'm convinced," Timmy said after Amelie and Annie had relayed their conversation with Patty. They were sitting at a table in the hotel bar. Charlotte Claire had insisted the group meet there immediately to hear what Patty had to say.

"I am, too," Charlotte Claire insisted. "That bitch."

"Me too," Annie added. "There are just too many pieces of the puzzle that fit for it not to be true."

"I have to admit that it seems possible," Amelie said warily. "But even if it is true, I don't really see what I could do about it."

"What *we* could do about it," Timmy said.

"What we could do about it," Amelie corrected herself. "But the fact remains, we have nothing in terms of evidence.

It's just a rumor, an unprovable rumor. We'd all look like a bunch of nut-jobs, and we could even be sued for slander."

"Let them sue me," Annie said defiantly. "I could give a shit."

"But there must be something…" Timmy was saying when Charlotte Claire interrupted him.

"Hold up, hold up," she said. "We do have evidence. We have the pink swan float."

"She's right," Annie said.

"But that could be any float," Timmy said. "We couldn't even prove it."

"No, you're wrong, Timmy," Amelie said. "We could prove it was Elizabeth's because of her initials on the bottom."

"They could say that we put those initials there," Annie said. "Then we'd *really* look like a bunch of nutjobs."

"Not true," Charlotte Claire said. "There's a process called ink dating to determine the age of ink and when it was used."

"How on Earth do you know that, Charlotte Claire?" Timmy asked.

"I saw it on Forensic Files," she replied. "You know how I love my crime shows. Anyway, it definitely can be done."

"Well, that's great and all, but there's just one problem," Annie said. "*We* don't have the float, *she does.*"

"God, you are being negative Nancy today," Charlotte Claire said, turning to Annie with a furrowed brow.

"Sorry!" Annie cried.

"So, let's get it," Timmy said.

"How are we supposed to do that?" Charlotte Claire asked.

"Now who's being Negative Nancy?" Annie teased.

"I'm not being negative," Charlotte Claire said impishly. "I'm being inquisitive."

"Yeah, Timmy," Amelie asked. "We can't just waltz up to the door and say, 'hey, you remember that pink swan float you stole that time you committed murder as a child? Well, we'd like it back."

"Really, girls," Timmy said. "Even collectively you have so little imagination. Tonight, we know that Leanne and Scotty will be here at the hotel for the reunion. After they get here I'll go to their house, let myself in and get it."

"But how will you get in?" Amelie asked.

"Simple," he said, pulling his cell phone from his pocket and dialing. "I'll go out there this afternoon. Scotty's having a beer and boudin thing at the river with some of his old cronies, so he won't be home. I'll say that I think my wallet fell out of the tote bag I had my swim suit in. I'll ask Leanne if I can look for it on the patio. If she lets me go out and look for it alone, I'll unlock the patio doors. There are so many of them, surely one has to be unlocked when I get there. I know where the master bedroom is. But Amelie, before tonight, you'll have to tell me in detail which closet it's in. Unlike *you,* I didn't open the closets when I took the tour. One or all of you will have to keep eyes on Scotty and Leanne the entire time I'm gone. If they leave, call me on my cell so I can make sure I'm out of there."

Timmy put a finger up and said into the phone, "Ralph! It's Timothy Tyler. How are you? Good, good! Hey, I hate to be a pain in the neck, but could you arrange for me to use the hotel's house car at 8 o'clock tonight?" He looked at the girls, rolled his eyes and made a yakkity-yak sign with his hand. "You are the best, you really are. And I promise to stop by the concierge desk and autograph your copy of *Summer Swan* this afternoon. No, you are. Thanks again, you're the best. All set," he said to the girls. "We have a plan."

"But why are you using the house car?" Amelie asked. "You already have the rental car."

"Just seems like a good idea to go in a different car, in case someone sees me driving away. People at the reunion and around town have seen me in the rental car. If the house car is seen near their house, it wouldn't be associated with me. They would have to do more investigation than they would do for a minor break-in or a trespasser. An over-abundance of caution, perhaps, but I feel a little safer doing it that way. By the way, I think Ralph has a crush on me."

At 4 o'clock Timmy pulled into the Piper's driveway, walked up to the front door and rang the bell. The cacophonous chimes rang out and within a minute he was ushered into the huge foyer by the maid. He stood looking around for a short time before Leanne greeted him. "Timmy?" she said, a quizzical look on her face. "What a surprise. To what do I owe this honor?"

"I seem to have misplaced my wallet," he said casually. "And I thought I may have dropped it from my bag when I was out by the pool. Do you mind if I go take a look?"

"I don't think it's there," she said. "I had the staff clean up the pool area this morning. I'm sure they'd have given it to me if they'd found it."

"You're probably right," he said. "But do you mind if I take a look, just to make sure?"

"Well yes, of course you're welcome to, but I don't think you'll find it there. Shall I help you look?"

"Oh no," he said, a little too quickly. "I know where I was hanging out, and I don't want to inconvenience you. I'm sure you have things to do."

"Well as a matter of fact, the maid and I were in the middle of putting the serving pieces from the party away. I have to supervise her every move. She never puts anything back where it's supposed to go. You know how it is."

"Do I?" he said. "I'm just the same way; everything in its place."

"Pop into the kitchen and say goodbye before you go."

"Absolutely."

Timmy walked toward the bank of French doors that led to the patio. He couldn't tell if Leanne was still standing behind him or if she'd gone back into the kitchen. He was afraid that if he turned around to check and she saw him that it would look suspicious, so he continued to the pool area. When he reached the row of chaise lounges that faced the house he pretended to look for his wallet. He moved on to the next chaise and again looked toward the house. Through a kitchen window he could see the back of Leanne's head as she faced the huge glass-fronted cabinets that held her serving pieces. She appeared deep into her task, so he walked briskly back to the bank of French doors and slipped inside the foyer, where he could hear Leanne barking out directions from the kitchen. Working from left to right he turned the latch on each of the French doors. He had just one latch to go when he heard Leanne's voice get louder as she drew nearer. His heart pounding, he quickly stepped back onto the veranda, quietly closed the door behind him, and made for the pergola midway between the pool area and the house. Leanne opened the door and called out, "Any luck?"

"Not yet," he called back. "I was all over the place last night. I'm just going to give it a few more minutes."

Timmy thought he would pretend to look for the wallet for a few more minutes when he noticed the French doors to the ground floor guest room where the barbecue guests had left their things. He glanced toward the house and saw that Leanne was back in the kitchen. It was very likely, he thought, that they would check to make sure the French doors from the foyer were locked before they left for the reunion, but there was a good possibility that it would not occur to them to check the guest room. He decided it was his best chance for gaining entry later. He crossed over to the veranda and let himself in as quietly as possible. Leanne was back in kitchen animatedly directing the maid in her task. He walked quietly across the foyer, toward the hallway that ran behind the library. He paused briefly to look at the staircase to the second floor. I could just get the float now, he said to himself, but it was too risky to get caught upstairs. Moving quickly down the hall, he reached the door to the guest room. He turned the door knob slowly, opened the door, stepped in and quietly closed the door behind him. The heavy drapes were closed, and the room was dark. He felt the wall beside the door until he found the light switch and flipped it on. Moving quickly to the patio door, he pulled back the drape and turned the latch until he heard the lock disengage. As he turned to leave, the door opened, and he found Leanne in the doorway, a suspicious look on her face. "What are you doing in here, Timmy?"

"Oh, I hope you don't mind," he sputtered. "I'd left my bag in here during the party last night, and I thought that maybe my wallet had fallen out in here. And guess what?" he said, pulling it from his back pocket. "It did! It must have fallen out of my bag and got kicked under the bed. What a relief!"

"Oh, good," Leanne said, softening her tone. "I'm so glad you found it. The maid only cleans this room on Mondays and Fridays, so you might have been back in New York by the time she found it."

"So true, I'd need to have my passport overnighted from New York or I'd have never made it onto a plane. Well, let me get out of your hair. I'm sure you've got lots to do before the reunion tonight." He followed Leanne back to the front door. "Thanks again, Leanne. I hope it wasn't too much of an inconvenience, my turning up unannounced like this."

"Of course not," she said unconvincingly. "It was just lucky I was home, since you didn't call ahead."

Leanne waited in the front doorway as Timmy made a concerted effort to walk to the car as casually as possible, but inside he felt like sprinting. Just as he put his hand on the door handle Leanne called out, "Timmy!"

"Yes?" he said, turning to look at her.

"It was *Happy Ending*."

"I beg your pardon?"

"Your book that I read, it was *Happy Ending*."

"Oh," he said with a chuckle. "Well, I hope you liked it." He didn't wait for her reply. He was sure she hadn't.

He returned to the hotel and gathered the girls to give them the details of his visit to Leanne's.

"How'd it go?" Charlotte Claire asked excitedly.

"It went," he laughed. "It was touch and go, so I touched and went."

"I'm impressed," Annie said. "You should be a cat burglar."

"No thanks," he said. "I haven't got the nerves for it. The important thing is I believe I'll have a way in tonight. Getting the float and getting out of there shouldn't take long. When I was driving there today I noticed the farm road on the old Duplechine property is pretty grown over with weeds, which means it doesn't get much use. And there are trees on either side of the road. I'll park there and walk across Leanne and Scotty's backyard to get to the house. I should be able to get there unseen. There's not that many houses out there, and none are particularly close. The important thing is we move into phase two of the plan tonight. We all need to be alert and ready."

"Timmy, thank you." Amelie said. "Thanks all of you."

At 6:30 that evening Charlotte Claire stood looking at her reflection in the full-length mirror in her hotel room. She'd dropped five pounds in the weeks leading up to the reunion, and the black Balenciaga dress she'd paid a fortune for hung on her body exactly as it ought to. Thirty-five hundred dollars for a dress, she thought, and no one here will even know what a Balenciaga is. Except for her friends, of course. She ran a hand over her blonde hair, snapped up her clutch and headed down the hall for the meeting.

She was the last to arrive and Timmy was already making cocktails. But the mood in the room was one of apprehension rather than celebration. Charlotte Claire tried to lighten the mood. "You look amazing Annie, who are you wearing?"

"Armani," she said, twirling around. "I love what you're wearing. Is that Balenciaga?"

"Yeah, thanks. And you look very handsome, Timmy," she said accepting her cocktail, "in your Tom Ford."

"Thanks," he replied. "Tom Ford, only and always Tom Ford."

"Listen to the three of you," Amelie said. "It's like an episode of Fashion Police."

"And who are you wearing, Amelie?" Timmy asked with exaggerated interest.

"Nordstrom, darling. You know me, only the best."

"We know, we know," Charlotte Claire said. "You think fashion is frivolous, which makes us shallow and you superior."

"She said it, I didn't," Amelie said.

"Okay, girls," Timmy said. "You're all cocktailed up so let's turn our attention to the plan. As soon as Leanne and Scotty arrive I'm going to make a point of spending a few minutes with them. If I spend a little time with them before I leave my absence is less likely to be noticed. After about ten minutes..."

"I come up and say that Annie is looking for you because she left something in your room," Charlotte Claire interrupted. "And then I stay and talk to them as long as I can."

"I watch this from a distance," Amelie said. "And if it looks like they are breaking away from Charlotte Claire I head them off at the pass. If they break away from me..."

"That's where I come in," Annie said. "If they split up, I stay with Scotty and Amelie stays with Leanne. Charlotte Claire watches from a safe distance in case they decide to leave early, and call you the minute they do. Timmy don't forget to put your cell on vibrate just in case, God forbid, they should somehow get back to the house while you're still in it."

"Don't even think it," Timmy said. "Okay, Amelie, the float is in the middle section of the bank of closets on the left..."

"Right!" she exclaimed.

"Right facing wall," he continued. "It's in a storage

container on the middle shelf of that closet, and it's labeled."

"Right," she said. "This is making me nervous. Are you sure you're up to this? You don't have to do it."

"I'm up to it. Let's go down. It's almost seven. People will be arriving now, plus I need a drink."

By the time they reached the casino ballroom it was nearly filled. A line had already formed at the registration table, where giddy alumni waited for their "Hello I'm..." tags. "This is where I must have gotten it from," Timmy whispered to Amelie. "I'm always ten minutes early for everything. People in Bayou Derkin are never fashionably late."

"I can't believe we have to wear these freaking name tags," Annie complained. "Our class wasn't that big. If we don't recognize one another we could just introduce ourselves."

"It's mostly for the spouses," Charlotte Claire said. "Besides, everybody recognizes you. You're on television once a week. We can't all be famous."

"We can't?" Amelie cried, in mock disappointment. "Well that's not fair!"

"You're famous," Charlotte Claire said. "I'm the only one of us who lives in total obscurity."

"Yes," Timmy said dryly. "The total obscurity of the Houston Chronicle society pages."

Once they were through the registration line and had cocktails, they split up to mingle with their former classmates, each of them keeping one eye on the door in anticipation of Scotty and Leanne's arrival. Just before 8 o'clock Amelie spotted the couple at the registration table. She pulled out her phone and group texted the other three with the single word "here." They responded with a single letter "R" to acknowledge that they'd received the text.

Timmy watched from a distance as they completed the

registration process and moved into the crowd that filled the ballroom. I'll give them five or ten minutes, Timmy thought, it may look suspicious if I approach too soon or seem too eager. He went to the bar where he found Annie, and ordered a diet tonic and lime.

"That's all you're having?" she asked in astonishment.

"Yeah, I decided I need to keep my wits about me," he said. "But I can promise you I'll be having an extra-large triple something when I get back."

"Are you nervous?" she asked.

"A little. Hang here with me for a few minutes. Then I'm going to go talk to them for five or ten minutes. Then I'll head out to their place."

"Did you see Jenny Karan?" Annie asked. "She was looking for you. She wants to pick your brain about *Summer Swan*."

"Oh joy," Timmy said sarcastically. "Is she still a chatter box?"

"Yes, some things never change."

"She's sweet, though. I always liked her. She was so funny in high school."

"Stop checking your watch every 30 seconds. It's making you appear nervous."

"I am nervous. Here," Timmy said, picking up Annie's drink and taking a big swallow, "Let's get this over with. I'm going to talk to them. Wish me luck."

"You can do it," Annie said. "Just ask about their kids and they'll do all the talking."

"Good suggestion, thanks."

Rather than walking directly over to where Scotty and Leanne were standing Timmy zigzagged through the crowd, saying hello and speaking briefly with different people, so that by the time he approached them it would seem coincidental. Leanne was wearing another of her tunics sets with an abundance of gold and diamond jewelry. Scotty looked uncomfortable in a suit that appeared new and that Leanne had probably picked out for him. They were talking to a woman that Timmy didn't recognize. After a couple of minutes, the woman stepped away and, taking a deep breath, he approached Leanne and Scotty.

"Hi guys," he said casually. "Hey, I wanted to thank you for last night. It was so nice of you to host the barbecue. I had a great time. It was great to see everyone and catch up."

"Thank you, Timmy," Leanne cooed. "It was our pleasure. We're so pleased that you came all the way from New York City."

"Yeah," Scotty said. "Must be pretty boring for you coming back to Bayou Derkin after living in New York."

"Not at all," Timmy said. "In fact, it's been pretty interesting to see all the changes since the last time I was here. It's really a different town. There's so much more to do. It looks like the town has really prospered since the casino came in."

"Yeah," Scotty said. "The times they are a 'changing. It used to be all those poor Indians driving drunk down the back roads in their old broken-down heaps, and now all the rich Indians are driving drunk down the back roads in their new luxury cars." Scotty laughed, amused by his own wit.

The three of them fell silent for an awkward few seconds. Scotty was looking around the room for a reason to excuse himself; Leanne's face was frozen in a counterfeit smile. To keep the conversation going, Timmy said, "Hey, Leanne, Scotty was telling me about your boy, Matthew. He said he was playing for LSU and doing really well."

Leanne's expression brightened; Scotty stopped looking around the room and began a long harangue involving positions and plays, scores and scouts, all of which could have been a foreign language to Timmy. Smiling, he listened intently while surreptitiously checking his watch for the time. Ten minutes later Charlotte Claire approached the three of them and cried, "Leanne, look at you! You look wonderful. Doesn't she look wonderful, Timmy? Oh, Timmy, Annie is looking for you. She left something in your suite. I can't remember what. She's by the entrance waiting for you."

"Sure," Timmy said. "Leanne, Scotty, would you excuse me? Duty calls!"

As he walked away he heard Charlotte Claire saying, "Leanne, where do you get these marvelous tunics? They're so chic...and so forgiving!" Timmy chuckled and made his way to find Annie at the ballrooms entrance.

"What's so funny?" she asked when he reached her.

"Oh, just Charlotte Claire being Charlotte Claire," he said. "She just told Leanne that her tunic was 'so marvelous and sooo forgiving."

"I love it."

"Okay, just for authenticity's sake, walk up to my suite, wait a minute and then head back to the ballroom."

"Okay," she said. "Can I have your keycard?"

"What for?"

"I have to go to the bathroom. If I have to go up there for authenticity's sake," she said making air quotes, "I may as well kill two birds with one stone."

"Okay, here," Timmy said, pulling his key from his breast pocket. "I need to make tracks. I want to get this over with as soon as possible."

"Good luck."

Timmy strode through the lobby to the concierge desk. An unfamiliar woman sat behind the desk. "Is Ralph available?" he asked.

"No, Ralph is on break," she told him. "Is there something I can help you with?"

"Yes, I'm Timothy Tyler..."

"Yes," she said beaming. "I'm a big fan. I read *Since You Went Away* three times. I..."

"Oh, thank you," Timmy said anxiously looking at his

watch. "I'm sorry, Ralph was arranging for me to use the house car. I was to pick up the keys here I believe. I'm in a bit of a rush."

"Keys...," she said, moving around papers and envelopes on the desk. "He didn't mention that you were coming by to pick up keys. But let me look around and see if I can find them."

"Thanks." Timmy looked at his watch again. He should be driving out of the parking lot by now. He watched the concierge open drawers and cabinets, pulling envelopes from numerous cubby holes, then finally disappearing into a room behind the concierge desk. When she returned empty handed, Timmy was about to explode.

"I'm so sorry," she said. "I just can't seem to find them."

"Perhaps you could call him?" Timmy asked, trying to conceal his irritation.

"I'll do that right now," she said. She dialed the phone and waited for an answer. She put the phone to her chest and looked dolefully at Timmy. "No answer, I'm afraid."

"This really isn't good," Timmy said testily. "I have some place I really need to be. There must be some way to locate those keys."

"Let me try again," she said apologetically. "Maybe he was speaking with someone. Although it seems like if he was speaking to someone the call would go..."

"Yes," Timmy said emphatically. "Do try again."

She re-entered the number and, head cocked to one side, listened as the phone rang. Finally, she put the phone down again. "I'm so sorry Mr. Tyler, he's just not picking up. I'm not sure..." As she was speaking the phone rang. She snapped up the phone and said, "Concierge desk. Oh Ralph, thank goodness! I've been trying to reach you. Yes, Mr. Timothy Tyler is here to pick up the keys for the house car and I can't seem to find...it's where? Oh, okay, okay. Thanks." She closed her laptop, and on the desk directly behind it was a white envelope with the name Mr. Timothy Tyler written on it. "Oh, my good-ness!" she exclaimed. "I feel like such a fool. It was right here all the time." She handed the envelope to Timmy with a little curtsy. "If it had been a snake it would've bitten me."

Timmy took the envelope and walked briskly toward the exit. "Where's a snake when you need one?" he muttered.

Annie scanned the ballroom in search of Amelie and Charlotte Claire. She spotted Amelie near the bar speaking to Jenny Karan. As Annie moved toward them Charlotte Claire approached her with a look of panic. "Where have you been?" she demanded.

"Pretending to retrieve something from Timmy's room," she said, slightly annoyed by Charlotte Claire's tone.

"Well, we have a problem," she said. "Leanne and Scotty gave me the brush and then went their separate ways. We need to track down Amelie and put her on Leanne's tail. And you need to locate Scotty and detain him as long as possible if it looks like he's making a move to leave."

"Man, you *do* watch a lot of crime shows," Annie said, scan-ning the room for Scotty. "Don't panic, he's right over there at the bar talking to that woman. Who's that? She's pretty."

"I don't know," Charlotte Claire said. "She's probably someone's trophy wife. She looks too young to be from our class."

"Speak for yourself," Annie replied. "Anyway, I'll keep an eye on him here and you go tell Amelie about developments. She's over there about fifteen feet from the bar talking to Jenny."

"Okay," Charlotte Claire said. "I'll check in with you later."

"Wait."

"What?"

"Look-no, don't look. They might catch us staring at them," Annie said. "I'll tell you what's happening. Leanne just went up to Scotty and this woman at the bar. She said something to him, and now he's saying something back to her, and they both look pissed. Now he's saying something to the woman. He's getting up. He's walking away with Leanne and they don't look happy. Now I've lost them in the crowd. You'd better go round up Amelie and I'll try to find them."

"Okay," Charlotte Claire said. "Text me where they are when you find them."

"Will do."

Timmy sped down the highway towards the Piper home worrying that everything that could possibly go wrong had. First the fiasco with the keys, then the overly conscientious parking attendant who felt the need to explain every one of the car's features, yet had failed to fill up the tank. So he'd had to stop for gas and now he'd fallen behind. Timmy glanced down at the speedometer. He was 15 miles above the speed limit, and his classmates had warned him about speed traps. He slowed the car to five miles above the speed limit. All I need now is to get a ticket, he thought, I'd have to give up, and then how would we ever get the damn float? He glanced down at his watch. Twenty minutes had passed since he left the ballroom and he still had to get to the other side of Bayou Derkin.

As he rounded the last curve before entering the town center he heard a deafening horn. He saw a freight train heading for the tracks a quarter mile ahead. Shit, I have to make it, he thought. He accelerated dramatically but the engine seemed only to rev louder, the acceleration sluggish. Now he wished he'd used the rented Mercedes which was much more responsive. Whether it actually did, or Timmy perceived it that way, the train seemed to be moving faster as it approached the highway crossing. Then the train crossing signal started dinging and the crossing gate slowly began to descend. Timmy slammed the brake pedal and, tires screeching wildly against the asphalt, the car careened violently, coming to a lurching stop less than six feet from the crossing gate and parallel with the tracks. He sat for a dazed moment, his heart racing, the smell of burned rubber in the air. After he'd collected himself, he put the car in gear and moved it to the proper position in the traffic lane. He sat, hands clenching the steering wheel, staring straight ahead as train car after seemingly endless train car moved past. I'm not sure this is meant to be, he thought. Maybe I should just turn around and go back. But then he thought of Amelie, and he knew that this would be his only chance to retrieve Elizabeth's float. So, he sat and watched the train cars roll by, hoping Leanne and Scotty were up for a long night.

Annie circled the ballroom three times and didn't see Leanne or Scotty anywhere. She'd just decided to call Timmy and tell him to get out of the house when she spotted Scotty talking to Andy Stoner. She positioned herself so that she could keep an eye on him without being seen. She'd been watching for several minutes when Andy, who was swaying from side to side and appeared very drunk, shook Scotty's hand, clapped him on the shoulder and staggered away. Scotty stood there briefly, shaking his head, before turning and walking towards the bar. Annie moved parallel to him in the same direction, making sure he didn't see her. He sat down at the bar and ordered a drink as Annie slipped her cell from her clutch and texted Charlotte Claire and Amelie. 'Eyes on Scotty, status on Leanne?' A few seconds later her cell phone pulsed. It was Amelie, 'Still looking.'

Timmy could hear the weeds crunching beneath the tires of the house car as he turned the lights off and backed slowly into the narrow farm road. After he'd determined that he was out of sight of the main road, he got out of the car and quietly shut the door. He pushed through the weeds, then through the trees, towards the Piper property. When he reached the property line he discovered an eight-foot-high chain link fence that had been obscured by the Cypress trees on the grounds of the Pipers' home. Shit, shit, shit, he thought, there is no way I'm going to be able to climb over this. He turned and pushed his way back through the trees and ran down the farm road toward the main road. He checked to see if a car was coming or if there was anyone around. Seeing nothing, he crossed to the other side of the road and walked briskly across the front of the property-but found there was no access due to the brick and wrought iron fence and the electronic entry gate. When he reached the opposite side of the property, he ran the length of it, looking for any means of gaining access. Beads of sweat covered his forehead, and his shirt was soaked underneath his jacket. He was losing hope with each step as he raced toward the rear corner of the property. Then he spotted a small opening between two metal poles that held up the chain link, no more than 12 inches wide, where the perpendicular property lines met. He considered the opening for a moment. Hell, he thought, I've come too far not to give it a try. He pushed himself sideways into the opening, but his chest was too thick to go through. He pulled himself out, took off his jacket, and tried again. He pushed fiercely, again and again, the rough iron poles pulling the buttons off his shirt and scratching his back and chest. With his arm he gave one hard shove to the pole and cleared the opening, almost falling to the ground. He ran along the periphery of the yard, past the pool area, until he reached the back of the house. The house was dark, except for the outdoor lighting and a dim light in the kitchen, which looked empty from where he stood. He crossed the yard to the veranda and the first set of French doors and slowly turned the knob. It was locked. He tried the second one, the third one, the fourth one, all locked. He ran to the end of the veranda where the French doors to the first-floor guest room were, and slowly turned the door knob. To his relief, the door opened. He let himself inside, pushed past the heavy drapes, and crossed noiselessly across the room. He opened the door and peered into the hall, checking both directions before walking carefully down the hall until he reached the foyer. Again, he checked in all directions before briskly walking towards the staircase. His shoes were making a clicking noise on the marble floor and he wished he had left them with his jacket on the other side of the chain link fence. He moved quickly up the stairs and down the second-floor hall to the master bedroom. He stopped outside the door, took a deep breath, and turned the doorknob. He opened the door just enough to see that the room was dark, and slowly entered. He opened the closet door and was startled when it was suddenly ablaze with light. They might have warned me about that, he thought. He quickly stepped inside the closet and closed the door behind him. He took a moment to recover, then went to the center cabinet, opened the door, and scanned the container labels until he found PINK SWAN FLOAT. With his cell phone he took a picture of the container, hurriedly pulled the lid off and took a picture of the deflated float in the container. Then he removed the float, reattached the lid and replaced it on the shelf. Just as he turned to leave, his cell phone pulsed.

After separately circling the ballroom for 20 minutes, Amelie texted Charlotte Claire and asked to meet her at the bar. Charlotte Claire could see immediately that Amelie was in a state of anxiety. "I think we need to text Timmy and tell him to get out of there," Amelie said.

"I don't think it's come to that yet," Charlotte Claire said. "Besides, Scotty's still here. Leanne may be in the casino hall. I know a group was going in to gamble."

"Then we need to check...now!"

"Let me call Annie," Charlotte Claire said, pulling her cell from her clutch. "Just to let her know where we are and to make sure she still has eyes on Scotty." She went silent, waiting for Annie to pick up. "Hey, it's me. Do you still have eyes on Scotty? Good. Amelie and I are going to the gambling hall to look for Leanne. Some of the guys were talking about doing that, so maybe that's where she is. If not, I think we need to text Timmy. Yeah, okay. Hey, and if Scotty starts to leave and you can't distract him, text Timmy. Yes, yes, I know. You can distract anything with a penis. Bye. Let's go," she said to Amelie. "We've got to nail down this bitch, now."

Annie was speaking to an old friend who'd been on the majorette squad with her when she saw Scotty getting up from the bar. She quickly excused herself and moved through the crowd, reaching the bar just as Scotty was putting his credit card back in his wallet. She stepped beside him and said, "I think someone owes me an apology." She could see that he was buzzed.

"Awe, man, I'm sorry," he said. "I was out of line. It's just that I always thought you were so sexy. Did you know I always thought that? Girl, I had a crush on you back in the day. Hell, I still think you're sexy. But you're right. I owe you an apology and I apologize. Here, let me make it up to you, let me buy you a drink."

Good God, Annie thought, he acts like an asshole and then spins on a dime and puts the moves on me. "That would be lovely. I'll have a vodka and cranberry with lime."

"The lady will have a vodka and cranberry with lime," he told the bartender, before turning back to Annie and saying, "So, did you ever have a crush on me?"

"Not even for a minute," Annie said, smiling flirtatiously.

"Awe, man, you're breaking my heart."

"Not that I didn't think you were good looking, Scotty, but you were too much of a player."

"Well, yeah, I guess I had my fair share," he said. "But you were the one I wanted to play with the most. See, if you'd given me half a chance I might even have toed the straight and narrow."

"Oh, right," Annie said laughing. "That was going to

happen."

"Awe, you got me," he moaned, clutching his heart with both hands and smiling broadly. "Shot down at point blank range."

When the bartender returned with Annie's drink, Scotty said, "Barkeep, bring me another one." He turned to Annie, and after a pause, said, "So Annie Squibb, oh sorry-I mean Anne Renee'-what's it like to be a big movie star?"

"Believe it or not, it's a lot of hard work and long hours."

"Come on," he said dubiously.

"No, really, I'm up at 5 a.m. and work some days goes to midnight. I have to be very disciplined when I'm working, maybe a glass of wine with dinner but that's about it. I'm in bed by 9 o'clock every night that I'm working."

"You're in bed by 9 o'clock," Scotty said. "But are you sleeping?"

"You have a one-track mind Scotty, a dirty one-track mind."

"You seeing anyone? You got a boyfriend?"

"I do."

"Who is he, some movie star or some big shot director?"

"Good guess, he's a big shot director. He's the director of *Philadelphia Law*. His name is Calder West."

"Oh, I see," Scotty said. "You must have given a very good, uh, audition." He grinned suggestively, and took a sip of his cocktail.

"No, you don't see, Scotty. The show was written for me. I chose *him* to direct, he didn't cast *me*."

"My apologies."

Annie checked her phone for a text from Amelie or Charlotte Claire but there were none. She hated talking to Scotty and she had to pee, but her first priority was to keep him at the reunion until she got word that Timmy was out. "Scotty, I'm going to run to the ladies' room. Would you order another drink for me?"

"Can't think of anything that would give me more pleasure," he said, smiling lasciviously.

Once the bartender had delivered the drinks Scotty reached into his pocket and pulled out a little blue and white capsule, surreptitiously emptied its contents into Annie's glass, and stirred the drink with a cocktail straw. "Come on, little Rufus," he said quietly to himself. "Do your stuff." Oh man, he thought to himself, I'm finally gonna get a piece of that.

Charlotte Claire and Amelie moved through rows of slot machines and around game tables. They asked every classmate they saw if they'd seen Leanne, but no one had seen her in the smoke-filled casino hall.

"I'm getting worried," Charlotte Claire said. "It's been a long time since either of us has seen her. She could be on her way home."

"Do you think she'd go home without Scotty?" Amelie asked.

"Who knows? I suspect they do a lot of things separately. They don't seem like the happiest couple. I mean, Scotty's a dick and Leanne is a total buzzkill. She might have wanted to go home, and Scotty might have told her to go."

"Maybe we should try the ladies' room? She might be in there."

"That's a good idea. It's off the hotel lobby," Charlotte Claire said. "Let's hurry."

"What if she's in a stall?"

"Just lean over and look for those black slacks she wears under her insipid tunics."

Amelie and Charlotte Claire raced across the hotel lobby. Just as they reached the ladies' room, Annie stepped through the doorway.

"What are you doing here?" Amelie cried. "You're supposed to be keeping an eye on Scotty!"

"That doesn't mean I'm suddenly blessed with the ability

to not pee, Amelie!" Annie protested. "Anyway, its fine, he's waiting at the bar, ordering me a drink. I think the dumb fuck thinks he's going to get lucky tonight."

"Well, you'd better get back there," Charlotte Claire said. "We still haven't found Leanne. This is making me nervous. Did you see her in the bathroom?"

"No, but I think there are a couple of women in the stalls."

"We need to check," Charlotte Claire said.

"How are you going to do that?" Annie asked.

"That's what I said," Amelie told her.

"Never mind how we're going to do it. Just get back to the bar. Now!"

Amelie and Charlotte Claire entered the bathroom and started checking beneath the stall doors. When they reached the third stall, the door opened, and Jenny Karan stepped out. "What on earth are y'all doing?" she cackled. "Looking for lost change? Y'all are crazy, crazy. Oh lord, how I have missed y'all. Remember how much fun we had in band, especially the out-of-town games? You wouldn't believe the Bayou Derkin band now! There's a hundred kids in the band, and the uniforms are so beautiful and new. Ever since the casino came in, the whole town is new and improved. Well, I guess there is a downside. Did you hear about old Miss Willa Picou? She gambled away all her money, poor thing, not a dime left. They say she's addicted to it, like an alcoholic. I guess that makes her a gamble-aholic!" Jenny erupted into peals of laughter.

"Actually, Jenny," Amelie said. "We were looking for Leanne. Have you seen her?"

"Oh, my God!" Jenny cried. "You haven't heard? I thought it'd gotten around the whole reunion by now. She and Scotty had a knock-down, drag-out fight in the parking lot. Ladonna Frey was there and saw the whole thing. Scotty was coming on to some woman at the bar and Leanne saw it. She was fit to be tied. She went and got him from the bar and said they were going home and Scotty said hell no he wasn't going home, and she slapped him, slapped him mind you, right across the face and then he called her the C word, I hate it when men use the C word, or women for that matter, but no woman I know uses it."

"But Leanne!" Charlotte Claire cried. "Where is Leanne?"

"Oh, she left," Jenny said. "She left about 20 minutes ago. I'd love to stay and chat girls, but I'd better get back to Leo. He hates these things. He only came on the condition that I didn't abandon him and here I am. I'll see y'all out there."

As soon as Jenny left the bathroom Charlotte Claire sent Timmy a two-word text. 'GET OUT!'

Timmy pulled his cell from his back pocket and read the text. Shit, shit, he thought, I need to get out. His body tensed, and his heart was pounding in his ears. Overcoming every impulse to panic, he slowly opened the closet doors and walked carefully across the master bedroom to the hallway door and opened it a crack. When he heard nothing, he stepped into the hallway and walked toward the gallery. Just as he reached the gallery he heard a key in the lock, a door slam, and Leanne's voice, teeming with rage. "You son of a bitch, you mother fucking piece of trash! I am used to your whoring around, but, at the reunion, really? You, at the very least, could have kept yourself under control during our reunion. Don't you realize that everyone at the reunion knows what you're up to? Do you realize how this makes me look? Jesus, you're pathetic, you miserable piece of trash. I should know better by now. That's all you've ever been and all you'll ever be, trash! Poor, white trash. If you make a fool of me, I swear, I'll send you packing, back to the poor white trash you came from!"

Timmy's heart was pounding as he turned back and inched his way down the hall. He wondered why Scotty wasn't arguing back. He stood still with his back to the wall and tried to figure out what to do. Then he realized he'd only heard one set of footsteps, so Leanne must be on her cell. When Leanne's voice trailed off he stepped out onto the second-floor gallery. But as he approached the top of the stairs he heard her voice grow louder again. When he heard the click-clack of her heels on the foyer's marble floor he retreated to the hallway. She was walking up the stairs now, moving quickly in her rage. He walked briskly down the hall and opened the first door he came to and ducked into a bedroom, carefully closing the door behind him. Standing perfectly still in the darkened room, he could hear Leanne's footsteps growing louder. Clutching the pink float to his chest, he held his breath until the sound of her footsteps grew fainter and the master bedroom door slammed loudly. Timmy exhaled and tried to calm himself. He folded the pink swan float in half and stuffed it into the back of his pants. He took his shoes off, slowly opened the bedroom door and peeked into the hall. Seeing the hallway empty, he walked slowly down the hall, down the stairs and across the foyer to the first-floor hall. When he reached the guest room he carefully opened the door, passed through it, then closed it behind him. He put on his shoes, crossed to the French doors and let himself out of the house. He moved slowly across the veranda until he reached the soft grass of the lawn, then broke into a full run until he reached the chain link fence. After he'd forced himself back through the small opening, he grabbed his jacket and ran the length of the property to the road. Breathing heavily and still shaken, he crossed the road and ran towards the narrow farm road where he'd parked, when he saw headlights in the distance. He immediately lay flat in the tall grass and waited for the car to pass before he stood and continued running until he reached the car. He pulled the pink float from the back of his pants and got into the driver's seat. Both hands gripping the steering wheel, he leaned his head against it and tried to calm himself. His hands were trembling, and he was drenched with sweat. He started the engine and, with the car lights off, drove slowly to main road. Once he was out of eyeshot of the house, he turned on the car lights and sped to the casino.

When Annie returned to the bar Scotty was facing her, watching her as she approached, with that same lascivious grin on his face. "I thought you might not come back," he said when she'd reached the bar.

"You can't get rid of me that easily."

"And I wouldn't want to," he said, handing her the drink. "You always drink vodka and cranberry?"

"No, I mostly drink them when I'm with Timmy," she said before taking a swallow. "He likes them."

"That figures."

"What figures?"

"Timmy would like a fruity drink," he said, snorting in disapproval.

"Watch it," she said flatly. "You're talking about one of my best friends. I expect people to treat my friends with respect or else I don't associate with those people."

"Okay," he said putting his hands in the air as if in surrender. "I hear you. I just don't understand those people. I may be just a humble country guy, but I don't understand how two men can be together that way. Now two women, put me in the room with them and I'm all over that."

"Well here's the good news, Scotty," Annie said casually. "You don't need to understand it. You just need to be respectful and, by the way, there's nothing humble about you."

Annie took another swallow of her drink and glanced at her cell; still nothing from Timmy or the girls. She was becoming increasingly anxious and wished she could leave, but knew that she was there for the duration. She was bored with Scotty, who kept rambling on and on about money, and his boat, and all the women who were after him. It was all making her feel very tired.

"Listen to me," he said, "I've been doing all the talking and you've been sitting there quiet as a lamb, just letting me yammer on."

"Oh no, it's interesting, really" she said without the slightest idea of what he'd been talking about. "I guess I'm just tired. What time is it?"

"Almost ten," he said.

"Oh," she said rubbing her forehead, "It's not even that late. I don't understand why I feel so tired all of the sudden. I'd better stop drinking for a while. Excuse me," she said to the bartender. "Could I get a glass of ice water, please?"

"You only have a sip or two left of your drink," Scotty said, handing her the cocktail. "You may as well polish it off."

Annie took another sip of the drink and wrinkled her nose. She tried to put the glass down, but the bar seemed to be moving. She focused on it as hard as she could, but when she tried to set the glass down, she knocked it over and stumbled forward. Scotty leapt to his feet and steadied her. "Oh, my goodness," she said, wiping her face with the back of her hand. "I don't know what's gotten into me. I don't think I feel well." Scotty handed her the ice-water the bartender had set down for her.

"Have some of this," he said.

"Is she okay?" the bartender asked.

"Oh, she's fine," Scotty said. "Just a little too much..." Scotty made a drinking motion with his hand.

"I need, I need..." Annie slurred.

"I know what you need," Scotty said. "You need to lay down a minute or two."

"No," she said wearily. "I need my clutch, I need my phone." Annie reached for her clutch on the bar. It seemed to take a herculean effort. What's wrong with me, she thought, am I having a stroke? She managed to reach her clutch, but when she tried to open it, it slipped from her hands and fell to the floor. She felt as if she may fall, but managed to get herself onto a barstool while Scotty collected her clutch and its spilled contents.

"My cell," she said. "Hand me my cell." She took the cell phone but couldn't focus well enough to see if there were any texts from Timmy or the girls. And now she felt as if she might pass out.

"I think we need to get you to your room," Scotty said.

"I can't," she said. But Scotty ignored her and helped her from the barstool onto her feet. Her knees buckled slightly but she stayed upright, one arm over Scotty's shoulders and his arm around her waist. "Can't..." she said weakly, but as Scotty propelled her through the ballroom she knew she had no power to stop him, and she couldn't remember why she was supposed to stay at the bar anyway.

When they reached the elevator bank Scotty opened Annie's clutch, removed the keycard envelope and checked the room number: 1015. He realized he'd need to get to the room quickly; she was having a harder and harder time staying on her feet, and he didn't want her entirely passed out when he fucked her. When he reached the room, he placed the key card over the sensor until he heard the mechanism turn and he opened the door. "A suite!" he said, helping Annie through the living room and into the bedroom. "You TV stars really know how to live." He put Annie on the bed, then went to the mini bar and took three small bottles of Jack Daniels. He opened one bottle and drank it down in one swallow before returning to the bedroom. In the bedroom he rolled Annie over and unzipped her dress, pulled it upward by the hem and slipped it over her head. Then he unhooked her bra, rolled her on her back and removed it. "Hot damn," he said, taking in Annie's nearly naked body. Annie watched helplessly as he picked up another Jack Daniels and drank it down, but she couldn't form any words. Why was he undressing her, she wondered, am I dreaming? Scotty pulled off his jacket, removed his tie and placed them neatly on a chair. He walked over to the side of the bed and stood in Annie's line of sight while he kicked off his shoes, pulled off his pants and boxers, and began to stroke himself until his penis was fully erect. After he opened the last bottle of Jack Daniel's and threw it back, he climbed onto the bed and violently ripped Annie's panties off. Just as she was losing consciousness, he climbed on top of her and forced himself inside of her.

When Timmy reached the casino parking lot, he pulled out his cell and texted the girls. I'M BACK. ALL IS WELL. MEET ME BY THE ELEVATORS. He checked himself in the rearview mirror. He looked like he'd been in a fight. He ran his hands through his hair and mopped his face with his handkerchief. His chest was scratched and bleeding and his shirt was ripped. He got out of the car and stuffed the folded pink swan float into the back of his pants. Then he put on his jacket and buttoned it all the way up. Blood was still visible on his shirt, so he walked around the back of the hotel to enter from the pool area, so he could access the elevator bank without having to pass the lobby or ballroom. When he reached the elevator bank Charlotte Claire and Amelie were already waiting.

"Where's Annie?" he asked.

"I don't know," Amelie told him. "We texted her, but she didn't text back. We left her at the bar with Scotty, but they were both gone when we circled back."

"Timmy, there's blood on your shirt," Charlotte Claire said. "Are you okay?"

"Yeah, I'm fine," he said pressing the elevator button. "That's why I wanted to meet you here, so no one would see me. I got scratched going through a fence. I didn't realize there are chain link fences around the whole property. They're covered up by those Cypress trees. Anyway, I'll give you the details when we get upstairs. Man, I need a drink." The elevator doors opened and the three stepped inside.

"Well, how'd it go?" Charlotte Claire asked anxiously. "Did you get it?"

Timmy unbuttoned his jacket and pulled the pink swan float from the back of his pants. "Got it," he said. "And a picture of it in the container in her closet, just in case she tries to deny it."

"I can't believe it," Amelie said, fighting back tears. "I can't believe it."

"And your text came just in the nick of time," he continued. "I was in the walk-in closet just about to leave. Leanne got back before I had time to get downstairs. I could hear her screaming at Scotty on her cell. I had to hide in one of the guest rooms until she went into the master bedroom. I almost shit my pants. They must have had a fight at the reunion."

"They did," Charlotte Claire said. "Motor mouth Jenny Karan filled us in on the details. I'll tell you later."

They exited the elevator and walked to Timmy's suite. Once they were inside Timmy immediately noticed the small, empty bottle of Jack Daniel's on the coffee table.

"Annie must have made herself a drink when she was up here before," he said. "I'm going to take a quick shower and change, if you guys don't mind. I won't be more than 15 minutes. Make yourselves a drink...and make me one too."

"You've earned it," Amelie said. "The pleasure is all mine."

Timmy opened the double doors to the bedroom, flipped on the lights and stopped in stunned silence. Annie lay naked on the bed, face up with her legs spread apart. Her ripped panties lay on the bed beside her and two empty Jack Daniels bottles sat on the bedside table. At first Timmy couldn't process what he was seeing, then he let out a gasp. "Charlotte Claire, Amelie!" he cried.

"Oh, my God!" Charlotte Claire shrieked. "Cover her!" Timmy grabbed a cashmere throw from the chair by the window and covered Annie with it. Amelie raced to the bed and felt for a pulse.

"Annie," she said, feeling underneath her chin for fever. "Annie!" she said again more loudly. She pulled back her eyelids and slapped her lightly on the face several times. "Her pulse is strong, and it doesn't feel like she has a fever, but she's out cold."

"I don't understand," Charlotte Claire said. "What's she doing in your room naked and passed out?"

"I don't know," Timmy said. "But I think we need to call the hotel doctor and have her checked out."

"Maybe we should bring her to the emergency room," Charlotte Claire said.

"She'll kill us if we bring her there unnecessarily," Timmy said. "It'll get around town and eventually to the press. And we can get a doctor here quicker. If he thinks we need to call an ambulance, we will."

The doctor arrived within five minutes and checked Annie's vital signs. Timmy explained how they'd returned from the reunion and found her on the bed, unconscious. "Her vital signs are all strong and her breathing is normal. I could admit her to the hospital for observation as a precaution if you want, but I think she just needs to sleep it off. Is she an alcoholic... or does she use drugs?" he asked, spying the empty whiskey bottles.

"No," Charlotte Claire said. "She drinks and gets buzzed every now and then...when she's with us. But normally when she's working she hardly drinks at all."

"And she hates whiskey," Amelie said. "I can't explain those empty whiskey bottles."

"It is curious," the doctor said. "She doesn't smell of alcohol at all, nothing on her breath. My guess is she over-imbibed, or else someone slipped her something. If she's not an excessive drinker, as you say, then she should be able to remember how she got here. But if she has no memory of how she got here, dollars to doughnuts someone at the reunion or at the bar slipped something into her drink. It happens more often than you might think. I've treated several women for it right here at the hotel. A casino is the kind of setting that lends itself to that sort of behavior...or crime, I should say." Before he left he turned to them and said gravely, "One more thing. There was what appeared to be semen on her stomach. Now, she may have had consensual sex with someone before she passed out; that's always a possibility. But if someone drugged Ms. Renee and brought her up here and took advantage of the state she was in, well now, that's sexual assault. I should report this as suspicious, but I understand your concerns, her being a public figure and all. And if, as you say, she would not want media attention, I wouldn't want to put her through that. With that in mind, when she wakes up tomorrow, you need to have a frank conversation with her. If she feels she's been violated and wants to pursue it through law enforcement, you need to warn her not to bathe and not to touch that room or the things in it, understand?

"Yes doctor," Timmy said grimly. "We understand...and thank you."

After the doctor left Charlotte Claire dressed Annie in a pair of Timmy's boxer briefs and a fresh T-shirt and got her under the bedcovers. Then the three of them sat in the living room trying, to figure out what could have possibly happened.

"Maybe she was drinking more that we realized," Amelie said. "But the last time we saw her was at the ladies' room and she seemed fine. I know she'd had a couple of vodkas but..."

"I think she was drugged and sexually assaulted," Charlotte Claire said with certainty. "There's no one here that Annie would sleep with, no one! She's in love with Calder and they're exclusive. I don't think that there's anyone in the world she'd sleep with but Calder at this point in time."

"I agree," Timmy said. "But who? It could be anybody at the reunion...or the whole hotel for that matter."

"Yeah," Amelie interjected. "And if she was drugged and can't remember, how on earth would she ever be able to find out?"

"That's easy," Charlotte Claire said. "Haven't you noticed that this hotel is crawling with CCTV? I'm sure there's one in the hall." She walked into the hallway and then back into the suite. "I found one already. Plus, I know the elevators and the elevator banks have them. All we need to do is get those DVDs from tonight and see if she got up here by herself or if someone helped her."

"But how are we going to get the DVDs?" Timmy asked.

"You're going to work your magic," she told him. "You said you think Ralph has a crush on you. You're going to charm the DVDs off him."

"I'll give it a try," he said skeptically. "But no promises."

"You underestimate your charms, Timmy," Amelie said.

"Just tell him you're researching CCTV for a new book," Charlotte Claire said. "He'll feel like he's part of the process. He'll be flattered. Ask him for the DVDs from tonight for the camera's located in the elevator, the elevator bank, and our hallway. It won't take us long to go through them, the window of time is pretty small. We saw her last around 9 o'clock and we got back here around 11 o'clock. Speaking of which, I'm exhausted. I've got to go to bed. What a night!"

"Okay, I'll go see Ralph first thing in the morning," Timmy said. "Someone should be here while I'm out, in case Annie wakes up while I'm gone."

"If you don't mind, Timmy," Amelie said. "I'd like to stay here tonight. I'll sleep in the bedroom with Annie. She's going to be freaked out when she wakes up and doesn't know how she got here."

"That's a good idea," Timmy said. "Charlotte Claire, come back tomorrow around 8 o'clock. I think we should all be here when she wakes up. This is going to be hard for her to hear. She's going to need as much moral support as we can give."

"Will do," Charlotte Claire said. "Poor Annie, I can't imagine what it would feel like to wake up one morning and have someone tell you what we're going to have to tell her."

Timmy woke up just before 6 o'clock the next morning. He lay on the sofa trying to go back to sleep but after half an hour he gave up. He'd hardly slept the night before, his mind racing with the possibilities of what had happened to Annie and how they were going to explain it to her. He ordered a pot of coffee from room service, took a quick shower, and dressed for his mission to charm Ralph. He put on jeans, sandals and his black Prada polo shirt, because it was clingy and form fitting. If I'm going to get this done, he thought, I'd better pull out all the stops. He combed his hair and dabbed some cologne on the back of his neck. Timmy checked himself out in the full-length mirror. "Not bad, not bad," he said aloud. He poured himself a cup of coffee, but thought better of it and poured it back into the pot. "Coffee breath," he said to himself, "is not sexy."

At 7:15 Timmy crossed the lobby to the concierge desk, where he found Ralph on the phone. He flashed a broad smile and gestured for him to take his time. When Ralph hung up the phone he said, "So sorry, Mr. Tyler, what can I do for you?"

"Oh, no worries, Ralph. I actually have a rather unusual favor to ask."

"Anything I can do, Mr. Tyler, I will be happy to help."

"Please Ralph, call me Timothy."

"Oh, okay...Timothy," Ralph said, laughing nervously.

"You see, I'm working on a new book..."

"How exciting!"

"And the main character is a detective. In the scene I'm working on right now..."

"You're working on a book while you're here in the hotel. Oh, that really is exciting."

"Yes, and in the scene, I'm working on presently, he's examining CCTV evidence from a DVD. I really need to describe how that looks as accurately as possible...for authenticity's sake...so I'd like to look at an actual CCTV DVD to make sure I get it right. So, I noticed the hotel has lots of CCTV cameras, and I was wondering if I could borrow a DVD from security. See, I told you it was an unusual favor."

"Sure, I'll just get a couple of old ones from security for you, wait..."

"Well, there's just one thing," Timmy continued. "This scene takes place at night when there's no ambient lighting, so I was wondering if I could get the DVD from last night. You see, the crime in the story takes place in a hotel, and the DVD that the character is viewing is from the elevator, the elevator bank and hotel corridor. So, I was wondering if I could get the DVDs from last night in my corridor and the elevator and elevator bank in the lobby."

Ralph looked at Timmy for several seconds, his brow furrowed, and lips pursed. "I'm not sure I understand..."

"As I said," Timmy said, leaning forward and resting his elbows on the concierge desk so that his biceps flexed. He saw Ralph swallow. "Authenticity is everything."

"I'm not sure security would let me remove those DVDs if they're still recording on them," Ralph said.

"But it would be so helpful for the book, Ralph," Timmy said plaintively. "And it would mean so much to me, personally."

"Well, I'll see what I can do, Mr. Tyler..."

"Timothy."

"Mr. uh, I mean Timothy. I'll do the best I can."

"Thank you, Ralph. I know you will."

When Timmy returned to his suite Charlotte Claire was already there, sipping a cup of coffee and reading the *Houston Chronicle*. "The gift shop didn't have the *New York Times* so I got you the *USA Today*, sorry," she said. "Well, how'd it go with little Ralphie?"

"Who knows?" he said dejectedly. "I'm not even sure it's

within his power to do it. He said he'd try. Maybe I haven't got it anymore."

"You got it," Charlotte Claire said. "Especially in that shirt."

Amelie stepped out of the bedroom and gently closed the door behind her. "Any more of that?" she asked gesturing toward the coffee.

"Yeah," Charlotte Claire said. "Help yourself. Is Annie still sleeping?"

"Yeah," she replied. "She's out like a light. I think she's still in the same position she was in when I went to bed. I even checked her pulse a couple of times to make sure she was alive. She'll probably sleep most of the morning. Timmy, how'd it go with the concierge?"

"Jury's still out," he said. "How'd you sleep?"

"Not so well," Amelie said. "I just couldn't stop thinking about this. It's so creepy. It's scary to think some stranger can get that kind of control over you and you are totally powerless to stop it. And I'm convinced Annie didn't have consensual sex, which leaves only one other option...and that is terrifying."

"I know," Charlotte Claire said fervently. "I agree."

"Have you thought about what we're going to say to her?" Timmy asked.

"Yes," Charlotte Claire said. "We're going to tell her, as plainly and simply and un-dramatically as possible, what the doctor said. Once that sinks in, we can tell her how we found her. I think that's going to be hard for Annie to hear."

"What's going to be hard for me to hear?" Annie said, standing in the bedroom doorway.

"Oh, you're up!" Amelie said in surprise.

"Y'all, what's going on?" Annie asked gravely. "How'd I end up here? I don't remember being in this suite...since...I was up here pretending to be retrieving something with you, Timmy. And how'd I get in this underwear? Are these yours, Timmy?"

"Yes," Timmy said. "That's my underwear and T-shirt, Amelie, and Charlotte Claire got you into them. Annie, what's the last thing you remember from last night?"

"I was having a drink with Scotty at the bar. That was right after I saw Charlotte Claire and Amelie outside the ladies' room. I went back out to the bar and had another drink. I remember starting to feel really tired, and I got a little dizzy. That's it, that's the last thing I remember."

Timmy and Charlotte Claire exchanged glances. Annie looked at the three of them and said, "What's going on? What do y'all know? Y'all are starting to scare me...somebody say something!"

"When we found you here you were unconscious," Charlotte Claire began gently. "We called in the hotel doctor to find out if we needed to call an ambulance or not. The doctor examined you and said you weren't in a serious medical emergency, only that you were either very, very drunk...or that you had possibly been drugged." Charlotte Claire paused to give Annie a moment to process what she was saying.

"I didn't have that much to drink," Annie said. "Maybe three cocktails over the course of four hours...and they were weak, at that. If someone drugged me, how'd I end up in Timmy's suite?"

"We don't know," Amelie said.

"No, I know," Timmy told them. "Remember I gave you my keycard just before I left for Leanne and Scotty's, and you put it in your purse. They must have gone through your purse and pulled out my keycard instead of yours. I stupidly left it in the keycard envelope, so it had my suite number on it."

"There's more," Charlotte Claire said. "Annie, he said there was evidence that you had been sexually assaulted."

Annie walked to a chair, sat and stared out the window. Timmy, Charlotte Claire and Amelie looked at one another, unsure of what to say. "What else?" she asked after a while.

"The doctor said," Timmy began. "That if you wanted to report this to the police..."

"No!" Annie said sharply before Timmy could finish. "No

police."

"That's what we thought you'd say," Charlotte Claire said. "Are you sure?"

"I'm sure," she said, as she continued staring out the window.

"Annie, do you want to have your urine tested?" Charlotte Claire asked.

"Why?" Amelie asked. "If she's not going to report it and do a rape kit, what is the point of a urine test?"

"So, she'll know what was in her system," Charlotte Claire said. "And to check for STDs."

"That's a good idea, Annie," Timmy told her.

"We could go see Patty Hammond," Amelie suggested. "Maybe she could get the testing done without using your name."

"No," Annie said flatly. "I'll go to my own doctor to test for STDs when I get back to LA. But I'm not doing that here."

"Are you sure, Annie?" Charlotte Claire urged. "There's a window of time to test for drugs. Once that window closes you'll never..."

"I don't want to find out," she said, turning to Charlotte Claire. "I'm going back to my room to take a shower and call Calder. I'll call later. Maybe we can go to lunch."

"Do you want me to come with you?" Amelie asked.

"No, thank you," she said, crossing towards the bedroom. When she reached the bedroom door she turned and said, "I'm fine, really. Let's not make a big deal out of this."

"Let's not make a big deal out of this?" Timmy cried after Annie had closed the door. "This is a big deal...a big fucking deal!"

"I think she's in shock," Amelie said.

"I wish she would take that urine test," Charlotte Claire, said just as there was a knock at the door. "Did you order room service or something?"

"No," Timmy told her as he crossed to the door. "It's probably the maid." He opened the door and found Ralph holding a large white envelope. "Ralph, hi!"

"It wasn't easy," Ralph said grinning. "But I got them, just like you asked; the elevator, elevator banks and the hallway. Patrick in security owed me a favor. He says you can have them for a couple of hours but then you'll need to return them."

"Oh Ralph, thank you so much," Timmy gushed. "You have no idea how helpful this is. I can't thank you enough...and I promise to get them back to you in a couple of hours."

"You're welcome, Timothy."

"Hold on, one second," Timmy said. He retrieved his wallet from the desk and pulled out a one-hundred-dollar bill and held it out to Ralph.

"Oh, no, thank you Timothy," Ralph told him as he waved the cash away. "You asked for a favor and that's what this was, a favor. And I was happy to do it. See you in a couple of hours."

"See you in a couple of hours," Timmy responded. "And thanks again!" Timmy closed the door and said, "Well I'll be god-damned. I've still got it."

"Are those the DVDs?" Charlotte Claire asked excitedly.

"Shh," Timmy said, putting his finger to his lips and pointing toward the bedroom. "We'll look at them after she goes to her room," he whispered. "Better to see what's on them without upsetting her."

When Annie got back to her room she hurriedly pulled her dress off and threw it in the trash. She could never wear it again; she didn't even want to see it again. Calder loved her in that dress. Calder. She couldn't tell Calder any of this. She wouldn't be able to endure the anguished look on his face, or the pity he might feel for her. She turned the shower on, grabbed a towel, and as she turned to get into the shower, glimpsed her reflection in the mirror. She stepped closer, pulled her hair back, and considered her face. Her makeup had smeared, and her eyes were red. She ran a hand over her face, down her breasts and then her belly. She felt a dry, sticky patch. Semen, she realized, someone's semen. A bit of a stranger left behind to remind her of what she can't remember. She stepped into the shower, closed her eyes and let the hot water wash over her. It made her think of tears, a shower of tears. She gasped, opened her eyes, and a deep wail burst forth from within her. She sank slowly to the shower floor, hugging her knees and crying the same way she'd cried as a girl when her mother died. She cried like it was the end of the world, because that is what it felt like.

Timmy pulled the DVDs from the envelope and crossed to the DVD player. "Okay," he said to Charlotte Claire and Amelie. "Someone else is going to have to do this. I don't know how to do those things."

"Men!" Charlotte Claire said in exasperation. "Men don't know how to do anything." She took the DVDs from Timmy and looked at their labels. "I'll put in the one marked ELEVATOR BANK first." She inserted the DVD and pushed "play."

"This starts with a time stamp of 6 o'clock," Amelie told them. "We saw Annie in the ladies' room around 9 o'clock, so super-fast-forward to 9 o'clock and then slow-fast-forward after 9.

"Thank you, Amelie," Charlotte Claire said sarcastically. "I would have never figured that out on my own."

"Now, girls," Timmy teased. "Play nice. Okay, stop, stop, stop!" he yelled. "You're at 9 o'clock."

"Not you too," Charlotte Claire complained. "Okay, slow-fast forward 9, 9:15, 9:30, 9:45, 10, 10:15..."

"Wait," Timmy shouted. "Go back!"

Charlotte Claire put the DVD player on rewind, then set the speed for real time. "There!"

"That's Annie," Amelie said. "And she's leaning on that guy. She looks out of it. I wish that he'd turn around. The quality of the DVD isn't that great." "He'll turn around when they get on the elevator," Timmy said. "Get ready to hit pause before the doors close."

"The elevator's opening," Amelie said.

"Dammit!" Timmy said. "He's not turning around! And the doors closed, shit! It's almost as if he's intentionally avoiding being seen by the camera."

"I'll put the one in from the elevator bank on this floor," Charlotte Claire said. "At least now we know we can super-fast-forward to 10:05." She inserted the DVD and fast-forwarded. When the DVD reached 10:05 she played it in real time. At 10:06 the doors opened, and Annie and Scotty stepped out of the elevator. When they reached the hallway, Scotty looked around the corner and then they went out of the frame. They were all silent for several seconds.

"That son of a bitch," Timmy said angrily.

"I can't believe it," Amelie cried.

"I can," Charlotte Claire said. "Now the question is, do we tell Annie? I wonder if she showered already and washed off the evidence."

"Slow-fast forward until you see him come back," Amelie suggested. "If he comes back within a minute or two it could mean that he was just helping her get back to her room, or what he thought was her room."

"Okay," Charlotte Claire said. "10:15, 10:30, 10:45, 11:00... look, there he is, 11:07. That son of a bitch was in there for an hour."

"That proves it for me," Timmy told them.

"Me too," Amelie agreed.

"Of course," Timmy said. "That explains the Jack Daniel's bottles. That disgusting piece of shit was drinking while he assaulted her."

"Unbelievable," Charlotte Claire declared. "Well, no, I guess not-so-unbelievable."

"We have to tell her," Timmy said. "She has a right to know.

I don't really think it would change her mind about pressing charges, but she may want to confront him."

"You're right, Timmy," Amelie agreed. "We don't have the right to keep this from her."

"Agreed," Charlotte Claire said.

"I'll call and tell her we're meeting here before lunch," Timmy said. "We'll tell her then. In the meantime, we need to collect those Jack Daniel's bottles for evidence. They'll have fingerprints and DNA."

"And the bedding too," Charlotte Claire added. "There may be semen or hairs."

"Good idea," Timmy said.

Timmy busied himself by straightening up the suite and repeatedly checking the time. Amelie and Charlotte Claire sat on the sofa nervously scrolling through their phones. The silence was deafening, but no one felt like talking. None of them was looking forward to what they had to do, and Annie's reaction to another traumatic revelation worried them. It was just after 12:30 when Annie knocked on the door. "Okay, she's here," Timmy said. "Who's doing the talking?"

"You wait until now to ask us?" Amelie asked.

"I'll do it," Charlotte Claire offered. "I'm just going to keep it simple and to the point."

Timmy opened the door and gave Annie a hug. She smiled at him and said, "I'm okay. I feel better now that I've had a shower."

Charlotte Claire looked at Amelie in disappointment. She'd been holding out hope that Annie would reconsider and go to the police; especially now that they had proof that it was Scotty who'd assaulted her. Now, she thought, he's gotten away with it again.

"Where do y'all want to have lunch?" Annie asked them. "Let's go to Boudin Barn. I'd love some boudin and a bowl of seafood gumbo."

"We need to talk to you first, Annie," Charlotte Claire said gently. "We know who assaulted you. It was Scotty."

Annie sat down and pushed against the seat of the lounge chair with her hands. She looked up at the three of them and asked, "How do you know?"

"CCTV video," Charlotte Claire continued. "We saw him getting in the elevator with you and coming out with you on this floor. You had your arm around his shoulder and he was helping you stay upright by holding you at the waist. You were clearly under the influence. It was obvious that you were having a hard time walking. He was in the room for a while. We played the video through until we saw him go back to the elevator."

"How long was he in the suite?" Annie asked.

"About an hour, sweetie," Timmy said.

"Oh, it makes me sick!" Annie cried. "Sick to my stomach... and angry. I'm so angry! I should have known. Of course, he's capable of that. Look at the way he tried to pull me into their bathroom Friday night at the barbecue, and the hateful way he talked to me when I turned him down. He was so full of rage, so quick to attack. It makes sense now. He must have dropped something in my drink when I was talking to y'all near the ladies' room. Of course, the last thing I remember is getting sleepy right after that. He ordered the drink while I was gone, so it would have been easy for him to drop something in it."

"We still have the DVD if you'd like to see it?" Charlotte Claire offered.

"No, no," she said thoughtfully. "I don't want to see it, but I'd like to keep it."

"I'm afraid you can't," Amelie said. "Timmy's supposed to return it to security this afternoon."

"That's true," Timmy said. "But I can run into town and have copies made first."

"Thanks, Timmy," Annie said. "And Amelie, I'd like to call Patty Hammond and see if we can arrange to get that urine test. I'm not sure how we'll manage that, but we're already sharing other confidences with her. I think she'll be receptive. But I guess we'd better do that right away, which means we'll have to skip our lunch."

"I'll call her now," Amelie said, stepping out of the room.

"Don't worry about that," Charlotte Claire told Annie. "I think this is a bit more important. If we get all this done quickly we can have a late lunch or maybe get a snack at happy hour to tide us over until dinner. They have a pretty good spread at the casino bar at happy hour. Timmy, I'll go into town with you to get the copies."

"I just got off the phone with Patty," Amelie said when she'd returned. "She's off today and said we could come at any time."

"Good," Annie said. "I feel better taking some action rather than doing nothing."

"Does this mean you'll go to the police?" Charlotte Claire asked.

"I don't know," she said. "I don't know. I just want to keep my options open. I'll figure out the rest once I've had time to process. But for now, this seems like the thing to do."

"We'd better get going then," Amelie told her.

"Oh wait!" Annie exclaimed. "In all this chaos I forgot to ask. What happened with the pink swan float?"

Patty Hammond hung up the phone in puzzlement. Why on earth would Amelie Ardoin need a urine test under a pseudonym? Perhaps she thought she had an STD, or maybe what she really wants is a pregnancy test. Half an hour later she was still considering the possible reasons for the unusual request when she heard a car pulling into her driveway. She went to the door and greeted Amelie and Annie. "I've enjoyed seeing you girls so much," she said, "but your visits are getting curious-er and curious-er."

"Hey, Patty," Annie said. "I really appreciate you doing

this. I run a risk of this getting to the press if I go to the hospital, and it can't wait until I get back to my own doctor in LA."

"Oh," she said in surprise. "I'm confused; I thought it was Amelie who wanted the urine test."

"No," Amelie said. "I'm sorry I wasn't clear, but it was a little too sensitive to share over the phone."

"Well, sit down and fill me in," Patty said.

Amelie described how they'd found Annie naked and unconscious in Timmy's bed, her inability to recall anything that happened, and the hotel doctor's conclusion that she had been sexually assaulted. And she explained how they'd proven that Scotty Piper was the rapist through the hotel security surveillance DVDs. "Oh, Annie," Patty said sympathetically. "Oh honey, I'm so sorry this happened to you. Those Pipers are evil. I never thought I would say that about anyone I actually knew. But they are evil to the core. And you want this test for what, rohypnol, pregnancy, STDs?"

"No," Annie said, "I had a hysterectomy five years ago. I can't get pregnant. Just test for the STDs and rohypnol. How do you handle this, with a pseudonym?"

"There's two ways to do it," Patty said. "We can put someone else's name on the sample. I'd do it under my name but if it comes back positive for rohypnol I could lose my job."

"You could use my name," Amelie volunteered.

"Or we could make up a name," Patty said. "And you just pay cash for the test."

"Let's do that," Annie said.

"I thought that's what you'd want to do," Patty said. "It's only $200 anyway."

"Here," Annie said, pulling her billfold from her purse and handing Patty $500. Patty took the bills and handed $300 back.

"Your money's no good here," she said, smiling.

The mood at dinner that evening was somber. The full

weight of the events of the last 48 hours had settled upon them like a suit of armor. They sat in silence for several minutes distractedly considering their menus as the 'ding-ding' of slot machines and the low rumble of a hundred conversations wafted in from the casino. It was Timmy who broke through the silence. "I'm not even reading this menu. I'm just staring at it. Where's the waiter? I need a drink."

"Did Patty say how long it would be until she had the results of the urine test?" Charlotte Claire asked.

"Just a couple days," Annie replied. "I don't know what I'm going to do with this information. I guess it's better to know. But if I don't go to the police, and I have decided that I'm not, how will knowing make any difference?"

"Knowing you had rohypnol in your system will tell you that you were definitely drugged. And Scotty fools around, so you need to know about STDs," Amelie told her.

"The CCTV is circumstantial, but the test results are hard evidence. Plus, we could hand over the whiskey bottles and bedding to the police to test for physical evidence. And what about you, Amelie?" Charlotte Claire said turning to her. "What are you going to do about Leanne?"

"Same," she said defensively. "I don't know either."

"Well, it seems like we spent the entire reunion running around playing amateur detective," Charlotte Claire said in frustration. "And for what, to have our evidence as souvenirs?"

"Charlotte Claire!" Timmy scolded. "A lot of shit has gone down in the last few hours. They need time to process. And I thought you were as invested in finding out as the rest of us were."

"I didn't mean it like that, Timmy," she snapped. "And I don't appreciate your tone."

"My tone?" he cried.

"Just stop!" Annie shouted.

Heads turned throughout the restaurant. The waitress approached the table and asked, "Is everything okay?"

"Yes," Timmy said. "We'd like a round of cosmos with Absolute vodka, Cointreau instead of Triple Sec, and Rose's Lime juice instead of fresh. And we'd like them as quickly as possible, please."

"Right away, Mr. Tyler," she said, skittering away.

"Thanks, Annie," Timmy said amusedly. "I guess that's how you get a drink around here. Look, we're all leaving in the morning and I don't want us leaving on a bad note. I knew what you meant, Charlotte Claire. It is incredibly frustrating to have gone through everything we went through this weekend, and have no idea if there is any hope of getting justice for anyone. But short of going to the police, which I am not willing to do, what are our options? What recourse do we have?"

"And if I went to the police with Elizabeth's float," Amelie interjected, "They would laugh me out of the police station."

"Or arrest you," Timmy added. "Remember what Tom Burnett told me; that Scotty had every cop and judge in the parish in his back pocket. It may be that there really is nothing we can do. And what you two have to decide is whether it was worth finding out. Maybe it would have been better not to know."

"Well," Amelie said resignedly. "That ship has sailed."

"And, Charlotte Claire," Timmy said. "I'm sorry I took a tone."

"And I'm sorry I snapped at you," she replied.

"Oh, praise the lord," Annie said good-naturedly. "Peace has been restored to our little banana republic. I'm leaving early tomorrow, so I won't see you before I go. I want to thank you all for taking care of me."

"That's what we do, Annie," Charlotte Claire said. "We take care of each other. We always have."

"And we always will," Timmy added.

"I love you guys," Amelie sang.

"I was thinking about something today," Annie said thoughtfully. "What if we'd never met? People come and go in your life, but we have lived each other's lives. We've known each other for almost 50 years, and through all those years we've been there for each other. You became my family when I had none. Your friendship has meant everything to me." Annie grew silent, her eyes welling with tears.

Bayou Derkin, Louisiana

August 20th, 2015

At 9 a.m. Patty Hammond strode through the hallway of Bayou Derkin Hospital with urgency. She'd just received the results of Annie's urine test and was eager to let her know. She stepped into a supply room and tapped Annie's number from her contacts. The call immediately went to voicemail, "Hi, this is Annie, leave me a message and I'll call you back."

"Hi Annie, its Patty Hammond, I have your results so give me a call when you can."

When 3 p.m. came and went with no response from Annie, she decided to call Amelie. Having this information felt like a burden and she wanted to be rid of it. She stepped into the supply room and tapped Amelie's number from her contacts. Amelie picked up on the second ring. "Oh, thank goodness," Patty said. "Hi, its Patty Hammond, how are you? Oh, good, look, I've been trying to reach Annie all day and haven't been able to and I thought you might have a better chance of reaching her. I have the test results from her urine sample. Yeah, I thought so. It was negative for STDs, but it was positive for rohypnol. Yeah, it looks like that son-of-bitch Scotty Piper drugged her, which almost guarantees that he raped her the night of the reunion. Do you think she'll go to the police? Well, I guess I don't blame her, but I'd make sure that bastard went to prison. He'd get a little taste of his own medicine there. And tell Annie to get a follow up test with her doctor for the STDs. Positive results don't always show up so soon after. You too honey, bye." There, she thought to herself, that's done.

As soon as she heard the supply room door close, Carla Courville stepped from behind the tall metal shelves, turned her cell phone on and called Tom Burnett. "You are never going to believe what I just heard!" she told him excitedly.

Carla's feet were aching by the end of her shift. She couldn't wait to get home and put them up. But she was mostly looking forward to discussing the revelation about Scotty Piper with Tom. When she got to the parking lot, Patty Hammond was just reaching her car. "Good night Patty," she said, secretly amused that she knew Patty's secret and Patty hadn't a clue. "Any big plans tonight?"

"Yes," Patty replied. "I'm going to take a long, hot bath and curl up with a good book."

"Sounds great after a day like today, enjoy!"

"Have a good one, Carla."

Carla had started out for home when she realized she didn't have coffee for the morning. She pulled into the Piggly Wiggly parking lot and rifled through her bag for her pocketbook. As she got out of her car she saw Leanne Piper walking toward her Mercedes. Leanne Piper, she thought to herself, what a snobby bitch, she and that husband of hers...always acting so superior. And the way they look down on Tom makes my blood boil. If she only knew what I knew, that would take her down a few pegs. "Well, hey there, Leanne," she called out, but Leanne kept walking, pretending not to hear her. This only made Carla more determined to engage her. She walked directly up to Leanne and said, "Hey there, Leanne. I guess you didn't hear me when I called out to you."

"Oh, Carla," Leanne said wearily. "I guess I was distracted."

"That must be it," she said, ignoring Leanne's tone. "You must have lots of things on your mind. How've you been?"

"Very busy, Carla, in fact I'd better be going now."

"Rushing home to that charming husband of yours?"

"Yes, Carla. And I suppose you'll be rushing home to that... Tom. Still a pipefitter...or no, a mechanic, isn't it?"

"Well, do rush home," Carla said happily. "You'll want to spend as much time with him as you can... while you can."

Leanne set her groceries in the backseat of her car and

slammed the car door. "What, Carla, in that oh-so-subtle way of yours, are you driving at?" There'd been rumors from time to time that Scotty was leaving her for one of his many affairs, and she braced herself for another.

"Well, I'm guessing that he'll end up in jail pretty soon. You know, if Anne Renee goes to the police and reports that Scotty drugged and raped her the night of the reunion. Or didn't you know about that?"

"What a ridiculous rumor," Leanne seethed. "And from such a ridiculous person. I'd advise you not to go around town saying that, because we'd be only too happy to sue you for slander. You won't even be able to afford that white trash trailer that you call home, so consider that. Besides, everyone knows you're the biggest gossip in Bayou Derkin. Everyone will know it's a lie."

"Patty Hammond just found out. She knows it's not a lie, and she has the piss to prove it."

"Carla, you don't even make sense," Leanne said, throwing her purse into the car and climbing into the driver's seat.

"It's results from a urine sample that tested positive for the date rape drug. And I'm positive it's positive," she said smiling. "So, run along home now. You'll want all the time you can get-if you enjoy spending time with a rapist, that is."

Leanne slammed the car door, started the car and willed herself not to floor the accelerator and speed away. "Oh," Carla said to herself, "that was fun."

Leanne was so angry she was shaking. When she got home she bolted straight into the house, forgetting the groceries in the back seat of the car. "Scotty!" she yelled. "Scotty, where are you? Scotty!"

"Goddammit, Leanne," he said, stepping out of the library. "What the fuck is wrong with you?"

"I'll tell you what's wrong with me," she said, throwing her purse on the hall table. "That horrible Carla Courville just told me that you slipped Annie a date rape drug at the reunion and raped her. She said that Patty Hammond has the results of a urine test for proof! She'll probably spread that all over town. You tell me right now if there's any truth to this." Scotty felt as if he'd been hit over the head with a baseball bat. He stood silent for several seconds, his mind racing. "Tell me!" she screamed again.

"Don't be ridiculous," he said at last. "Carla Courville is a shit-stirrer and she hates us. It's so outrageous, how could you even ask me that?"

"Because I know you, Scotty," she said evenly. "I know what you're capable of. And you were there at the reunion for hours after I left, and you reeked of perfume when you got home. You have a track record and I don't put anything past you. And I'll tell you this; if there's any truth to this you'd better fix it, by whatever means necessary. Don't forget the company is mine, and if this comes to light, you're out. I'm not going to have everyone in town call me a fool whose husband is a rapist. I won't have my name associated with a lurid scandal. So, fix it!"

"Thank you, Leanne," he said heatedly. "Thank you for the fucking vote of confidence. This is too ridiculous to even talk about." As he walked out of the room they both wondered if she believed him.

By the following morning Scotty Piper had devised a plan. He'd spent most of the sleepless night before concocting it. Patty Hammond and Carla Courville had to go. He had too much to lose to let these bitches ruin him, or worse, get him locked up. He knew that hospital employees worked in shifts. He just needed to ascertain which days Patty and Carla worked the night shift. He hoped it would be soon. At 6 AM he went into the library and closed the doors. He'd call the hospital to find out the two women's schedules. He reasoned that Patty and Carla most likely didn't work the graveyard shifts, and if he called before the start of the seven-to-three shift, they wouldn't be at the hospital-which would give him the opportunity to ask when they would. He picked up the phone on his desk and dialed the number for Bayou Derkin Hospital. He could feel himself tensing as the phone rang one, two, three times. "Bayou Derkin Hospital," an elderly sounding woman answered. "How can I help you?"

"I'd like to speak to Patty Hammond."

"Hold on while I transfer you to the nurse's station." He heard a click and then elevator music-"Close to You" by the Carpenters. He was thinking how much he hated the song when a voice came on the line.

"Nurse's station, this is Rhonda, what can I do you for?"

"Could I speak to Patty Hammond?"

"Sorry, Patty's not in until three today. Is there something I can help you with?"

"No, but uh, is Carla Courville around by any chance?"

"I'm afraid not, she's...," she paused, the sound of papers shuffling in the background. "She's also not here until three today. Are you sure there's nothing I can help you with?"

"You've already been very helpful."

"Who's calling, please?"

Scotty placed the receiver gently back on the phone and sat down behind the big mahogany desk. That was almost too easy, he thought. Now if everything else falls this easily into place, this will all be taken care of before I go to bed tonight.

At 10:30 Scotty told Leanne that he was running out for cigarettes, and she said okay without ever turning away from the television. He pulled on a black leather jacket and went out through the kitchen, removing a large carving knife from the knife block as he did so. He climbed into his son's old Ford F-150 pick-up and drove toward the hospital on the old gravel road that farmers and their farmhands used during the day. He was aware that his plan had many variables, and a lot would depend on luck.

He pulled into the parking lot and parked beside Carla Courville's old Chevy Malibu. Without turning off his truck, he hopped out, moved quickly to the rear of the Malibu, and shoved the knife into a rear tire-one, two, three times-until he could hear the air being released. He moved to the other rear tire and did the same. He jumped back into his truck, parked two cars away, rolled down his window and slumped down in his seat. At 11:05 Carla emerged from the front door of the hospital and walked quickly to her car. She opened the back door, threw her bag in, climbed into the driver's seat and started the car. Her headlights popped on and the car began to move sluggishly back. Carla stopped and then moved sluggishly forward, back into the space. She got out of the car, walked around to the back and bent towards the rear tire. "Shit!" Scotty heard her say.

Two more people, a man and a woman, stepped out through the front door of the hospital and walked toward the parking lot. In the semi-darkness Scotty couldn't tell if the woman was Patty or someone else. When they saw Carla, the man said, "Hey, Carla, what's up?"

"Flat," she said grimly. "Or *flats* I should say. Both of my rear tires are flat."

"I'd be happy to change them for you," he said. "But I'm assuming you only have one spare."

"Oh Mel, that's so sweet to offer but, right-only one spare, and ironically, it's flat too. I've been meaning to get it repaired but I kept putting it off. Not that it would've made any difference tonight. It's just so weird; I've never had two flats at the same time before. I'll just call Tom to come pick me up. Or, any chance you could give me a ride, Mel?"

Scotty braced for his reply. The wrong answer could derail his plan. And if the woman with her back to him wasn't Patty, that would be a problem too.

"Any other time I'd be glad to," Mel said apologetically.

"But Mama's in bad shape with the cancer. I promised Dad I'd swing by and check in on her after my shift. If you lived a little closer I'd be glad to, but you're a little far out, sorry, Carla."

"Don't be, I totally understand. I'll just call Tom."

Scotty clutched the steering wheel of his truck as he waited to see what happened next.

"I'll take you," the woman said. "I'm going in that direction and it's not that far for me. Grab your stuff."

"Really? That would be great," Carla said. "Thanks so much! You are the best, Patty."

"Bingo," Scotty said to himself. He waited until Patty pulled onto the road before he started his engine and slowly followed them, at a safe distance. He was familiar with Guidry Pass, the narrow road that wound through the woods and across the Bayou Derkin River. Carla's trailer was on the other side of that bridge.

They'd had heavy rains, so the river would be high. He could see the two women talking animatedly as they drove off the main highway and onto Guidry Pass. He accelerated slightly, so that when they approached the bridge he could advance on them quickly. The waning moon was still large enough to cast some light on the narrow road, so Scotty turned off his headlights and pulled a few feet behind the women. He could see Carla turn in her seat and look out the rear window.

"There's someone right behind you with their lights off," she said nervously.

"That's weird," Patty said. "Probably lost their headlights and are using me in their place. But that's not safe. What if a deer ran out into the road and I had to come to a sudden stop?" As the cars reached the bridge, Scotty floored the accelerator and pulled into the opposite lane, his truck even with their car. "What's he doing?" Patty shrieked.

Scotty jerked the steering wheel and hit Patty's car with a tinny thud, sending both vehicles rocking. "Oh, my God!" Carla screamed, "He's trying to run us off the road!"

He gunned the engine, pulled a few feet ahead of Patty's car, and again jerked the wheel to the right, smashing his truck into the front half of her car and sending it off the road to the right-crashing through the guard rail of the old wooden bridge and careening over the edge. He drove on for a mile, breathing heavily, before he turned the truck around. When he got back to the bridge he stopped his truck, walked to the smashed guard rail, and peered over the edge. Patty's car lay upside down in the shallow river, only its chassis and wheels visible above the water. He got back in his truck, reached into the glove compartment, pulled out a pint of bourbon and took a long swallow before he sped away. By the time he reached the highway he was smiling, pleased with himself that his plan went off so easily. He took another long swallow of bourbon and thought, that reminds me of the time I ran that faggot Timmy Tyler off the road. Oh man, that was funny. I should let him know he got lucky.

When Scotty got home, he backed the old pickup into the garage so the damaged side wouldn't be seen by Leanne when she went to and from her car. He would take it over the state line to Texas, in a few days and have it repaired. He went into the library, poured a bourbon, knocked it back and then went up to bed. As he lay there, the bourbon lulling him to sleep, he felt strangely happy...and proud.

The following morning Leanne was at the hairdresser's when she heard about the accident. She could barely sit through the end of her appointment. As soon as she was done she drove to Scotty's office, walked past his secretary without saying hello, and closed the office door behind her. "What have you done?" she asked him urgently.

"I haven't got the faintest idea of what the hell you're talking about," he said dismissively.

Charlotte Claire awoke to dappled light playing on the wall of her childhood bedroom. She rolled over and looked at the clock, 7:30. Her mother will have probably been awake since 6 o'clock, she thought, so she climbed out of bed, put on her robe and went to the kitchen, where her mother sat with a cup of coffee and the newspaper. "Anything interesting in the paper?" she asked.

"Good morning, sweetie," her mother sang. "How'd you sleep?"

"Great."

"No, nothing much; Fredrick's is closing. I hate to see it go. Bayou Derkin is not the same town since the casino came in. All the old businesses are closing up. Oh, Andy Stoner's daughter's wedding announcement is in the social section. She got his looks, poor girl."

"Oh, Mama," she laughed. "You are too funny." She poured herself a cup of coffee and joined her mother at the table.

"I wish you didn't have to leave today," her mother said. "Aunt Sadie and I are going into Lake Charles for a movie and dinner. If you stayed an extra night you could come with us."

"I'd love to, Mama, but Stanley has a dinner thing and the wives are invited. Believe me, I'd rather stay here. Some of those women are so boring, and the men are worse!"

"Stanley's a good man," she told her. "It's your duty to support him, so I understand."

"I thought I'd run into town and stock you up on a few things. Do you want to come with me?" Charlotte Claire asked.

"I'd love to, but I have a Ladies Auxiliary meeting at the church this morning. We're electing officers, so I don't want to miss it. That horrible Thelma Allemande is running for president, so I have to go vote against her. And you don't have to stock me up every time you come for a visit," she insisted. "I can buy my own groceries."

"I like to," Charlotte said. "It gives me pleasure."

"You're a good daughter Charlotte Claire," she said looking

at her lovingly. "I guess we did something right."

"I guess you did."

Later that morning, after she'd showered and dressed, Charlotte Claire drove the narrow, twisting road into Bayou Derkin and parked in front of the Piggly Wiggly. As soon as she got out of the car she saw Jenny Karan walking quickly towards her in the parking lot. "Oh, hey you!" Jenny sang. "Still in town?"

"Yeah, just for a few more hours. I thought I'd stock up on some things for Mama before I leave. She's so thin. I worry she's not eating enough."

"I wish I had that problem. Oh, did you hear the terrible news?" Jenny asked excitedly.

"No."

"Oh, it's terrible. Patty Hammond and Carla Courville were killed in a car accident last night," she said, shaking her head. "You know they work together, or worked I should say, at the hospital."

"What happened?" Charlotte Claire asked, incredulously.

"Well," Jenny said, only too happy to repeat the grim news, "Patty was giving Carla a ride home from the hospital because she had a flat tire and no spare, and they went off that old wooden bridge on Guidry Pass; went right through the railing and into the river. You know Carla lived with Tom Burnett in a trailer way out on Guidry Pass. They really ought to do something about that old bridge. This was bound to happen sooner or later. Poor, poor Tom, he has had so much heartache the last few years. You know about his boy?"

"Yeah, I'd heard about that at Scotty and Leanne's barbecue Friday night. That's so sad."

"They're having the wake for Carla tonight and Patty tomorrow," she continued. "The funeral home is going to be overwhelmed the next couple of days; the flower shop too, I imagine. Patty was such a good person; never married. When

Mama was in the hospital with her gallbladder Patty was so good to her. Mama is just devastated."

"I imagine so," Charlotte Claire said distractedly. "Give your Mama my love. I'm sorry, Jenny, I have to run. I have a lot to do before I leave this afternoon."

"Well, of course you do, and I'm here running at the mouth like you haven't got a thing to do in the world. You run along and next time you're in Bayou Derkin give me a ring and I'll get some of the old crowd together for a gumbo or something."

"I sure will, take care."

"Take care!"

Charlotte Claire got back in her car and sat motionless for several minutes before starting the car and driving away. She was reeling from the shock as images and snippets of conversations from the last few days replayed in her mind. Could there be a connection to the rape, or was all of this just a terrible coincidence? She pulled into her mother's driveway and tapped out a text to Annie, Amelie and Timmy.

Charlotte Claire

I just found out that Patty Hammond and Carla Courville were killed in a car accident last night. What do you think?

When she went inside her mother said, "I've just heard the most terrible news."

"I know," Charlotte Claire said. "I ran into Jenny Karan at the store. Oh, the store! I completely forgot to buy anything." Her phone dinged, and she saw an incoming text. "Mama, I'm going to check my texts in my room. I'll be out in a minute."

"Go ahead, dear. And you don't need to buy me any groceries," she called after her as she left the room.

By the time she got to her room she'd gotten texts from all three of them.

Timmy

What? That's terrible.

Annie

That so sad; I can't believe it. We just saw her.

Amelie

I know-poor Patty.

Timmy

What do you mean by "what do we think?"

Charlotte Claire

Patty and Carla went off the bridge on Guidry Pass. No other car was involved.

Annie

So?

Charlotte Claire

We just got the urine test results. Patty knew about the thing with Scotty. Carla works with Patty at the hospital. What if she got wind?

Amelie

I think it's unlikely...but not impossible.

Annie

Patty would never tell her. Everyone says Carla's (was) a big gossip.

Charlotte Claire

Exactly; she may have found out another way.

Timmy

If Carla knew, then Tom would know. You need to talk to Tom.

Annie

Wait...are you suggesting that Scotty had something to do with this?

Charlotte Claire

Yes...or Leanne. We all know killing isn't beneath her.

Timmy

Or Scotty-if he could do what he did to Annie I don't put anything past him. You need to talk to Tom.

Charlotte Claire

The wake is tonight. I was planning to go back to Houston

this afternoon, but I'll stay for the wake. If I get a chance I'll speak with him tonight, or I'll go see him tomorrow. I'll let y'all know what I find out tomorrow. Need to run. Mama's waiting for me in the kitchen.

That evening Charlotte Claire put on the same black dress she'd worn to the reunion two nights earlier and prepared to drive into Bayou Derkin. She regarded herself in the mirror and thought how much had changed since the last time she'd worn the dress.

The funeral home was packed. Funerals and wakes, she knew, were social events in Bayou Derkin. She knew so many people there that she had a hard time getting across the room. Every few feet someone stopped her to tsk-tsk about the tragedy before launching into small talk and gossip. When she made it to the viewing room she was relieved to see there was a closed casket. She hated seeing dead bodies, especially someone as young as Carla. People who she supposed to be Carla's parents and siblings were seated in the front row, but she didn't see Tom. Jenny Karan sidled up beside her and whispered, "So sad, so sad. I hear that she was pretty messed up. That's why the closed casket."

"Oh, really?" Charlotte Claire asked, thinking what poor taste it was to bring that up.

"Yes," she said. "So, you decided to stay for the funeral? I didn't know you knew Carla that well."

"No, just the wake. I didn't really know Carla at all. I wanted to pay my respects to Tom. Have you seen him? I would've thought he'd be in the front row."

"He was," Jenny said. "You just missed him. He's probably out on the front porch smoking or behind the funeral home with a pint of bourbon."

"Okay, thanks," Charlotte Claire told her. "I think I'll step out and see if I can find him. Talk to you later."

"Later!"

Charlotte Claire found Tom in the parking lot behind the funeral home. He was smoking a cigarette and taking slugs from a pint. She could tell from his bearing that he'd been drinking for a while. When she approached him, the look on his face made her profoundly sad.

"Tom," she said sympathetically. "I'm so sorry. How are you doing?"

"Oh, you know," he said sadly.

"I can only imagine. Is someone here with you?"

He laughed bitterly. "I don't have no one. My parents are gone, my boy's gone. I don't speak with my brother no more. Carla was my family...and now she's gone." Tears rolled down his cheeks. He took another slug of bourbon and a drag from his cigarette. Charlotte Claire found it all heartbreaking. She put her arms around him and patted him gently on the back. The unexpected act of kindness unleashed a well of emotion in Tom. He sobbed for the first time since getting the news of Carla's death.

"Here," Charlotte Claire said. "Let's go sit for a minute." They sat on the steps to the back door of the funeral home and Tom took another slug of bourbon. "Go easy on that, Tom."

"You're right."

"Did they determine the cause of the accident?" she asked.

"Accident, my ass," he snorted. "That wasn't no accident. Of course, I'd never be able to prove it. And even if I could, nobody'd do shit about it."

"What are you talking about, Tom?"

"Scotty ran them off the road...or had someone do it for him."

"Why would you say that?"

"The day before she was killed she called me from the hospital. She'd overheard Patty talking to someone on the phone about the results of a urine test that proved that Scotty had drugged Annie at the reunion. She even went on to say that it was likely that he raped her."

"Did Patty know that Carla overheard her?"

"No, she'd been standing behind some shelves in the supply room. She just stood there listening until Patty hung up and left the room. Carla was so excited to have a scoop. I don't think it occurred to her to consider what Annie must've went through. Carla was a bit of a gossip...she liked to have the scoop."

"Did Carla know who Patty was talking to on the phone?" Charlotte Claire asked apprehensively.

"No," Tom said. "Or if she did, she didn't say."

"But how does that prove that Scotty had anything to do with the crash?"

"Like I said, Carla's, I mean Carla was a bit of a gossip. It wasn't that she had no good qualities," he said. "She did, she had a lot. But this wasn't one of them. On her way home from work that night she ran into Leanne at the Piggly Wiggly and told her what she'd heard."

"What?" Charlotte Claire cried. "Why on earth would she do that?"

"To get Leanne's goat," he said. "And Scotty's too; she hated the both of them."

"Oh, my God, Tom!" Charlotte Claire exclaimed. "That means that Leanne knew, which means that Scotty most likely knew too. You may be right."

"It was a damn fool thing to do, and I told her so," he said. "And I think, no, I know, it got her killed. And I'll tell you what else. Carla had two flat tires that night. The tires on her car weren't brand new, but they were in good shape. And what are the odds that she'd have two flat tires at the same time? I went and got Carla's car from the parking lot at the hospital today. When I changed the tires do you know what I found? Three thin, fine cuts about two and a half inches wide in each tire, the kind of cuts that'd be made by a butcher knife. Her tires didn't go flat on their own...someone made them flat."

"Listen, Tom, you can't tell this to anyone else," she told

him. "It could be very dangerous for you if it's true."

"It's true and I know it. But I'm no fool. I got no proof...not even proof of the conversation with Carla. And if I tell them about the tires they'll just say that it could've been anyone. I got no proof of murder, no proof of rape, no proof that son of a bitch drugged anyone. What I do have is a fucking heartless killer who's in bed with the law. And as for Scotty himself, he'd kill me soon as look at me. So, no, Charlotte Claire, I'm not telling anyone else nothing."

On the drive back to her mother's house that night Charlotte Claire compared the facts she knew with Tom's theories. That's what they were after all, just theories. As he said, he had no proof, but she felt he'd made a powerful case. Scotty may have been desperate enough to want to shut them up, but what were the odds that, even if he did slash her tires, Patty would be the one to end up driving Carla home? There were so many things that could have gone wrong, least of which was the fact the Patty may have been off that night. Though Charlotte Claire supposed that finding out what nights Patty and Carla worked together would be easy. And it was also true that Patty may not have offered to drive Carla home. No, Charlotte Claire thought, that's just exactly the kind of thing Patty *would* do. And Bayou Derkin Hospital is small, just a clinic with a few rooms really, there can't be many nurses on any given shift. Everything she'd heard about Scotty since the reunion made a compelling argument for Scotty being capable of murder.

When she got home she found her mother with a cup of tea, watching TV. "How was the wake?" her mother asked.

"Sad...and strange," she replied, wearily.

"Strange?"

"Oh, I don't know. I guess I've always found wakes and funerals strange. When I die I want everyone to wait a month and then throw a big cocktail party." Charlotte Claire sat quietly for a few seconds, overwhelmed by all that she'd learned that evening. "I'm going to change, Mama, and then I'll come sit with you."

"That sounds nice, honey."

Alone in her bedroom Charlotte Claire texted the group.

Charlotte Claire

Lots of revelations tonight.

She slipped off her dress and threw it on a chair, looked at it guiltily for a second, then hung it up. In the time it took her to put on her pajamas, her phone dinged three times. They must have all been waiting, she thought. The first text was from Annie.

Annie

Tell!

Timmy

I'm here.

Amelie

Me too.

Charlotte Claire

Tom thinks Scotty forced them off the bridge. Carla told Leanne about the urine test and rape and that Patty had proof. She overheard Patty call Amelie. If Leanne knows it probably means Scotty knows. Tom said that Carla's tires were slashed so she had to ride home with Patty.

Amelie

Does Scotty know that Patty was talking to me on the phone?

Charlotte Claire

No.

Amelie

Sheesh! Wiping my brow.

Timmy

How was Tom?

Charlotte Claire

Terrible. Broke my heart. Says he has no one now.

Annie

Were Leanne and Scotty at the wake?

Charlotte Claire

Conspicuously absent.

Annie

Will Tom go to the police?

Charlotte Claire

No, he says no one will believe him with no proof. Says Scotty has law enforcement in his back pocket. And he wouldn't put it past Scotty to kill him too.

Amelie

He's probably right.

Timmy

Do you think he did it?

Charlotte Claire

Yes. Do y'all?

Annie

Yes.

Amelie

Yes.

Timmy

Yes.

The week following the murder was stressful for Scotty, thinking another shoe might drop at any time. His normally confident swagger was tempered by a simmering dread. What if the cops were to come sniffing around? How would he react and what would he say? They'd no reason to suspect him, but what if Patty and Carla told other people about the rape? What if those people went to the police? He had friends in law enforcement, loyal friends, but he knew that even they wouldn't be able to turn a blind eye to a double murder. He'd conceived and executed the plan calmly and efficiently, but hadn't bargained for the anxiety and the fear of being caught.

A week after the accident Scotty drove the old Ford pick-up across the state line into Texas. When the repairs were complete a week later, he returned to Texas and traded in the old truck for a new one-which he presented to his son for his 'great work on the football field.' He tried to present only a casual interest in the accident when speaking with his friends in law enforcement, but made a point of keeping up with the state of the investigation. How long before they close this fucking investigation, he wondered, so I can get back to my god-damned life?

Leanne tried to block the thought from her mind, but every day it kept coming back; am I living with a murderer? She tried to act as she normally did around Scotty, which wasn't difficult; even before the accident their marriage was chilly at best. But Scotty seemed different to her. She'd never known him to be quiet or pensive, but now he seemed preoccupied, distracted. And he'd taken off to Texas unannounced to buy that truck. In her private moments she wondered if she ever really knew him. He'd cheated on her numerous times, he could be crude and uncaring, but rape, murder? She could only wonder...and worry. What else is he capable of? Am I safe? If something happened to me he'd have a lot to gain.

In less than a month the investigation into the accident deemed it exactly that, an accident. Even though the dents and black paint on the front left side of the car appeared suspicious, inconsistent with the direction the car exited the bridge, it was determined that if there were another vehicle involved there was little evidence and no witnesses-so any pursuit by law enforcement would be expensive and fruitless. Scotty's old pals at the Sherriff's office just weren't that interested. The matter was officially closed.

After word came that the investigation was closed, Scotty no longer felt as if he were constantly looking over his shoulder. He began to relax and feel like his old self again. His old swagger was back, perhaps more so than ever, because he'd pulled off the perfect murder. The following week he was in his office reviewing October sales stats with his team when he noticed the message light on his phone start to flicker. He finished his meeting then called his secretary into his office.

"Lisa, I thought I asked you to take a written message and bring it in to me when I'm in a meeting. Sometimes these calls are urgent enough for me to pause the meeting and take the call."

"Yes, I remember Scotty, but this guy refused to give me his name and insisted on leaving a voicemail. I thought you'd prefer me to do that rather than miss the message altogether."

"Well, try to insist back," he said firmly.

"I did," she replied impatiently.

"Well, try harder," he said, dismissing her with a wave of his hand.

"Yes, Scotty."

He picked up the phone, grabbed a pen and played the message. "I know what you did," a monstrous voice said. "You are a killer and you will pay." His face went ashen and a chill shot through him. He slammed the phone down and leaned back in his chair. Who could this be? The voice was so unearthly, so sinister. It must have been a voice distortion device like they use on the news to interview people who want to remain anonymous. His heart was racing as he picked up the phone again and pressed the button. The monstrous voice repeated, "You are a killer and you will pay."

Someone knows, but who? And how would they find out? He replayed the night of the murder in his mind. He'd passed no one on the old farm road on his way to the hospital. As far as he knew, no one saw him in or leaving the parking lot. There had been no other cars on Guidry Pass the entire time he was there. The truck was God knows where now, and even if they tracked it down, the repairs were made before he traded it in-so they'd have no proof that it was involved in an accident. The only way someone might suspect he was responsible was if Patty or Carla told someone else about the rape and the test results, and that someone put two and two together. But, he reminded himself, suspicion isn't proof.

On Halloween afternoon Leanne arrived home with bags full of candy for the annual Halloween party she hosted for the Catechism children at St. Bethany's. She threw her coat on a chair and called out to her maid as she rifled through the mail on the foyer table. "Lena!"

"Yes ma'am?" the old lady asked.

"Lena, there are a dozen shopping bags filled with candy in the car. Bring them in and we'll fill up the goody bags for the party. I'll do the first one, so you can see how I want them done and then you can do the rest."

"Yes ma'am."

Leanne took her mail into the kitchen and played the messages on the answering machine. The Catholic Daughter's meeting was cancelled. The landscaper could come on Monday to wrap the rose bushes for the winter. The Cormier's would like them for dinner on Saturday. Then she heard it. She dropped the mail and stepped back from the answering machine in horror; that terrible voice, so hideous, so evil-sounding. Most horrifying of all was the message: "I know what you did. You are a child killer and you will pay." She slammed her hand down on the machine so hard she thought she'd broken it. She raced to the foyer, where she could see the maid through the window, still struggling with the shopping bags. She returned to the kitchen and played the message again, "I know what you did. You are a child killer and you will pay."

Leanne sat down hard on a kitchen chair and covered her mouth, her eyes wild with fear, confused thoughts swirling in her mind like a hurricane. Who? Why now? Is this blackmail? They said she would pay, maybe that's what they meant. But, if she paid blackmail, it would be proof that she'd done it. And what proof could they have? Had someone seen her all those years ago and kept it a secret all this time? It was so long ago, surely any proof would have been destroyed by now. No, there was no proof. Then her memory stopped her short. She raced upstairs to her bedroom and went into the walk-in closet, over to the middle right, and flung open the doors. She withdrew the storage container marked PINK SWAN FLOAT, threw the lid on the floor and looked in horror at the empty box. She laughed involuntarily and fell back against the closet door. It was all too absurd, she thought. How can this be happening now? She picked up the lid, put it back on the box and replaced the box on the shelf. Maybe this was a Halloween prank that turned out to be horrible coincidence. That's it, she thought, it's just an unfortunately coincidental prank. She needed to get a grip. She went downstairs to the dining room where she poured two fingers of bourbon and drank it down in one long swallow.

In the weeks that followed, having received no further threatening voicemails, Leanne convinced herself that the whole thing was a tasteless Halloween prank. She still had a nagging feeling about the missing swan float, though. She wasn't even sure why she'd held onto it. It was a gruesome memory, yet it had given her a perverse sense of satisfaction to know she had a secret so outrageous, so extreme that if she told it to anyone they wouldn't believe her. There were so many things about her, she thought, that would shock people if they knew. Everyone in Bayou Derkin saw her as the wife, the hostess, the church going member of the ladies' auxiliary. It made her laugh at how stupid people could be. She knew she was smarter than all of them. How could she have gotten so rattled by one prank call? No one in Bayou Derkin would be smart enough to figure out what she'd done. Anyway, she thought, that was a long time ago, just a childish impulse gone awry. She wasn't a serial killer. She hadn't killed anyone else; though she knew she could if she had to.

After receiving the ominous voicemail, Scotty's recently recovered swagger left him again. He drank more, to ease the stress of not knowing who left the voice mail or if he'd get another. Everyone he came into contact with fell under suspicion. It could be anyone, male or female; with that voice distortion device he couldn't even pin down the gender. It could be anybody who had contact with Carla or Patty, though Carla would be the more likely candidate, she was such a gossip. Patty Hammond was of a more judicious nature. And if it was Carla, the obvious conclusion to draw would be that she told Tom Burnett and he was exacting some juvenile revenge for something he would never be able to prove. The only problem was that it was working. Scotty had to reluctantly admit to himself that it was taking a toll. But how could he approach Tom about the voicemail without giving all the rest away? The answer was simple; he couldn't. He could only hope that Tom would grow weary of his sick prank.

On Thanksgiving Day, Leanne mingled with her extended family while Scotty supervised the preparation of the deep-fried turkey in the backyard. It was a Thanksgiving tradition that they both looked forward to. But today Scotty seemed preoccupied, even depressed. When she thought about it, she realized he'd been like that for weeks. She'd ignored it the way she ignored most things about Scotty, but today it annoyed her because they were hosting, and she expected him to be a gracious host. She'd have pulled him aside and reprimanded him for it, but she wanted to avoid a scene. She decided to take a different tack. She poured herself another glass of wine, grabbed a beer from the refrigerator and joined him in the backyard. When she held the beer out to him he looked up in surprise. "Well, thanks. Not used to this kind of service from you."

"I'm full of surprises," she said, smiling. "How's the turkey coming?"

"Good. Should be ready in half an hour."

It irritated her that he always dropped his pronouns. It reminded her of the rough edges she had tried so hard to smooth over. "Has Matt called you? I'm a little irritated with him for being late."

"Called about an hour ago. Just leaving Baton Rouge. Told him not to speed. I'm tired of paying damn speeding tickets."

"Well, it's very inconsiderate," she complained. "Mother is dying to see him and she's fading. She'll probably be napping when he gets here. Is he still bringing that girl?"

"What's wrong with the girl?" he asked. "She's a good-looking girl."

Leanne frowned, as she always did when she felt he was being tiresome. "Her father is a high school custodian and her mother is a waitress. I want Matt to marry into a family with breeding."

"Like you did?" he asked sarcastically.

"Do as I say, not as I do," she joked, to keep things light. She was about to ask if Scotty needed anything from the kitchen when both their cellphones sounded. "That's probably Matt," she said, slipping her phone from the pocket of her tunic. "Hello? And you'd better be close."

"I know what you did," the horrible voice said. "You are a child killer and you are going to pay."

She gasped and dropped her phone on the grass. When she looked up she saw Scotty wore the same look of shock as she.

"What is it?" he asked anxiously. "What's wrong?"

"Nothing," she said, trying to regain her composure. "There must be something wrong with my cell. It gave me a little shock. Are you okay? Was that bad news? It's not Matthew, is it?"

"No, just a work problem I've got to figure out on Monday."

"I'd better get back inside," she said nervously. "I don't want to ignore our guests. I'll bring you another beer later."

"Okay, thanks."

When Leanne walked into the house her mother noticed immediately that she was upset. "Honey is everything okay?"

"I'm fine, Mother," she said, walking past her. She went into the library, closed the big walnut doors behind her, poured herself some bourbon and drank it down. She poured another and downed that one too. Who is doing this, she wondered, why did I answer my phone without looking at the caller ID? "What do they want?" she said aloud. "This is no prank."

Scotty replayed the message. It was identical to the first; the cadence, the timing. It was probably a recording. His phone had identified the caller as UNKNOWN. No fucking kidding unknown, he thought, but how the fuck do I make them known?

Christmas morning Leanne woke up early, went down to the kitchen and put on a pot of coffee. She opened a cookbook and ran her finger down the list of ingredients for Quiche Lorraine, even though she'd made it dozens of times. She did this every year. It was a tradition she loved. The house was still quiet, and she had some time to herself to cook while she had coffee and watched a Christmas movie on TCM. The sun hadn't come up yet. She sipped her coffee and gazed out the window at the little white lights twinkling on the cypress trees. She was thinking about the day ahead when she was startled by the ring of her cellphone. It must be one of the kids, she thought, asking what time they should arrive. She picked up her cellphone and looked at the caller ID, UNKNOWN. "Who could that be?" she asked herself. "Hello."

"I know what you did...," the frightening voice said.

"Who is this?" she demanded. But the caller kept talking. "What do you want?" she pleaded but the voice continued. "I have money," she said.

"...are going to pay," was the last thing she heard before the line went dead.

Scotty stumbled sleepily into the bathroom and sat on the toilet. When he was done he walked over to the vanity and looked at himself in the mirror. A little worse for the wear, he thought, probably should have stuck with beer. He ran a hand over his stubble and decided he'd have to shave. Leanne would have a fit if he didn't shave on Christmas. He walked over to the nightstand, picked up his phone and turned it on. When the phone came to life he scrolled through his messages hoping there weren't any work emergencies to cut into his holiday plans. When he saw UNKNOWN he stopped scrolling and sat down on the bed. He thought about whether he wanted to listen to the message or not. It could be a random sales call, he thought, I've gotten those from UNKNOWN before. But every time an UNKNOWN call came through, his heart raced and fear overcame him. Would any company be making sales calls on Christmas Day? He doubted it. He tapped the message and listened.

"I know what you did. You are a killer and you are going

to pay."

"Who is…" But the call dropped before he could finish his sentence. "Merry fucking Christmas."

The calls came again on New Year's Day, Valentine's Day, and March 15th, the ides of March. Scotty and Leanne didn't reveal to one another their menacing calls, and the mounting stress of keeping their terrible secrets was taking a toll on both. Scotty's drinking escalated dramatically. He kept bottles of bourbon in his car and desk. He drank in the mornings before work, at work and all night. He'd even started a couple of drunken brawls in public, and the Bayou Derkin rumor mill was saying that he was an alcoholic and unhinged. Leanne suspected as much but had no idea to what extent the problem existed. She was too preoccupied with her own fear of exposure or violence. She worried that the payment the caller referenced in his threat wasn't just blackmail, but payment with her life. She only went out at night if Scotty was with her. She withdrew from her cherished social organizations and kept a low profile, only venturing out to the grocery or shopping during the day. Her drinking had escalated too, and her mother worried that she had a problem. They were both shutting down, their lives shrinking into knotted fists of tension and fear, and there was nothing they could do to stop it.

On April Fool's day they each received the last call they would ever get from UNKNOWN. Scotty was at his office when it came, Leanne was at her mother's house. But this time the message was different. "I know what you did. You are a killer and you're going to pay. Before the month is over your sins will be avenged. Your time is up killer, and this is no April Fool."

Houston

February, 2016

Charlotte Claire sat at the kitchen island having a cup of coffee and scribbling out a guest list. She'd pulled out an old yearbook to make sure to leave no one out. Memories flooded back as she leafed through the pages filled with tiny head-shots of her senior class. How young they all looked, the boys with their shaggy, shoulder-length hair; the girls still wearing Farrah Fawcett hairdos long after the rest of the country had moved on to Madonna. Her hair, though, was long, straight and parted down the middle the way her mother insisted. In hindsight she realized the reason her mother had forbid Charlotte Claire to get a trendy hairdo was that they couldn't afford the expense of going to the hairdresser. She ran her fingers through a lock of her own hair and wondered what her mother would think if she knew how much she spent on a cut and color now. She guessed she spent as much on her hair in a month as her mother earned in the same time period working in the school cafeteria. What a great idea Timmy had in suggesting a class of '85 girls weekend in Houston. She could take them shopping, out to eat in some fun restaurants, take in a museum, and maybe even a nightclub if the super-religious ones didn't come. Even if Leanne didn't accept the invitation, it would still be fun to see the others. But Timmy's calculation was a good one. Leanne never skipped reunions or class gatherings because, despite her active social life and because of her snobbery, she had very few friends in Bayou Derkin. After she'd entered the guest list, Charlotte Claire started tapping out the evite.

Charlotte Claire Parker Latimer

Invites you to a

Bayou Derkin Class of '85 Girls Weekend

March 12-14

300 Newbury Circle

Houston, Texas

Food, Fun and Frolics for all

Come on girls, let's keep the reunion going!

RSVP by March 1ˢᵗ

Life is good!

She reviewed the text with satisfaction and clicked send. Now all she could do is wait and see who responded.

The first thing Charlotte Claire did every morning since sending the evite was check the RSVPs. Responses from the girls who usually attended these types of get-togethers came dribbling in daily, but a week went by with no response from Leanne. Charlotte Claire was getting anxious and frustrated. Even though she was looking forward to the weekend for its own merits, getting Leanne to Houston was the point.

At the end of two weeks she was beside herself. Timmy,

Amelie and Annie were texting daily for updates, which only made her more nervous. The cutoff date to RSVP was in three days and she knew that Leanne, a stickler for etiquette, would reply; but the waiting was difficult. She was reviewing the responses when she noticed that Annie had yet to reply as well. This wasn't unusual. Annie's shooting schedule was such that she frequently procrastinated responding to the group texts and emails. Charlotte Claire immediately texted the group.

Charlotte Claire

Annie, I noticed that you haven't responded to the evite. Maybe that's why Leanne hasn't RSVP'd. Too uncomfortable with you here. Please RSVP immediately that you can't come. And, sorry, you can't come.

Timmy

I think you're right.

Amelie

Me too.

Annie

Done.

Later that evening Charlotte Claire opened her email and saw the response from Leanne. She nervously opened the email. It read;

Dearest Charlotte Claire,

You are such a darling to host us "ole" gals. I wouldn't dream of missing this wonderful weekend and seeing your lovely home. Thank you for your kindness and generosity. This couldn't come at a better time.

Regards,

Leanne

Charlotte Claire was relieved, but also apprehensive. What they were planning could have serious consequences. She immediately sent a text to the others.

Charlotte Claire

She's coming.

Annie

Okay then.

Timmy

I knew she would come.

Amelie

What did she say?

Charlotte Claire

Usual gracious RSVP. Too bad she's never that gracious in person. One interesting thing, she said, "it couldn't come at a better time."

Annie

That IS interesting.

Charlotte Claire

Timmy how are things coming on your end?

Timmy

Well, apparently.

Charlotte Claire

Timmy, I wish you were coming.

Timmy

Thanks, but it's best I stay here and do what I'm doing.

Charlotte Claire

Must run kids. Lots to do.

Over the next two weeks Charlotte Claire organized menus, made reservations for meals and events, and prepared her house for the ten women who'd accepted her invitation. Like a seating chart for a formal dinner, she thoughtfully considered who'd share her guest rooms. She'd put two women in each bedroom, and she would stay alone in her own room. Stanley would go to a hotel for the weekend. Amelie would share with Leanne, to observe her behavior and glean any useful information. Every detail, including the baby monitors that would be put beneath Leanne's bed and in her bathroom, had been carefully considered and executed. Their plan, to seduce and manipulate Leanne into accepting the next unlikely invitation.

Flowers filled Charlotte Claire's home on the day the women were to arrive. The scent of rose's, tulips, and hydrangea left a sweet fragrance throughout the house. The group was driving three hours from Bayou Derkin in a caravan, and were due to arrive for a late lunch at 2 o'clock. Amelie had taken an early flight from Asheville, so they could discuss strategy. "We'll have to keep her drinking," Charlotte Claire said. "Not the whole time, but we want to get her drunk around bedtime when the two of you are alone in your room. You'll be very solicitous and sympathetic, ask her how things are going at home. Ask her if she's happy and how things with Scotty are."

"Won't she think that's a little forward?" Amelie asked. "We're not close, she may tell me to mind my own damn business."

"Not if she's drunk. She'd definitely say that if she were sober. But unhappy people love to unload when they're drunk."

"That makes sense."

"And if it looks like she's leaving the room to use her cell, volunteer to give her some privacy. Then head straight to my room and listen to the baby monitor. That's why I put you in that room, proximity."

"We should also pay attention to her interactions and general state of mind. Is she nervous, suspicious or depressed?"

"Obviously," Charlotte Claire said. "Also, one of us should have eyes on her at all times. If she's not with the group, chances are she could be on the phone with Scotty. I'm going to become her best friend this weekend. I'll make the invitation on the last day just before everyone is leaving. Hopefully I'll have buttered her up enough that she'll accept."

"Well, if there's anyone who can do that, Miss Charlotte Claire..." Amelie sang in Charlotte Claire's southern drawl.

"By the way, what's with all the flowers? It smells like a funeral home in here."

"I guess I went a little overboard."

"A little," Amelie teased.

Just before 2 o'clock that afternoon the caravan pulled into Charlotte Claire's circular driveway. She and Amelie greeted the women under the portico and directed them into the large foyer, where Charlotte Claire had put out champagne and hors d'oeuvres. The mood was festive. Amelie noted that Leanne was interacting naturally enough, though her smile seemed forced: most notably, her usual superior bearing was somewhat diminished. Was it worry, or maybe anxiety? Amelie exchanged glances with Charlotte Claire, who raised her eyebrows slightly. Yes, she'd noticed, too.

After the women had champagne, Charlotte Claire announced to the group, "Okay girls, let's have lunch." She showed them into the dining room, where a place card sat beside each of the elegant place settings. Charlotte Claire sat at the head of the table, flanked by Amelie on her right and Leanne on her left. Once the group chatter had broken down into smaller conversations, Charlotte Claire turned to Leanne and asked, "How are things back in Bayou Derkin?"

"Oh, I guess they're about the same as always," she said weakly. "You know, garden club, Catholic Daughter's...club stuff. Though I've pulled back a bit."

"Oh, really," Charlotte Claire asked. "Why?"

"It must be so time-consuming," Amelie said. "I've never been into any of that. When I get home from the office all I want to do is kick back and watch something on TV." Amelie is losing focus, Charlotte Claire thought; we need to keep Leanne on topic. She shot her a scolding glance.

"It is time-consuming," Leanne said.

"I know what you mean," Charlotte Claire said. "I'm on a

couple of boards and even with the kids living away I'm busy all the time. Did you lose interest...or are you just not enjoying it anymore?"

"Yes, that would be fair to say. And Mama's getting older. I've spent a lot of time with her the last few months."

"And how is Scotty these days?" Amelie asked.

Leanne put her fork down and took a swallow of wine. "Scotty seems distracted these days," she said with uncharacteristic candor. "It's probably work. Isn't it always work with men? Mama used to say the only things Daddy worried about was work and the Saints. I think I married my Daddy." Leanne laughed and took another long swallow of wine.

"Come with me, girls," Charlotte Claire said to the women after they'd finished lunch. "I'll show you where you're staying, and I'll have Alma bring your bags to your rooms. Amelie, you can show Leanne to hers since you're sharing."

"Come with me, roomie," Amelie said cheerfully. "I'll give you the grand tour."

Leanne unpacked while Amelie sat on the bed beside her. "It's terrible about Patty Hammond, isn't it?" Though she couldn't see Leanne's face, Amelie saw her back stiffen and she stopped unpacking for a moment.

"Yes," she said softly. "Death is always the most terrible when it comes without warning."

"I knew her well," Amelie said casually. "I mean, I knew her well when I was a kid. She and Mama worked together at the hospital. She used to come to our house a lot. I really liked her."

"Yes, Patty was well liked in town."

"She was really there for Mama when Elizabeth died."

Leanne continued putting items from her suitcase into the chest of drawers. Her face was expressionless, and her gaze never met Amelie's.

"Yes, Patty was very helpful...I mean...kind to everyone."

"And that Carla girl; I didn't really know her. She didn't grow up in Bayou Derkin. Did you know her?"

"Yes," she said as she hung her clothes in the closet, her back still to Amelie. "Carla Courville. We weren't friends." Leanne turned suddenly to Amelie as if she'd misspoken. "I mean we weren't enemies, we just weren't friends, really. I'd see her around town. Bayou Derkin is bigger than it used to be. Not everyone knows everyone like when we were young."

"Wasn't she dating Tom Burnett?"

"They were living together."

"Poor Tom, he's been through so much; losing his son, then his divorce and now this. It just seems unfair that some people have to endure so much hardship and others don't."

"No one should have to endure hardship, Amelie, but that's the way the world works. You just take care to make sure that you're not the one who does." Leanne put her empty suitcase in the closet and picked up her makeup kit. "If you'll excuse me for a bit, I'm going to freshen up." She went into the bathroom and closed the door before Amelie could respond. Amelie raced to Charlotte Claire's room, turned up the baby monitor and texted Charlotte Claire.

Amelie

Think I hit a nerve. In your room w/baby monitor.

Charlotte Claire

Be right up.

After a couple of minutes of rustling with what Amelie determined to be her cosmetics, the baby monitor went completely quiet. At first, she feared Leanne had discovered it and turned it off. But then she heard a pounding, as if Leanne were pounding on the counter top with her fist, followed by the sound of Leanne weeping softly. Charlotte Claire burst into the room and asked, "What?"

"No conversation, but I got quite a reaction." Amelie repeated the conversation and Leanne's reaction to it.

"This may be even easier than I thought," Charlotte Claire told her. "By the end of this weekend she'll be so happy to get out of Bayou Derkin she'd accept an invitation to hell."

"Well, isn't that what it is?"

Since the group had been out to dinner on Friday evening and out all day Saturday, Charlotte Claire thought a barbecue on the terrace would be a respite from all the activity. She was pleased, in all respects, with the way the weekend had progressed. It'd been a window into Leanne's current emotional state and her level of vulnerability. It was clear to Amelie and Charlotte Claire that Leanne was not the same haughty woman they'd seen at the reunion. She appeared shaken, even frightened at times; it not only confirmed their suspicions but would ultimately lend itself to the successful execution of their plan.

That evening the women sat under a tangerine sunset, gossiping, laughing and recounting high school exploits. "Do y'all remember old Mr. Dubois?" Jenny Karan asked. "He was a hateful old buzzard. He gave me so much hell in French because I'd slip into Cajun French instead of Parisian sometime. I couldn't help it. That's what Mama and Daddy spoke at home."

"Oh, I couldn't stand him, either," Amelie said. "And he had bad breath, old man breath."

"Do you remember the time junior year...?" Linda Howe asked through a fit of laughter. "In fifth hour French when he sneezed, and his false teeth went flying into the front row of the class? Oh, my God I never laughed so hard in my life!"

"Oh, that's right," Charlotte Claire giggled. "I'd forgotten all about that. Weren't you in that class too, Marla?"

"Yeah, and guess who sat to my right, Leanne?"

"Scotty?"

"Oh, I had such a crush on Scotty junior year," Marla crooned. "But alas, he had eyes for another."

"You sure dodged a bullet," Leanne said dryly.

"Leanne!" Paula Stone cried. "You don't mean that."

"Of course not; well, some days," Leanne joked. The women erupted in laughter. Charlotte Claire realized it was the first time she'd seen Leanne smile all evening.

"I think we could all say that about our husbands every now and then," Mary Ann Patterson agreed.

"Not me," Dorie Calhoun said, letting her words hang in the air for a moment. "I could say that every day." Again, the women burst into raucous laughter, none of them able to speak. As the merriment began to subside, Leanne's cellphone buzzed. Amelie crossed from where she'd been standing and stood behind Leanne so that she could see the name or number that came up on the screen.

"Hello?" Leanne said. Leanne's face tensed, her eyes narrowed, and her brow furrowed. "I have to take this," she said, standing and walking into the house.

"I hope everything's all right," Mary Ann said sympathetically after Leanne had gone into the house.

"Me, too," Linda added.

"She's been different lately," Dorie whispered. "I think something's going on with her."

"Yeah," Marla said sardonically. "I think it's the bullet I dodged."

"Marla!" Paula exclaimed. "You should be ashamed."

"You should have another drink, Paula," Marla responded dryly.

"No, I agree with Dorie," Jenny said. "She's been withdrawn; she hardly ever comes to Catholic Daughters anymore.

She's not running for president this year. She's been the president for the last three years and you know how she likes to be the boss."

"Do y'all see her often in Bayou Derkin?" Charlotte Claire asked.

"Rarely, and when I do it seems like she wants to get away as fast as she can," Paula responded.

"Maybe someone should go check on her," Amelie suggested.

"I'll go," Charlotte Claire said. "Y'all keep an eye on the grill. I'll be back in a minute. Amelie, can I see you for a second?" Once they were inside Charlotte Claire asked, "Who was the call from?"

"Unknown," she told her.

Charlotte Claire knocked gently on the guest room door. "Come in," Leanne said softly, wiping tears from her eyes. She looked at Charlotte Claire with a helpless smile and said, "I don't know what's gotten into me. I'm so emotional lately. I'd say it's menopause, but that ship's sailed."

"Is everything okay?" Charlotte Claire asked. "I hope the call wasn't bad news."

"No, no," she said. "Everything's fine. It was Mama. She sounded, oh, weak I guess, and it gave me a start-but she's fine, really."

"Is there anything I can do?"

"You've already done it. Just getting me out of town was a godsend. Maybe I should convince Scotty to take some time off and travel a bit."

"That gives me a great idea, Leanne." Seeing an opening, Charlotte Claire said, "I'm hosting an event in Miami for major donors to the Houston Opera Company. It's in mid-April. All the hoity-toity of Houston will be there. Timmy and Amelie are coming too. You and Scotty should join us. It's going to be quite an event. We have a block of rooms at the Ritz-Carlton

South Beach. I can hold a room for you. You could spend days at the pool or on the beach. It would be so good for you to get away. What do you say?"

"Charlotte Claire, that's so nice. I'd have to talk to Scotty. And you say Timmy and Amelie will be there, is Annie going?"

"Unfortunately, she can't come. She's on location in Philadelphia then."

"Oh, that's too bad. It would've been great to see her."

"In fact, maybe y'all should come a couple of days early. I don't think Stanley could come early, but I'll be there. I bet Timmy and Amelie would be up for it too. It would be fun."

"I'll talk to Scotty and get back to you."

"Sure, just let me know. I'd better get downstairs. There's no telling what those crazy bitches are up to."

"I'll be down in a minute. I just want to freshen up a bit."

"Take your time," Charlotte Claire told her. "We're not going anywhere."

On a hunch Charlotte Claire went into her bedroom and turned up the volume on the baby monitor. She could hear Leanne sniffling and rummaging around; probably fixing her makeup, she thought. Then she heard the tell-tale beep of a cell phone being dialed and Leanne's rapid-fire, "Why haven't you returned my calls? Busy is no excuse. When I call, you answer and if you can't, return the call. I won't be treated like a common bill collector. Yes. Yes. No, not really that much fun, but it's good being away. It's an impressive house. They must have more money than we realized. Yes, it's one of the best neighborhoods in Houston. Yes. What have you been doing? Well, please don't drink too much and make sure Lena comes in to clean in the morning. I'm not coming home to your mess. Well, tell her she'll have to skip church or find another job! We're going to have breakfast here and leave around noon, so I should be home by 3 o'clock. Charlotte Claire invited us to a fundraiser she's hosting in Miami for the Houston Opera

Company in mid-April and I think I'd like for us to go. I don't know the exact dates yet but who cares? You run the company and I own it; you can come and go as you please. Oh, really Scotty. I don't know why they are having an event in Miami to support the Houston Opera and she didn't ask me for a dona-tion...though it wouldn't be a bad idea. The cream of Houston society will be there. There's a shock, but I do care. These are well-connected families and we have two unmarried sons, and one of them is dating trailer trash. Besides, we need to get away. You haven't been yourself for months and I need to get out of Bayou Derkin sometimes. The town is so small it's smothering me. Well, it's either a long weekend in Miami or a month in Europe, your call. Yes, I thought you'd see it my way. I'll find out the exact dates and you can have your secretary block them out on your calendar. Okay, I will. I will. Bye."

Charlotte Claire turned off the baby monitor and went downstairs to find Amelie. When she reached the patio she said, "Hey girls, everyone doing okay out here? Everybody got what you need?"

"I could use some more champagne," Marla said.

"Me, too," Linda added.

"More champagne!" Jenny chanted.

"More champagne, more champagne..." The women joined in chanting merrily.

"Crazy bitches," Charlotte Claire joked. "Amelie, you want to give me a hand?"

"I think we got her," Charlotte Claire said as soon as she and Amelie entered the kitchen.

"Did she say yes?"

"Not yet, but I heard her talking to Scotty over the baby monitor and she pretty much bullied him into it."

"That's a bit of karma Timmy would love."

"I suspect she'll tell me tomorrow before they leave. Or

she'll send me one of her painfully gracious thank you notes accepting the invitation. But based on what she said to Scotty, I think they'll come."

The following Wednesday Charlotte Claire was rifling through the mail when she noticed a small ecru colored envelope made from extremely fine paper stock. She flipped the card over and saw *Leanne Reed Piper* engraved on the flap. Jesus, Charlotte Claire thought, she must have written this Sunday when she got home and mailed it first thing Monday morning; always the perfect hostess and gracious guest. She tore open the envelope and withdrew the card.

Dear Charlotte Claire,

Thank you for a truly extraordinary weekend. You are such a gracious hostess and your home is lovely. It was such fun spending time with you and the other girls. It's so good to spend time with old friends.

And thank you also for your kind invitation to the Houston Opera Company event in Miami. Scotty and I would love to come, and we would be pleased to make a donation, as well. We are both looking forward to some time away, meeting your lovely friends from Houston, but most of all seeing you.

Most Sincerely,

Leanne

Charlotte Claire texted the group immediately:

Charlotte Claire
We got'em.

Miami

Wednesday, April 13, 2016

Charlotte Claire lay with her eyes closed beside the pool at the Ritz- Carlton South Beach, relishing the warmth of the sun on her skin. Even the splashing and shrieks of children playing in the pool didn't bother her. She'd spent three days in Miami nailing down the last details for the Opera fundraiser that was to start the following Saturday. This was the first time she'd been able to relax and enjoy herself. Amelie and Timmy would be arriving from the airport at any minute, and she was looking forward to reviewing their plans for the following day. She reached for her cellphone to check the time and as she did, it rang. "Hey," she said happily upon seeing Timmy's name on the caller ID. "Where are y'all?"

"In the lobby," he replied. "Where are you?"

"At the pool; why don't you get changed and come meet me. I saved a couple of chaises for y'all."

"Great, we'll just be a few minutes."

Twenty minutes later Charlotte Claire was startled by something rubbing her foot. "Oh, Timmy, you dirty dog! You almost gave me a heart attack." Timmy laughed and dropped his bag on the chaise next to her's.

"I told him you'd jump out of your skin," Amelie laughed as she reached over to give her a hug. "He's like the bratty little brother we never had."

"You got that right," Charlotte Claire said. "How were your flights? They must have been on time because you showed up right on schedule."

"Uneventful," Amelie said.

"Mine was uneventful except the woman sitting next to me in First was reading *Happy Ending* and recognized me from the photo on the sleeve," he complained. "I'd wanted to sleep a little, but she talked practically the whole flight. I don't know how Annie does it. It's got to be way worse for her. People don't usually recognize me.

"Are you all squared away for the fundraiser?" Amelie asked.

"Yeah, just finished this morning," Charlotte Claire told them. "I'm totally free until the fundraiser starts on Saturday."

"What time are Scotty and Leanne arriving?" Timmy asked.

"They should get to the hotel around five, so they'll be with us for dinner I'm afraid," Charlotte Claire said. "I made a reservation for us at the Matador Room at 8 o'clock. I left a note for them with the front desk saying that we'd meet in the mezzanine bar at 7 o'clock for a drink before we go."

"I'll be curious to see how they act around us," Amelie said, as she sat on the chaise facing Charlotte Claire. "I still can't believe they accepted the invitation. They don't even particularly like us and vice versa. It was such a long shot."

"It was a bit of a long shot," Timmy offered. He pulled off his shirt and spread out on the chaise. "But not a total long shot. Remember that they must be pretty rattled these days, and getting out of Bayou Derkin had to sound good. And Leanne is such a social climber, I figured she'd jump at the chance to hobnob with the Opera donors. By the way, Charlotte Claire, did she make good on the donation?"

"Yes, believe it or not; five thousand. I was impressed. I mean, it's a fraction of what most of the donors attending gave, but still. I suspect she'll want to weasel her way on to the board but as we all know that won't be possible."

"Nope," Amelie agreed.

"Where's the waiter?" Timmy asked, looking around the pool area anxiously. "I've been here ten minutes and I'm still not holding a cocktail."

"Oh, Lord," Charlotte Claire laughed. "Look, there's a waiter over there. Flag him down."

Timmy stood and waived until the waiter took notice

and approached the group. He was a young, good-looking Hispanic man with broad shoulders and a muscular build. "What can I get for you?" he asked, his broad smile revealing perfect, white teeth.

"I'll have another Ketel One bloody," Charlotte Claire said.

"That sounds good," Amelie said. "I'll have that as well."

"And you, sir?" he asked Timmy.

"Absolut rocks with a splash of cranberry and a squeeze of lime."

"Absolutely," the waiter replied flirtatiously. "I'll be right back with that squeeze."

"Oh, my God," Amelie exclaimed. "That man is stunning. If I were 20 years younger..."

"You'd still need a penis," Charlotte Claire said dryly. "I don't think you're his type...at any age. He was flirting with you, Timmy."

"I know, right? He just made my day. Are we all set for tomorrow?" Timmy asked Charlotte Claire.

"Yeah, I have a driver picking us up here at 11:30 for the drive to Key Largo. That takes a little under an hour and a half. That will give us an hour and change to sightsee. I made a reservation at The Pilot House at 2 o'clock. Then we'll board the Sweet Revenge after lunch."

"Have you told Leanne and Scotty that Annie is joining us?" Amelie asked.

"No, Timmy and I discussed it, and we both think that if they know before we get to Key Largo, one or both may make some excuse to beg off. Once we have them in Key Largo, they're stuck."

"But how are you going to break it to them without it seeming suspicious?"

"They don't know which of us knows what," Timmy explained. "Charlotte Claire will just say she was saving it as a surprise for all of us. She'll tell them we're going to see Key Largo and have lunch. At lunch she'll say she has a couple of surprises for us and one is a boat tour of the coast. Then when we get to the marina and board, Annie will step out and... surprise!"

"And don't forget to act surprised," Charlotte Claire told them.

"What about the other stuff?" Amelie asked.

"Annie's taking care of that," Timmy explained. "The other supplies are already on the boat. So, as long as the weather holds, and so far, that's looking good, we're all set."

"I can't believe this is really happening," Amelie said.

"Well, it is," Charlotte Claire said soberly. "And if you're having any second thoughts, now is the time to say so. Nobody will blame you if you do." Charlotte Claire looked earnestly from Amelie to Timmy, awaiting their reply.

"Not me," Timmy said.

"Me either," Amelie said. "It has to be done."

"Okay then," Charlotte Claire said. "Okay."

"This is a nice hotel," Scotty said, after the bellhop left their room. "How the hell much am I paying for this?"

"Don't worry about it," Leanne said. She opened the envelope from Charlotte Claire and read the note. "They want us to meet them in the mezzanine bar at 7 and then dinner out at 8 o'clock; the Matador Room, hmm, sounds fancy."

"Sounds pricey to me."

"Oh, for Christ's sake Scotty, are you going to complain about the cost of everything the entire time we're here? We haven't been on a vacation in years and I'd like to enjoy myself."

"I don't see what possessed you to want to come to this thing in the first place. You don't even like Charlotte Claire and Amelie, and I could take them or leave them. And I sure don't feel like hanging around with that faggot for a weekend."

"I'd be willing to bet he's not thrilled about the prospect of hanging around with you, either. And we're not only going to be around them. Once the event starts on Saturday I for one am going to mingle and meet some of these people from Houston. Of course, I'll need a couple of introductions from Charlotte Claire, but once I've made a couple of connections I won't need her. Who would have ever thought that I would need social introductions from Charlotte Claire Parker?"

"Afraid of being shown up?"

"Hardly, afraid of being slowed down. There will be a lot of Houston oil money here this week, and we have two unmarried sons, one of whom is on the verge of getting serious with that poor white trash."

"You're a dog with a bone with that."

"I want our boys to marry well and to have access and opportunities beyond Bayou Derkin, and if I can make some connections to aid in that goal, then I will."

"Do you think those people are going to want to have anything to do with you? We're just country hicks with a little money as far as they're concerned; just a couple rungs up from trailer trash. As long as the boys can support themselves and stay out of jail...I don't give a shit about who they marry."

"That's a rather low bar."

"Whatever you say," Scotty said in exasperation. "I'm going to shower."

"Okay," she replied. "I'll unpack while you're in the bathroom." She was feeling more like her old self. Making Houston connections for her boys had given her a purpose, something to focus on. She was putting Scotty's sport jacket in the closet, going through the pockets, as she routinely did. She withdrew his cellphone from the breast pocket and scrolled through a vast number of undeleted voicemails. You'd think that someone who cheats, she thought, would have the common sense to delete them. She'd had suspicions over the previous couple of months that he'd been fooling around. He'd seemed jumpy and secretive, but as she scrolled through days of voicemails she didn't notice any unfamiliar numbers; work, the kids,

Andy Stoner, hers. Then she reached April 1ˢᵗ and stopped in shock. Scotty had a voicemail on April 1ˢᵗ from Unknown. I'm sure it's just a coincidence, she reassured herself as she selected the voicemail and played the message. "I know what you did and you're going to pay..." It was the same horrible voice that had been calling her on all the holidays. It was the same threatening warning as those she'd received. She nervously scrolled down to Valentine's Day: Unknown, New Year's Day: Unknown, Christmas: Unknown, Thanksgiving: Unknown, Halloween: Unknown. She put the phone back in Scotty's breast pocket and hung up the jacket. She opened her suitcase and began distractedly putting her clothes away. Who was this lunatic harassing the two of them, and what did they have on Scotty? Were her suspicions about Scotty being involved in the deaths of Patty Hammond and Carla Courville correct? Or was it the crazy accusations that he raped Annie? But, if it were true, the only people who knew about that are dead... except for Annie. Leanne sat on the edge of the bed for a moment, letting the thought sink in. That's it, she decided, it's Annie. She probably got some special effects person from her show to record the messages. They were always the same, except for the last one. She was probably doing this as some juvenile form of revenge. She took a bottle of bourbon from the mini-bar and poured herself a drink. She liked the idea that it was Annie making the threatening calls. If it is Annie, that's all it will be; threatening. Annie would never do anything violent, and she had plenty of money so why would she blackmail them? And she has no real proof that she or Scotty did anything. She relaxed at the thought of Annie as her surreptitious tormentor. After all, how dangerous could Annie be? But her relief waned when she realized that Annie wouldn't have any information to threaten *her* with. Her anxiety returned as her theory melted away. Who would hate them both enough to carry out this sadistic harassment? She could think of a few.

Timmy returned to his room to get ready for the evening. He felt heavy, as if the weight of doubt, worry-and, yes, maybe regret-had settled on him. It wasn't too late, he thought, we could abandon the plan and just get on with our lives, our very happy lives. Was this worth the risk? Now all he could think about was Joe. He would never want anything he did to jeopardize his life with Joe and the kids. He felt homesick, even though he'd just seen Joe that morning. He pulled out his phone and called him. Joe picked up on the second ring, "Hey, sweetie. How's Miami?"

"Good, good," he replied. "I spent most of the afternoon at the pool with the girls."

"Is the weather cooperating?"

"Yeah, it's good; warm and sunny. How are things up there?"

"You know," he said with a laugh, "typical work day; it's non-stop. How are the girls?"

"They're good," he replied half-heartedly. "It's great to see them."

"Is everything okay? For someone who's hanging out at the beach with his beloved girls, you sound a little down in the mouth."

"No, I'm fine, just a little homesick. I miss you already. And I'm..."

"What?"

"I guess I'm just second-guessing coming here. I'm not sure I should have."

"That's a first," he laughed. "I never heard you second-guess a trip with the girls before. And, hey, I'm glad you miss me. It would suck if you didn't, but I'm fine here, just missing you, too, but fine."

"I know."

"Look, these are your oldest and best friends. You guys have a bond and a loyalty that most people envy. You're always there for each other, you depend on each other and you never let each other down. I think Charlotte Claire wanted a little star power for her big event and she'd have been disappointed if you'd said no."

"I guess so."

"I know so. So, shake off the homesickness and concentrate on being there with your friends. This funk will pass in an hour or two and you'll have a blast. I love you for showing up for your friends. And I'll be here waiting with our girls and two excited little pups when you get home."

"Thanks, Joey; you always know what to say."

"I'll remind you of that the next time I say something you don't like."

"I love you, Joe."

"I love you too, sweetie. Now go have some fun!"

"Delia?" Amelie said into the phone.

"Why, Amelie Ardoin, is that you?" Delia asked excitedly. "What a nice surprise. I feel as if we haven't spoken in ages. How are you, honey?"

"I'm good," she replied weakly.

"What's wrong?" Delia asked. Amelie knew she would. Isn't that what she wanted? Isn't that the reason she'd called in the first place? Since moving to Asheville, Delia had become a mother figure, someone she turned to for comfort and support. She'd even thought Delia was a lot like her mother; gentle, kind, upbeat. Now, hearing her voice made her ache for her mother.

"Is everything okay with Deedee, Elizabeth?" Delia asked anxiously, "Pierre?"

"No, they're all fine. We're all fine. I guess I'm just a little homesick. I miss you. It's so ridiculous that we live in the same town and see so little of each other, and then I wait until I'm out of town to call. I get so wrapped up at work, but I need to make the time."

"Out of town?" Delia asked. "Where are you?"

"Miami."

"Lucky you," she crowed. "What are you doing in Miami, work or fun?"

"Fun," she said with laugh. "But it feels a little like work. I'm with my old friends from Bayou Derkin. One of them is hosting a boondoggle for major contributors to the Houston Opera Company, and she invited us to meet her here. Anyway, I'm just here for a few days and I was thinking about my mother, which made me think of you too, so I thought I'd give you a call."

"That's so sweet, Amelie. You've made my day, but, tell me, why do you sound so sad?"

"Oh, I don't know," she lied. "I guess being around my old friends from home brings back memories of my mother...and my sisters."

"How is Sara?"

"Oh, she's good. She and her husband live in north Louisiana now. But I was thinking of my other sister, Elizabeth, the one who died when we were kids."

"Yes, I remember you telling me about her. You poor dear, there's nothing worse than losing a child. What your mother must have gone through. What all of you must have gone through."

"You see, I was supposed to be watching her that day. I was the one who was supposed to take care of her," she said. Her eyes filled with tears and she placed her phone against her chest, so Delia wouldn't hear her cry.

"But you were just a child yourself."

"I let her down, and I want to make it right...but the thing is I can never make it right, can I? I can't bring her back."

"Oh Amelie, after all these years you're still grieving, and that's appropriate. But search your heart and your head and try to separate the pain of your loss from guilt you've placed on yourself. You're a grown woman now, and you must know in your heart that you're not to blame. That's what you'd say to anyone else, and that's what you need to accept. *That* is something you can make right. And that's the thing Elizabeth would want you to do."

"See?" Amelie said, wiping away tears, "That's why I call you. You always have wisdom to impart. And you're right, that is something I can make right."

When she hung up the phone Amelie sat on her bed and thought about their conversation. She realized this was why she was here. She'd failed Elizabeth all those years ago, but now she was here in Miami, and she was going to make things right.

Charlotte Claire took off her swimsuit, put on a robe and rifled through the mini bar for something to drink. She opened a split of champagne, poured herself a glass and curled up on the sofa with the current issue of *Vogue*. Her cell phone dinged. It was Annie.

Annie

How are things going over there? Have you seen them yet?

Charlotte Claire

Yes, Timmy and Amelie are here. Call me. I don't want to text.

A minute later her cell rang. "Hey," she said.

"Why didn't you want to text?" Annie asked.

"I wasn't sure where the conversation was going to go, and I don't think it's smart to write things down. Unless someone is recording us, our conversation will stay private. I've already mentioned that to Timmy and Amelie, too. For the time being we should send only the most mundane text messages, nothing about tomorrow."

"Good idea," Annie agreed. "You really should have gone into law enforcement...or crime. Anyway, have you seen them yet?"

"I'm assuming you're referring to Scotty and Leanne. No, we haven't seen them yet, but I know they checked in. The envelope I left for them with the front desk got picked up. We're meeting in the mezzanine bar for drinks at 7 o'clock. I'll tell them about the day trip to Key Largo tonight. There's no reason to think that everything won't go according to plan."

"I hope so. I'm just a little afraid that one of them will find some reason to beg off. If we can't get them to Key Largo tomorrow, the whole plan falls apart."

"I don't think you have to worry about *that*," Charlotte-Claire said ominously.

"What do you mean?" Annie asked. "What *do* I have to worry about then?"

"I'm a little worried about Timmy and Amelie. When we were at the pool today, they seemed, I don't know, conflicted."

"Did they say that?"

"No, not in so many words," Charlotte Claire conceded. "There was something about their demeanors that struck me today. They seemed apprehensive. And at one point I saw them exchange a look like; oh, shit what are we about to do?"

"Did you say anything; ask them if they were changing their minds?"

"Yeah, I asked them directly. They said they were all in. Maybe you could give them a call after we hang up just to make sure. Maybe it's just a case of nerves."

"I will."

"And what about you?" Charlotte Claire asked. "Do you have a case of nerves?"

"A little, I guess, but it hasn't lessened my resolve. And you?"

"Not in the slightest," Charlotte Claire said resolutely.

"You're a cool customer."

"Just a woman with a plan," Charlotte Claire said, "a very good plan."

Timmy walked through the lobby of the Ritz-Carlton South Beach with a sense of dread. He hated these two people, and now he was going to sit through not only drinks but dinner for the next couple of hours. He glanced down at his watch; 7:15. He was late, and he wasn't sorry. They would need to leave for dinner at 7:45, so now he only had to sit with that smug bitch and her bloviating asshole for half an hour. As soon as he stepped into the mezzanine bar he saw the group at a table across the room. Even from that distance he could read the look of admonition on Charlotte Claire's face. If she had been his mother, he would have been quaking in his boots. "Hi guys," he called out cheerfully, then changed his tone to one of contrition. "I'm so sorry I'm late. Just as I was walking out the door, my publisher called. My agent I can put off, but my publisher, never."

The group chuckled half-heartedly as Timmy took his seat. "Well, I wondered where you'd got to," Charlotte Claire said, giving him a coded look that was at once scolding and forgiving.

"Leanne, Scotty, great to see you. How was your trip?"

"It was fine," Leanne said. "Though New Orleans to Miami First Class is nothing to write home about."

"Oh yeah?" Scotty asked sardonically. "American Express is going to beg to differ when I get my statement at the end of the month." He let out a belly laugh. Leanne looked annoyed.

"We've been catching up with Charlotte Claire and Amelie, but Timmy, how've you been? Any new books coming out?" Leanne asked.

"As a matter of fact, I'm working on a new one now."

"What's it about?"

"Go on, Timmy," Amelie said mischievously.

"It's about a group of friends who return home for their

25th high school reunion."

"Oh!" Leanne cried.

"On the count of three," Scotty boomed, "Get out your cell phones and call your lawyers."

"I'm not worried," Charlotte Claire said confidently, "I'm one of the group of friends who returns."

"Me too," Amelie sang.

"Who said either of you were in the book?" Timmy asked playfully.

"Oh, I guess that means we're all in trouble now," Leanne said, looking around the table as she gulped her drink.

"Not all," Timmy said. "Just a couple. Where's that waiter?"

It was a warm, balmy night when the group stepped out of the hotel at 7:45 to wait for their Uber. When she noticed that Scotty and Leanne had hung back a bit and were deep in conversation, Charlotte Claire moved beside Timmy and said, "I should kill you for leaving us alone with them for the first 15 minutes."

"But you love me," he said. "So, you won't. But truly, I'm sorry. I just couldn't bring myself to *greet* Scotty Piper. I'm not that good an actor. Leanne I can manage, but Scotty not so much."

"Oh, I know Timmy, I'm just teasing you, not to be confused with bullying, which is never appropriate."

"Oh, so cool to tease someone who spent their childhood being bullied."

"I wish we could have taken them to Key Largo today," Amelie complained. "Instead of having to spend the whole evening with them and then the whole day again tomorrow."

"I would've tried that," Charlotte Claire said. "But I thought Leanne might say that they were too tired from traveling for a day trip; I would. I didn't feel I could push it. You heard them at drinks; it sounds as if they're looking forward to it. I want them to be in good spirits and feel totally comfortable."

"And, we want them three quarters of the way to being shit-faced by the time they get on the boat," Timmy added.

"That shouldn't be too hard," Amelie said. "Did you see the way they were throwing their drinks back tonight? They'll probably be fully shit-faced by the time they get on the boat."

"We just can't let either of them pass out too early. We need them mobile and semi-coherent for at least an hour," Timmy said.

"I wonder what they're talking about." Amelie asked. "They look so serious."

"Who knows? Who to kill next? Our Uber is here. Scotty, Leanne," Charlotte Claire called out. "Our car is here."

As they made the short drive from the hotel to The Matador Room, Scotty rolled down the tinted window and watched the hotels along Collins Avenue fly past.

"What do they call this kind of architecture?" Scotty asked.

"Depends on which buildings you're looking at," Timmy said. "The ones you're seeing now are mostly Art Deco from the 1930s. Further up you'll see some Mid-Century from the 1950s. It's all playful architecture. I think it's what gives Miami Beach such a whimsical vibe."

"Feels sort of like Disney World, only bigger," he replied.

"I'm sure that's just what everyone was thinking," Leanne said sarcastically.

"Whimsical," Scotty said derisively. "Who uses a word like whimsical? Well, I guess you would Timmy being you're a... writer and all." He knew he shouldn't let it bother him, but Timmy felt stung by the comment and even more so by the pause. Insert "faggot" here. There was an uncomfortable silence. I think I'll fuck with him, Timmy decided. Timmy slipped his cell phone from his jacket pocket and texted Charlotte Claire.

Timmy

Call my cell.

From the back-seat Timmy could see Charlotte Claire look at her phone and then turn toward him as if to say, huh? She turned back toward the front, slipped out her phone and surreptitiously dialed his number. When his phone rang he made a show of glancing at it before replacing it in his pocket. "Unknown," he blurted. Leanne turned toward him with a stricken look and Scotty leaned slowly back in his seat and rolled up the window.

"I never answer calls from Unknown," Timmy said.

Though they travelled occasionally, Leanne and Scotty were not accustomed to places like The Matador Room, with its elaborate gardens, velveteen-and-silk banquettes, and uniformly glamourous patrons. As they followed the maître d' through to their table Leanne tugged at her tunic with one hand, and placed the other over the gold chains on her chest, hoping she didn't look out of place.

When they'd reached the large round dining room in the center of the restaurant the maître d' stopped at a banquette, turned with a flourish and said, "Your table."

"This is lovely," Charlotte Claire said.

"Ladies?" Timmy asked. "Banquette or chairs?"

"I prefer a chair," Leanne said.

"Then why don't you and Scotty take the chairs," Timmy said. "Amelie, Charlotte Claire and I will take the banquette." They sat in an awkward silence reviewing the menus until drinks were served. Charlotte Claire, Amelie, and Timmy had agreed to have only minimal wine or champagne, so they could keep control of the evening and glean whatever information they might. By the time they ordered a second round of drinks, the tension receded and the conversation was more fluid.

"This place is pretty pricey," Scotty said, apropos of nothing.

"Scotty!" Leanne scolded. "You can dress him up, but you can't get him to stop talking about how much everything costs." She laughed at her own joke and took a long swallow from her cocktail.

"It is expensive," Charlotte Claire agreed. "But good news, kiddos, this one is on The Matador Room. We're hosting one of our events for the opera company here this week, so they invited me to bring some friends for dinner on them."

"Then I guess I'll be having that ribeye after all," Scotty said, laughing and polishing off his second martini.

"Pace yourself Scotty," Leanne warned. "That's your fourth martini tonight."

"And that's your third bourbon," he said slyly. "Woman, you've got some catching up to do."

As the two laughed at Scotty's joke, Timmy realized it was the closest he'd ever come to seeing them appear happy together. But it was alcohol, not love or goodwill that made them mirthful. Amelie and Charlotte Claire exchanged concerned glances, each for a different reason. Charlotte Claire hoped that they wouldn't make spectacles of themselves now that she was working with the restaurant for the opera company event, and Amelie feared that their drinking was such that they may not be able to pace themselves in Key Largo the next day. Amelie decided it might be the right time to steer the conversation toward Patty Hammond and Carla Courville. "What's the latest from Bayou Derkin?" she asked.

"Well, you know," Leanne said, "Nothing much ever happens in Bayou Derkin."

"How's your Mama?" Charlotte Claire asked, before Amelie could ask her follow-up question.

"As well as can be expected for her age," Leanne replied. "Her heart's not good, but she gets around pretty well. I try to spend as much time with her as I can."

"Hell," Scotty said. "You're with her all the time. Or else she comes over to our place. Leanne hardly sees anyone *but* her Mama."

"That's not true," Leanne protested.

"Damn sure is," he replied testily.

"How are the kids?" Timmy asked, fearing the conversation might escalate into a fight.

"They're doing great," Scotty boasted. "Matthew is killing it for the Tigers, but sports probably don't interest you too much, Timmy. Scotty Jr. is out of school and working full time for a law firm in New Orleans. He's got the world by the balls. Matt's dating a hot girl..."

"Oh please," Leanne said wearily. "Let's not get into that."

"Leanne doesn't think she comes from the right kind of people," he said putting air quotes around 'right.' "Now you know how your Mama felt when you married me."

"And your daughter?" Charlotte Claire asked.

"She is doing great," Leanne said proudly. "She's turned into such a wonderful mother. She loves being a stay-at-home mom. Tiffy is four now. And the baby, little Riley, she just gets more precious every day."

"Oh good," Charlotte Claire said. "I loved being a full-time mom when my kids were small."

"So, did I," Leanne agreed.

"I wish I could have," Amelie said. "I always had to work. But once I started the company I could bring Deedee to work with me and she loved it."

"I guess that made you a stay-at-work mom," Timmy joked.

"Guess so," Amelie laughed.

"And look how great it turned out," he continued. "Now she's working in the company with you."

"And she loves it," Amelie said. "The company will be hers one day."

"Oh, that's nice, too," Leanne said dismissively.

The waiter approached the table and another round of drinks was ordered. Amelie noticed that Scotty's eyelids were drooping, and Leanne had begun to slur her words. Worrying that they might need to leave soon, she decided that if they were to broach the subject of Patty and Carla tonight, now was the time. "It was terrible what happened to Patty Hammond and Carla Courville. Charlotte Claire was telling us about it. It really is so sad." Scotty placed his drink on the table and looked angrily at Amelie. Leanne's face turned ashen as she took another long swallow from her cocktail.

"Yeah, well, shit happens," Scotty said.

"Do they know how it happened?" Timmy asked.

"Yeah," Amelie said. "Do they know what the cause of the accident was? It seems so strange just to go off the bridge like that."

"What caused it?" Scotty barked. "Who the hell knows? Bad driving or a deer, maybe she had a blowout."

"No, it wasn't a blowout," Charlotte Claire told him. "I spoke to Tom Burnett at the wake. They had already pulled the car out of the river and inspected it. He said it wasn't a blowout. Poor Tom, first he loses his son and then this." Scotty looked around the dining room anxiously. Leanne downed the rest of her drink.

"Maybe someone ran her off the road," Leanne slurred. "Right, Scotty? That could have happened. Maybe someone just pulled up behind them or beside them and just ran them off the bridge."

Scotty turned to her angrily, his face growing red with rage. "Shut up, Leanne! You're drunk. You don't know what you're talking about." The waiter returned with the drinks and the group fell silent while he served them. Timmy looked at Charlotte Claire meaningfully, then he turned to Amelie.

After the waiter stepped away Timmy said carefully, "I suppose you're right, Leanne. Someone could have run them off the bridge. It's not unheard of, but why would someone do that? Patty was a great girl; seems like everyone liked her."

"Maybe she pissed someone off," she said pointedly. She stared straight at Timmy. "Maybe she got on someone's bad side, or maybe she knew something that she shouldn't have."

"That's enough, Leanne," Scotty said into his cocktail.

"I suppose it's a possibility," Amelie prodded. "But what could she have known that would be so bad that it would prompt someone to do something that extreme? It's hard to believe that something like that could happen in Bayou Derkin."

"Well you know what Miss Marple used to say," Timmy said.

"Who's Miss Marple?" Scotty asked.

"She's a character in a series of novels by Agatha Christie. She's a little old lady in a small English village who's brilliant and solves murders," Timmy replied.

"What did she say?" Amelie asked.

"All of the evil that you can find in the world can be found in a small English village...or, in this case, a small Southern town."

Scotty abruptly slid his chair away from the table, stood up and threw his napkin on his chair. "Excuse me," he said. "Men's room." He strode off.

Leanne picked up her drink and, with a drunken smile, took another sip of bourbon.

"I hope we didn't upset him," Charlotte Claire said. "He seemed upset by the conversation. It probably wasn't the best topic for dinner conversation anyway."

"Oh, don't worry," she said, swaying slightly in her chair. "He's a big boy. He'll get over it." She took another sip of her cocktail, smiled and said, "Or, maybe you should worry. Maybe he'll run you off the road one day too."

It took three rings to rouse Leanne from a deep, death-like sleep. It was only when she picked up the phone that she realized she'd gone to bed in her bra and panties, makeup and jewelry still on. "Yes, thank you," she said hoarsely into the receiver. "Scotty," she said. "Scotty, it's time to get up. That's our wake-up call. We have to be ready to go in an hour. Scotty!"

"All right, all right," he responded crossly. "I'm getting up, shit!"

She sat on the side of the bed and removed her necklace, watch and earrings. A sharp pain seemed as if it was piercing her brain. "Oh hell," she said. "I drank too much last night."

"No shit," Scotty said testily.

"Why didn't you stop me?"

"If I'd tried to stop you last night, I'd have lost a limb. Besides, I had my own fair share, didn't I?"

"I don't even remember coming back to the hotel."

"I'm not surprised. You probably also don't remember the conversation about Patty Hammond and Carla Courville. You probably don't remember suggesting that someone may have run them off the road. Have you lost your mind?"

"Oh no," she said, turning to him and putting her hand over her mouth.

"Look, I don't know what you know or what you think you know. What I do know is that you need to keep your mouth shut. Do you hear me? And today you need to lay off the booze...or at least dial it back. I don't know why they brought that up anyway. Why the fuck would they care about Patty Hammond?"

"I'm sure they brought it up just because it's hometown gossip, that's all." She stood up and crossed over to him. "I don't think it's anything more significant than that."

"Now we have to spend the entire day with them. I hope they don't bring that shit up again."

"Let's not go, Scotty," Leanne said suddenly.

"What?"

"Let's not go. We can beg off, tell them we're too hung over. It's not even a lie."

"We're going."

"But…"

"We're going," he repeated emphatically. "Charlotte Claire planned the whole day and we're going. Hell, seeing Key Largo is about the only thing that sounds like any fun on this trip. Besides, it will look…" He stopped himself before he said 'suspicious.' "It'd be rude to beg off at the last minute. I can't believe I have to tell you that. You're the one who's usually the etiquette police."

"I know," she conceded. "I know. It's just that I have a bad feeling. I don't know why, but I do."

"Bad feeling or not, we're going. You'd better start getting ready."

"All right," she said softly. She crossed to the phone and pushed the button for room service. "Would you send up two Bloody Mary's'…and make them doubles."

"There they are," Charlotte Claire said as Leanne and Scotty stepped out of the hotel into the blazing sunlight. "The car's here," she called out to them, pointing to a large, black SUV. "Climb on in. Who wants where?"

"I'll take the way back," Timmy volunteered.

"Okay then," Charlotte Claire said cheerfully. "Amelie and I will take the middle seat and Leanne and Scotty, y'all can have the first seat." As the driver pulled away from the hotel Charlotte Claire asked, "How are y'all feeling this morning?" They all began to laugh.

"Better now," Leanne said, turning in her seat to face the others. "A little hair of the dog put things right."

"I hope y'all saved room, because I brought us a little surprise," Charlotte Claire said, opening a cooler on the floor beside her.

"Oh, what?" Amelie asked, "I love surprises!"

"Bloody Marys' for the road, you're welcome." Charlotte Claire passed out covered plastic cups filled with the spicy, red drinks. "Enjoy."

"You know how to travel, Charlotte Claire," Timmy said. "Let's not forget the man in the way back."

The hour and a half drive from Miami Beach to Key Largo passed quickly. The day was clear and sunny, and once they'd reached the Southern Glades the vistas unfolded like a panoramic postcard. While Scotty was mostly quiet, the others chattered about high school, teachers, and old crushes, which kept the mood pleasant and light-hearted. It wasn't until they'd passed Manatee Bay, where the light played on the water like stars, that Scotty seemed to relax and join in the conversation. It all felt so normal that Timmy had to remind himself of what they'd come to do.

When they reached Key Largo, Charlotte Claire instructed the driver to let them out on Overseas Highway, the main tourist drag. The women shopped along the way, but except for the smoke shop, where Scotty bought a cigar and Timmy a pack of cigarettes, the men found little of interest. Filling the empty silence with awkward small talk was wearing on them both. At his first opportunity Timmy pulled Charlotte Claire aside. "We need to go somewhere for a drink. I think it's important to keep a steady stream of alcohol in them. Besides, if I have to keep making conversation with Scotty, I'm going to kill myself."

"Do you think it's any easier with Leanne?"

"Yes."

"You're probably right."

"Look, there's a place I spotted on the next block, Snook's Bayside, why don't you suggest we pop in for a cocktail...or two."

When Amelie and Leanne emerged from a craft shop, Charlotte Claire said, "How about a cocktail, ladies? I think Timmy and Scotty are less enthusiastic shoppers than we are."

"That's a great suggestion," Scotty said.

"I'm in," Amelie said cheerfully. "I'm always up for a cocktail."

"Great," Timmy said. "I spotted a place on the next block that looks fun, full of Key Largo color."

"You weren't kidding about the Key Largo color," Charlotte Claire said when they were seated. "Let's see: Thatched roof, tiki torches, conch shells, and palm trees. All that's missing are some hula dancers."

"They actually have hula dancers. See?" Timmy said, turning over the menu and indicating the photo inside. "But they don't start performing until evening."

"I think it's fun," Amelie said.

"It's cute," Leanne agreed.

After they'd placed their drink orders Leanne excused herself to go to the ladies' room. "That's a good idea," Scotty said. "I think I'll go unload before I load up again."

"Thank God, I needed a break," Amelie said when they'd left the table.

"Me, too," Timmy agreed. "Making small talk with Scotty is like pulling teeth...with your fingers."

"Oh shit," Charlotte Claire said under her breath.

"What?" Timmy asked urgently.

"The couple that just walked in; I know them. Amelie, switch seats with me." Charlotte Claire moved to the other side of the table so her back was to the restaurants entrance. "That's Ernie and Rita Goldman. They're here for the opera event. They live near us. We have dinner with them from time to time. If they see me they'll want to join us, and that would ruin everything."

"What do you mean?" Amelie asked.

"We're going to try to get Scotty and Leanne drunk. They'll notice, and they'll think it odd; especially if the three of us aren't drinking that much. And what if Scotty or Leanne mentions that we're going to the marina for lunch? They'll want to join us. I know them. They are socially aggressive, and they'll ask. We've spent too much time, energy and money to abort at this point."

"Just keep your back to them," Timmy said. "They're seated near the entrance. We'll just have to wait them out. Let's hope they're not ordering a meal."

"Scotty's coming back," Amelie warned.

"Shit," Timmy said. "Rita looks like she's headed to the ladies' room. She's coming this way. Don't say anything and turn your head a little to the left."

Scotty reached the table just as Rita was passing. To make room for her to pass he turned his back to the table, standing directly between Charlotte Claire and Rita. "Thank God," she mouthed to Timmy and Amelie as Rita walked past. Just as Rita reached the ladies' room Leanne walked out. Charlotte Claire's heart raced at the thought of Rita's return trip and how she might avoid being seen. As Leanne took her seat, the waitress approached with their drinks.

"Perfect timing," Timmy said to Leanne.

"I pride myself on never being late for a cocktail," she joked.

"Okay, let's see," the pretty blonde waitress said. "I have a Bloody for the lady, a gin martini for the gentleman, and three Chardonnay's for the other gentlemen and ladies. Can I get you anything else? Would you like to order something from the menu?"

"No, thank you," Charlotte Claire said. "We're having lunch at the marina."

"You'll have to try us next time," she suggested. "The food is really great here."

"We will," Charlotte Claire was saying when she noticed Rita exiting the ladies room and walking toward their table. As the waitress was turning to walk away Charlotte Claire's hand flew out in front of her and knocked over her wine glass.

Just as Rita was about to reach them the waitress turned back, standing beside Charlotte Claire and blocking her from Rita's view.

"Oh goodness, you had a little accident," the waitress said sweetly. "Let me clear this up and I'll get you another Chardonnay."

"Thank you," Charlotte Claire said apologetically. "That was so clumsy of me. I'm so sorry."

"Not a problem," she said.

After an hour and two more rounds of drinks, Ernie and Rita Goldman paid their check and left the restaurant. "They're leaving," Timmy whispered to Charlotte Claire.

"Thank God, I've got to pee," she whispered back. Her nerves were frayed from modulating her voice so she wouldn't be heard, and worrying about how she would manage avoiding them again should one of them make another trip to the bathroom. "What say we get the check and head over to the marina?" Charlotte Claire suggested.

"Sounds like a plan," Scotty slurred.

"Great idea," Timmy agreed.

"I love a marina," Leanne said, setting her cocktail down heavily on the table.

"Excellent," Charlotte Claire said. "I'll just call the driver to pick us up after I visit the ladies' room. Timmy, here's my credit card."

"You don't have to pay for us," Amelie said.

"Today's on me," she replied. "No arguments."

Leaving the restaurant Leanne was swaying and Scotty stumbled, instinctively grabbing Timmy's shoulder for support. "Thanks, old man," he slurred.

"No worries...old man." Timmy looked over at Charlotte Claire and Amelie and gave them the thumbs up. "Drunk," he mouthed to them.

On the short drive to the marina Charlotte Claire pulled out her phone and texted Annie.

Charlotte Claire

How far away are you?

Annie

About an hour.

Charlotte Claire

Good, see you at 6.

"I'm getting a little peckish," Leanne called out from the first set of seats in the SUV. "It's kind of on the late side for lunch. I probably shouldn't have had all those Bloody Marys on an empty stomach."

"You probably shouldn't have them on a full stomach neither," Scotty said sarcastically. Leanne turned and glared at him.

"I think y'all are going to like The Pilot House," Charlotte Claire said, hoping to distract Leanne and Scotty from what she feared could become a drunken brawl. All they needed was for one of them to get pissy and storm off. "It was very highly recommended by the concierge at the hotel."

"I'm sure we'll love it," Leanne told her.

It was 2 o'clock when they arrived at the restaurant. Leanne and Scotty were unsteady on their feet as they made their way from the SUV to the entrance. The hostess asked if they'd prefer to dine in the indoor dining room or The Glass Bottom Bar, which was outdoors and faced the water. "Oh, outside by the water," Leanne said immediately. "We may get to see the sunset on the water if we're here long enough."

"You'll definitely see sunset on the water," Charlotte Claire assured her. The Pilot House turned out to be a little rougher than Charlotte Claire would have liked, but it was at the marina and they'd be able to walk to Annie's boat. The waitress approached them for a drink order as soon as they were seated. "I'll have a Chardonnay," Charlotte Claire said.

"Me too," Amelie agreed.

"Make that three," Timmy added.

"And you, Miss?" the waitress asked.

"I think I'll just have a tonic and lime," Leanne told her. Amelie looked at Charlotte Claire and Timmy anxiously. "I think I'd better slow it down a bit. All those Bloody Marys and no food; I think I'll wait and have wine with dinner."

"I think I'll do the same," Scotty said. "Just club soda and lime for me."

"Are you sure?" Amelie asked, as casually as she could.

"Well," Scotty said, seeming to reconsider. "What the hell. I'm not in Key Largo every day. I'll have a vodka martini; Absolut if you have it."

"Scotty," Leanne snapped.

"What?" he asked loudly. "I'll have a goddamned drink if I want a goddamned drink."

"Lower your voice, you're making as ass of yourself," she hissed. "And don't you dare speak to me that way."

"I'll speak as loud as I want, goddammit," Scotty yelled, his face red with fury, as he slammed his fist on the table. Everyone grew silent and within seconds the manager, a tall lanky man with overly tanned skin, approached the table.

"Is there a problem here?" he asked.

"No," Scotty said. "There's no problem. Just a little disagreement that got out of hand. But it's over now."

"Good," he said with a wary smile. "We like our patrons to have a good time and enjoy themselves."

He walked away, leaving the frightened waitress standing

by timidly, not sure of what to do. Scotty said, "Why don't you cancel that martini after all."

"Yes, sir," she said softly, skittering away.

Amelie gently kicked Charlotte Claire under the table and said, "Excuse me, I'm going to visit the ladies' room."

"I'll go with you," Charlotte Claire said. "Excuse us, we won't be long." Once they got there she asked, "Why are you kicking me under the table?"

"If they stop drinking it could ruin everything," Amelie said excitedly.

"I thought that's what it was. The look on your face when they didn't order cocktails was priceless. You need to get a poker face."

"Aren't you concerned?"

"Not really, you've seen the way they drink. You don't think they're going to suddenly stop drinking, do you?"

"I guess not."

"We're in control here. We'll encourage them to have wine with dinner and once we're on the boat we'll make cocktails or open a bottle of wine. And we have our secret weapon on the boat. Try to relax. If you get too jumpy they're going to think something's up. We have to get them on that boat. When they see Annie, they may get panicky, so we need to be as casual and relaxed as possible. We just have to make sure they're on the boat before Annie comes out from below deck. It would be too awkward for them to leave at that point."

"Right," Amelie agreed.

"Amelie, we've come too far to turn back now. We're almost there. Are you going to be able to hold it together? "

"I think so."

"We'd better get back to the table. If they don't order a glass of wine, I'll order a bottle. It might make it easier to convince them to have a drink. Just don't worry."

"You're right, I won't. By the way, pretty smooth move, knocking your wine glass over so that your friend wouldn't see you."

"Yeah, I always wanted to do that."

When they ordered lunch, Charlotte Claire ordered a bottle of wine to have before the meal, and when the wine was served she ordered another to be served with the meal. As she predicted, Leanne and Scotty couldn't resist the temptation to drink. After lunch Charlotte Claire suggested a bottle of champagne with dessert, and after dessert she ordered another. They'd been at the restaurant for three and a half hours when Charlotte Claire asked for the check. She felt that Leanne and Scotty were sufficiently buzzed but not too drunk. As they walked to the edge of the deck to take in the view Charlotte Claire whispereds to Amelie, "See? All according to plan."

"It's been a beautiful day, Charlotte Claire," Leanne slurred. "Just beautiful, and we have you to thank for it. It was so generous of you to treat us to Key Largo."

"Yes, thank you, Charlotte Claire," Timmy added. "It has been a fun day."

"Well," Charlotte Claire said, "It's not over yet. I have a little surprise for y'all."

"Ooh," Amelie said, feigning surprise. "I love surprises. What is it?"

"I've chartered a boat, a small yacht actually, to take us out on the water. They'll take us up and down the coast for a couple of hours. That's why we had lunch at the marina. We can walk to the boat from here."

"You're full of surprises," Timmy said.

"I love being on the water," Scotty said. "And it'll be a nice night for it. That must have set you back a pretty penny."

"Scotty!" Leanne snapped. "Does it always have to be about money?"

"It wasn't so much," Charlotte Claire interjected, fearing that the tension between the couple might escalate.

"Do you have someone to pilot the boat?" Scotty asked,

pointedly ignoring Leanne's remark.

"Oh yes, we have someone." Charlotte Claire glanced at Timmy and Amelie conspiratorially.

"It's a chartered boat, Scotty," Leanne told him impatiently. "Of course, there's someone to pilot the boat."

"Let's see," Charlotte Claire was saying as the group walked past rows of watercraft. "I think it should be down this way. Right, she said turn left at the center of the marina and walk down to the end. It's slip 51."

"The pilot is a woman?" Scotty asked with a lascivious grin.

"Try and control yourself," Leanne warned.

Charlotte Claire felt a wave of panic over the slip. But she composed herself and said, "Yes, we women do all kinds of things now-a-days." The group grew silent as they walked toward the yacht, the clatter of their footfall on the boardwalk, the din from The Pilot House and the sound of splashing water filling the void. When they'd reached slip 51 Charlotte Claire said, "She told us just to come aboard if we don't see her on deck. I'll go down below to let her know we're here."

"What a beautiful vessel," Timmy said as they boarded.

"Sure as hell is," Scotty agreed. "Like to have one of these for myself."

"Don't get any ideas," Leanne told him.

"I've got another surprise for everyone," Charlotte Claire announced once they'd all boarded. "You can come out now," she called out towards below deck. Annie climbed the steps and appeared on deck, smiling broadly.

"Surprise!"

Scotty and Leanne turned stunned gazes on one another.

"Oh, my God!" Amelie called out. "I can't believe you're here!"

"I thought you had location shooting. This is fantastic. Isn't this great, guys?" Timmy asked Leanne and Scotty.

"This really is a surprise," Leanne said brightly, trying to recover herself. "A really, really nice surprise. Don't you think so, Scotty?"

"Hell yes," he lied. "The more the merrier. Charlotte Claire, you sure know how to pull the wool over our eyes."

"I thought you'd be pleased."

"Oh, we definitely are...pleased," Leanne gushed.

"We can all sit around and catch up once I get us out of the marina," Annie said, crossing the deck to free the stern line. "Timmy, can you untie the bow line?" He looked at her helplessly. "The rope at the very front of the boat," she instructed.

"Aye-aye, captain," he said, saluting.

"Wait a minute," Scotty said in disbelief. "Is there someone else down there, or are you piloting the boat?"

"Just call me Captain Annie," she said, looking back over her shoulder at him.

"Do you know what you're doing?" Leanne asked anxiously. "I mean have you done this before?"

"Oh sure," she replied. "Dozens of times. We have a boat in California and this boat is mine. It's relatively new, but I've taken it out a few times already."

"I thought you said you'd chartered a boat," Scotty said to Charlotte Claire.

"Just a little white lie," she said coquettishly. "I couldn't very well tell you we'd being going out on Annie's boat without spoiling the surprise."

Leanne looked at Scotty anxiously and then at the dock. Every impulse was telling her to get off the boat. Scotty stood speechless looking at Annie as she took her seat behind the wheel."

"Okay," Annie called out, pulling slowly out of the slip.

Leanne looked at Scotty, barely able to mask her horror. What are they playing at, she wondered, something doesn't feel right. She sat away from the others, who'd gathered around Annie as she drove them away from the marina and into the open water. They were talking and laughing, the wind blowing their hair and the orange light of the sunset bathing their faces. It all seemed so normal, picturesque even, but all she felt was apprehension. Scotty sat down beside her and seemed oddly sober, she thought. "What have you gotten us into?" he whispered.

"I could ask you the same thing," she replied.

Timmy looked back from the pilot house toward Leanne and Scotty. "They looked shell-shocked," he told them.

"We'd better call them over here," Charlotte Claire said. "We need to make conversation with them; keep it light."

"I'll anchor soon so we can all sit together and have a glass of wine and some hors d'oeuvres," Annie whispered. "The Xanax is in the galley. Timmy, you can help me with that. Call them over, Amelie."

"Hey, guys," Amelie called out cheerfully. "Come on over. You're missing the sunset."

Scotty and Leanne made their way gingerly toward the pilot house. "Y'all were missing all the fun back there," Annie said cheerfully. "This is where the action is."

"This is some boat, Annie," Scotty said. "How many feet is she?"

"Sixty-five, I can't wait to show you below deck; it's spectacular."

"This must have cost...oh wait. I'm not supposed to talk about money anymore." The group chuckled good-naturedly. "Leanne disapproves."

"You're learning, though," she replied. "Who says you can't teach an old dog new tricks?"

"My husband," Timmy joked.

"I'm so glad y'all could make it to Miami," Annie said to the group. "And especially you guys, Leanne and Scotty."

"Hey," Amelie said, "Timmy, I think we've just been

insulted."

"Now, Amelie, you know what I mean. I see you guys fairly often. But when Charlotte Claire told me you were coming I was elated. In fact, that was one of the reasons that I changed my plans and decided to come."

"Really?" Leanne asked incredulously. "Annie, what a really sweet thing to say."

"I mean it. You're really the reason I'm here."

"And I want to thank all of you for coming to Miami," Charlotte Claire said. "You're good friends for coming all this way to show support for the opera company. And the event is going to be a lot more fun because you're here."

"Wouldn't have missed it for the world," Amelie said.

"Timmy, why don't you go to the galley and grab a couple bottles of wine and some glasses," Annie suggested. "Cruising is always more fun with wine."

"How does this spot look to you guys?" Annie asked after they'd cruised the coast for two hours and consumed several more bottles of wine. "How does it look to anchor?"

"Well, to be perfectly honest Annie," Timmy said, "We're in the middle of the ocean. It all looks pretty much the same to me."

"I think I'll drop anchor here." Annie slowed the boat gradually before turning off the engine. "I'm ready for another glass of wine. Shall we?"

"Let's do it," Timmy said.

When the group moved from the pilot house to the deck, Leanne and Scotty hung back. Once she was sure that the others were out of earshot Leanne said, "I think we over-reacted."

"Yeah, I guess so." Scotty admitted.

"I could use another glass of wine now, too." Leanne looked at him and smiled uncertainly.

"Me, too."

"Well, that wine's not going to pour itself," Timmy said after Leanne and Scotty joined the others on deck.

"Oh, right," Annie laughed. "I forgot, that's my job; we'll be right back."

"Can you open this for me?" Annie handed Timmy the corkscrew and a bottle of red wine. She glanced toward the deck and saw Leanne and Scotty sitting on the upholstered bench that faced the wet bar in the galley. Leanne was looking towards Amelie, but Scotty's line of sight directly faced Annie. "Timmy, stand right there, facing me." Timmy moved so that he blocked Scotty's view of Annie. She slipped two tiny, plastic packets from the pocket of her shorts.

"What did you get?" Timmy asked.

"Xanax, Leanne had a prescription for them in her medicine cabinet, so did Scotty."

"How much are you going to give them?"

"Eight milligrams each," she said, emptying the contents of one of the packets into the wine glass. "My therapist said that eight milligrams would put someone to sleep for an hour or so. Considering what they've been drinking today, it shouldn't take long."

"Do you think it was wise to ask your therapist that?"

"I told him I was researching a role, and anyway, doctor-patient confidentiality would apply." She poured the second packet into another wine glass and filled them both with wine. "Here," she said, handing Timmy the two glasses, "Go ahead and bring theirs out. I don't want to risk mixing up the glasses by mistake."

Timmy took the glasses to the deck and handed the first to Leanne and the second to Scotty.

"Scotty," Leanne said in alarm. "Really, where are your manners? Ladies first; give that glass to Amelie."

"Oh, sorry, Amelie," he said in surprise as he offered the

glass to her.

Timmy and Amelie looked at each other for a moment. "Oh, that's all right. I don't think I'm really in the mood for red. I think I'll see if Annie has a bottle of white on board."

"I'll ask her when I go back in," Timmy said, relieved. "I'll bring it out to you." Timmy went back into the galley, leaned on the wet bar with both hands and breathed a sigh of relief. "That was close," he told Annie.

"What was close?"

"Leanne just insisted to Scotty that Amelie take one of the glasses of wine; ladies first and all that. I almost had a heart attack."

"What about Charlotte Claire?"

"Luckily she was in the bathroom."

"How'd you deal with it?"

"Some quick thinking on Amelie's part. Oh yeah, that reminds me. Do you have white wine?"

"In the wine fridge...*Oh!* That *was* quick thinking."

As he uncorked the white wine Timmy looked out to find Leanne and Scotty sipping their wine, and Charlotte Claire, who'd returned from the bathroom. "When is he ever going to take that fucking blazer off?" he asked in frustration. "We need to get him out of that jacket before he passes out. Otherwise it could be difficult to get off. He's a big guy."

"I'll take care of it," Annie said.

"We'd better get back out there. Grab Charlotte Claire's wine, would you?"

"There's no way in hell I'm throwing my hard-earned money away," Scotty was saying, "on the damn Houston Opera Company. No offense Charlotte Claire."

"None taken."

"I didn't mind the 5K donation," he went on. "But that was for this event. That was a one-time thing."

"What's going on out here?" Timmy asked, handing the

glass of wine to Amelie.

"Leanne got it in her head that she wants to join up..."

"Support and contribute," Leanne interrupted.

"Support and contribute to the Houston Opera Company. Fuck, it's in Houston, three hours away! How much sense does that make?"

"Three hours is not that far. We drive that far to see the Saints play, at least four or five times a season. And I'd like to support the arts and expand our social circle. Oh, never mind, we'll talk about it later."

"Not if I see you first," he said, laughing loudly at his own joke. "What you really want is to hob-nob with those Houston snobs. Oh, no offense, Charlotte Claire."

"None taken."

"She wants to fix our boy up..."

"I said we'd talk about it later," Leanne said harshly.

Scotty put both his hands up in mock surrender. As Annie refilled their glasses she said, "Scotty, why don't you take off your blazer? You'll be more comfortable. Here, let me hang it up for you." He removed the blazer and handed it to her. He was starting to look tired, she thought. His eyes were droopy, and his body was draped across the bench like a heavy, wet blanket. The feel of his jacket in her hand filled her with disgust. She'd not touched him since he boarded the yacht; no kiss hello, no shaking hands. The thought of him and what he had done to her made her almost physically ill. "Be right back." Inside the galley she quickly hung up the jacket and retreated to a corner where she couldn't be seen. Tears welled up in her eyes and she had to put her hand over her mouth to keep from being heard. After a moment she recovered her composure. She checked herself in the mirror and blotted her eyes with a tissue. She returned to the deck carrying a small case. "Hey guys, look what I bought." She set the case on the table, opened it and removed a small handgun. A jolt went through Leanne. She turned to Scotty, panicked, but he was too drunk and seemed unfazed.

"Oh, my God," Timmy said in mock disbelief. "You bought a gun!"

"Yup,"

"Why on earth would you buy a gun?" he asked her.

"Protection, why else?"

"I could never own a gun," he said. "They give me the creeps."

"Me too," Amelie agreed.

"I feel the same, no guns for me," Leanne said, as casually as she could.

"I have a handgun," Charlotte Claire said. "Stanley bought it for me. There are a lot of bad people out there. I feel safer with it. I keep it in my car."

"Can I see that?" Scotty asked.

"Sure," Annie said. She replaced the gun in its container, closed the lid and slid it across the table to Scotty. He opened the container and removed the gun.

"How's she handle?" he asked Annie.

"Pretty smoothly. She's got a little kick, but once you get used to it, it's not bad. You want to give it a try?"

"Out here?" he asked. "Sure."

"Oh, Scotty," Leanne protested. "No, it's not safe."

"Oh, it's perfectly safe," Annie told her. "Especially out here. He can just fire it up into the air."

"Sure," Charlotte Claire agreed. "Scotty knows how to handle a firearm safely."

"Calm down, Leanne," Scotty said. "I know what I'm doing."

"Let's go to the bow, away from the second amendment haters," Annie suggested. "Charlotte Claire, do you want to come with us?"

"No, I'm good. I'll stay here with my wine."

Annie and Scotty walked to the bow of the boat, Scotty carrying the gun in its case. "It's a Sig Saur P226. The clip holds up to twenty rounds. The clip is already in," she told him. He removed the gun, glanced over at Annie excitedly, pointed the gun in the air and fired.

"Oh, that's nice," he said.

"Go ahead, try it again." He pointed the gun in the air and fired again.

"How much did this set you back?"

"A little over a thousand. I think if you fire that way, it's safe," she said, pointing east. "As long as you don't see another boat, it should be harmless." He turned facing east and fired directly in front of him. He looked at Annie with a loopy smile. "Go ahead, take a couple more." He pointed the gun east and fired again. "We should get back to the others," Annie said, after he'd fired several times. She asked Scotty to replace the gun in its case and then they joined the others.

"Would anyone like more wine?" Amelie asked when they'd returned.

"Oh, good lord, no," Leanne said. "I couldn't possibly. I am so sleepy."

"Why don't you go to one of the staterooms below and lie down for a few minutes," Annie suggested.

"I think a catnap would do me a world of good; maybe just 10 or 15 minutes to give me a second wind. Would you mind?"

"Not at all," Annie told her. "Y'all had a long day. It's no wonder you're sleepy. Come with me. I'll put you in one of the staterooms."

"This boat is to die for," Leanne said as Annie led her to the stateroom.

"That's exactly how I feel," Annie replied.

"I have to confess I'm a little embarrassed about needing a nap."

"Don't be. Anyway, no one ever died of embarrassment."

By the time Annie had returned from below deck, Scotty

had become visibly altered. "Are you feeling alright, Scotty?"

"Well, I believe I'm feeling fine," he slurred. He leaned forward awkwardly to pick up his glass.

"If you'd like to lie down, you could join Leanne in the stateroom," she offered.

"No, I want to stay here and talk with you girls," he said drunkenly. "I'm not a party pooper like that one." He grimaced and pointed wildly with his thumb in the direction of the staterooms. He took another long swallow and tried to set the glass on the table, but instead it fell to the deck floor and shattered.

"Oops," he said. "I'm sorry. Here, let me clean it up." When he reached down to pick up the shards of glass with his bare hand, Timmy grabbed his arm to stop him.

"Get off me, faggot," he snarled, jerking his arm away. I don't need a filthy faggot to..." he trailed off.

"He hasn't changed a bit," Timmy said.

"Let us help you below deck, Scotty," Charlotte Claire said authoritatively. "I think you've had too much, and the drugs we put in your wine will have you passing out right here."

"Charlotte Claire!" Amelie gasped.

"Don't worry, he's too out of it now to know what's what," she said. Scotty was slumped over on the bench, his head hanging down and his hair disheveled. "We need to get him below deck while he can still walk. Amelie, will you help me. I'm afraid of what he'll do if Timmy tries to help him."

"Oh God," Amelie sighed. "This is actually happening, isn't it?

"Are you okay?" Annie asked.

"Yes, I think so."

"Okay, Scotty," Charlotte Claire coaxed. "Can you stand up for me?" She put her hands firmly on his arm. "Amelie, take his other arm. Okay, Scotty, we're going to help you stand up and then we're going to bring you to a stateroom where you can rest. I'm going to count to three and when I say stand, you stand. Okay, one, two, three, stand!" Scotty got up on his feet, but his knees didn't lock, and he went back down."

"What if we can't get him below deck?" Amelie asked frantically.

"We have to get him there," Charlotte Claire said impatiently, "so, we will. Sit on the bench beside him, put his arm around your shoulder and hold onto his hand. We're going to use all of our weight as leverage to get him on his feet."

"I'm going home," Scotty slurred weakly. "I'm…"

"Again," Charlotte Claire said. "Okay Scotty, we're going to take you home, but in order for us to do that, you need to stand up and walk with us, okay? Now I'm going to count to three again and then we'll stand up. You got his arm, Amelie?"

"Got it," she replied.

"One, two, three, stand!"

With all the strength they had, they propelled Scotty upward until he was on his feet. They moved carefully from behind the cocktail table and walked him to the top of the stairs leading to the staterooms. Charlotte Claire looked at the daunting pitch of the stairs. "We're never going to get him down the stairs," she told them, "He's too heavy and we're not strong enough."

"Sit him down on the top step," Annie told her. "Timmy and I will go down first. We'll take his legs, and y'all hold him by the arms, and we'll slide him down slowly."

"That's a good idea," Charlotte Claire said. "If the son of a bitch would have gone to lay down when we told him, we wouldn't have to do this."

"Okay, ready?" Timmy asked. "Let's start." With Annie and Timmy holding his legs and Amelie and Charlotte Claire holding his arms, they moved him slowly down the steps, his rump landing on each step as they did so. Scotty groaned and slurred something, but was incoherent and very close to being unconscious.

When they'd reached the bottom step Charlotte Claire said

breathlessly, "I need a minute."

"Me too," Amelie said. "I need to catch my breath."

"Now's not the time to rest," Timmy said. "He's still conscious. If we can get him on his feet again maybe we can get him to the stateroom. You guys just help us get him upright and then Annie and I will take over. Okay, on three. One, two, three!" With great effort they got Scotty to his feet and the three moved sideways down the narrow hall and through the stateroom door. They lay him on his back, on the floor at the foot of the bed. The four of them stood silently, taking a moment to catch their breath.

"Okay, where are the supplies?" Charlotte Claire asked.

"In the closet, in the Louis Vuitton bag," Annie told her. Charlotte Claire removed the large duffel bag from the closet and withdrew rolls of foam strips, duct tape, scissors, two pairs of handcuffs and a hand gun.

"Hand me the foam strips and duct tape. I'll start wrapping his wrists. Annie, you get the other one," he told her.

"That was a great idea, Charlotte Claire, wrapping their wrists so there wouldn't be marks from the handcuffs," Amelie said.

"Where did you get the handcuffs, Annie?" Charlotte Claire asked.

"Props department," she replied. "I had my handyman in LA buy the duct tape and foam strips. The scissors I pinched from the CVS."

"You stole the scissors from the CVS? Are you crazy?" Amelie asked. "You could have gotten caught."

"I didn't want them traced back to me. They'll have fibers from the duct tape and foam on them. It was worth the risk of getting caught for a petty theft. I could just say I had Winona Ryder syndrome."

"But we're going to throw them overboard when we're done," Timmy told her. "Even if they thought to look for them, they'd never find them.

"I know," she agreed. "An overabundance of caution, I guess."

"You think?" he replied. Timmy cut a length of foam strip and wrapper it around Scotty's ankles, then covered it in duct tape, tearing it with his hands. Annie wrapped foam around his wrists and closed the handcuffs over it as tightly as she could.

"Okay," Charlotte Claire said, "Now let's take care of Leanne." Amelie and Charlotte Claire applied the foam and duct tape to her ankles. They worked silently and efficiently, as if they'd done it a thousand times. When they'd finished Charlotte Claire said, "Okay, *now* let's go review our strategy for how this next part is going to go."

"How long do you think they'll be out?" Annie asked, after they'd settled back on the deck.

"You're asking us?" Amelie said. "You're the one who got the Xanax. By the way, where did you get it?"

"Are you kidding? I live in LA. You can practically get them at the grocery store. Well, you probably can get them in the parking lot at the grocery store. Anyway, my therapist said they could knock you out for an hour or two, but with all that booze it's a wild card."

"I think Leanne will wake up first," Amelie offered. "She didn't drink quite as much as Scotty, and she went to sleep first."

"Yeah, but Scotty is bigger," Timmy said. "He can handle more."

"It doesn't really matter who wakes up first," Charlotte Claire told them. "Whoever wakes up first we'll deal with first."

"And how do y'all want to handle that part?" Annie asked.

"I think the first thing is, we tell them what we know," Charlotte Claire suggested. "They'll deny everything, of course, so then we present our evidence. And we scare them until we get a confession. They're never going to give anything up unless they think their lives are in danger."

"I don't know," Amelie said, "They would probably do any-thing, say anything, to avoid going to jail. Scotty already has."

"This could go in a number of directions when we confront them," Timmy said. "I think we just have to roll with it, play it by ear."

"I think it's important that we make them feel powerless and afraid from the get-go," Charlotte Claire said. "They need to know this is serious."

"Deadly serious," Timmy agreed.

Leanne was trying to wake up, as if fighting to reach the water's surface, but so far in the deep it seemed impossible. Finally, she opened her eyes, saw the stateroom ceiling and remembered where she was. When she tried to sit up she became aware of the handcuffs and duct tape on her ankles. She thought, 'is this some sophomoric prank, am I dreaming?' Then she remembered her apprehension after boarding the yacht and was filled with panic. "Scotty!" she screamed. "Scotty! Someone get me out of here! Someone take these things off! Scotty!"

They could hear Leanne screaming from the deck. "We're up," Timmy said.

"Do you have the float?" Charlotte Claire asked Amelie. "And the gun that Scotty fired, don't forget that."

"Yeah, it's in my bag."

"Let's go," Annie instructed.

"Scotty!" Leanne shrieked, her face wild with fear. "These people are crazy. Help me! Scotty!" She wriggled backwards until she was able to sit up, her back against the headboard. She'd hoped this was just a tasteless joke, but the expressions of their faces as they entered the stateroom told her that it wasn't.

"Scotty can't help you now," Annie said calmly, as they stood together beside the bed. "He's all tied up."

"He's on the floor at the foot of the bed, still passed out," Amelie told her.

"What have you done to him?" Leanne demanded.

"We haven't done anything to him...yet," Timmy said.

"We gave him a cocktail like the one we gave you," Charlotte Claire told her.

"You know," Annie continued, "a red wine and Xanax spritzer."

"What is wrong with you people?" she cried. "Why are you doing this? You're all crazy. Unlock these things and let me go. Take me back to Key Largo now!"

"No can do, Leanne," Charlotte Claire said. "We have some issues that need clearing up first."

"What issues?" she asked urgently. "What are you talking about? There no issues to clear up."

Timmy removed his cellphone from his pocket. He opened his voicemail and put it on speaker. The familiar message from the horrific, disembodied voice said, "I know what you did, you are a killer and you will pay." Leanne looked at Timmy in horror. Her eyes were wild, and her mouth hung open.

"You!" she said accusingly. "It's you whose been making those calls and leaving those messages. And you left them on Scotty's phone too. What's wrong with you? What's this all about?"

Amelie stepped towards her. "This." She withdrew the pink swan float from her bag and tossed it on the bed beside Leanne. Her eyes still wild with fear, she said nothing for several moments.

"What is that?" she asked, feigning ignorance. "I don't know what that is. What does that have to do with me?"

"Does this ring a bell?" Timmy asked. He removed the phone from his pocket and showed her the picture he took of the float in its container in her closet.

"How did you..." she said, her voice trailing off as she recalled the house tour on the weekend of the reunion.

"Ah," Timmy laughed. "I see a look of recognition. Yes, I think you know. We know the significance of this float; this child's toy that you kept all of these years as some sick trophy."

"I don't know what you're talking about," she protested.

"Oh, please, Leanne," Amelie erupted. "You know what we're talking about. So just stop pretending and start talking. I want to know how it happened. I want to know exactly how it happened."

"I'm telling you, I don't!" Leanne screamed.

"Here," Amelie hissed, thrusting it toward Leanne. "E A! Elizabeth Ardoin! My little sister's float. She had it with her on the day she died. And you just happened to be coming from where they found her, at the same time. So, stop lying, and tell me how it happened."

"Patty Hammond told us what you said when you were under anesthetic," Charlotte Claire said. "You basically confessed as much."

"What did I say? I don't..."

"You said that you killed her, that you hit her with a rock, that you didn't want to go to hell. But guess what? You're in hell now."

"So now we want to hear it from the horse's mouth," Annie barked. "Start talking."

"You're all crazy!" Leanne screamed, tears rolling down her cheeks. "I don't know anything about that. I didn't have anything to do with that."

"Start talking," Annie took the gun from the duffel bag and pointed it at Leanne's head."

"All right, all right," she cried. "I didn't know what I was doing. She wouldn't give me the float. I just wanted to play with it and she kept saying no. She should have just given it to me and nothing would have happened. It wasn't my fault. She should have just given it to me." Leanne turned her face away from them, sobbing, then turned back and screamed, "It was not my fault! She was a terrible child, a selfish child!"

Amelie lunged at her, grabbing her by the hair. "Shut up!" Amelie cried. "My sister was a sweet, gentle child. She was an innocent!" Charlotte Claire pulled her away; Amelie fell into her arms. She turned to Leanne, still crying, "I've spent my whole life thinking it was my fault that she died. That if I'd been with her, she wouldn't have fallen and hit her head. Do you have any idea what that feels like? Do you? No, I'm sure you don't. You'd have to have a soul to know what that feels like."

"Keep talking," Annie said, still pointing the gun at Leanne. "We want details. How did you do it?" Leanne looked around the room, helplessly saying nothing. "I'm not afraid to use this, so start talking."

"I hit her," she said softly.

"Details," Timmy said sternly. Annie cocked the gun.

"I hit her with a rock," she bellowed. "I picked up a big rock and hit her on the side of the head as hard as I could. She fell down at the edge of the river and I took the float. I was afraid she'd tell, so I left her there. It wasn't my fault. She should have just let me have it."

"One more question," Amelie said, "The float, the pink swan float. You didn't have it with you that day when I saw you in the school yard. How did you come to have it if you didn't take it with you after?"

"I hid it in the woods. I went back for it after they found her."

"You knew that you killed her, and you still went back for that stupid, fucking float? That's all you cared about? You really are something, Leanne," Timmy said in disgust.

"What are you going to do with me?" she asked.

"Don't know yet," Charlotte Claire said, "Maybe we'll turn you in to the police. There's no statute of limitations on murder."

"No one will believe you," she said defiantly. "I'll tell them you made it up."

"That's why we've recorded all of this on our phones," Timmy told her. "Your confession is on record."

"I'll tell them that you held me against my will and forced me to confess to something I didn't do. You've basically kidnapped me. Maybe I'll be the one telling the police about you."

"You're still being recorded, dumb-ass," Annie said. "But you're right about the kidnapping part. That might not pan out well for us. So, maybe we'll do something else. But first I think we'll deal with your husband."

"Let's wake him up," Timmy said. He kicked at Scotty's foot several times to no avail. He leaned down and shook him by his shoulders. "Wake up, you son of a bitch!" he commanded. Scotty murmured something unintelligible and passed out again. "I said, wake up!" Timmy lifted Scotty's head by the hair and slapped him hard across the face. Scotty's eyes popped open and he stared up at Timmy in disbelief. "We have some business to discuss."

"What's happening?" Scotty asked, still dazed. "What the fuck? Where's Leanne? I want to see Leanne."

"Scotty, they're crazy," Leanne screamed. "I'm here on the bed. They've got me tied up. Help me!"

Scotty inched his way across the floor until he could prop himself up against the wall. He saw Leanne's horrified expression. "How'd I get here?" he demanded angrily, now fully conscious. "How'd I end up in handcuffs?"

"We took a page from your playbook, you rapist prick," Amelie told him. "We drugged you. Only we were smart about it. We used Xanax. Lots of people take Xanax, so it won't send up any red flags when they perform an autopsy on you."

A hot flush coursed through Scotty's body as he frantically tried to push himself upright. "An autopsy?" he asked frantically. "Why would there be an autopsy?" He lost his footing and fell back to the floor.

"Because you'll be dead, stupid," Charlotte Claire said. "You'll be dead because you went crazy and killed your wife and then tried to kill us, so we had to shoot you. But it was self-defense, promise. Annie had to shoot you in self-defense, and we're her witnesses."

"You're crazy!" he yelled. "You're all crazy. Leanne, Leanne!"

"Scotty!" Leanne yelled from the bed. "Scotty, help me! They're crazy!"

"Shut up, Leanne," Annie said calmly. "One more peep out of you and I'm going to come over there and pistol-whip you until you pass out."

"They'll never believe you," Scotty said, defiantly.

"Oh, I think they will," Amelie said. "Because Leanne is going to call the Coast Guard and report that you are trying to break in to her stateroom. That you're drunk and have a gun." Right Leanne?"

"Mayday, mayday," Annie said, affecting Leanne's southern drawl. "My husband's gone crazy, he's got a gun and I think he's trying to kill me!"

"You see, we can finish the both of you off and you get blamed for all of it," Timmy told him. "You go crazy and kill your wife and then kill yourself. Oldest story in the book. With Xanax and all that alcohol in your system, it won't be hard to believe that you went off your nut. See? We have options."

"And your hands are covered in gunshot residue," Annie added. "Thanks to our target practice this afternoon."

"And you made such a drunken scene at lunch today," Amelie pointed out, "That the manager had to come to the table. So, we have a credible witness with no personal connection to any of us."

"So, you see Scotty," Charlotte Claire explained, "We've got witnesses, we've got evidence. Which story sounds more laudable? The one where a drunken, drugged up, middle-aged husband loses it? Or the one where four well-known, successful people with everything to lose risk committing a double murder?"

"Oh, I don't know if it's murder, Charlotte Claire. More like the pursuit of justice," Timmy said. "You see, Scotty and Leanne, we've got you dead to rights, emphasis on dead."

"What do you want?" Scotty asked nervously. "None of you needs money, so what do you want?" His mind was racing. He knew he could overpower them, but they had weapons and he was tied up. He had to find a way to get at that gun.

"Confessions," Annie told him. She moved to where he was lying at the foot of the bed. "We want confessions."

"If you tell us the truth we'll consider getting you back to Key Largo alive," Amelie said.

"Tell the truth about what, you fucking cunt?" He pulled wildly at the handcuffs. "You're all fucking crazy. I have no idea what any of you are talking about."

"Oh dear, you two are so tiresome. We'll start with the small stuff," Timmy said. "You made my life a living hell. You stalked me. You beat me. You humiliated me every day that I lived in Bayou Derkin. And not once in all that time did you show any remorse. You drove me off the road and very nearly killed me. Tormenting me was just a pastime for you. You drove me to a nervous breakdown, and you very nearly drove me to suicide. Your bigotry and cruelty did drive Tom Burnett's son to suicide. Even as a grown man you show no remorse, only contempt for the people you victimize. You were a hateful, callous boy and you are a hateful and callous man. You are a blight on humanity. Oh, by the way, that reminds me." Timmy pulled out his cell and played the threatening message from "Unknown."

"You son of a bitch!" Scotty said contemptuously.

"Yeah, me. How does it feel?"

"It feels like I'm going to kick your faggot ass when I get out of these fucking handcuffs."

"Well then I guess we'll have to keep you in those fucking

handcuffs indefinitely." Timmy forcefully kicked him in his side, and Scotty groaned and doubled over in pain. "And by the way, that word you like to call me, faggot? That word and your use of it no longer have any power. It just reveals you to be the dumb, backward, bigoted piece of shit that you are."

"Now me," Charlotte Claire said. "You raped me sophomore year. I don't need a confession for that. I was there. You were there. We both know it happened."

"What is she talking about, Scotty?" Leanne cried. "Scotty, is this true?"

"You wanted it," Scotty raged.

"Scotty!" Leanne cried again.

"I did not want it!" Charlotte Claire shrieked, startling everyone in the crowded stateroom. "You stupid thug! Do you think your daughter would want that? You have no idea, no idea what I went through for years after that. I blamed myself. I wasn't able to trust anyone. I felt shame. But the shame is yours, Scotty, if you were a decent enough person to feel shame. You're guilty, Scotty. I find you guilty."

"I'll go now," Annie said solemnly. "You raped me, too, Scotty. You thought I didn't know, didn't you?"

Scotty looked at the group nervously. "I didn't..."

"Don't bother," Timmy interrupted. "We have evidence."

"What evidence?" he asked.

"CCTV of you taking Annie to my suite during the reunion, and of you leaving after the assault. And we know that you spiked her drink, because she had her blood tested the next day. We saved the whiskey bottles and the bedding, so we have physical evidence of you at the scene. It was a bit of bad luck for you that you unwittingly took her to my suite. Otherwise we wouldn't have found her that night, and she might have slept through the morning without even knowing she'd been drugged. That must sting."

"And you can't pretend that I wanted it. I was unconscious. Now I want to hear it from you," Annie told him. "I know it's true, but I need to hear it from you. I want a confession...and an apology."

"I'm not confessing anything."

Annie pointed the gun at Scotty and he pushed wildly against the floor with his feet until his back was once again up against the wall. "You see this gun, Scotty? I'm very comfortable with shooting you. But I'm not going to shoot to kill. I'm going to shoot you in the stomach and watch you suffer. I hear that's the most painful place to get shot. It'll take longer, but you'll still die. So, what's it going to be?" Annie cocked the gun and aimed it at Scotty's stomach. He twisted sideways toward the wall, shielding his face with his arms.

"Okay, okay," he pleaded. "I did it. Just don't shoot me. I did it, I did it. I'm sorry. I apologize!"

"So, it's true, Scotty?" Leanne asked. "What Carla told me was true?"

"Shut up, Leanne!" Scotty barked.

"Tell me what you did, the whole thing, from the beginning," Annie demanded.

"I put a roofie in your drink. When you started to feel the effects of it, I walked you to your room."

"Go on," she said.

"I took your clothes off...and we had sex."

"We didn't have sex, you fucking pig," she snapped. "You raped me. Say it! Say you raped me."

"I raped you alright, I raped you," he confessed. His eyes were wild with fear and he began to cry. "Please don't shoot me! I don't want to die, I don't want to die."

"Not such a tough guy now, are you, Scotty?" Timmy chided.

"So, you raped me 35 years ago," Charlotte Claire said, "And you raped Annie last year. How many others have you raped in the last thirty-five years?"

"None...some," he cried. After a while he straightened up and looked at Annie. "Go ahead and shoot me, then," he shouted. "You don't have the guts. The fucking gun probably isn't even loaded. You'd never..." Annie raised the gun and fired it, striking the foot of the bed only inches away from him, then she pointed at his stomach. "No, no," he cried. "Don't, please don't. I'll do whatever you want. I'll go to the police and turn myself in if you want. Please just don't kill me." He hung his head, still crying.

"We'll get around to that," Amelie said. "But you're not through confessing just yet. If you want us to spare your life, we want to know the full story about the murders of Patty Hammond and Carla Courville." Scotty looked up in shock at the four of them. Amelie's words landed like a shot through his chest. "Yes, we know," she continued. "Patty knew you'd raped Annie. She's the one who had the urine test done that proved you had put Rohypnol in her drink. We also know that Carla overheard Patty on the phone telling someone that the results were positive for Rohypnol, and that it proved you raped Annie."

"How do you know that?" Scotty demanded.

"Because she called Tom Burnett from the hospital and told him what she'd heard, the day before you killed her," Charlotte Claire told him. "He also told me that she ran into Leanne and told her, too. That's how you found out what Patty and Carla knew."

"Do you know who that was Patty was talking to?" Amelie asked him. "That was me. So, yes, we knew. We've all known for months."

"So, you killed Patty and Carla for nothing, Scotty. We were going to make sure you were prosecuted for the rape anyway. That was poor planning on your part," Annie said. "Weren't you worried about the person on the other end of Patty's phone call?"

Scotty rested his head against his knees. When he looked up again, bitter resignation had settled on his face. "No," he said at last. "I figured that if Patty was dead, it would just sound like gossip. What is it you call it, secondhand information?"

"Hearsay, you moron," Charlotte Claire told him.

"Yeah," Timmy said. "Leanne, how could you marry such a dumb fuck. I gave you more credit."

"And you figured the Keystone Cops in Bayou Derkin, most of whom are your friends I'm told, would make the rumor go away and not investigate," Annie said.

"Something like that," Scotty admitted. "But then that fucking Carla Courville had to stick her nose in it. And if she was willing to tell Leanne within hours, or hell, minutes, then God knows who else she'd tell. She would have been running all over town with her story."

"And you had a reputation to protect," Charlotte Claire suggested.

"And a business to protect, and a marriage to protect," he added.

"Oh, really, Scotty," Leanne moaned.

"And if we kill you, you'll be known as the man who murdered his wife," Annie said. "If we force you to turn yourself in, you'll be known as a murderer and rapist. Either way you'll be remembered for the degenerate, soulless pile of shit that you are."

"Tell us exactly what happened," Amelie told him.

"Why?" he replied bitterly. "You're all so fucking smart. Why don't you tell me?"

"We probably could, with a relatively high degree of accuracy," Timmy told him. "But we want to hear it from you. Otherwise, Annie will just shoot you in the stomach now."

"Fuck it," Scotty said. "There's not that much to tell. I called the hospital and found out that they were both working the night shift. I went to the hospital parking lot and slashed Carla's tires and then waited for them to come out. And then I followed them."

"How'd you know that Patty would offer Carla a ride?" Amelie asked.

"I didn't know for sure. But there's never more than two or three nurses on a shift. I knew they were on the same shift. And I figured if anybody would offer her a ride it would be that goody-goody, Patty Hammond."

"Go on," Annie told him, still pointing the gun at him.

"I followed them to Guidry Pass, that's all. When we got to the bridge I sped up beside them and forced them off the bridge. Those old wooden guardrails on the Bayou Derkin Bridge are shit. I knew they'd go right through."

"But how'd you know the crash would kill them?" Charlotte Claire asked.

"I didn't know for sure," he admitted. "But I knew if I hit the right part of the car at the right angle they'd land upside down in the river. The water was pretty high. I figured if the impact didn't kill them, they'd drown."

Charlotte Claire looked around at the others. She felt sick to her stomach, disgusted by this man who'd become so matter-of-fact in the telling of his monstrous act of self-centeredness and murder.

"Anyway, if they'd survived they'd never have been able to identify me. It was dark as hell, I was in a truck they wouldn't recognize, and I'd turned my lights off. Not that they had time to see."

They were all quiet for a while. Timmy said, "You're a psychopath."

"I'm just a man who was protecting myself and my business and my family," he replied.

"You took the lives of two innocent people to cover up the fact that you are a serial rapist," Charlotte Claire said. "That makes you a sociopath and a psychopath. I never thought I'd say this to another human being, but I hope you rot in hell."

"What time is it?" Amelie asked.

"Eleven o'clock," Annie told her.

"We'd better get on with it," Timmy said.

"Get on with what?" Scotty asked anxiously.

"The rest of our evening," Charlotte Claire replied.

"What are you going to do with me? Please don't shoot me. You can turn me in in Key Largo. I swear I'll confess everything. They can send me back to Bayou Derkin to be arrested. They can put me in jail. I don't care, but please just don't shoot me."

"Yes, Scotty," Annie said. "That's exactly what you're going to do."

"We're taking you to the Key Largo police and they can take it from there. We'll show them your confessions on our cell phones. We have enough evidence-CCTV at the casino, the bedding from the hotel, and your DNA on the whiskey bottles. And the pink swan float should be at least enough evidence to bring you to trial, Leanne. Even if you're not convicted, you'd have to live through the scandal of a trial. You'll be ruined in Bayou Derkin."

"What pink swan float?" Scotty asked. "What the hell are you talking about?"

"Ah, so you don't know?" Amelie asked him. "Well Leanne, you are the secret-keeper. Do you want to tell him, or shall I?"

"Yes, I did it," Leanne screamed. "But I was just a child. I didn't know what I was doing. Scotty, I didn't know what I was doing!"

"Tell me what?" Scotty demanded. "Did what? Tell me!"

"I killed Elizabeth," she cried. "I killed Amelie's little sister."

"So that she could have her float," Amelie added. She picked up the float and thrust it towards Scotty. "The pink swan float that I'm holding in my hand. The float that she kept as a souvenir, which I found in your house." Scotty looked at Leanne in disbelief.

"What?" he asked in bewilderment. "You...I..."

"Well, what's this?" Annie said. "The asshole's speechless."

"So, you see. We've built our case," Timmy told them. "We have the float, the CCTV footage, the urine test, the whiskey bottles, the bedding-and your recorded confessions. Now it's more than hearsay. If Patty's car is still impounded, there's probably paint evidence as well."

"Scotty and Leanne, you were tried and convicted before you got on the boat," Charlotte Claire told him. "We just needed to hear it from you directly."

"We're your judge and jury and you've been found guilty on all counts," Annie said.

"Without warning, Scotty lunged at Annie, hitting her legs and knocking the gun from her hands. He scooped it up and awkwardly pointed it at the four of them. "Okay, now this is how it's going to go," he told them. "Someone is going to take this tape off my ankles. And then they're going to take the handcuffs off me, understand?"

"What do we do?" Amelie asked the others.

"You do what I say," Scotty replied evenly. "Or else I start shooting. You're fish in a barrel. One, or even two of you may get away, but the other two are going to die."

His captors looked from one to the other. Timmy said, "We don't have a choice." He knelt at Scotty's feet and slowly began to remove the duct tape. Amelie quickly reached into the Louis Vuitton bag, pulled out the second gun and held it at Leanne's head. Leanne screamed.

"If you don't drop that gun, I'll kill her," Amelie told him.

Scotty laughed sardonically. "Go ahead," he told her. "You'd be doing me a favor."

"You bastard!" Leanne shrieked.

"Go ahead," he insisted. "No, I didn't think so. You haven't got the balls."

Amelie froze. She hated herself for it, but she couldn't pull the trigger. She looked at the others helplessly.

"Don't worry about it, Amelie," Timmy told her. "Everybody *runs* out of nerve sometime. Right Charlotte Claire, Annie? Everybody *runs* out of nerve." He looked at each of them meaningfully, still unwrapping Scotty's ankles and hoping he'd gotten his meaning across.

"Now help me up," Scotty barked when Timmy had finished.

"Going for a *run*?" Timmy asked.

"Shut up, faggot! Just get me up. Take me by the arm and don't try anything funny. And don't forget I have this gun."

Timmy stood and grabbed Scotty's right arm. "Okay, Scotty, on three. One, two, three." Timmy lifted, Scotty struggled to his feet. Timmy slammed him against the wall, screaming, "Run! Run!" The women fled the stateroom. Timmy shoved him again to make him drop the gun, but Scotty held on tight. He tried to wrestle the gun from his hands, but Scotty managed to point the gun directly at Timmy's face. Terrified, Timmy let go and backed away. They stood, silently panting, eyes locked on one another. Timmy thought of making a run for the door. He was close and might just make it, but Scotty would still have the gun and be free to roam the boat in pursuit of the others.

"That was stupid, faggot," Scotty said, breaking the silence.

"Shoot him!' Leanne screamed.

"Shut up," he told her. "I'm not going to shoot him."

"What are you going to do?" Timmy asked him, nervously.

"That bitch has a gun. You're going to be my bulletproof vest. Unlock these handcuffs."

"I can't."

"Or, I could shoot you in the leg, for starters. Then maybe work my way around your body. Not kill you. Just to make you suffer until you decide to get smart and unlock these handcuffs."

"No, I mean I don't have the keys, Annie does. I can go get them," Timmy offered.

Scotty considered Timmy's suggestion. "Alright then," he said. "But no funny business." Timmy turned to leave the room, but Scotty shouted, "No! Stay where you are." He motioned for Timmy to move to the opposite end of the stateroom. He walked to the open door and called out, "Annie! Bring me the keys to these handcuffs."

"No, Annie, don't!" Timmy yelled.

"Annie, bring me those keys!" he bellowed. "Or I'll shoot your fucking queer boy in the face."

"No, Annie! He won't shoot me, if I'm dead he won't have any leverage to get the keys. And he knows Amelie has a gun."

"Shut the fuck up, faggot, or I will shoot you. Annie!" he screamed out the door.

"What should I do?" Annie asked Charlotte Claire and Amelie. "We can't stay locked up in this stateroom while he kills Timmy."

"Bring him the key," Amelie cried.

"He's not going to kill Timmy as long as he and Leanne are locked up in those handcuffs, knowing we have a gun and there's three of us." Charlotte Claire told them. "We have to find another way to put him at a disadvantage, disorient him in some way."

"The lights," Annie said. "I can go to the pilothouse and turn off all the lights on the boat. It'll be pitch black below deck. I'll come to the bottom of the stairs to cover that area. Charlotte Claire, you stay in the stateroom with the gun. Leave the door open but stay to one side of the door. Amelie you go to the bathroom off the hall and do the same, keep the door open and stay to one side of it. Once the lights go out, he'll have to come out if he wants the keys."

"It may also give Timmy a chance to escape," Charlotte Claire added.

"But how are we going to overtake him in the dark?" Amelie asked.

"I have a flash light in the pilot house," Annie told her. "Once I hear them in the hall I'll tell Timmy to hit the deck and blind Scotty with the flashlight. Amelie, when he passes the bathroom, grab his ankles to knock him off his feet and take him down. He'll almost certainly drop the gun, so grab it if you can. Charlotte Claire, come out with your gun, too, and hold it on him. I think that's our best option."

"I hope you're right," Charlotte Claire said.

"Get over here, faggot. If they're not going to bring those keys, we're going to have to go get them." Scotty motioned for Timmy to stand directly in front of him.

"What about me!" Leanne screamed.

In an instant Scotty turned the gun on Leanne, shot her in the forehead and turned the gun back on Timmy.

"Oh!" Timmy cried. It was so sudden that he could barely take in what he'd just seen. He realized the others would think it was he who'd been shot. "I'm alright, girls! I'm okay!" he yelled.

"I really should thank you," Scotty said casually. "I'd have never gotten away with that in Bayou Derkin. Now I can frame one of your dead asses, and the money's all mine. Hell, I can file wrongful death lawsuits against all of your estates and then I'll..."

Everything went black. Timmy tried to bolt but Scotty grabbed the back of his collar, the barrel of the gun wedged precariously against the side of his head.

"No funny business," Scotty barked, jerking Timmy back. "We're going to walk slowly out into the hall and then up onto the deck. Try anything and I'll kill you."

Annie perched on the bottom of the stairs and waited to hear Scotty and Timmy enter the hall. "Take it slow, faggot, and no one gets hurt...yet." Annie listened intently as she heard their footsteps moving slowly across the hall. When she guessed they'd had passed the bathroom, she shined the flashlight down the hallway.

"Hit the deck, Timmy!" Annie yelled.

"Who's there?" Scotty demanded. Amelie crawled into the

hallway behind them, grabbed both of Scotty's ankles and pulled back with all her strength. Scotty fell forward, bringing Timmy down with him. They hit the floor with a tremendous thud. Annie stepped into the hallway and shone the flashlight on the two men. Timmy could see the gun had fallen and was just inches away, but he was pinned beneath Scotty's considerable weight and couldn't move. They both lurched forward, reaching for the gun, but Timmy was closer and grabbed the weapon. Scotty struck him on the back of his head with clenched fists. Amelie and Annie watched in terror as the two men struggled for control of the gun. Charlotte Claire held her fire for fear of shooting Timmy by accident. Timmy pushed against the wall with his legs and turned them both over; he was straddling Scotty now. Scotty grabbed at the gun with his bound hands, but Timmy had managed to turn it in his direction. "I'll kill you, you son of a bitch," he snarled at Timmy. They were locked in battle, pitting their strength against each other. Timmy forced the gun towards Scotty's face but couldn't get his finger on the trigger. Annie, frantic to help, kicked Scotty in the groin. Scotty screamed loudly, and when he did, Timmy thrust the barrel of the gun into his mouth. A shot rang out in the hall. Scotty was dead. Timmy sat up and let the gun fall to the floor.

"Annie, turn the lights on," Amelie told her.

"Are you alright?" Charlotte Claire asked anxiously.

"Yeah." Timmy remained straddling Scotty, breathing heavily and unable to move. Suddenly the boat was awash in light and music began playing on the upper deck. The music abruptly stopped, and Annie reappeared, gripped by the scene.

"Timmy, get off him," Amelie said softly, but he stayed there, staring at Scotty's face blankly and saying nothing. He could see brain matter and blood on the floor, but strangely, his face looked unharmed. "Help me, Charlotte Claire," Amelie said. "Be careful not to walk in the blood." They each took one of Timmy's arms and helped him to his feet, then stepped carefully away from the body.

"What are we going to tell Leanne?" Charlotte Claire asked.

"Nothing," Timmy told her.

"What do you mean, nothing?" she said.

"She's dead."

"What?" Amelie gasped. "Did you..."

"No, Scotty did."

"Oh, my God!" Annie muttered.

"He said he'd never have gotten away with it in Bayou Derkin. He thanked me...us."

"Thanked us?" Charlotte Claire asked.

"He planned to kill us all, then blame it on one of us."

"What a stupid idea," Annie remarked. "He'd never have gotten away with it."

"I'm not so sure," Charlotte Claire told them. "He got away with Patty and Carla's murders."

"The question is, what are we going to do now?" Amelie said. "This wasn't supposed to happen. We were just going to scare them into confessing and record it on our phones! Now we have two dead bodies on our hands. We could explain Leanne's death, not that they'd necessarily believe us, but Timmy's killed Scotty!"

"No, I didn't," he said. "Not technically. I was just trying to get the gun away from him. I just shoved the gun into his mouth to scare him into letting it go. My finger was never on the trigger; Scotty's hands were wrapped around that part of the gun. He accidentally pulled the trigger when he was trying to get the gun away from me."

"We are all responsible for them being dead," Amelie said. "If we'd never invited them here, if we'd never come up with this stupid plan to make them confess, none of this would have happened."

"That's enough, Amelie!" Charlotte Claire shouted. "We were trying to get justice for ourselves, Elizabeth, Patty, and

Carla. Listen to the list of their victims! There's no way we could have foreseen this happening. For now, we need to keep cool heads and figure out what to do next."

"We should just call the police and explain what happened," Amelie told her.

"Do you want to go to jail?" Annie asked her.

"We have guns," Timmy said. "We bound and handcuffed them, we drugged them."

"They'd never believe us," Charlotte Claire added. "No, we have to figure out a story and eliminate any evidence that doesn't completely support that story. Put on your thinking caps. It's time to brain storm."

In half an hour they had a plan. They would flesh out the fictional plan they'd told Scotty and Leanne. Timmy would need to shower and change to eliminate any gunshot residue. The handcuffs, foam stripping and duct tape and all the contents of the Louis Vuitton bag-including the second gun-would be weighted down and thrown overboard. Annie would move the boat a mile or so away from where the items were dumped. They would clean the gun and, since Annie's fingerprints on the gun would be explainable, she would place it in Scotty's hand for fingerprints. It was decided that leaving the bodies as they lay was the most convincing scenario. They crafted their story of what unfolded and executed the supporting evidence: The smashed cabinet on the upper deck, the mattresses pulled from the bunks, the broken stateroom door. Timmy created the script for the calls to the coast guard, and they were ready to begin.

Just before midnight they gathered in the stateroom where Leanne Piper lay dead. "Are you ready?" Annie asked Timmy.

"Ready," he said. He stepped into the hall, leaving the door open to maintain eye contact with Annie. She dialed the coast guard and looked at Timmy fixedly. She nodded and began to speak.

"Mayday, mayday, mayday!" she said excitedly in Leanne's southern drawl. "This is Leanne Piper, oh God, oh God, please!" After several seconds she said, "I don't know. I don't know. I don't know boats and I don't know how to read the position thing." Annie's voice grew more panicked with each word. "Off the coast of Key Largo is all I know." A beat and she said, "The Sweet Revenge."

Annie pointed to Timmy who began banging on the door and kicking at the wall. He turned his head facing away from her and growled in a low voice as he pounded the walls, "I'm going to kill you, you fucking bitch!"

"My husband, Scotty Piper, he's trying to kill me! I'm locked in a stateroom and he's trying to break in! He's got a gun and..." Timmy continued to pound the walls and bellow.

"Let me in," he yelled. "Let me in, you fucking bitch!"

"Oh my God, he's going to kill me! He's going to kill us all." Timmy slammed the door back against the wall and Annie let out a blood curdling scream, which she sustained as she disengaged the call. She looked at the others and asked, "How was that?"

"It sounded convincing to me," Charlotte Claire said.

"Me too," Amelie agreed.

"You must be exhausted, Timmy," Annie said. "Yelling and screaming, kicking the doors in and now all that banging."

"I'm fine," he said.

"How long before the next call?" Amelie asked.

"Fifteen minutes," Charlotte Claire told her.

FBI Miami Field Office

Miramar, Florida

April 29, 2016

"So, explain to me why the Miami Field Office is in Miramar?" Coast Guard Officer Matthew Clayton asked. "I thought we might get a little Miami time in after we pick up the report."

"I don't know," Officer Max Price responded. "I think it used to be in Miami back in the 1930s."

"Well, what say we drive into South Beach after, for a couple of drinks?"

"What say we don't. It's Friday and I want to get home to my family."

"Right."

They were near the end of the 45 minute drive from Key Largo to Miramar. There was a wide-open, cloudless sky and the late April weather was already warmer than Max Price liked. He was fond of Clayton, but there was a little too much of the frat boy in him, and Max was finding the conversation tedious. "Here we are," Max said, turning into the rear parking lot. "Try not to embarrass me." Clayton looked at him like a wounded puppy. "I'm just kidding," he said. "But let me take the lead. They're handing this off to me personally as a favor. They may have questions and they may not. They may take questions and they may not. So, follow my lead...quietly."

It was a typical office space: Large banks of cubicles for the underlings, surrounded by small, glass-partitioned offices for their superiors. It smelled of synthetic carpet and toner. Officer Clayton looked from left to right, taking in all he could. "Haven't you ever been to an FBI office before?" Price asked.

"No," he said excitedly. "It's awesome...but kind of boring too. I mean, come to think of it, it looks like any old office."

"Officer Price," an athletic looking young man said to them, "The agents are ready for you." They were escorted into one of the glass-partitioned offices in the corner of the building.

"Officer Price?" a middle-aged Hispanic man asked.

"Agent Anthony Lopez," Max responded. "It's good to meet you in person."

"This is Agent Laura Alison, who's been working on the case with me."

"How are you, Officer Price?" asked Agent Alison, a very businesslike and attractive woman in her late thirties.

"Great," he responded, "And you?"

"Well, thank you."

"This is Officer Matt Clayton, who's been assisting with the investigation on our end."

"Good to meet you both," Clayton said.

"I want to thank you both for allowing me to pick up the report in person," Price told them. "I thought given the high profile of the people involved in the case, it would save them and us a lot of unwanted attention- especially given the facts of the case and that is was closed out fairly quickly."

"Please have a seat," Agent Lopez instructed. "Publicity in a case of this type is just a distraction from cases that need publicity." Agent Alison looked down and to the side which Price immediately caught as a "tell." She's not on board, he thought.

"It's a little hard to believe the media didn't pick up on it," Lopez remarked.

"Considering that it happened offshore and we didn't dock until well after two o'clock in the morning, it's not that surprising. Key Largo is hardly a media mecca."

"It was helpful that you docked in Key Largo," Agent Alison agreed. "If you'd docked in Miami your...the others on the boat might not have been so lucky."

"That's true," Clayton agreed, forgetting Price's admonition to remain silent.

"But all things being equal," Agent Lopez continued, "There was nothing that pointed to foul play among the surviving passengers. All of their statements were consistent..."

"If not too consistent," Agent Alison said suggestively.

"I should have warned you," Agent Lopez said laughing. "I have a conspiracy theorist on my hands here."

"You're the lead on this case," she said. "It's just a gut feeling."

"I don't operate on feelings," Lopez said authoritatively. "I operate on facts and evidence. And the facts are these. Unless others boarded the boat and committed the crimes, the only people who could've committed the crimes are Renee', Tyler, Ardoin and Latimer; four people who are well known and have a lot to lose and nothing to gain. Hell, the four of them hadn't lived in their hometown in over 30 years. We spoke to Leanne Piper's mother, who referred to them as lovely people and friends since childhood. She, and the Piper's grown children, acknowledged that friction in the marriage had increased in the last few months, and that, aside from this visit and their high school reunion last October, the four had had little to no contact with the Pipers for the last 30 years. Plus, there was information from the family, from the other passengers, from the restaurant in Key Largo and the restaurant in Miami that they'd had drunken arguments in public."

"And there is the physical evidence," Price added. "Everything was consistent with what the four survivors told us; the damage to the boat, the shell casings, the gunshot residue test. Their blood alcohol was through the roof, and they both had high levels of Xanax in their systems, which both had prescriptions for."

"And the bullets' trajectories were all consistent with what they described," Lopez told them. "Hell, they'd have to be criminal masterminds to set that up."

"Or have a very well thought-out and executed plan," Agent Alison said cynically.

"That and a whole hell of a lot of good luck," Lopez responded. "Look at who we're talking about here: An actress, a writer, a socialite, and a woman who sells expensive sheets. Even if they were able to accomplish a crime that sophisticated, why would they do it? There's no motive."

"Maybe it's something that happened before they moved away 30 years ago," Clayton offered. The others turned toward him in surprise, having forgotten he was in the room.

"Or from their childhoods," Agent Alison offered.

Lopez let out a big, hearty laugh. "Now there's an investigation we should embark on," he said. "With no motive and no physical evidence, we should go back, what, 49 years, through six people's childhoods, to look for a motive for murder. No thanks. The FBI will pass. But I admire your commitment, Officer Clayton."

"Well, we've taken up enough of your time," Price said. He stood silent for a few seconds.

"Oh, the report," Lopez said. "Here you go." Lopez handed him a thin volume. "It's all in there. This case is officially closed."

"I really appreciate the special consideration," Price said. "If there's ever anything I can do from our end, just say the word."

"You may regret that, Officer Price," Lopez said genially.

"Agent Alison, it was a pleasure to meet you," Price told her. "And thank you too, for your help."

"Not a problem," she replied, in such a way that made him think that it was.

"Sorry, I forgot to keep my mouth shut," Clayton said as they drove toward Key Largo.

"No worries," Price replied. "Just slow down a little, you've got a case of the lead-foot." He was in too good a mood to be annoyed. He felt like he'd done something good for some good people. Why put them through it, he thought. He pulled his cell from his pocket and dialed.

"Hello Miss Renee, its Officer Max Price from the Coast Guard. I'm well, thank you for asking. I've just left the FBI Miami Field Office, and I wanted let you know that I have their final report. The case is officially closed."

Bayou Derkin, Louisiana

April 29, 2016

"Mama, Mama!" Charlotte Claire cried out from her childhood bedroom. "I'm leaving. I'm running late." She stopped to check herself out in full-length mirror on her closet door. She tugged at the black Armani jacket and turned to see how the skirt hung in back. "This is probably a little outré for Bayou Derkin," she said to herself. "But there's no way in hell I'm wearing something from Dress Barn just to fit in." She found her mother at the kitchen table with a cup of coffee and the newspaper.

"Don't you look pretty," her mother said.

"Thank you, Mama. I wish I were going to a cocktail party instead of a memorial service."

"Oh, I know," her mother said, putting down the paper. "It's so sad. I'm glad you came for the service though, what with you being there when it happened. I'm sure the family will appreciate the gesture."

"I hope so," Charlotte Claire replied doubtfully.

"Oh, they will," her mother insisted. "Why, your whole little group is here; Timmy from New York and Annie from Hollywood, Amelie from North Carolina. I think it's wonderful. Tell them all I said hello."

"I will, Mama." She leaned over and kissed her mother on the cheek. "We're going to the casino for a drink after the reception, so I'll be gone a few hours. Call me on my cell if you need anything."

It was two weeks since the killings. She didn't think of it often, but when she did, that was what she called it: The killings. Not the accident, or the incident, but the killings, and it surprised her how comfortable she was doing so. Charlotte Claire had very little contact with the others in that time. She assumed that was true for all of them. They'd decided it was best to minimize communication until the investigation was complete. It was only when she heard about the plans for the memorial service from her mother that she finally called each of them, to urge them to attend the service. "It'll look strange if we don't go," she'd told them, and they'd all readily agreed. Now she was looking forward to seeing her old friends, though she knew they would be in for a grilling from the locals, who were, no doubt, mesmerized by the shocking tragedy. It was the most salacious thing ever to happen to anyone from Bayou Derkin. She dialed Timmy's cell on her console and waited for him to pick up.

"Hey, Charlotte Claire. Where are you?"

"I'm running late," she replied. "Can you guys wait out front? I don't have time to park the car and get out, so I'll just swing by the front door and pick y'all up."

"Okay," he said. "See you out front."

Charlotte Claire pulled up to the front of the casino hotel and saw the three of them standing in the lobby waiting. They were all dressed in black, conspicuously stylish attire for a Bayou Derkin funeral. Most of the locals would be dressed as they normally were, the women in their Sunday dresses, the men in open-collared shirts and jeans or khaki pants. Timmy and Annie smiled faintly and waved as they approached the car, but Amelie wore the tense expression of someone about to do something they'd rather not do. "Are you alright?" Charlotte Claire asked her once they'd gotten into the car.

"Should I be?"

"I know," Charlotte Claire told her. "But it's just an hour, then we'll make a quick appearance at the reception, and it's done."

"It'll be done when the investigation is over," Annie said.

"When will that be, I wonder?" Timmy asked.

"Soon, I hope," she responded.

They sat in silence throughout the short drive to the church. The parking lot was full, and the overflow of cars lined the street for two blocks in every direction. "Holy shit," Timmy said, breaking the silence. "It looks like everyone in town is here."

"I didn't think Leanne was that popular," Amelie said.

"She's not," Charlotte Claire told her.

"Why else would so many people be here?" she asked.

"To see us."

When they entered the church vestibule they were surprised to find Scotty and Leanne's three children: Matthew the LSU football star, Scotty Jr. the New Orleans attorney, and Caroline with her husband, Clay. "We were waiting for you," Caroline told them.

"Oh, I'm so sorry that we're late," Charlotte Claire said apologetically. "It's my fault. I'm so sorry."

"No, no," Caroline said, "It's alright. You're just ten minutes late and we'd have held back for that time anyway."

"We wanted to thank you all for coming all this way to attend the service," Scotty Jr. said.

"We all felt that we should be here," Timmy said.

"Thank you," Matthew said.

"We're so sorry for your loss," Annie told them.

"Yes," Amelie added. "It's hard enough to lose one parent, but two at the same time, I can't even imagine how difficult this must be."

"Yes," Caroline said gravely. "And under these circumstances it's been particularly so. That's one reason we wanted to wait for you and speak with you before the service. We wanted to say how sorry we are for what Daddy has put you through."

"Oh no, please don't..." Amelie said, her words trailing off.

"No, really," Caroline said. "We know what you went through that night. It must have been horrifying. We know that what happened to Mama might have just as easily have happened to you. Daddy could be callous, we know that, even a little cruel sometimes. But none of us thought he'd be capable of this. His drinking had gotten out of control over the last few months. The agent from the FBI told us his blood alcohol level was through the roof, and there was Xanax in his system. I didn't even know he took Xanax," she said, looking quizzically at her brothers. "Anyway, the only thing I can think of is that the mixture of the drugs and alcohol made him not responsible for his actions. That's the only thing I can think of. I have to think of it that way or I..." her voice trailed off as she fought back tears.

"I'm sure that's what it was," Charlotte Claire said. She took Caroline's hand in hers and patted it consolingly. "Will you have a memorial service for your father?" she asked.

"We did already," Scotty Jr. told her. "Something private, just for the family. We didn't let anyone know we were doing it."

"We couldn't possibly have Mama and Daddy's services together," Caroline said. "It would have been too... inappropriate."

"I see," Charlotte Claire said.

"You did the right thing," Timmy said.

"Well, we tried," she said, smiling weakly. "There's no book of etiquette for this kind of thing."

"If there were, Mama would have had it," Matthew joked, and they all laughed a little.

"Indeed, she would," Annie said.

"Well, I guess we should be getting started," Scotty Jr. told them.

"Yes," Caroline said. "We saved a pew for you behind the family."

"Oh, my goodness," Amelie said looking nervously at the others. "You didn't need to do that."

"No, we don't want to intrude," Timmy added.

"It's not an intrusion at all," Caroline told them. "We'd like you to be near, and it's an expression of our, oh, I don't know, our way of saying that we're sorry for what Daddy put you through." They fell silent, looking from one to the other, unsure of what to do. "Please," Caroline said. "It would mean a lot to us."

"Well, sure," Annie said. "We'd be honored."

"Yes, of course," Charlotte Claire said.

"Thank you," Timmy added.

"Why don't y'all go in now," Scotty Jr. said. "We're going to hold back a bit for Grandma and the aunts. They're waiting in the lounge."

"You'll see the empty pew, third row on the right," Caroline told them. "That's for you. And we hope you'll come by the house afterward."

"Of course, we will," Charlotte Claire told her.

The sound of the organ swelled as they stepped through the heavily carved wooden doors to the nave. They looked at each other apprehensively and Timmy said, "That aisle looks mighty long."

"And the church is packed to the rafters," Annie added.

"It feels like the walk of shame," Amelie said warily.

"Let's just get this over with," Charlotte Claire told them. "And don't walk too slowly." As soon as they'd passed the first few rows heads began to turn in their direction. Murmurs could be heard as news of their arrival got passed toward the front of the church, one whisper at a time. By the time they'd reached the middle of the church all eyes were on them. Jenny Karan waved and smiled from her pew. Further up, Paula Stone and Dorie Calhoun nodded in unison at the four of them. Out of the corner of his eye Timmy caught sight of Tom Burnett. He looked tired and haggard from drinking. He nodded gravely at Timmy and gave him a discreet thumbs-up.

"That was weird," Timmy whispered to Annie.

"What was?"

"Tell you later."

"That was seriously bizarre," Charlotte Claire announced, after the service in the privacy of her car.

"I know," Timmy said. "I felt so guilty standing there, with their kids being so gracious and apologetic."

"Guilty?" Amelie asked. "We're beyond guilty, worse than guilty. We're irredeemable. We tricked them into that trip. If we'd just let it go, none of this would have happened."

"I don't want to hear that, Amelie," Charlotte Claire scolded. "We know what we did. We own it among ourselves. But we own it *only* among ourselves. And we know why we did it. Between the two of them they killed four people, three of whom were innocent people-one a little girl-and raped two of us. God knows how many others Scotty has raped. And if he could kill three people and live with himself, who's to say he wouldn't do it again? If he'd found out we knew what he did, what's to say he wouldn't have come after us? His hatefulness is also indirectly responsible for the death of Tom Burnett's boy. He stalked and bullied Timmy for practically his entire childhood and drove him to a nervous breakdown. And she killed your little sister and seemed to not only be able to live with it, but she kept that pink swan float like a trophy. It's sick. She was sick."

"I know," Amelie conceded. "But I'm having trouble living with this. It haunts me."

"It haunts all of us," Timmy said. "But it's just a couple of weeks since it happened. In time you'll find a way to compartmentalize it, to accept that you did it and move on."

"You say 'since it happened' like it was an accident," she replied, "like we didn't orchestrate the whole thing."

"Okay," he snapped. "Since we orchestrated the whole thing, happy now?"

"Pull it together, guys," Charlotte Claire told them. "We have to stick together." They fell silent. Rice fields, trees and houses slid by as they drove the old farm road towards Leanne and Scotty's house.

"We're never going to feel good about what we did," Annie said after a while. "Nor happy nor proud of it, but we just have to remember why we did it and find a way to live with that. And let's not lose sight of the fact that we didn't actually kill anyone."

"She's right," Charlotte Claire said. "You need to focus on that, Amelie. We've always had a bond, but now we have an even deeper bond. We have to be strong and we have to be strong together."

"I know," Amelie said. "You're right, and we will."

"Damn," Annie said. "I hope they have some booze at this reception. I need a drink."

"It's Bayou Derkin," Charlotte Claire said. "There's always booze."

People filled the entire first level of Scotty and Leanne's house and spilled on to the patio and lawn. There were tables with catered food and a bar had been set up outside. Caroline and her brothers worked the room like a cocktail party. "She's a lot like Leanne," Charlotte Claire said.

"What do you mean?" Amelie asked.

"Circulating among the guests, being the perfect hostess," she replied. "Leanne would be proud."

"How many people do you think are here?" Annie mused.

"It looks like at least 200," Timmy told her.

"It's a small town," Charlotte Claire said. "And it's Bayou Derkin. Funerals are social events." They were standing in the foyer; a crush of people surrounded them.

"Let's make our way to the patio," Timmy suggested. "It's too crowded in here."

"Good idea," Annie said. "And I overheard someone say there was a bar out there." They made their way toward the rear of the house, occasionally stopping to say hello and express their sorrow over the tragic turn of events. As soon as they'd stepped outside, Jenny Karan made a beeline toward the group.

"Oh, I hoped you'd turn up," she said when she reached them. "Isn't it just terrible? Well, of course if anybody knows how terrible it is, it would be the four of you. It must have been horrible to go through. Though I don't know any of the details, but I can only guess it was a horrifying experience. And then to have to go through that whole investigation must have been nerve-racking too. I just can't even imagine." She fell silent, wearing a look of anticipation that communicated that she was waiting for the scoop.

"It's good to see you, Jenny," Timmy said after a moment. "Would you excuse me? I could use a drink."

"That sounds like a great idea," Annie said. "I think I'll join you. Good to see you, Jenny."

After they'd left Jenny turned to Charlotte Claire and Amelie and said defensively, "Well, I guess they don't like to talk about it."

"No," Charlotte Claire said. "None of us do, really. It was such a terrible experience and it's only been a couple of weeks. I guess we're all just trying to process it."

"Of course, I understand," she said. "It's just such a terrible thing; a murder suicide. It's so shocking. But you know what the funny thing is? It kind of wasn't shocking. And I'm not the only person who thinks that. A lot of people I've talked to say the same thing. It was almost as if, in hindsight, it was building up to something like this with Leanne and Scotty." She looked around to see if anybody was in earshot. "They'd both been acting so strange in the months leading up to the… to this. Leanne had practically become a recluse. She dropped out of Catholic Daughters and the garden club. Her maid told my maid that she was drinking heavily…at home…during the day! She also said that they were fighting like cats and dogs. My husband saw Scotty out several times and said he was so drunk he could barely stand up. And he'd become belligerent. He got into a couple of bar fights. Scotty always was a bit of a bully, but this was something much worse."

"Well," Amelie said when Jenny finally stopped talking. "I guess that a marriage under stress can lead to such things. It's not unheard of."

"No," she agreed. "Not unheard of at all. Can you get over this crowd?"

"It is quite a crowd," Charlotte Claire said. "I suppose they were well-loved in Bayou Derkin." Jenny snorted, then clapped her hand over her mouth.

"Are you kidding?" she asked. "They weren't well-loved at all. In fact, most people I know didn't even like them. I didn't know you and she were so close, Charlotte Claire."

"We weren't, really."

"You were close enough that you invited her to Miami."

"Oh, that was a fundraising thing. They donated to the opera company I raise money for, so they got invited to the fundraising event in Miami."

"Oh," she said. "Well, that makes sense. A lot of us were wondering. But, no, they were not well-liked in Bayou Derkin. I've even heard some people say, not me of course, that they got what was coming to them."

"That's a terrible thing to say," Amelie scolded.

"I agree," Jenny said. "But they weren't very nice to people. Some would even say coldhearted. And they were incredibly snobby. I wasn't a fan."

"Then why did you come to the memorial service?" Charlotte Claire asked her.

"For their kids," she replied. "They were friends with my kids, and my kids all live out of town, so I'm sort of here on their behalf. But I don't have much use for them, either."

"Really?" Amelie asked. "They seem like such nice people."

"Yes," she replied dryly. "They're good at appearances. Truth is, those apples didn't fall far from the tree. They're very like their parents; cold, snobby, money-obsessed. They were all over town, telling anyone who'd listen that Annie and Timmy were coming to the memorial service. The younger boy, Mathew, he's big man on campus at LSU. He was accused of date rape. Everyone says that Scotty and Leanne paid the girl to keep quiet. Scotty Jr. got a girl pregnant when he was a freshman in college and she was a senior in high school. He refused to admit it was his, even though they'd been dating exclusively for over a year. He claimed that she cheated on him and broke it off with her, and he wouldn't take a paternity test when she asked him to, so she could prove it was his. But everyone knows it's his now. The little boy looks just like Scotty Jr. And he's a big wig lawyer in New Orleans now, probably making millions and never offers a penny of support."

"It must be so strange to come back to Bayou Derkin and know that you have a child that you've never met," Amelie wondered.

"He'd have to have a heart for that," Jenny told her. "And Caroline, that one, she was one of the mean girls in high school. Oh, she bullied this one poor little girl mercilessly; almost drove her to a nervous breakdown. The girl had to change schools. So, what did Caroline do? She found another poor child to make miserable."

"That's terrible," Charlotte Claire said.

"And they spoke terribly about Scotty and Leanne to anyone who'd listen. They're probably already celebrating their inheritance. No, they're horrible people. And you don't have to take my word for it. Ask anyone here."

"Goodness, Jenny," Amelie exclaimed. "Why are all these people here if they feel that way?"

"They're here to see the four of you, because you were there when it happened and you're all famous," Jenny replied. "And besides, it's a funeral, it's Bayou Derkin. That's what we do."

"I'll have a vodka rocks," Timmy said to the bartender.

"What'll you have Annie?"

"Same."

"Jenny can talk a blue streak," Timmy said. "I had to get away. And look, she's still over there. Charlotte Claire and Amelie are going to kill us."

"Ms. Renee'," the bartender said, handing her a drink. "I'm a big fan."

"Aren't you sweet, thank you."

"What am I? Chopped liver?" Timmy said after the bartender was out of earshot. "Guess he's not a reader."

"Poor Timmy got your ego bruised," Annie crooned as her cellphone began to pulse. She looked at the caller ID. "It's Price from the Coast Guard."

"Oh God," Timmy's eyebrows shot up and his face betrayed his apprehension. "Please let this be good news."

"Hello," Annie said into the phone. "Oh, hello, Officer Price. Yes, how are you? Oh, is it? Well that's good news," she said, smiling at Timmy and giving him thumbs up. "I can't thank you enough for the way you've treated us throughout the investigation. You made a very difficult time much less so. You too. Thanks again." Annie put her phone in her purse and said to Timmy, "The investigation is officially closed. The determination is murder-suicide."

"Oh, thank God," Timmy sighed. "I can finally get a good night's sleep. This is great news."

"I feel so relieved," she said. "We should go tell the girls. They'll be so happy." As they started for Charlotte Claire and Amelie, Timmy noticed Tom Burnett, standing alone under the pergola, smoking a cigarette. It was the same spot where they'd spoken last August at the barbecue and, but for the fact that he was dressed for a funeral instead of a barbecue, he looked the same.

"Hey," Timmy said to Annie. "You go on without me. I want to talk to Tom. Do you remember what I whispered to you in the church?"

"No."

"I whispered 'that was weird'."

"Oh, right. What were you talking about?"

"Tom Burnett nodded and at me and gave a thumbs-up."

"He did? What do you think he meant?"

"I don't know, but I'm going to see if I can find out. I'll catch up to you guys in a minute." Timmy crossed the lawn to the pergola. "Can I bum a cigarette?"

"I didn't know you smoked," he said.

"Only on special occasions," Tom let out a short, bitter laugh. He slapped the pack of cigarettes against the side of his hand until a couple of them sprang partially out of the pack. His hands were calloused and had the same weary look as his face.

"It's a special occasion, alright," he said. "I wouldn't have missed this for the world."

"Are you thinking all of this was a colossal bit of karma?" Timmy asked him. Tom looked up at Timmy from under his furrowed brow. He squinted his eyes as if deep in thought and looked off towards the house.

"You could say that; karma or something like karma."

Timmy looked directly into his eyes and asked, "What do you mean?"

"Well," he replied. "Karma is a naturally occurring phenomenon; murder, not so much."

"I see what you mean."

"I'm not sure you do."

"You mean because it was a murder-suicide, right?"

"Well, it was definitely a murder...or two." Tom took a drag from his cigarette and blew the smoke out of the side of his mouth. Timmy took a drag from his cigarette and slowly exhaled. He was buying time to figure out what to say and wondering where the conversation was going.

"Or two?" Timmy asked as casually as he could. "Tom, I'm not sure I know what you mean."

"I think you do," he replied. "But you don't have to say anything. In fact, you shouldn't say anything. Best if we just leave it alone. But it *is* strange that this would just coincidentally happen with the four of you there. And it was a surprise that Charlotte Claire should just happen to invite the two of them to Miami when, as far as I know, up until the reunion they hadn't seen each other in years. And it's odd that you'd be there when I know you hated him or that Annie would be there in light of the fact that-if what Carla told me was true-Scotty raped her. And Amelie was there, too. Even despite the rumors that Leanne killed her little sister. That's 50 pounds of unlikely coincidences in a five-pound sack, wouldn't you say?"

Timmy looked at Tom for a long time, his mind racing for a reply. "Is that the reason for the thumbs up in the church?" he said at last.

"I think the less said the better. I haven't shared these thoughts with anybody and I don't plan to. And no one around here has said anything of that nature to me. But I will say this, Timmy, I'd like to shake your hand." Tom tossed his cigarette to the ground and extended his hand. "Don't be a stranger, Timmy." He turned and walked toward the house.

"Oh, my God," Charlotte Claire cried as they drove out of the long driveway and onto the old farm road. "That was definitely the strangest memorial service I've ever been to."

"And informative," Amelie added.

"Timmy, wait until you hear what Jenny told us," Charlotte Claire said, launching into Jenny Karan's laundry list of vices, character defects, sins and outright crimes that flowed through and out of the Piper family.

"Unbelievable," Timmy said. But what he found more unbelievable was how this information made him feel, better. He knew it shouldn't, but it did. The weight he'd been carrying wasn't lifted, but it was lighter. He could see the road ahead, the road that they all were going to have to navigate from that dark night in Key Largo to a brighter place ahead, where guilt and fear of discovery were placed in a box, labeled and set on a shelf in a closet, like Elizabeth's pink swan float.

"Oh, Timmy," Annie said excitedly. "What happened with your conversation with Tom?"

"Oh, nothing," he said casually. "Just small talk."

The next morning Timmy put on a pair of khaki shorts and a polo shirt and his most comfortable sneakers. He went down to the lobby where he found Amelie and Annie waiting and similarly dressed. "Well, I can see we all got the memo."

"Yes," Annie said. "She called first thing this morning and told us to wear comfortable shoes."

"That's Charlotte Claire," Amelie said, "Leader of the pack. What would we do without her?"

"Ruin a pair of good shoes, I guess," Annie replied.

"Did you bring the float?" Timmy asked.

"Yeah, it's in my bag. I'll inflate it in the car on the way there."

"Hey gang," Charlotte Claire called out from across the lobby. "Y'all ready?"

Instead of taking the highway into town, Charlotte Claire took the back roads that divided the huge farms with vast acres of rice and soy beans. Sunlight bounced on the water of the mirror-like flooded fields and reflected the vivid green of the rice blades swaying in the April breeze. An enormous, cloudless sky extended spectacularly down to the flat Louisiana landscape; it looked as if you could drive off the edge of the earth and into the sky. With all the windows down the wind blew loudly through the car, so no one spoke. They each took in the view, the wind blowing through their hair, a million memories reflected in their eyes.

When they reached town, Charlotte Claire pulled into the

parking lot and the four friends walked across the schoolyard, through the woods, and down to the river bank. The sun reflected on the water gave the scene an other-worldly quality. The river's steady current moved through the pines on either side, like a brown snake sliding through the grass. They stood taking in the scene for several minutes before anyone spoke.

"Is this the spot?" Annie asked.

"Yeah," Amelie said. "This is it."

At the river's edge Amelie knelt and set the pink swan float on the water's surface. She gave it a gentle shove until it was taken into the current. They stood together as the little swan bobbed and tilted like a happy child, passing below the bridge, down the river and out of sight.

Lightning Source UK Ltd.
Milton Keynes UK
UKHW010624080621
385138UK00001B/269